SUPREME MANDATE

Supreme Mandate

Book 1

Tarizon Saga

by

William Manchee

Top Publications, Ltd.

Supreme Mandate
Book 1
Tarizon Saga

© COPYRIGHT
William Manchee
2019

Cover Design by Raido Design

Top Publications, Ltd.
Plano, Texas

Paperback ISBN 978-1-935722-96-0
Library of Congress Control No. 2018963475

To Alex

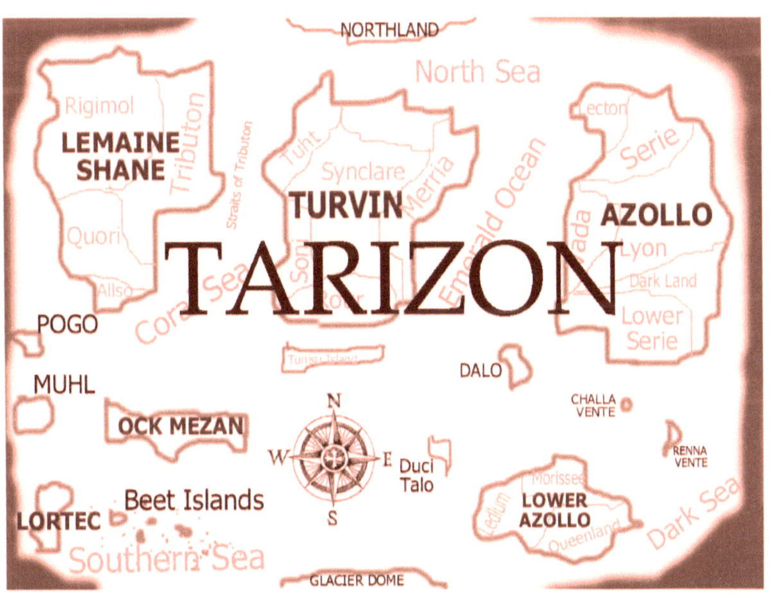

NORTHLAND
North Sea
Rigimol
Lecton
LEMAINE
SHANE
Serie
Tributon
Tuht
AZOLLO
Straits of Tributon
Synclare
Lyon
Merria
TURVIN
Dark Land
Quori
Emerald Ocean
TARIZON
Lower
Serie
Allso
Coral Sea
Sona River
POGO
Turisa Island
DALO
MUHL
CHALLA
VENTE
OCK MEZAN
N
RENNA
VENTE
W   E
Duci
Talo
Ledium
Morissee
Beet Islands
S
LOWER
AZOLLO
LORTEC
Queenland
Dark Sea
Southern Sea
GLACIER DOME

Prelude

Tarizon's historical manuscripts claimed there was a much larger and greater human civilization far away in another galaxy called Pharidon. It was said that this civilization was so advanced that the people there sometimes lived for nearly a thousand cycles. Consequently, Pharidon became overcrowded and the planet's natural resources could not support the growing population. When the situation became critical, explorers began searching other solar systems and even other galaxies for inhabitable planets where its citizens could relocate. One of these groups of explorers came to Tarizon and another to Earth.

It is believed that these settlers brought with them many animals, plants, insects, and other organisms from Pharidon. They were raised and nurtured by the first settlers and then released to live and evolve on their own. Although the settlers, presumably, brought with them Pharidon's advanced technology, it was lost through war or natural disaster, and these early settlers were forced to start over. In terms of technology, Tarizon was further advanced than its sister-planet, Earth.

It is the cycle 20237 on Tarizon according to the Pharidon Calendar and the mid-1960's on Earth. While both planets had suffered the effects of numerous worldwide wars, the nation-states of Tarizon had been waging nuclear wars for over a hundred years with devastating effect on the planet and its inhabitants. Now with Tarizon's atmosphere so polluted, only in the domed cities were people provided law and order, clean air and water and protection from the radiation storms that were now as common as the dew. Millions lived under these domed cities but tens of millions lived outside the domes in sickness, poverty, chaos, and desperation.

While many of the rich and elite of Tarizon were evacuating Tarizon to seek refuge on Earth, a boy with a rhutz as an unlikely companion emerges from the wilderness with a message that will change everything.

1
Almighty Pelgrem

19 BU

Eleven-cycle-old Sandee Brahn climbed to the top of a nearby hill to look out over what used to be the Brahn Ranch. A stiff fall breeze rustled his sandy blond hair. He used to love sitting high on the hilltop, known as Five Trees, where he could look in every direction over the Hills of Loctula that stretched from Lago Lat to Baca Rue across northern Lecton and Serie. But now the view sickened him. The once lush green hills had turned a ghastly black and grey. The five trees that once proudly crowned this hill had been vaporized in less than thirty tiks after a nuclear strike on nearby Lago Lat Airbase. What the bomb hadn't destroyed the radiation took care of in the days that followed.

After the strike, each day was an impossible struggle for survival. Warned of the imminent strike by the alarm on their wrist arrays, his family had survived by retreating into a deep cave, but most of their herds and all of their orchards had been wiped out. This once proud Brahn family was now, five cycles later, with few productive assets. Of course, it didn't much matter anymore, Sandee thought, there wasn't a road or a bridge still intact in all of Lecton and Serie on which to take their products to market. He wasn't sure about the rest of Tarizon but he suspected it was the same everywhere. The rulers of the world had gone insane and now each citizen was on his own to live or die depending on his own wits or good fortune.

After a while, Sandee hiked to the east bank of the Loctula River which was the eastern boundary of Lecton. The once clear blue water had turned a dark green and was cluttered with debris, dead fish and animals as well as an occasional human corpse. The water wasn't fit for human consumption without a complicated and time-consuming filtration process. First, the water had to be collected and allowed to settle for several kyloons. Once the sediment settled, the water was poured through a wire mesh to remove any debris. After the debris was removed, the water had to be treated with chemicals to remove the radiation poisoning and finally boiled to destroy any bacteria that had survived the radiation. Even rainwater and water from deep wells had to be treated, and every member of the family spent several kyloons every single day just doing this tedious chore.

Sandee held his nose as the river's smell made him sick. He thought back to the days he could breathe deeply, relishing the wonderful scent of the river. Now the stench made him gag. He recalled many days that he would actually wade into the water and immerse himself, letting the current carry him downstream. Being a good swimmer it took little effort to make it back to shore. But those days were over, and he knew it would be many cycles before he'd ever set a foot in the river again.

It was starting to get dark and he was expected home, so he began walking toward the family's reconstructed ranch house. The new house wasn't nearly as nice as the original one that had burned to the ground, but it was a roof over their heads which he knew was more than most people had these days.

As he started up the last hill overlooking the house, he saw smoke rising into the sky. Frowning and feeling uneasy he picked up his pace until he got to the top of the hill. The sight of the homestead burning sent a jolt of fear and foreboding through him. He began running. As he got closer to the house, he saw a body laying lifeless twenty strides ahead of him. He knelt next to it, his heart racing, and felt his brother's wrist for a pulse. His heart sank as he felt nothing.

Overcome with grief and panic, he got up and began to run mindlessly toward the smoldering house. Along the way, he couldn't help but notice that the pribett pens were empty and the barn door wide open. Bounding up the front porch steps he kicked the front door open and ran inside. His mother's charred body was lying in the kitchen with a bullet hole in her forehead. Sandee gasped in shock and horror, then kneeled in utter despair. Gathering her into his arms he rocked her back and forth, crying and moaning hysterically. Their life together raced through his mind. She had been a wonderful mother and he had so dearly loved her. *Who did this? Why would anyone kill my mother and my brother?*

It took a while for him to collect himself, but eventually, he got up and started searching the rest of the house. It wasn't long before he found his sister lying in a pool of blood, her throat slit. *Why God? Why have you allowed this to happen?*

He gagged at the stench of burnt blood then let out an agonizing scream. "Father! Are you alive?" His pulse quickened as he moved to the next room, another dead body but not someone he recognized. A deserter from the Lecton Army he surmised by the patch on his uniform. The soldier's skull had been cracked open. He assumed it was the handiwork of his father. When he'd searched the entire house, he went out back and there he found his father and two more dead soldiers. There had been a fierce struggle from the looks of it, he thought. He knew his father wouldn't have gone down without a tenacious fight.

Kneeling down at his father's side, he wept.

Everything he loved was now gone. *Why God!? Why has this happened?* Sandee's father had been a devout Pelgremist. Pelgrem was the God who reigned over Tarizon's mother-planet, Pharidon. The Pelgrem Church was the largest on Tarizon but there were others. The Forsaken was its most formidable rival. Its advocates believed in Pelgrem but insisted his domain did not extend beyond Pharidon's solar system, and therefore there wasn't a god looking out for the people of Tarizon. This is why so many people believed Tarizon was doomed from the beginning of its human habitation and one day would self-destruct. No civilization could survive without spiritual guidance and an occasional divine intervention, they argued. Sandee was starting to wonder if they had been right and the day of reckoning was at hand.

He sat there next to his father for some time feeling empty and listless. The horror of the day had drained every bit of his energy. He felt guilty that he was still alive and wondered if there was any point in his living in such a hostile world, especially without his family. His father's knife lay beside his still body. Sandee picked it up and gazed at its sharp blade. One quick slice to his wrists and his suffering would be over. If ending his life would have taken him to the place his parents and siblings had gone, he would have done it then and there. But he had been taught in his religious training that those who gave up on the gift of life would not transcend to the second stage of existence but would be expelled into the void and lost forever.

A door slammed and there were voices in the distance. Alarmed, Sandee stood up and rushed to the side of the house. He peered around the corner and saw two soldiers coming out of the barn and heading his way. Retreating quickly, he took off running back up the hill. The soldiers saw him and yelled for him to stop. He ignored them and kept on running. A bullet passed over his head, so close that he felt a whisper of wind on his ear. He hit the dirt fearing the next bullet would pierce his back. *If I can just get to the top of the hill, I can lose them.* On his feet again, he ran in a zig-zag pattern this time, hoping it would make him a difficult target. Bullets hit the dirt beside and behind him but none of them found his flesh. A surge of relief washed over him as he crested the hill, but it didn't last.

A huge, greenish-grey, four-legged beast stood before him and gave him a ferocious growl. Sandee recognized it immediately as a rhutz and figured it was twice his weight. Feeling like the wind had been knocked out of him, he froze for a moment and then just sank to the ground. There was nothing he could do. The rhutz could easily outrun him if he tried to get away, and then there was the beast's third hand to consider. The rhutz were telekinetic. *At least if I am shot or killed by this beast I will go onto the second stage of life and be with my family.* The soldiers' footsteps grew louder and louder. Sandee closed his eyes wondering if his death would come from a vicious bite from the rhutz or from a bullet to his brain.

He waited with clenched teeth for the final blow, but nothing happened. Opening his eyes he saw the rhutz rush past him and launch itself at the first soldier. Taken by surprise, the soldier could do nothing to stop its razor-sharp teeth from sinking into his throat. Blood spurted from the gash as the soldier tumbled onto his back. The other soldier looked on in shock and when he finally pulled up his rifle to take aim, the rifle shot out of his hand and landed twenty feet away. As the rhutz was finishing off the second soldier and turning back toward him, he was again overwhelmed with fear. *Am I next?*

Normally it was unusual for a rhutz to attack a human but these were not normal times. Since the rhutz had attacked the soldiers, Sandee figured he would suffer the same fate. Sandee turned and began running away. He knew he had no hope of outrunning the rhutz but he hoped the rhutz might be occupied long enough with his kill that he wouldn't notice that he had slipped away. When he looked back, however, his hopes were dashed as he saw the rhutz trotting after him. Quickening his pace he prayed the rhutz would lose interest and end the pursuit, but after two kyloons the rhutz was still behind him but keeping his distance.

Exhausted, Sandee stopped and sat on a large rock. It was almost dark now and he had to think about finding food and water and getting some sleep. His anxiety over the rhutz following him had waned. *If you were going to kill me, you'd have done it by now. What do you want from me? Why did you save my life?*

The rhutz's behavior was baffling to Sandee. Rhutz were savage beasts but they weren't stupid. They knew better than to attack humans because, even with their strength, speed, and telekinetic abilities, they were no match for the humans' long guns and jet copters. *Is it because I am unarmed that you are stalking me?* Sandee gave the rhutz a hard look. The rhutz, who was sitting now, watched him intently. Finally, Sandee looked away and began listening. In the distance, he could hear the sound of the rushing river.

The sound made him thirsty. Unfortunately, he couldn't drink contaminated water and live very long. He didn't have his decontamination kit with him, it was back at the ranch, but he didn't dare go back there for fear other soldiers might be lurking about.

Sandee looked at the rhutz wondering how he had survived without clean water. The rhutz perked up, stood, and then started trotting away. Sandee was glad to see him leaving but wondered why he'd suddenly lost interest in him. The rhutz stopped and looked back expectantly. Sandee frowned, wondering what he wanted. Then it hit him. *You want me to follow you?* Sandee didn't know where the thought came from. It just popped into his head. The rhutz continued on and Sandee felt compelled to follow him.

The rhutz trotted north several kyloons through the scorched terrain, over a hill, through a canyon and then up a steep embankment. Sandee struggled to keep up with the beast, and several times nearly gave up the pursuit. Finally, the rhutz came to the mouth of a cave, stopped and looked back. Sandee gasped for air. *Don't worry, my friend. I'm still here.* The rhutz seemed almost to nod and then continued on into the cave.

Sandee hesitated. It was against all his instincts to go into a dark cave that he knew was occupied by a pack of rhutz. He'd been in caves before with a light stick and knew how dangerous they could be even if they were unoccupied. He could easily trip and fall and injure himself, or walk off a cliff into a bottomless pit. He wondered if the rhutz was bringing him home to his pack to be their next meal. If they were sentient beings, they were probably laughing at his stupidity in walking into their den. But, he also knew the rhutz could have killed him earlier or just let him die at the hands of the soldiers. So, summoning all his courage, he cautiously moved forward.

Twenty strides into the cave it was pitch dark. Sandee stopped to let his eyes adjust to the darkness. After a few loons, he began to see shadows and could make out the walls of the cavern. He heard the trickling of water, so he carefully followed the sound praying the ground beneath him wouldn't give way. Several loons later he felt a fine mist and knew the water was nearby. He heard the rhutz lapping up water, so he got on his knees and felt around. His left hand found the shallow pool of water. It was cool and smelled delicious. Since the rhutz was drinking freely,

Sandee assumed the water was somehow clean. *Perhaps it comes from a deep artisan well that hasn't been contaminated or has been cleaned over time.* After his thirst was quenched, he thought about food. *Okay, my friend, now what are we going to do to quench our hunger?*

Without hesitation, the rhutz was on his feet and trotted off. He went so quickly Sandee didn't even think about following him. He heard a scuffle in the distance and then a deathly squeal from some kind of small animal. A few tiks later the rhutz came back with a furry rodent in his mouth. Sandee recoiled at the sight of the small lump of fur with its grotesquely twisted face and bulging red eyes. *Pelgrem help me! I'll starve before I'll eat a cave rat.*

The rhutz dropped the rat, sat and waited patiently. Sandee turned away. "I'm not going to eat that thing! Take it away. I don't even want to look at it." The rhutz did nothing.

Suddenly feeling very tired, Sandee looked around for a place he might sleep. The ground was mainly rock and gravel but he managed to find a sandy spot where he curled into a ball and closed his eyes. Neither the rhutz nor the rat moved.

Kyloons later, he woke with a start. He'd been dreaming about his family and his life in Lecton but the dream hadn't ended well. His mind had conjured up a version of his family's last day and it had been violent and ugly. He noticed his hands were shaking and he felt a terrible pain in his gut. *Was it the water? Have I been poisoned by the water?*

Finally, he realized he was hungry. He hadn't eaten for a full day, and he had no spare fat on him for his body to metabolize. He looked over and saw the furry rat still there as ugly as ever and now smelling foul as well. His body involuntarily convulsed at the thought of eating the rodent, but he felt weak and knew he didn't have the strength to find or kill a more appetizing game in the hills around them.

Reluctantly, he crawled over and took the offering. He smelled it and nearly gagged again. *Now, what am I going to do with this?* The rhutz didn't respond but just watched with great interest as Sandee continued to inspect the creature. Finally, he got out his knife and began to skin it. When he was done, it was no more appetizing and he certainly wasn't going to eat it raw. Not only would that be disgusting, but the rodent would likely be carrying a whole host of infectious diseases. Sandee finally decided he'd have to make a fire and cook the meat to be safe.

He remembered seeing a partially charred tree just outside the entrance to the cave. He wondered if he dared try to find his way out. The rhutz stood up like he had read Sandee's mind, and headed in the direction in which they had come. Sandee struggled to catch up. After a few loons, the light began to filter into the cave indicating to Sandee that they were close to the entrance. Sandee breathed a sigh of relief as he stepped out of the darkness into the dim light of Clarion, Tarizon's largest moon.

His eyes lifted to the hazy red jewel in the sky and a sense of foreboding washed over him again. After pondering the feeling a few tiks, he shook his head to break the trance and looked around for the charred wood. Spotting it, he broke off an adequate supply and stacked it in a square configuration like he'd seen his father do a hundred times over. Then he stuffed the center of the structure with small twigs and leaves for quick combustion. Finally, he took a stone out of his pocket and began striking it against the backside of his knife. A steady stream of sparks began to fall onto a flat piece of charred wood. A moment later it began to smolder and smoke rose into the air. He blew on the embers until they had sufficiently spread and then he dropped the charred wood into the leaves and small twigs. A tik later he had a blazing fire.

After cutting off the vermin's ugly head, he soon was roasting his dinner on a stick and eating it gingerly. It tasted horrible but felt good in his stomach. He looked over at the rhutz, who hadn't taken his eyes off his new friend for a moment, and smiled. Thank you.

Once Sandee had eaten, he went over the day's events in his mind. He didn't understand why his family had been murdered. *Why didn't the soldiers just take what they wanted and leave my family alone? What was the point of killing them?*

"Skutz!" he screamed angrily.

The rhutz stood up and walked over to him. Fear shot through Sandee's body. "Sorry, friend," he said aloud. "I'm not mad at you."

The rhutz inched closer and looked directly into Sandee's eyes. Their eyes locked and Sandee suddenly felt a rush of energy through his mind. He closed his eyes and tried to shake off the sensation but it only intensified. He held his head with both hands, fearing it would explode if he didn't, then he began to twitch and shake violently. A jolt of fear shot through him.

"What are you doing to me?" he screamed as he scrambled away from the rhutz in fear and terror. After a few tiks, the rhutz backed off and sat a few strides away. Sandee took a deep breath and tried to calm himself. He could feel his heart pounding from the pain of his splitting headache.

"What did you do to me?" he asked angrily.

The rhutz just stared back at him without making a sound. Suddenly, the fire exploded into a magnificent display of glowing embers. He looked at it in awe, mesmerized by a thousand points of light seemingly hovering in suspended animation. Sandee's eyelids became heavy. He struggled to keep them open but to no avail.

They involuntarily closed and his mind opened to a desolate landscape that he recognized.

It was Lake Orage that once supplied water to Lago Lat. During the nuclear missile attack, one of the bombs hit near the lake and created an explosion so hot that it evaporated the entire lake in a few tiks. Since it had been an artificial lake and the dam had been destroyed, the lake did not refill after the explosion. Now it was flat, dry, and without vegetation. What appeared to be an old man in a brown robe stood tall with his hands raised to the sky. The ground shook and his voice echoed over the land as He spoke.

"I am Pelgrem, God of Pharidon and all the multiverse. The human inhabitants of Tarizon, through their selfishness and greed, are destroying this wondrous planet which was my gift to them. Unless a leader emerges soon to restore sanity to the human race, all will be lost."

Sandee said nothing, being completely thunderstruck and overwhelmed by the images before him. The rhutz walked over and sat at Sandee's side. Sandee looked down at him curiously.

"You, Sandee Brahn, are Tarizon's last hope," Pelgrem continued. "You must go forth and lead the people of Tarizon out of the shadow of doom and into the glorious light of peace and renewal."

Sandee swallowed hard. He wasn't sure if Pelgrem would allow him to speak but he felt he must try. "But how could I possibly do what you ask? I am but an orphan child without even food for my next meal."

"You have a quick mind and a kind heart. You are one of but a few humans on Tarizon who have not been corrupted by other humans. I have ordered the rhutz to provide you with food, water, counsel, and protection while you work to bring the human race to its senses. Do not fear, although the journey will be long and treacherous, you are resourceful and have what it takes to save mankind."

"But what do I tell them?" Sandee pressed.

"Tell them their God Pelgrem is here with them on Tarizon and is watching over them. Tell them they must turn from selfishness and greed, and respect and cherish all that I have created. For it is my will that there are peace, justice, and liberty on Tarizon and that the world is returned to its original wonder and splendor. Go forth and do as I command!"

The ground shook again and a lightning bolt struck the ground beside them. Sandee closed his eyes and turned away quickly from the blinding flash of light. Suddenly, in his mind's eye, he saw bombs falling and exploding around him. People were screaming, moaning and crying out in great pain and despair. In the distance he saw glowing mushroom clouds billowing up into the sky, planes crashing, forests burning, troops marching, and people dying everywhere.

When he opened his eyes, Pelgrem was gone and he was back in the cave. He looked curiously at the flickering light of the campfire and the rhutz sleeping nearby. *Was that a dream? Or, was I really visited by the almighty Pelgrem himself?* It didn't feel like anything had changed. He tried to dismiss the dream. *But what if it is true?* He wondered about this until weariness overcame him and he fell asleep. Again vivid dreams came to him, and he saw Tarizon as it had been given to mankind at the beginning of time. He marveled at the clear air, bright sun, high mountains, never-ending plains, gorgeous deserts, and vast oceans, and then understood what God expected of him. When he awoke, he remembered his dreams and wondered how he could accomplish such an impossible task.

2
Evacuation Earth

Tarizon: The city of Vaceen, State of Tributon
13 BU

Romas Garciah walked into the conference room and took a seat at the head of the long glass table around which were seated the men who controlled the twenty most wealthy and powerful companies on Tarizon. Known as the Group of Twenty, the GOT included most of the major players on Tarizon in medicine, agriculture, transportation, electronics, pharmaceuticals, and textiles. They were meeting to discuss the implementation of their evacuation plans now that most of Tarizon's infrastructure had been destroyed and the atmosphere so polluted by nuclear fallout that life, as they knew it on Tarizon, could no longer exist. Romas was the most prestigious of the GOT members being the Chief Justice on the Supreme Council of Interpreters for the state of Tributon.

"Fellow members, for cycles we have been planning for this unpleasant eventuality. We all knew, save divine intervention, that one day the politicians and generals would destroy our planet," Romas said sighing deeply. "Well, I believe the day has arrived that we must implement our evacuation plans. Therefore, I move that final preparations be started immediately for operations Orbital Hibernation and Evacuation Earth."

The chairman of the GOT, Jox Machlyn, a tall, stout man with reddish-brown hair, cleared his throat and replied, "Do I have supporters for the motion?"

Under the groups' charter, it took three members to sponsor a resolution.

"Second," Paya Alt said. Several other members raised their hands to join in supporting the motion.

Paya Alt was the owner of Alt Fuel Corporation, the largest fuel exploration and production company on Tarizon. Unfortunately, with the world's infrastructure in shambles and the environment in such dire straits, demand for oil and gas had been drastically reduced. In fact, the company's main customers now were the nation-states who still had armies to support with vehicles and fighters that needed fuel to operate.

Jox nodded. "There has been a motion properly supported, is there any debate?"

A tall, elderly man with stark white hair stood up. "Yes, the chair recognizes Rama Sloken."

"What if we have changed our minds and want to switch operations?"

Romas shook his head. "The only way that can be done is if you can find someone willing to swap places with you. Otherwise, you are stuck with the choices you have made."

"But my wife is afraid of hibernation. She's in a near panic over the thought of it."

"Just tell her it's like going to bed at night and waking up the next morning."

"She's worried that something will go wrong with the hibernation pods and we'll never wake up."

"That's highly unlikely. The onboard computers are very reliable, and every system has triple redundancy."

"But what if it takes longer than ten cycles for the pollution to clear? How long can we be left in hibernation?"

"Twenty-five cycles, give or take one or two, so I have been told. But you already know this," Romas said impatiently. "There is no guarantee the rest of us will make it to Earth either, or if we do that we will be allowed to settle there. So, there is a great risk for all of us no matter what choice we have made. The debate right now should be on whether it is time to abandon our beloved Tarizon. Is there any hope that our planet can be saved?"

"Every major city on every continent has suffered multiple nuclear strikes," Jox replied. "Millions of our citizens have been killed and billions injured from all the bombs and even more will die from the radiation. Most of our armies have been so decimated by deaths and desertion that they are no longer viable forces for war or even disaster relief. Our governments are in such turmoil that anarchy is the norm. As much as I hate to admit it, Tarizon is lost and the time has come to evacuate."

"And we don't have any time to lose," another member said. "If word gets out that we have an Earth shuttle ready for evacuation, I know of several generals who will try to appropriate it for their own personal use."

"Yes. That is a danger we cannot afford to ignore," Romas agreed. "I think it is time for a vote."

The chairman nodded and said, "All those in favor raise their hands."

There was nearly a unanimous show of hands.

"All right. It is agreed that operations Evacuation Earth and Orbital Hibernation be immediately commenced. You each have 27 kyloons to report to your launch sites. A kyloon was a little longer than an Earth-hour as Tarizon was a little larger than Earth, and there were 27 kyloons in a day. Good luck, and I hope to see all of you on Earth or back on Tarizon someday if the atmosphere clears up, and it is safe to return and rebuild."

After the meeting broke up, everyone said their goodbyes and then rushed off to gather their families together and prepare for the evacuation. Romas caught an air taxi to his compartment near the Capitol Building in

Vaceen, Tributon's capital city. His wife Celius, a jaunty woman with a pale complexion and long, light auburn hair, was anxiously waiting with the children when he came through the door.

Their eldest son Rammel, age 12, bursting with excitement asked, "Are we going to Earth?"

Romas nodded. "Yes, the board agreed it was time."

"Yes!" Rammel said smiling broadly to his sister and brother who were looking a little green.

"Oh, no!" Celius said. "You can't be serious."

"I am quite serious. The vote was unanimous. We leave tomorrow at 1200 kyloons."

"But we will never be ready," she moaned.

"We are as ready as we can be for something like this. There is nothing to pack other than a few clothes. Everything we need is already on the shuttle."

"What about my brother and your sister?"

"I have told Argusto and Elainess to be ready to leave tomorrow."

"I have to say goodbye to my parents and friends," Celius noted.

"No. You can tell no one that we are leaving," Romas said looking sternly at his children. "No one must know we have gone to Earth until we are safely out of Tarizon's atmosphere. You will have two kyloons once we leave to call all your family and friends and give them the news."

"I so wish my mother and father were coming with us. What will become of them?"

"They could have come had they wanted. We can't force them to leave."

"I know, but I fear for them. The streets are not safe; they can't even leave their compartment anymore. How will they get groceries?"

"I will tell my friend Lusus Tomol to look after them but not until after we leave."

"Can you depend on him? He has his own family."

"He is a good man. He'll do everything possible to keep them safe."

"But his family will come first."

Romas sighed. "Of course, but he'll still look after your parents. We've had this conversation before."

"I know, but I'm still worried."

"Father," Eroh, their 11-cycle-old said. "What is Earth like?"

Eroh was tall and muscular with deep blue eyes. He wasn't as outgoing as his elder brother but was just as smart.

"They say it is like Tarizon used to be before the wars," Romas replied.

"The sky is so clear it is blue, and the clouds are pure white," Rammel interjected. "They say there are vast forests and mountains so high, birds can't fly to their summits."

Eroh smiled. "I can't wait to see it."

"Well, tomorrow night you will go to sleep on the shuttle in a hibernation chamber and when you wake up we will almost be to Earth."

"How long will I sleep?"

"A little more than a cycle but it will seem like just one night."

A cycle was the equivalent of an Earth-year.

"Where on Earth are we going to land?" Rammel asked.

Rammel was tall like his brother but had a slim physique. He was brilliant and charismatic, and most everyone thought he would follow in his father's footsteps and become an advocate or counselor.

"We don't know yet. Somewhere in North America probably. That seems to be the most hospitable place to try to set up a settlement."

"Will we contact the authorities on Earth?" Celius asked.

"No. Probably not. The people of Earth do not know of our existence. They may not welcome our arrival, so it is better for us to land and try to blend in with the local population. Later, if the situation seems right, then we might make contact with the authorities and make our presence known."

"What if they see us land?" Rammel asked.

"They won't. They are not as technologically advanced as we are. The stealth capabilities of our Earth shuttles should prevent them from discovering our arrival."

"All right, children. Go wash up," Celius commanded. "Dinner is in thirty loons. After dinner, you will need to do your last-loon packing."

After dinner, when the children were fast asleep, Romas and Celius went out on their balcony to view Vaceen at night one last time. The city was beautiful with its tall buildings internally lit in a rainbow of colors. The darkness of the night hid the chaos on the streets and the burnt yellow pollution that was suffocating the planet. For a moment Celius tried to forget about the reality of their situation. She sighed and smiled at Romas.

"Remember when we first moved into this compartment?" she said.

Romas nodded. "Yes, I do. I had just been appointed to the Supreme Council of Interpreters and we had to find a place to live in a hurry."

"We were lucky to get these accommodations. It has been a wonderful place to raise our family."

"Yes, it has."

"So, I hate to leave it," Celius moaned.

"It's no longer safe," Romas replied. "The public enforcers won't be able to handle the roving mobs of sick and homeless much longer. There was almost a breach just yesterday."

"I know. I've been watching the VC."

"We are lucky that Vaceen's air defenses were able to protect the city from the last nuclear attack. One of the missiles almost made it through. We may not be so lucky next time."

A tear rolled down Celius's cheek. Romas wiped it with his thumb and embraced his wife of twenty-five cycles. "We will get through this. I promise. And one day, when all the lunatic politicians and generals are dead, we can return and rebuild Tarizon."

"I don't think so," Celius said. "If Earth is as wonderful as everyone says, there would be no reason to return."

"Well, I'm going to return some day. The only reason we are leaving now is we don't have a choice. If we stay, we will likely die."

"I know. That's why I am so scared to leave my parents behind."

"Your parents are almost 100 cycles old. If they die soon they will still have lived a long life."

"On Pharidon people often live to be one thousand," Celius reminded him.

"So the history books say, but Pharidon was at peace for ten-thousand cycles. Just think if Tarizon could be at peace for that long."

"Yes. If only that were possible, but I fear human nature won't allow it. If only Pelgrem had come to Tarizon. We need a God to help fight off the evil that is in each of us."

"You don't need a God to keep evil out of your life, just a strong desire to do what's right."

"Most people think anything to their advantage is good and right. They have no clear understanding of good or evil."

"True. Selfishness and greed have been Tarizon's downfalls," Romas agreed. He took one last look at the magnificent lights of the city. "We should go to bed. Tomorrow will be a hectic day and we must leave before dawn to avoid the mobs."

Celius nodded and they went inside to take one last inventory of what they were taking with them. A kyloon before dawn they were up and getting ready to leave. A long line of air taxis was hovering above their building waiting for their passengers. When Romas saw them, he shuddered. "Skutz! If anyone in the media sees all these taxis, they will know something is up. We should have staggered our departures throughout the day."

"It's too late now," Celius said. "Let's get to the roof quickly and just hope all the reporters are still asleep."

They rushed to the elevators but when Romas pushed the call button nothing happened. "They're really busy," Romas said. "We will have to take the stairs."

"The stairs?" Celius repeated. "You can't be serious. It's thirty floors to the roof."

"We don't have a choice. We could be waiting for an elevator tube for kyloons."

Romas began walking quickly to the stairwells. Celius and the children followed him reluctantly. When he opened the door, another family was walking past. "Come on! Hurry!" he said, waving Celius and the children past as he held the door. The noise of many feet echoed in the stairwell. It was a long hard climb and they were all exhausted when they finally reached the roof.

"I'll summon our taxi," Romas said as they stepped out onto the landing pad. He spoke into his wrist array. Five families were already milling around waiting for their taxi to land. Romas looked up at Celius. "It's here, number 2407."

A few tiks later, a taxi descended from above.

Romas's wrist array flashed. "It's here, come on." Several taxis were on the roof and Romas was afraid there was going to be a collision. Just as they were boarding their taxi they heard a sharp clash of metal on metal. Romas looked out and saw two taxis collide. One of them managed to set back down on the roof but the other one lost power and disappeared off the side of the building. A tik later there was an explosion.

"Oh, my God!" Celius exclained. "Let's get out of here."

Their copter took flight and soon they were flying fast above the city toward the spaceport.

"I wonder who that was," Romas said. "What a horrible thing to happen. We should have anticipated this. I thought we had thought of every contingency."

"The media will be all over this now," Rammel said.

"What's going to happen?"

"The spaceport will be mobbed, and we'll be lucky to get off without killing a lot of people in the process."

"Oh, Romas. What if the crowds block us? We won't be able to leave."

"Don't worry about that. Our security forces can handle any contingency. I just didn't want us to have to fight our way to the ship. A lot of people will die needlessly if that happens."

Romas tapped on his wrist array to call up a video of the local news. A reporter was talking.

"In Vaceen it seems there has been a taxi collision on the Continental Building causing the death or injury of at least five citizens. Reportedly, more than a hundred taxis were operating in the immediate area. There is no word as to why so many taxis were in one place."

There was a moment of silence as the reporter

listened to his earpiece.

"I have just been informed several buildings have had heavy taxi traffic and there is speculation that the long-anticipated evacuation by the Group of Twenty is underway. We have dispatched reporters to the spaceport to confirm this report."

Romas shook his head and shut off the video. "This is all we need."

"Will we make it before the mobs, father?" Rammel asked.

"I don't know. I have put the security forces on alert just in case we don't."

A few loons later the Vaceen Spaceport came into view. Mobs of people could be seen rushing toward the facility. "Hurry," Romas commanded the pilot. People were climbing over the fences to the heliport as they landed. Several security policemen were firing warning shots into the air, but the mob just came pouring over the fences. Finally, the security officers started firing into the crowd. People began to fall, and the flow of humanity briefly slowed. This gave Romas and his family just enough time to enter the terminal and disappear. Ten loons later they were walking aboard Earth Shuttle 7.

An officer saluted Romas as he stepped aboard. Romas nodded and asked, "Captain Linde, what's the status of our departure?"

Captain Linde was a retired test pilot from the Rigimol Air Force (RAF). Upon retirement at age thirty-two, the blue-eyed blond from Fasoon had been recruited by Khor Aerodynamics to test-fly the first Earth Shuttles which were in development at the time. Being highly recommended as the best shuttle pilot available, Romas had hired him to command Earth Shuttle 7 for the

GOT.

"The ship is ready for flight. We have 1731 passengers on board with 269 on their way."

"I'm not sure any more will make it. The Spaceport is under siege."

"We will depart on your command, sir," Captain Linde replied

"Any other problems?"

"I have been informed a squadron of T17s has taken off from Ce Lat with orders to stop us from leaving."

"What! How much time do we have?"

"We must be in the air in seventeen loons to avoid contact with the T17s."

"Then prepare for takeoff in fifteen loons."

"Yes, sir."

"Does everyone have to be in their hibernation pods before we take off?"

"No. We can put people in pods after takeoff, but anyone not in a pod will have to suffer through a rather unpleasant takeoff."

"Well, they will just have to suffer through it."

"Do you want to go to your pod now, Councilor?"

"No. Take my family to a safe place. I want to stay awake until everyone is on board and we are safely in space."

"Very well. I'll have someone take you to the bridge."

"Romas," Celius called out as they were taking her and the kids away. "I want to stay with you."

"No. Go with the children. I'll see you when we are safely on our way."

"But Romas," she moaned as they were led away.

"It will be okay," Romas assured her.

An explosion rocked the ship. Dust and debris fell down on them as Romas grabbed a railing for support.

"What was that?" Romas asked worriedly.

"A missile attack," Captain Linde said irritably. Apparently, they realized the fighters would not get here in time.

"Take off immediately. We can't afford to wait any longer."

"Yes, sir," Captain Linde said as they rushed toward the bridge. "I just hope it's not already too late."

Romas swallowed hard and prayed none of the missiles would hit their target.

3
Takeoff

Romas took a place in one of the spectator seats on the bridge and strapped himself in. Captain Linde began barking orders to the crew. The ship rocked again from a missile strike too close for comfort. The ship began to vibrate harshly as the thrusters came to life.

"Get us out of here," Captain Linde ordered as the ship started to slowly rise off the ground.

As each tik went by the big shuttle gained speed and soon it was rapidly ascending through the clouds. Romas looked out his window and saw Vaceen growing smaller and smaller beneath them. Soon the town, where he had lived most of his life, disappeared and all he could see was a layer of yellowish grey clouds beneath them. Romas felt a tinge of remorse knowing that he might never see Vaceen again.

As the shuttle gained speed in its effort to escape Tarizon's gravity, Romas reeled from the g-forces that felt like they would crush his skull. He struggled to breathe and retain his consciousness. Passengers were usually spared the trauma of takeoff and reentry by being placed in their hibernation pods immediately, but the missile attack had prevented that on this trip. Romas wondered how his wife and children were taking the pain and discomfort of takeoff.

When they had escaped Tarizon's atmosphere, Romas rushed to where they had taken his family. As he approached, he could hear Celius trying to comfort their daughter Tillie who was visibly shaken.

Tillie was seven-cycles-old and had always been a frail child. Romas had feared the trip to Earth might be too much for her.

"Oh, I am so glad you are here. That was horrible! Poor Tillie. I wanted to hold her, but I was strapped into my chair."

"Are you all right, Tillie?" Romas asked.

Tillie nodded. "Now I am. What happened? I thought the ship was going to break apart and we were going to die."

Rammel laughed. "No, you dirkbird, that happens every time you take off or land."

"Rammel," Celius scolded. "Your sister didn't know that. I was scared too."

"Why didn't you warn me about that?" Eroh complained.

"We thought you'd be in your hibernation pod and wouldn't feel it," Romas replied.

"So, since we didn't have time to get in the pods, does that mean we get to stay awake the rest of the trip?" Rammel asked.

Romas smiled. "No. I'm afraid not. We don't have enough food for everyone to stay awake. Besides, you'd be bored to tears in a confined space for a cycle."

Rammel sighed. "Then let's get this over with. I want to go to sleep and wake up on Earth."

"Okay. But before we go into our pods I want to take you to the bridge and let you see Tarizon from space."

"Oh, good!" Eroh said.

Celius smiled. "Yes, that would be nice."

Romas led them back to the bridge and introduced them to Captain Linde. The captain switched the big video screen to a rear view and they saw Tarizon in the distance.

"Wow!" Rammel said. "I can't believe that is where we lived. It looks so small from up here."

"Yes, it does," Romas agreed.

"What are all the little lights?" Eroh asked.

Romas frowned. "Oh, that's right. You have never seen a star."

"Those are stars?"

"Yes. Tarizon's atmosphere is so polluted you can't see them from the ground anymore."

"There are so many of them."

"Yes. More stars than you could count in a lifetime."

"Okay. Enough star gazing," Celius said. "I'm sure the captain has more important things to attend to. Come on. Let's get back to the hibernation deck. I want to get this part of our journey over with."

Romas looked at Celius. "You aren't scared, are you?"

She nodded. "Yes, aren't you?"

"Sure, a little. It's only natural. But there's really nothing to worry about."

"Good. So, let's just get it over with. I will feel better when I am back on solid ground."

"Okay, children. You heard your mother. Back to the hibernation deck."

Eroh, Tillie, and Rammel reluctantly followed their mother out of the bridge and back to the hibernation deck. There was a line of people waiting to be fitted and placed in their pods. Tillie grabbed her mother's arm and held it tightly.

"I will go first, so you can see that it won't hurt and will be perfectly safe."

A crewman took Celius by the arm and escorted her to an empty pod. After helping her get into it, he hooked up several monitors to her, fixed a mask over her face, and then injected her with a sleep serum. Tillie watched worriedly and looked up at her father.

"It will all right, Love. I'll see you on Earth," Romas

assured her.

Tillie looked at her father and swallowed hard.

"Be brave," Romas said, stifling a tear.

Romas watched anxiously as each of his family members were put in their pods and put into a deep sleep. As he was being situated in his own pod, he prayed to Pelgrem that he and his family would arrive safely on Earth and awake to a better life.

4
Whisper

Sandee lived with the rhutz and his pack in Lecton for nearly a cycle. He hunted with them, ate, even played their games and slept in their den. It wasn't easy keeping up with them but over time he became very fast, strong and developed tremendous endurance. He even learned to talk to them without speaking.

It began just after the pack had fed on a morning kill and had left some meat for Sandee to eat. Whisper looked up and Sandee felt a strange feeling in his head. He closed his eyes and saw the image of a campfire.

"That meat is for me?" Sandee said out loud. "I should make a fire."

Whisper nodded slightly and thought about the sound he'd heard, "Make a fire."

For many phases of the moon Clarion, Whisper continued to send images into Sandee's head and Sandee would describe them out loud in Tari, the primary language of Tarizon.

One day Sandee got an image of Whisper leading him away from the cave. Sandee was carrying provisions, so Sandee realized it wasn't going to be a short excursion somewhere.

"We must leave this place." Whisper thought.

The voice was soft like a whisper. He looked around and saw Whisper looking at him.

"This is the way the rhutz communicate," Whisper thought.

Sandee nodded. *"Yes, I figured that out. What shall I call you?"*

"My voice is soft, so I am called Whisper."

"Yes, I noticed that. I could barely feel it."

"It will get stronger as our bond strengthens."

Sandee nodded again. *"So, why must we leave?"*

"Pelgrem says your task must begin in Lyon."

"Why?"

"Pelgrem did not explain. He said to lead you to Lyon and stay with you until your destiny has been fulfilled."

"My destiny? To lead the world to peace? How am I supposed to end the war and bring peace? I'm but a boy."

"A boy with the hand of God to guide him."

"You sure that wasn't a meaningless dream?"

"No. It was our first time to meet. Our dreams could not have brought about such events. Pelgrem came to me earlier in a dream and told me I would be meeting you. He said I must teach you the ways of the rhutz because the rhutz had been living in peace and harmony with the land for centuries. Then you appeared just as He said, so I knew it was really Him."

"Well, my family has been murdered, so there is nothing keeping me in Lecton," Sandee thought bitterly.

"Yes. I'm so sorry about that. I wish I could have helped you save them, but that was not part of God's plan."

"Why not? They could have helped me with this impossible task."

"I can't answer that question, but your task isn't impossible. Pelgrem said it would be a long and difficult struggle, but that you could bring about peace."

"So, how have the rhutz managed to live in peace for so long?" Sandee asked.

"Every rhutz puts the pack first. Every important decision is made through the collective consciousness and

not by any individual rhutz. Only when we have a consensus do we act."

"What is the collective consciousness?" Sandee asked.

"It's when all rhutz think together. Our minds are linked and a decision is reached that is best for all of us."

"But humans can't do that," Sandee noted.

"True. But you have other methods of communication that could work as well. It's just a matter of always thinking of the good of Tarizon rather than what's good for one individual or one nation-state. Humans must learn to consider the consequences of their actions and restrain from doing things that will harm the environment or other life-forms."

"What happens if one of your pack doesn't like the collective decision and refuses to go along with it?"

"That isn't allowed and no rhutz would dare challenge the decision of the collective."

"But so many humans are selfish, stubborn and independent. They won't be easily brought in line."

"With Pelgrem's guidance, you will persuade them," Whisper assured him.

"Right," Sandee thought skeptically. *"So, I guess we should figure out how to get to Lyon, then."*

"Yes," Whisper thought. *"To get to Lyon we have to cross the Green Mountains and winter is fast approaching. It's at least five hundred kylods to the base of the mountains. We will be lucky to get there before the passes become impassable."*

"Have you been there before?"

"No. But there are packs along the way who will give us food and shelter."

"Okay. When do we leave?"

Sandee hadn't been convinced he'd really met Pelgrem. He thought it could have been a wild dream or hallucination. He wondered if he'd been poisoned by the rodent he ate that first night and none of what he thought he'd seen was real. But he had been living with a pack of rhutz and felt Whisper's presence in his mind now. He couldn't deny that. To think he had the gift of telepathy and could communicate without speaking was mind-boggling. Only a small percentage of humans had this gift and he never suspected he was one of them.

None of his family had the gift to his knowledge. He couldn't believe he was so lucky. He pondered his dream of Pelgrem. Why would God pick him to lead a movement to save the world? What was so special about him? He didn't feel special. He felt tired and often depressed when he thought of his family and his circumstances. In his mind he was nobody. He was just a boy and, right then, wanted to do nothing more than find something tasty to eat.

What bothered him the most was why Pelgrem had waited so long to intervene. After all, Tarizon had been at war for over a century. *Why now? Isn't it a little late to be trying to save the planet? How many millions of lives have been lost already?* Then he remembered Pelgrem had said this was mankind's last chance. So, perhaps other messengers had been sent but each had failed. I have no choice but to be successful or see Tarizon destroyed. Still, why me?

Later that day Whisper found Sandee and they started their journey south along the west bank of the Loctula River. Whisper told him they'd take it toward Pala Uza, the capital city of Serie, but turn east toward the Green Mountains before they reached it. Pala Uza had sustained several nuclear strikes during the Lecton-Serie war and what was left of the Serie government had reportedly moved north to Marna.

Late in the afternoon, two days later after traveling more than 30 kylods, Whisper stopped and looked around.

They were nearing the Green Mountains once known for its vast forests, clear mountain streams and plentiful game. Unfortunately, much of it had burned during the war and the forests were now just starting to come back. "This is where the river turns west. We must continue south. There is a tube that leads to Pala Uza but it will be well-traveled."

Tubes were enclosed highways that had been built to protect travelers from the toxic atmosphere and bad weather. If properly maintained they made high-speed vehicular travel between domed cities possible. Unfortunately, they were often attacked by enemy forces to disrupt troop movements and sever supply lines. The Pala Uza Tube hadn't been spared, and since the war, the tube had become a place of refuge for mutants who weren't allowed into the domed cities. Most of the traffic was on foot since fuel was now a scarce commodity.

"Do you think it will be safe?" Sandee thought.

"Not for a child or a rhutz, I'm afraid."

"What are we going to do, then?"

"We can walk parallel to the tube but not inside. There will be a few places, like bridges and mountain passes, where we will need to travel inside, but if we are careful it should be all right."

"I'm tired and hungry," Sandee complained.

"Yes, it will be dark soon. I will reach out to my rhutz brothers and sisters nearby and arrange for a place for us to stay."

They stopped in a clearing close enough to the tube that they could hear people inside talking. It was starting to snow as Sandee sat and leaned back against a tree that somehow had survived the war. Whisper looked around, sniffed the cold air and then sat next to Sandee.

"A rhutz named Snowflake will be here in a loon. She will bring us food and show us where we can get clean

water."

"How come I didn't feel her presence?" Sandee asked.

"Because you are not a rhutz, you are not linked to the collective consciousness."

"The collective consciousness? What's that again?"

"It's a channel of communication between packs."

"So, you are really connected to all the other rhutz on Tarizon?"

"Yes, but the collective consciousness is not always open. It can only be invoked when it is necessary for the survival of one or more packs."

Sandee looked up and saw a white rhutz running up to them. Whisper got to his feet and allowed Snowflake to sniff him. The beautiful rhutz then turned to Sandee bowing slightly. Sandee smiled and stuck out his hand for her to sniff.

Sandee felt Snowflake in his head and saw images of water and range deer. It was snowing harder now and getting colder. As they walked, a flood of images came through his mind, images of Snowflake's pack and the surrounding terrain. He assumed she was sharing these images to make their next day's journey easier. Snowflake led them into a cave where the sweet sound of dripping water could be heard in the distance. Finally, they got to the pool of water and drank deeply.

Feeling better with his thirst quenched, Sandee started to think about food. He hoped their host would provide them with something better than the rodents he often had to endure. As they left the cave Sandee's spirits soared seeing two freshly killed range deer on the ground in front of them.

"I hope one of those is for us. I'm starving," Sandee thought.

"Yes, cut off what you want to cook and leave the rest

for the pack."

"Sure, no problem," Sandee thought as he pulled out his knife.

Once he had cut off a good sized steak from the hind quarter, he set it aside to make a fire. The pack pulled the remains of the carcass a few strides away and began feeding on it. Soon he had a raging fire going, and was enjoying its warmth and the scent of the roasting range deer that permeated the air. Ten loons later he put the steak on a metal plate he had been carrying in his backpack and began to eat. He watched snowflakes land on his plate and melt before his eyes.

As he was chewing his first bite, one of the rhutz began to growl. Sandee looked over in the direction of the disturbance and saw an elderly man standing there looking rather pale. He had long grey hair that came to his shoulders with a beard and mustache to match.

"Excuse me, boy!" the man said. "Can you control these beasts?"

Sandee looked up and smiled. "Don't worry. They won't hurt you unless you try to harm me."

"No. No. I smelt your range deer cooking and wondered who was eating so well."

"Well, I would have cut some off for you had I known you were coming."

"That's okay. I don't want to impose," the man said taking in the strange scene before him. "So, you have a rhutz protecting you?"

Sandee smiled. "Yes. I guess I do."

The man inched closer to the fire and put out his hands to take in its warmth. He stared into the flames as Sandee took another bite.

"I haven't eaten range deer in cycles," the man said. "Haven't even seen one in these parts since the war began. Thought maybe they'd all died off."

Sandee grinned. "Hey, I doubt I can eat this whole piece, why don't I split it with you?"

"Really?"

"Yes, I insist," Sandee said, stifling a laugh.

The man walked over eagerly and sat down. Sandee took his knife and cut the steak into two pieces and put one on a clean plate. He gave the man the plate, a knife, and a fork and they ate together in silence for a few moments.

"My name is Mill Talvihn. I'm the ambassador of Lyon."

"The ambassador?" Sandee said, taken aback.

"Yes. We are traveling from Pompelus to Marna, the capital of Serie."

Sandee frowned, "You're traveling alone in the wilderness?"

"No. No. I'm not alone. My entourage is just over there inside the tube."

"Oh. Well, I'm glad to hear that. It's warmer in there, I hope."

"No, not really, but there's no snow and we're protected from the chill of the wind."

"Good. We can't travel in the tube. The rhutz aren't welcome there."

"No. I expect not."

Sandee extended his hand. "I'm Sandee Brahn from Lecton."

The Ambassador glanced warily at the rhutz chewing on its prey, then took Sandee's hand and shook it. "Nice to meet you. How is it that you came to live with a pack of rhutz?"

Sandee winced at the question. He'd almost purged his mind of the haunting memory. Thoughts of his family's brutal murder still haunted him. He looked down trying to suppress his anger and bitterness. After a tik, he took a deep breath and replied, "Well, my family was murdered actually and that rhutz over there, Whisper, saved my life."

"Oh, my God!" Ambassador Talvihn exclaimed. "Your whole family?"

"Yes, my mother and father and brother and sister."

"You poor child."

Tears welled in Sandee's eyes and he struggled to keep his composure. "I can't really accept it yet. It all just seems like a bad dream."

"Yes. I can imagine. I have never heard of a rhutz saving a human's life. Do you have any idea why they have taken you in?"

Sandee wasn't sure if he should answer the question. He feared the old man would think he was crazy. But he was an ambassador and seemed to be wise and understanding, so he decided to confide in him. He told the Ambassador about his encounter with Pelgrem and the task that had been thrust upon him.

"Pelgrem actually appeared before you?" the Ambassador questioned.

"I think so, but it could have been a dream or hallucination. Whisper assures me it was not a dream, though."

"So, you communicate with Whisper?"

"Yes. We open our minds and trade thoughts. It is very strange. I never knew I had the gift."

"Forgive me if I am a bit skeptical, but could you give me a demonstration? I want to believe you, but—"

"No. I understand. I scarcely believe it myself. What would you like me to do?"

"I don't know," Ambassador Talvihn said apologetically and then bent over and whispered into Sandee's ear. "Tell your rhutz to get up and walk around the campfire two times, but tell him with your mind."

Sandee smiled and looked at Whisper. *I'm sorry to bother you, Whisper, but would you mind getting up and circling the campfire a couple times? The Ambassador doesn't believe we can communicate telepathically."*

Whisper jumped up and looked back at Sandee. *"Humans. They think they are the only life-form with a brain in their head."*

"Thank you," Sandee thought.

Whisper started walking and did a complete circle around the campfire, hesitated, and then did it again. The Ambassador watched him intently and then shook his head.

"Wow! It's true. You can really communicate with him."

Sandee laughed. "I told you."

"I know. I'm sorry I didn't believe you. This is all a bit hard to fathom."

"Yes, it is," Sandee agreed. "So, tell me. What brings you to Serie?"

"I am on a diplomatic mission. Rikin Linzcot, our new chancellor, wants me to try to negotiate a truce with Serie. This war has gone on too long and further death and destruction aren't going to accomplish anything. It is time for peace."

"Do you think they will listen to you?"

"Probably not, but I have to try."

"I wish there were some way I could help?" Sandee said. "But I really don't know how."

The Ambassador gave Sandee a thoughtful look. "Didn't Pelgrem tell you how to bring about peace?"

Sandee shook his head. "Not really. He gave me a message of sorts to convey to the people. He said getting the people to listen would be a long and difficult process but that he would help guide me along the way."

"You know. Our meeting may not have been a chance encounter then. I don't usually wander away from my entourage, particularly my security, but I felt an uncontrollable yearning for a walk in the cold, damp woods and then smelled the range deer cooking. That couldn't be a coincidence. You should come with me to Marna and be there when I meet with Chancellor Dosimo. You might be able to help me negotiate a truce."

"But I'm still just a child. They will laugh at me when I tell them Pelgrem sent me."

"Not if your rhutz is at your side and we tell your story to the media before we meet with the Chancellor. If the people believe God has sent you, the Chancellor will have to listen."

Sandee frowned. He wasn't sure he was ready to start negotiating with heads of state. After all, not too long ago he had been just a poor boy trying to help his family survive one day at a time. He had no special education, no training or political experience. How could he possibly be expected to bring peace to a world that had been at war for over a century?

5
Salina Gill

Sandee liked Ambassador Talvihn's confidence and enthusiasm but he didn't share his optimism that anyone would believe that Pelgrem had sent him to bring peace to Tarizon. He was torn as whether he should follow this man or continue on to Lyon where he thought his destiny was to be fulfilled. Finally, he succumbed to Mill's insistence that he accompany him to Marna in search of the Serie government and Chancellor Dosimo. He just hoped he was making the right decision.

The next morning they entered the tube and joined the Ambassador's delegation headed to Marna. Sandee had never been in a tube before and marveled at how huge it was inside. He thought it must be ten times as big as any cave he'd ever seen. There were numerous cracks in the otherwise smooth inner surface. He surmised it was the result of bombing or tremors, and wondered if the tube was still structurally sound.

Although the tubes had been built for high-speed vehicular traffic, there were no PTVs or trucks operating anymore. Serie had long since run out of fuel and the electrical grid hadn't been operational in many cycles. So, most of the travelers in the tube were on foot, riding on a cart behind a zodillo, which looked like a large Earth buffalo, or on a zach which resembled an Earth zebra with the exception that its stripes were black and yellow.

Mill assured them they would be okay in the tube even with a rhutz in their company as he had an entourage of government officials and a security team. But Rack Brodie, his chief of security, was alarmed when he saw Whisper at Sandee's side when they were introduced that morning.

"Are we taking a rhutz along with us?" he asked warily.

"Yes," Mill replied. "Whisper has been assigned by Pelgrem to protect Sandee. He cannot leave his side."

Brodie laughed. "Oh, really? That could cause some concern from fellow travelers in the tube."

Mill shrugged. "True. But it will also attract interest and speculation about our mission, which is something we desperately need. I'm hoping word will get out to the media that we are coming."

Sandee spotted a young woman with long blond hair approaching. She smiled warmly and her pearl white teeth sparkled even in the dim light of the tube. He gazed at her shyly and when she extended her hand shook it eagerly.

"Hello, I'm Salina Gill, Mr. Talvihn's chief of staff."

Sandee wasn't sure how to react. He finally bowed awkwardly and smiled. "It's a pleasure to meet you."

Salina took his arm and said, "Come with me. The Ambassador has asked me to make you comfortable on our journey. My carriage is this way."

"Thank you," Sandee said as she guided him through the crowd. He looked back to make sure Whisper was following. He was, and this reassured him.

"So, you and your rhutz were traveling alone?"

"Yes, we were on our way to Lyon."

"Do you have family there?"

"No. I have no family. They were all killed."

"Oh, that's right!" she cringed. "The Ambassador told me that. I'm so sorry."

"Thank you," Sandee replied uncomfortably.

"Your rhutz is beautiful," Salina said looking back at

him and wanting to change the subject. "What's his name?"

"Whisper."

"Well, welcome to our delegation, Whisper."

Whisper looked up at Salina cautiously.

Salina smiled and turned back to Sandee. "Mill tells me you and Whisper were on your own personal mission of peace."

"You could say that, but we really don't have much of a plan yet."

"Well, perhaps by joining together we can develop one."

"Absolutely," Sandee said feeling relieved and excited by Salina's confidence and enthusiasm. "And we shall succeed," he heard himself say, "It is God's will."

Salina smiled. "That's good to hear. You and your rhutz will ride with me. I have plenty of room in my carriage and we have so much to talk about."

Sandee nodded appreciatively. Salina excited him and he liked the idea that he would be spending time with her. It would be a welcome change from living with a pack of rhutz.

"Careful my friend," Whisper thought. *"You can't let anything distract you from your mission."*

Sandee looked over at Whisper. *"She's not a distraction. She is just a nice person and pleasant to be around."*

"That's true. Just don't spend so much time thinking about her that you lose focus."

He laughed to himself. *"Lose focus? I'm only eleven-cycles-old, I don't even know how to focus."*

"That's not true. You helped your family survive for cycles after the nuclear strikes. That took a lot of focus."

"But it was a much simpler task than bringing about world peace. Why do people fight, anyway? Why don't they

get along? I have no idea what I should be doing to bring about peace. I feel so inadequate."

"Don't worry. You are already doing what needs to be done. Pelgrem is guiding you. He brought you to the Ambassador and now Salina. You must have faith."

"Right," Sandee thought. *"My father talked a lot about faith and look where that got him."*

Whisper turned away feeling rather inadequate himself. He wondered why he had been chosen to be a companion to a human. He'd had no experience with human beings, particularly one so young.

"Pelgrem should have chosen a wise one rather than me for this job."

The oldest rhutz in each pack was called the wise one and routinely consulted in difficult situations.

"What do I know of humans and their politics? How am I supposed to be of any help to you in this sacred mission?"

"You saved my life, provided me with food and shelter and now are protecting me along my journey. You know exactly what Pelgrem asked you to do and you're doing it. I wasn't given any specific instructions, just an expected result? It's not fair."

Sandee followed Salina to a large carriage that was being pulled behind a zodillo. The beast stomped its feet impatiently and let out an intense wail that echoed off the walls of the tube forcing Sandee to cover his ears or suffer broken eardrums.

Salina laughed. "Burkha is a noisy one, but you'll get used to her."

"Are you sure?" Sandee replied skeptically.

"Yes. You wouldn't want to walk to Marna. It's a hundred and fifty kylods and the nights are very cold in the mountains, not to mention that zodillos walk three times as fast as we do."

"How do you control them? I wouldn't think they would be easily tamed."

"We communicate with them as you communicate with your rhutz."

"Seriously? They are not slaves?"

"No. We feed and protect their herds in Lyon in exchange for transport."

Sandee raised his eyebrows. He'd heard about zodillos but had never seen one in person. His father had told him about visiting zodillo runs and betting on their races. But he had understood that zodillos were slaves and cruelly treated.

Sandee looked at Whisper. *"Can you communicate with the zodillos?"*

"Yes." Whisper thought. *"If there is a need. The rhutz and zodillos have always been at peace. They feed on grass and we hunt game, so there is no reason for us to fight."*

The interior of the carriage was spacious and lavishly decorated. Salina showed Sandee to a bank of soft chairs where they sat and relaxed. After a few loons, the carriage began to move forward in a rhythmic motion.

"So, what about you?" Sandee asked. "How did you get involved with the ambassador?"

"My father and he were friends and he was like an uncle to me when I was growing up. I have always admired his efforts to settle disputes peacefully and avoid war, so when it was time for me to choose a career I asked him if I could work for him. He agreed, so here I am."

"You don't have a mate?"

"No. There hasn't been time for that. I'm on the road most of the time."

"So, do you like your job?"

"Yes, I do. It's frustrating at times, but we have to do all we can to stop the fighting. So many people have died."

Sandee nodded and they continued to talk as their caravan slowly made its way northeast toward Marna. When night came, they stopped to let the zodillo eat and rest for the night. Sandee wondered if he should ask Whisper to find them something to eat. He didn't know what the Ambassador's Chief of Staff had planned for dinner.

Salina seeing the confusion on his face said, "I have plenty of field rations if you are hungry."

Sandee frowned. "Field rations?"

"Yes. It's the only alternative when you are traveling these days, but they are not so bad. Just swallow them quickly."

"Ah. Maybe Whisper can find us something more appetizing."

Upon hearing this suggestion Whisper took off in a run. They saw him leave the tube through a crack in the wall and disappear. Ten loons later he returned with a rabbit in his mouth. Sandee smiled at the sight and gratefully took it from Whisper.

"You like rabbit meat?" Sandee asked.

Salina shrugged. "I don't know. I've never had it before."

"I'll get a fire going and we can find out."

Salina smiled. "Good. I can't wait."

As Sandee was making a fire, Mill walked over to them. "Your rhutz found you some game, huh?"

Sandee nodded. "You want him to catch you a rabbit?"

"No. No. I'm sure it wasn't easy for him to find it. Rabbits are scarce these days. No. I just wanted to ask if you could come to the media bus later for a news conference."

"A news conference?"

"Yes, I have arranged a remote link with the local

Marna media. I want to give them time to stir things up a bit before we arrive there tomorrow afternoon."

"They have media in Marna?"

"Yes. It's censored by the government, of course, but they have agreed to cover the peace initiative."

"Do they know about me?"

"I mentioned your name but didn't tell them much. I want you to be a surprise."

"What about Whisper?"

"You can introduce him when the time is right."

"Okay. But I'm not sure what to tell them. I haven't really put together a . . . ah . . . speech yet."

"Don't worry about that. I will give them simple questions to ask you to get the ball rolling. Just answer from your heart. I am sure you will do fine."

Sandee swallowed hard. "I'm not sure I'm ready for the media. This is all happening so fast."

"You'll do fine," Salina assured him. "After all, you'll have Pelgrem at your side."

Sandee's stomach twisted. He nodded uncertainly. "I guess."

Sandee wondered if Salina and Mill really believed he had talked to Pelgrem. They were difficult to read. They seemed sincere but they were politicians and his father had warned him about politicians. They couldn't be trusted, he often said, as they would say or do anything to get what they wanted.

After eating the rabbit, Sandee and Salina went for a walk in the forest outside the tube. It was a cold night but Sandee thought the air here was much cleaner and easier to breathe than it was on the plains of Lecton. He mentioned it to Salina.

"It's not so bad in Ya Lat either," Salina said. "We get a stiff breeze off the Coral Sea that disburses the pollutants and drives them into the Oringo Desert."

"Have you lived at Ya Lat long?" Sandee asked.

"All my life. My father has always been in one political position or another, so Ya Lat has always been my home. We'll take you there once we are done in Marna."

"Good. I'm looking forward to it."

"Tell me, does Pelgrem talk to you frequently?"

"No. Just that one time. I wish he would, though. I'd have a lot of questions."

She laughed. "I'm sure you would. I can't imagine the pressure you must feel."

He nodded. "Yes. Mainly I worry that I will fail. Ending the war seems like such an impossible task."

Salina smiled warmly. "Yes it does, but I believe in you. I don't think you will fail. You have an aura of divinity around you that is unmistakable."

Sandee laughed. "Really? Nobody has ever told me that before."

"No. It's true. It's in your eyes, your calm demeanor, and humility. Most men, if they believed they were an instrument of God, would be arrogant and condescending, but you are kind and respectful of others and wise beyond your age."

He smiled. "And you are very generous in your praise for someone who has known me for only a day."

"Well, I'm a good judge of character. I have to be in my position."

After their walk, Salina took Sandee to Ambassador Mill's media bus for the news conference. The rear of the bus had a communications center complete with a remote video communicator which Salina referred to as a VC. The middle of the bus contained dressing rooms, bathroom and make-up stations. When they were traveling, the media staff rode in the front of the bus behind the driver. The media bus had an engine but with no fuel, so, it too was being pulled by a zodillo.

Sandee was taken to the communication's section and seated in front of the VC next to the Ambassador. After a few moments, a technician advised them the conference would begin in 10 tiks.

"9...8...7...6...5...4...3...2...you are live!" he said.

The screen came to life and a group of about twenty-five reporters and cameramen appeared on the screen looking less than enthusiastic. Ambassador Mill cleared his throat. "Hello. I'm Ambassador Mill Talvihn from your neighbor Lyon. As I informed some of you last night I have been sent by Chancellor Rikin Linzcot to commence negotiations with Serie for an end to the war between our two countries.

"As you may have heard the Group of Twenty has already made plans to abandon Tarizon. Some of them are planning to go to our sister world Earth and others are going to live in hibernation pods on indefinite orbit around Tarizon. Unfortunately, most of our citizens don't have the option to sit out these wars off-planet, so it is incumbent upon our leaders to try to stop them.

"Since Lyon and Serie have been at each other's throats for nearly a century, Chancellor Linzcot thought a cease-fire between our two governments could be a good start toward that objective. On our way here we had a chance encounter with a fascinating boy who has been living with a pack of rhutz."

There was a buzz of excitement and curiosity in the audience.

"Yes, a pack of rhutz, but I'll let him tell you all about that later. After several long conversations with this boy over the last couple of days, I am convinced that a lasting peace may finally be possible. Okay, I will take a few questions now, and then if you have any questions for this remarkable boy, Sandee Brahn, or Whisper the rhutz they will be happy to answer them."

Hands shot up for permission to speak but the Ambassador reminded them that they had previously drawn for the order of asking questions. Everyone took their seat and the selected reporter stood up. "As you know the rights to the water of the Pinnela River have been a recurrent source of conflict between our two countries. How do you propose to end that dispute?"

"As you know the Pinnela River is so polluted at this time that the water isn't worth much to anyone. We need to jointly address this issue first and then agree to the fair use of the water by both countries once the water is drinkable again."

"Do you represent your allies in this peace initiative, Lower Serie and Darkland?" the second reporter asked."

Ambassador Talvihn nodded. "They agree that it is time for peace and will join these talks if progress is made."

The third reporter stood up. "Can you tell us more about this boy and his rhutz and what they have to do with bringing peace to our nations or to Tarizon?"

"Yes. It was my good fortune to run into this boy, Sandee Brahn, and a rhutz named Whisper. They were traveling together on a pilgrimage to Lyon."

"What kind of a pilgrimage?" the reporter asked.

"I'm going to let them tell you about it," Mill advised nodding to Sandee.

Sandee sat up straight and looked into the camera nervously. "Ah . . . well . . . a cycle ago, I came back to my home in Lecton to find that my family, my mother, father, brother, and sister, had been murdered."

There were sympathetic moans from the reporters.

"I didn't have time to grieve as the killers were still there and came after me. Luckily a rhutz showed up and saved my life. I know that must seem hard to believe, but it is true. Whisper the rhutz saved my life and has been assigned the task of protecting me while I work to bring about peace to Tarizon."

"Assigned by who?" Reporter #1 asked.

"God, . . . Pelgrem. He appeared and told me it was my task to bring peace to Tarizon."

The reporters were silent save a few that couldn't stifle their laughter.

Reporter #3 said, "Where is this rhutz you speak of?"

Sandee looked over at Whisper and nodded for him to come in front of the camera. He obeyed and positioned himself between Sandee and the Ambassador.

The reporters broke out in whispered conversation.

Reporter #3 continued, "Okay. So, you had never met this rhutz before?"

"That's right. After Whisper saved my life he took me to his den and that night Pelgrem appeared before us in the form of a man and told me that I was Tarizon's last hope for peace. He said He ordered the rhutz to guide and protect me while I worked to bring a lasting peace to our planet."

"Pelgrem, the God of Pharidon, appeared before you?" the reporter repeated skeptically.

"Yes. So, the pack took me in and I lived with them for nearly a cycle, then we left for Lyon because Pelgrem told Whisper that was where I should start my mission."

Reporter #4 stood up. "I'm sure you realize many will consider your story a joke. In fact, a large segment of our population doesn't believe Pelgrem even came to Tarizon."

"That is true, but in time it will become apparent that I am telling the truth."

Several of the reporters began shaking their heads and dismissing Sandee with laughter and heckling. Taking offense to this Whisper stood up and began to growl. The reporters quieted for a moment but soon were laughing even harder since Whisper posed no threat to them over a

VC monitor.

A few moments later the press room in Marna suddenly quieted. Everyone turned to the back of the room where two rhutz had appeared in the flesh and began growling as if they were about to attack. The reporters quickly scrambled away from the rhutz and huddled together against the back wall. Several picked up chairs to use to fend off the rhutz if they were attacked. A few moments later the rhutz let out a deafening howl, then turned and ran off.

Mill motioned for the technician to cut the feed. "That went better than I could have ever dreamed," he said.

"I'm sorry. I don't know what got into Whisper."

"Don't worry about it. He was perfect. How did he arrange to have the two rhutz in Marna show up for the media conference?"

Sandee told him about the collective consciousness and the ability of the rhutz to communicate over long distances.

"That will come in handy."

Sandee nodded. "So, you think it went well?"

"Yes. You will be a household name in Marna by the time we get there unless the Chancellor suppresses the story."

"Do you think he will?"

"He might, but the word will still get out. Don't worry. You can't stop something momentous like this from leaking out."

Sandee had his doubts about how well the rhutz scare would play in Marne. He worried that he and Whisper might be arrested when they arrived there. But he soon realized the Ambassador had been right when he noticed many people were now following them. By the time they got to the outskirts of Marna hundreds of curious spectators had joined the delegation. This made for an impressive entry into the city, particularly when they were joined by a squad of public enforcers who led them to the government's temporary offices.

The government of Serie had moved to the campus of the University of Serie which had ceased operations cycles earlier when most of the students there had been conscripted into the military. They were led to a large conference room where they were welcomed by Chancellor Drath Dosimo and his staff. They all stiffened when they saw Whisper.

"Can you guarantee that rhutz won't attack us?" Drath asked worriedly.

Sandee smiled. "Don't worry. He won't hurt anyone as long as we are not harmed or threatened."

"Alright," Drath replied warily. "But if he growls the way he did at the media last night I have instructed the enforcers to shoot him."

Sandee stiffened but said nothing.

"So, with that understanding," Drath continued. "Welcome to Serie. Please take a seat."

When everyone had been seated around the large conference table, Ambassador Talvihn began the negotiations.

"Thank you for agreeing to meet to discuss this most important matter."

Drath nodded. "Well, we are all weary of the war, but I can't say that I am optimistic that you will be willing to give us the concessions necessary to bring about peace."

"I don't think either of our nations has a choice," Talvihn replied. "We must find a way to resolve our differences or the human race faces extinction."

"Is it the human race who faces extinction or the people of Lyon?"

Talvihn shook his head. "Even, for the sake of argument, if you do have a superior arsenal of weapons and eventually are victorious. What is such a victory worth if there is no oxygen left to breathe after your victory?"

"I think you underestimate the ability of the atmosphere to repair itself over time. We may have to live in an artificial environment for a while but I doubt Tarizon would ever be uninhabitable."

"Well, our scientists don't agree."

"Everything they say is pure speculation."

Talvihn sighed deeply. "Even Pelgrem believes the end is near."

Everyone turned to Sandee.

"Yes," Drath chuckled. "So, I have heard."

Sandee swallowed hard and then said, "It is true. Pelgrem came to me to tell me of his concern for the future of Tarizon. He said that if the nations of Tarizon can't learn to live in peace very soon that all the life-forms on the planet will be destroyed."

There was laughter from Drath and his staff. Drath said, "Everyone knows Pelgrem didn't come to Tarizon. He is the God of Pharidon and has never intervened here on Tarizon in the history of mankind. But if he has now decided to intervene to save the planet, why would He entrust such an important mission to a child like yourself?"

"I cannot answer that question. I asked Him the same question, but He was insistent that I assume this task, and who am I to question a God?"

Drath didn't respond immediately. He just slowly shook his head. Finally, he said, "Alright. Let's get down to business. I assume you have a proposal."

"I do," Mill replied.

For the rest of the day, Ambassador Talvihn laid out his proposal and for the three days following the parties discussed it in detail. On the fifth day, a tentative agreement for a cease-fire was reached subject to the ratification by each nation's general assembly.

During that fateful week, Sandee visited the homes of many of Marna's most influential citizens and visited churches of every denomination. Many were skeptical of his claim to being Pelgrem's emissary, but they listened to him because of his natural charisma, obvious intelligence, wisdom well beyond his age and apparent ability to tame a ferocious rhutz.

6
Preparations

Thirty days out from Earth the crew of Earth Shuttle 7 woke everyone from deep sleep hibernation. Unfortunately, eleven passengers didn't wake up including Tillie Garciah. Romas and Celius were grief-stricken when they got the news.

"How could this happen?" Celius moaned. "I wouldn't have come had I known one of us might die."

"It's very unusual," Captain Linde said. "Our ship's doctor says she was weakened and traumatized by the take-off and that made the long hibernation more difficult."

"It was that damn hover taxi that crashed that alerted the media to our departure," Romas said angrily. "We should have planned our departure better. I'm so sorry, Celius. It never occurred to me that I was putting any of us at risk."

"It's not your fault," Captain Linde said. "No matter how well you plan something like this, you can't anticipate everything."

"I just hope the mission is a success. Otherwise, Tillie's death will have been for nothing," Celius said bitterly.

In respect for those who had died, the captain delayed his schedule one day so that anyone who lost a loved one could have some time to grieve. At the end of the day, everyone gathered in the main storage bay where an atomizer had been set up. It was the custom on Tarizon to have the remains of the dead reduced to their original atomic state. The atoms would then be released into the atmosphere, or in this case, into space.

The next day, as soon as they had showered and dressed, Romas,, Rammel and Eroh went to the Officer's Dining Room and joined Captain Linde for breakfast. Celius remained in her quarters, still too upset over Tillie's death to do anything but grieve. The food on a shuttle was nutritious, but not particularly tasty since it had to be stored for such a long period of time. But Romas, Eroh, and Rammel didn't complain because, despite the bland taste, it eased their hunger pains considerably.

Joining them at breakfast were Jox Machlyn, Paya Alt, Sarna and Markis Lai, their two teenager twins Blinh and Bellah, and Rama Sloken and his son, Ritz.

"What are you doing here, Rama?" Romas asked. "I thought you were going into hibernation?"

Rama nodded. "I arranged a swap with another family as you suggested. As it turned out, it was an unnecessary exercise as many evacuees didn't make it to the spaceport before we took off."

"Well, it's good to have you aboard," Paya said.

Paya Alt was the GOT member in charge of the Evacuation Earth Project. He had been planning it for several cycles including a dry run to Earth and back. The Officer's Dining Room had a large observation portal which provided an impressive view of the solar system through which they were traveling.

"So, what is this solar system we are in now?" Romas asked.

"We call it the Terra System, but on Earth, they simply call it the Solar System like it is the only one in the universe," Paya replied.

"Why are we so far ahead of Earth technologically?

Weren't we settled about the same time?"

"No one knows for sure, but our historians believe Earth was hit by a meteorite which wiped out most of the human population. That slowed down their development dramatically."

"What planet is that with the ring around it?" Rammel asked.

"On Earth, they call it Saturn," Paya replied.

"It is magnificent!"

"Yes, it is," Captain Linde agreed, "but not a place any human could live."

"So, through all the galaxies that the settlers from Pharidon traveled they only found two habitable planets?" Blinh asked.

"Yes," Paya replied. "Human life is very fragile and will only thrive if the right conditions exist. That is the tragedy of Tarizon. It was the perfect habitat for the human race until the human race destroyed it."

"Why haven't the humans on Earth destroyed their planet?" Bellah asked.

Bellah had dark, curly hair like her parents but had already surpassed Sarna in height. She had her mother's good looks, her father's serious demeanor, and was obviously very intelligent. Today, though, she looked a little thin and pale from being in hibernation for so long.

Paya smiled. "Oh, they're working on it, but so far they have managed to avoid nuclear wars. Still, it's just a matter of time if they don't change their ways."

"That's something we might be able to help them with if we ever can establish communication," Romas added.

"Do we plan to try to communicate with them?" Rammel asked.

Rammel had a square, handsome face and black hair. His lips were thin, and his ears were a bit too big, so he kept his hair long to cover them. Like his father, he was a near genius, but he didn't let that go to his head and got along with almost everyone.

"No, the people of Earth do not know of Pharidon and the origin of the human race," Paya replied. "They believe they are alone in the universe and that gives them great comfort and allows them to ignore the skies above them. If they found out alien life existed there is no telling how they would react. If we decide to make contact it will only be after we've been on Earth long enough to know the best way to do it."

"Won't they know when we land?" Rammel asked.

"No," Captain Linde replied. "We have stealth technology, so our landing will not be detected by their radars. The only risk is that someone on the ground sees us land, but we have defenses against that too."

"What kind of defenses?" Blinh asked.

"Well," Captain Linde replied. "We have the blue light. It sweeps the terrain around us when we land and anyone who sees it will pass out, and their immediate memory will be erased."

"Does it do them any harm?" Bellah asked.

"Not usually. They become disoriented and pass out before there can be any serious brain damage."

Bellah raised her eyebrows.

"We have a portable version of the blue light, a memory gun that can be used if someone sees something they shouldn't. That way we won't have to kill anyone.

"Now, many of you, I'm sure are feeling a bit tired and weak. This is normal. Your muscles have deteriorated due to lack of use and a zero gravity. So, every day you will be expected to engage in an exercise regimen designed to restore your body to a healthy state that will be able to function on Earth. This will not be a pleasant task, but luckily we have drugs that will help ease your pain."

Everyone looked around at each other with anxiety in their eyes.

"Where are we going to land?" Rammel asked.

"Well, we have chosen North America and specifically the United States," Paya said. "It has the strongest and most stable government on Earth. And it is a free country with much ethnic diversity, so it's less likely anyone would be suspicious of us."

"Where in America will we go?" Rammel asked.

"Texas," Paya replied. "It is a big state with a lot of unoccupied land. We have picked a spot in Central Texas in a place called Possum Kingdom."

"What's a possum?" Bellah asked.

"It's a funny looking animal that is common in Texas. It has no apparent value, but they have named a manmade lake after it for some reason. We will bury the ship on an island in the lake."

"Bury the ship?" Bellah asked wide-eyed.

Captain Linde laughed. "Yes, actually the ship will burrow into the ground until it is no longer visible from above. This will give us an initial base of operations and provide a means of escape should that be necessary."

"How are we going to communicate with the people on Earth?" Rammel asked. "We don't speak the Earth language."

Paya nodded. "English is the language they speak in Texas, so we will all have to learn it before we land. You will also have to learn to speak a second language, as well."

"We have to learn two languages? Why?" Rammel complained.

"Because no matter how prepared we might be, it will be obvious to the local people that we are not from Texas or anywhere in the United States. So, we will tell them that we are immigrants from Hungary. It is a small country far away from Texas, and their language is very strange to Texans, so they will most likely believe our story. But just in case we encounter someone from Hungary, we must learn their language as well."

"Do we have enough time to learn two languages?" Rammel asked.

"Of course, we have equipped the ship with two language labs and we have plenty of parazene," Paya replied. "We have an instructor in both languages too, so it shouldn't be a problem."

"Another thing you will have to learn is the terminology in Texas for various measurements. For instance our kyloon is similar to an Earth-hour. Our tik is similar to a second, a loon is a minute and a cycle is a year on Earth. A kylod is close to a mile and a stride will be called a yard once we land. The term one foot is the same on Tarizon as it is on Earth. From now on we will use Earth terminology for all measurements."

The process of educating people on Tarizon was far more advanced than on Earth. A typical language course was twenty days or the equivalent of a month on Earth. So, it was expected that everyone would master English and Hungarian long before they reached Earth. The process involved the use of a drug called parazene. It was a mind stimulant that would make a student feel very awake and keenly focused. At the language lab, the crew would attach electrodes behind their ears and on their foreheads that would further stimulate the brain. In the lab, the students would sit in front of VC monitors where an on-screen teacher would present the course at a very rapid pace. The students usually had no trouble following the course and would feel exhilarated when the session was over.

After each instructional session, the class broke up into small groups where they only spoke English or Hungarian, depending on the class they were in. Normally, after the first half-day session group members would be communicating amongst themselves fairly well. In the evenings, they were going to let the students watch movies produced on Earth and spoken in English or Hungarian. Even though they wouldn't understand them completely, they would be surprised how well they would be able to follow what was going on.

"How did you get an American movie?" Rammel asked. "And how is it that you know so much about Earth?"

Paya smiled. "You think this is our first trip to Earth? . . . It's not. We have been here before gathering intelligence in preparation for this mission. So, just follow our instructions and everything should go smoothly."

"I will," young Rammel replied.

"Now before bed each night your earphones and monitors will be attached to your chests and foreheads again. We will play music at first to put you to sleep but then the instruction will begin.

"Once you have mastered English and Hungarian, you will learn about the customs of each country, the music, history, politics, sports, entertainment, and geography. Finally, you will each create and memorize a personal biography that you will be able to recite if you are ever asked about growing up in Hungary.

"I know this is a lot to process and you may feel overwhelmed at first, but it is necessary for a seamless assimilation into the Possum Kingdom community."

"Where will we live when we arrive?" Rammel asked.

"On the ship at first until we acquire a place for everyone to stay. It will probably be a ranch or camp at first. But eventually, every family will have their own place. This is the American way.

"Finally, you will all need an identity card and some American money. Getting these things will be our first priority upon arrival.

"One more thing," Paya said. "Although we will be settling into a new life in America, do not get involved with the local population any more than necessary. We are only temporary visitors and will one day leave. So, it is best that you do not make friends with the local citizens, particularly with persons of the opposite sex. Although we are all humans, there are significant differences between humans from Tarizon and humans from Earth.

"So, no sex with the local citizens and don't ever go to one of their doctors. We will set up our own clinic and if any medical treatment is necessary it will be done there. Should you be examined by an American doctor your unique identity will likely be discovered.

"Finally, if anyone disobeys these rules they will be subject to severe punishment, including termination if you put the project at risk. Is that clear?"

Everyone nodded solemnly.

"General rule. Don't make yourself conspicuous. Don't volunteer for anything, join any clubs or churches and don't get involved in politics. Keep to yourselves and don't ever use our advanced technology in front of the local citizens.

"Alright," Paya said, "during lunch, I will post a training schedule right outside this door. After you eat, you will report to your assigned training room. Any questions?"

No one spoke up so Paya stood up. "Enjoy the rest of the morning because it will be the last free time you have before we land."

7
Secret Mission

Paya, Ramos and Captain Linde left the dining room. The others began talking amongst themselves about what they'd just heard. It was a lot to digest particularly since they had been asleep for nearly a cycle and had just awakened.

Markis and Sarna Lai and their two children Blinh and Bellah were sitting together at one corner of the dining room. Markis Lai had managed one of Petri Volk's company mines in northern Rigimol. He had started off at the bottom as a common laborer, but eighteen cycles earlier fortune had smiled on him when he met Petri's sister Sarna. Being a handsome, muscular man with dark hair and deep blue eyes, Sarna fell in love with him the day they met. Not wanting his sister to mate a man beneath her, Petri made sure Markis rose quickly through the ranks until he got into management. But his rise to the position of Director of Operations wasn't entirely a gift. Markis turned out to be a cunning, if not ruthless, businessman and would have probably risen to his current position on his own.

Markis had always been the outdoors type and loved sports, camping, hunting and regularly rode a jet cycle. When the GOT started talking about going to Earth he got very excited. He didn't agree that Tarizon was lost but simply wanted to go to Earth for the fun and adventure of it. Sarna and his children Blinh and Bellah were okay with the idea too as long as they had assurances that someday they'd come back home to Tarizon.

Blinh and Bellah were fraternal twins, now thirteen cycles old. They both had fair skin, blond hair, and blue eyes and had inherited their parent's natural charisma. Blinh had already worked for a Public Investigator in Vaceen before leaving Tarizon. Bellah had been an intern at a media company training to become a VC reporter.

Markis and Sarna had always kept their children on a tight leash. They knew what their children were doing at any moment and no major decisions were made about their lives without their knowledge and prior consent. Blinh and Bellah didn't complain too much about their parent's micro-management of their lives as the rewards of being in the Lai family were quite generous.

Markis looked at Bellah and Blinh solemnly and said, "There is something you need to know."

Bellah and Blinh looked at each other curiously, then back at their father.

"We have been charged with another assignment while we are here on Tarizon. Some of us, your mother and I included, aren't as optimistic as Romas and Paya about the future of Tarizon and its ability to recover even if the fighting stops. So, as a precaution, someone must prepare the way for many more Tarizonians to come to Earth."

"How many more?" Bellah asked.

"Hundreds of thousands, maybe millions."

"What?" Blinh said wide-eyed.

"You heard me," Markis replied. "So, you are going to have to disregard what Paya just said about staying to ourselves, and not mingling with the Earth-citizens. If we are going to pave the way for millions of our citizens to come to Earth, we are going to need lots of friends and allies outside our community. So, your job will be to find these friends and allies, and learn as much as possible about Earth, its government, its commerce and its citizens as you possibly can."

"But how can we do that without Paya finding out?" Blinh asked.

"It will be hard while we are on the shuttle, but once we get our own place Paya won't be able to keep track of you. Your mother and I will cover for you if Paya or one of his staff come by looking for you."

"What exactly do you want us to do?" Bellah asked.

"Besides getting involved in the community, you will need to help us recruit other Tarizonians to become agents. The four of us can't do this alone. We will need hundreds more to help."

"What will we tell them?" Bellah asked.

Sarna leaned in and whispered, "Our cover story will be that the government of Soni has instructed us to set up this covert operation on Earth and we are recruiting volunteers for the network."

"But what if they don't like the idea and decline our offer? What's to keep them from going to Paya and telling him what we are up to?"

Markis sat forward. "There will be incentives to make it worthwhile for them to participate. I doubt many will refuse."

"But what if they do?" Bellah pressed.

"Then we will have no choice but to kill them."

Bellah's mouth dropped open. Blinh stiffened.

Sarna put her hand on Blinh's shoulder. "Don't worry. We won't ask anybody to join unless we have gotten to know them and are fairly certain they will want to do it."

Bellah and Blinh didn't say anything for a few tiks, just kept looking at their parents uncomfortably. Finally, Blinh shrugged. "Fine. I guess since I have military and PI training, I'll be in charge of clean-up."

Markis smiled. "That was my thought as well. We will call your job security and intelligence."

"And what about me?" Bellah asked.

"Yours will be public relations and propaganda since you're already skilled in those areas."

She nodded. "Good. So, when do we start?"

"The moment we land," Sarna said. "In the meantime, start meeting people and getting to know them. We don't have time to lose."

8
The Landing

July 22, 1960

Earth Shuttle 7 dipped into Earth's atmosphere and descended quickly. The exterior of the shuttle began to glow from the intense heat generated during entry but the thick limdidium shell insulated the shuttle's interior from the heat. There, however, wasn't any insulation from the intense vibration and turbulence felt by the crew and passengers within.

Eroh gripped the arms of his chair for dear life and looked over at his mother worriedly. "What's happening? Are we going to die?"

Romas smiled at his youngest son. "No. Don't worry, this is normal. It will be over in a few loons."

As predicted the shuttle leveled off, the vibration and turbulence came to an abrupt end, and Eroh breathed a sigh of relief.

"Thank God," Celius said. "That was quite unpleasant."

"I loved it!" Rammel exclaimed. "It was better than the takeoff."

"How long until we land?" Eroh asked.

"I don't know," Romas said. "Let's go ask the Captain. He said we could come to the bridge once we were in Earth's atmosphere."

They all unbuckled their seat belts and shoulder restraints and headed for the bridge. A few loons later they were standing before the door to the bridge. Romas spoke into the control array by the door and announced their presence. The door slid open and they entered and were directed to a row of spectator seats behind the Captain's chair. In front of them was a large portal. They were traveling through a clear blue sky over a blanket of puffy white clouds.

"Oh, my God!" Eroh said. "Look at that momma. Is it snow?"

"No," the Captain replied. "Those are clouds. Beneath them is the ground where we will be landing soon."

"They are so white," Rammel observed. "I have never seen white clouds before."

"That's because Earth isn't polluted like Tarizon. You are looking at clusters of pure, clean water vapors, so they appear white unless they become so thick that they choke out the sun's light."

"Where are we right now?" Celius asked.

"We are over a nation called Mexico. Soon we will be crossing over the border of the United States near a city they call El Paso. In less than twenty loons we will be at our destination, Possum Kingdom Lake."

"Has anyone spotted us, you think?" Rammel asked.

"No," the Captain assured them. "We won't have to worry about that until we dip below this cloud cover. Then we will have to turn on our blue light in case we are spotted."

Twenty loons later the shuttle started its descent toward Cactus Island on Possum Kingdom Lake in Central Texas. The blinding blue light immediately began sweeping the area in front and to both sides. Ahead a large lake appeared, and Earth Shuttle 7 began to slow. Two fishermen in a small boat looked up as the shuttle passed over them. The blue light swept over them and one collapsed in the boat and the other one fell overboard.

Ahead a large, deserted island came into view. Soon they were hovering over a large flat area the size of a football field in the midst of it. The ship slowly descended to the surface and immediately began burrowing into the loose gravel surface.

Rammel and Eroh were silent as the ship vibrated sharply while it burrowed into the ground. Rammel held Celius' hand as she was beginning to get very pale. Ten loons later the ship was out of sight and Cactus Island once again appeared deserted.

When the vibrating had stopped, the Captain announced they had arrived at their destination undetected. The crew broke out in cheers and they all gave the Captain a round of applause. Celius frowned at the ritual.

"That's what they do here on Earth when someone achieves something important. They clap their hands," Romas explained.

Celius nodded. "Really? That's very strange."

"Well, it will be the first of many strange customs, I promise you."

The Captain stood. "Now, let's go see what shape the caves are in."

Romas nodded and looked at Rammel and Eroh. "Okay. Follow the Captain. We'll be right behind you."

The Captain left the bridge and led them down a corridor to an elevator that would take them to the lower deck of the ship. When they got to the lower deck, they followed another corridor to a ramp that led out of the ship and into the large cavern under Cactus Island. Several lanterns illuminated the cold damp expanse.

"The cave leads under the lake and exits on the eastern shore," the Captain said. "The crew is checking it out to see what condition it is in. Sometimes there are cave-ins that must be cleared before we can get through."

"Do they ever flood?" Romas asked.

"No. They haven't in the past."

A crew member ran up and reported. "There's a cave-in about two-thirds of the way to the shore."

"Hmm. Well, it's too late to clear it today. We'll have to do it in the morning. Right now, we should all go back to our rooms and get ready for dinner. After dinner, we'll have a little celebration in honor of our safe arrival, and then we can talk about the immediate tasks ahead."

They all turned and returned to the ship. That night the ship's cook prepared a special dinner for everyone complete with desserts and Tekari, an extravagance they hadn't seen since they left Tarizon. After they had eaten, the Captain announced that in America it was a tradition to dance at parties and celebrations such as they were having, so they were going to do that now as part of their assimilation training.

With that introduction, they were shown video clips from old movies of people engaged in various types of dancing. When it was over music was played and instructors circulated showing everyone how each step was supposed to be done. Although it was a very strange experience for most, everyone seemed to enjoy it.

At the end of the evening, Jox asked for their attention once again. "Now, I don't expect you all to be perfect dancers after this simple demonstration tonight, but it doesn't matter. Most Americans are not good dancers, so it is common to decline to dance because you are not very good at it, and if you do give it a try no one will give your clumsiness a second thought. The important thing is that you know that dancing is an American tradition. Later we will instruct you in Hungarian dancing in case that topic ever comes up.

"Now tomorrow most of you will stay aboard the shuttle and continue your cultural studies. But some of you will have to go out and scout the local area to find suitable housing, sources of food and water, transportation and figure out how to acquire local currency. Assignments will be posted during breakfast. Now go back to your quarters and get a good night's sleep. I'll see you in the morning."

The next morning Romas and Celius learned that their assignment for the next few days would be to find out what documentation everyone would need to live and work in Texas and figure out how to acquire it. After breakfast, they said goodbye to Rammel and Eroh, admonished them to work hard and be good during their absence, and took the elevator to the lower deck. A crowd had already gathered outside the shuttle at the entrance to the tunnels in anticipation of their imminent clearing.

While they were all waiting, Jox addressed the group. "Now, it is very important that you not attract undue attention to yourselves while out today. Be respectful and go about your business with confidence as if you were a member of the community. You can ask questions but just ask a few at a time and move on. If anyone asks who you are or what you are doing in Possum Kingdom just say you are tourists from Hungary. That will explain why you don't know your way around and seem a bit lost.

"Now, you all have communicators. If you get in trouble there will always be help close by, so don't hesitate to send for assistance. So, good luck and have a productive day."

The crowd began to move slowly as the entrance to the tunnel was opened. After a few loons, Romas and Celius ducked their heads as they stepped into the dark passageway. There were lanterns every fifty yards that just provided enough light to avoid tripping on the rocky floor. It was almost two miles to the eastern shore, so it took almost an hour to make the trek. The tunnel ended inside a large barn constructed so that neighbors would not see a large number of people emerging from it. When Celius stepped out into the bright Texas sun, she gasped.

"Oh my God! It is so bright and hot out here. Look at the blue sky."

"I know, isn't it amazing?" Romas said. "We'll need to buy sunglasses first thing when we get into town."

A school bus pulled up and the driver got out and announced he was taking people to Palo Pinto, the county seat of Palo Pinto County. Romas knew that's where he wanted to go so he took Celius' hand and led her to the front of the bus where people were beginning to climb aboard.

"This is a strange vehicle," Celius observed. "I have never seen anything like it."

"It's called a bus. It is propelled by an internal combustion engine. It has been a hundred cycles since anything like this was used on Tarizon."

"Is it reliable? It makes a lot of noise and smells horrible."

Romas laughed. "That's its exhaust. One of the drawbacks of this type of engine. Wait until we get started. I have heard it's going to be a very bumpy ride."

Once they were all seated, the bus pulled out onto the dirt road that led up to the barn. The ride was every bit as rough as expected, and Celius held onto the armrest so hard her knuckles turned white. The area was sparsely populated so they didn't see anyone for nearly twenty loons. Celius strained to see some children playing by the road.

"Look. Earth-children!"

"Yes, they look much like children on Tarizon, except much healthier."

"What are they riding?"

"I think they are called bikes, a very primitive type of transportation."

"So, what are we going to do in Palo Pinto?" Celius

asked.

"There is supposed to be a courthouse there where they keep records of births and deaths in the county. We need 1731 unique identities for everyone aboard."

"How will that work?"

"I don't know yet. That's what we have to figure out."

Celius raised her eyebrows. "Hmm. Sounds like we've got a difficult task ahead."

"Maybe, but we'll figure it out. We have no choice."

Celius nodded.

As the bus neared Palo Pinto, the courthouse could be seen protruding above the tree line. The bus turned off the main highway and turned onto the street that led to the courthouse square. It stopped in front of the imposing building and let Romas, Celius and several other passengers off. Downtown Palo Pinto only amounted to several square blocks. There was a restaurant, a newspaper, a florist, a professional building occupied by several doctors, lawyers, and accountants, a title company, a pawn shop and a public park with benches, tables and a playground under a canopy of large oak trees. "This isn't much of a town," Celius observed.

"No. It's not, but it will do. Let's start with the pawn shop. We'll need some local currency."

Celius nodded and they walked to the end of the block to Big Tex Pawn & Jewelry and went inside. The shop was cluttered with assorted merchandise including guns, stereos, TVs, tools and display tables packed with jewelry. A sign on the wall read: WE BUY GOLD AND SILVER. A large, bald man wearing blue jeans and chewing a wad of tobacco sat behind the display cases cleaning an old watch. A name tag identified him as Ben.

"Can I help you?" Ben asked.

Romas walked over to him. "Yes. Your sign says you

buy gold and silver."

"Yes, we pay the highest prices in the county."

"What about diamonds?"

"Sure. What you got?"

Romas pulled a fabric bag out of his pocket and set it on the counter. He opened it and pulled out a large diamond pendant. The man picked it up and examined it. Celius wandered away to look at the jewelry on display. After a moment, Ben looked up.

"This isn't too bad. It's got decent clarity. I could give you two hundred dollars for it."

Celius looked back at them and frowned. "Two hundred dollars? But you have one right here that is half the size but priced at $1,500.00."

"Ah. Well, that's nearly a perfect stone, Ma'am."

"Actually, it doesn't look as nice as the one we have for sale."

Ben sighed. "Well, let me take a look at it again," he said, taking another look. "Where did you get this? It's not stolen, is it?"

"No, of course not. I bought it as an investment many years ago but I'm a little short on cash right now, so I decided to sell it."

"Well, the best I can do is $1,000. Take it or leave it."

"All right. You drive a hard bargain. It's a deal."

The man smiled broadly. "Good. I'll go write this up and get you your money."

"Thanks," Romas said.

Celius walked over and whispered in Romas's ear. "Isn't it worth a lot more?"

"Yes, but it doesn't matter. We have barrels of them back at the ship."

Diamonds had once been valuable on Tarizon but with so much death and destruction over the years and the collapse of most of the world's economies, nobody could afford them as a luxury item anymore, and they had lost their value. The situation got even worse when a much harder and more easily malleable substance called Limdidium was discovered. Many of the commercial uses of diamonds simply disappeared.

Ben came back and counted out ten one-hundred-dollar-bills. Romas picked up one of the bills and examined it carefully.

"What other denominations do you have?"

"Huh?" the man said.

"You must have other, smaller bills."

"Oh, you want change for one of these?"

"Yes, please."

"Sure," he said and took one of the bills to the back room. When he returned, he counted out four twenty-dollar bills, a ten and two fives.

"Thank you," Romas said as he gathered up his money.

The man started to say something, closed his mouth, and then opened it again. "Is that bag full of diamonds?"

Romas shook his head. "Oh, no. Just some old costume jewelry and a few trinkets."

The man nodded but didn't look convinced. "Okay, then. Well, it was a pleasure doing business with you. You have a nice day."

With their first task accomplished, they left the pawn shop and went to the diner. Romas stopped on the way to look at a newspaper dispenser, wondering how to go about purchasing a newspaper. He finally gave up and followed Celius to the front door. A sign read Dave's Diner, Established 1904. Romas pushed the door open, held it for Celius and then entered behind her. The room was furnished with a dozen wooden tables and a long bar. Pictures of famous people the proprietor had served over the years adorned the wall. A middle-aged waitress wearing a faded blue uniform walked over and showed them to a table. When they were seated, she asked if they wanted coffee.

"Coffee?" Romas repeated. Coffee had been mentioned in some of the movies they'd watched. He looked at Celius.

She smiled. "Yes, two coffees, thank you."

She handed them each a menu and then went back into the kitchen. When she was gone, Romas and Celius carefully opened their menus. After a few loons, the waitress returned with their coffees and took out an order pad.

"So, what can I get you?"

"Ah. What do you recommend?" Celius asked, not trusting her own judgment.

"Well, our specialty is chicken-fried steak. The gravy is to die for, best in the county."

Celius looked at Romas and he nodded. "Well, that sounds good. We'll both have that," she replied.

The waitress wrote down the order and was about to leave when Romas asked. "Ah. That newspaper dispenser out front, how do you work it?"

The waitress frowned. "You mean the newspaper rack. Oh, it takes quarters. You need some change?"

Romas nodded. "Yes, change, that would be good."

The waitress waited and when Romas didn't do anything she said. "Give me a dollar, honey, and I'll give you four quarters."

Romas nodded. "Oh, sorry," he said and pulled out his wallet. He took out a five-dollar bill and handed it to her. She frowned, then turned and walked over to the cash register. After hitting a few keys, the register opened, and she pulled out four ones and four quarters. She brought them back to the table and counted them out into Romas' outstretched hand.

Romas smiled and stood up. "Just one of these?"

The waitress laughed. "Yes, put it in the slot and pull back on the handle."

Romas smiled and went out the front door. A moment later he walked back in proudly carrying a copy of the *Fort Worth Star-Telegram*.

While they were waiting for their chicken-fried steak, Celius and Romas silently read the entire newspaper cover to cover. Even though they had only learned English a few weeks earlier they had no trouble reading it.

"It is amazing how much you can learn from reading the newspaper," Celius observed. "Did you know children go to school until they are in their early to mid-twenties? That's incredible. Our kids were done with school by age fourteen."

"I know. They haven't discovered our rapid learning technology yet."

"The local government is called a city and there is an outlying authority called a county," Celius went on. "Then there is the state which makes all of the laws they must adhere to."

"Right," Romas agreed. "And then there is a federal government that controls all the fifty states."

"Yes. Did you know people here still have to drive their own personal transporters?"

"Cars or automobiles are what they call them."

"That is so unreal. I have never driven a car."

"Me either, but I remember my grandfather telling me about driving his personal transporter before hover taxis were invented. He said he enjoyed driving and felt sad when driving became obsolete."

"Yes, and they have a big problem with people driving while they are intoxicated."

"Oh, really, they don't have sobriety pills?"

"No. So, people often drive drunk and get into

accidents. Many citizens are killed each year by drunk drivers, so it is against the law to drink and drive. Citizens are sent to prison if they get caught doing it."

"That's very interesting and sad too," Romas noted.

When their lunch finally arrived, they put aside the paper and dug in. A smile came over Romas' face.

"This is quite good. What do you think?" he asked.

Celius nodded and took another bite. "Yes, it's very good. What is a chicken again?"

"Ah. A little bird-like creature."

"Oh, right. Very tasty."

As they were eating, two men in khaki uniforms and cowboy hats walked in and were seated. Romas looked over at them wondering what the uniforms meant. Celius gave him a worried look. He smiled back at her hoping to reassure her. When they were done, Romas wondered how they should pay for their meal. He stood up and walked over to the register hoping that was the correct protocol. When the waitress saw him there, she walked over quickly.

"In a hurry, huh?"

"Well, we have business to attend to."

She handed him a ticket that indicated he owed eight dollars and seventy-seven cents. He took out a ten and handed it to her. She hesitated so he wondered if he'd done something wrong. He frowned.

"Do you want change?" she said irritably.

Then he remembered something in one of the movies about tipping. "Oh, no. You keep it. Great service. Thank you."

When he turned to leave, he noticed the two uniformed men watching him. He smiled and went back to his table.

"Okay, dear. Time to go."

Celius stood up, grabbed her purse and they made a hasty exit.

Once outside Celius asked, "Were those soldiers?"

"No. I don't think so. Local public enforcers probably. Best stay clear of them."

"Indeed. . . . So, now where?" Celius asked.

"Let's go to the courthouse now and check out the birth and death records."

It took them only a few minutes to walk over to the courthouse. Once inside they went to the directory but couldn't decide what office would have birth and death records, so they asked the first person who walked by.

A skinny man in a short sleeve white shirt told them those records were kept in the county clerk's office down the hall to their right. They thanked him and walked to the office and stepped inside.

It was a busy place with many people mingling around. Romas scanned the room and saw a sign that read: Birth and Death Certificates. They walked over to it and stood. A few minutes later a woman came up to the counter and asked if she could help them.

"We are looking for a death certificate for a relative who we think died in this county ten or fifteen years ago."

The woman nodded. "Okay, those records are on microfiche. Do you know how to work the machine?"

"No. Could you show us?"

"Sure, come with me."

They followed the woman over to a large machine and watched her demonstrate how it worked. Once they got the hang of it, she left them alone.

"What are we looking for?" Celius asked.

"Two things, we need a copy of a death certificate to take back to the ship and we need 1731 names of persons who are dead, so we can assume their identities."

"That will take a long time to gather all that information. Don't you think they will get suspicious?"

"We're not going to do it all today and we're not

going to get the names here. We'll have to go to another county to lessen the chance that we might pick a name that someone might recognize. We're just scouting today."

As they were working, one of the uniformed men they'd seen in the diner walked into the County Clerk's Office. He saw them and gave them a hard look.

"Good, because that public enforcer is looking at us again. I think he's suspicious," Celius said worriedly.

Romas looked over at the man. "Right. Let's buy a copy of one of these birth certificates and get out of here."

Celius nodded. "Yes, do it quickly."

Romas went over to the counter and gave the clerk the page and volume of the death certificate they wanted. She said she'd get it for them and pointed to a row of chairs where they could wait. They walked over and sat down. A few moments later the uniformed officer walked over to them.

"Hello. I'm Sheriff Wilkins. I saw you over at the diner."

"Oh, yes. Excellent food," Romas said nervously.

"Ah. You all aren't from around these parts, are you?"

"No. We're tourists. Just seeing the sights."

"Where are you staying?"

"Ah. . . . Over at Possum Kingdom Lake."

"Yes. It's nice over there. What are you doing here in the county clerk's office?"

"Oh, we had an aunt who lived here in Palo Pinto County. She died a few years ago and we needed a copy of her death certificate."

"Oh, I see. Is there a probate pending?"

"Probate? Ah. No. We just wanted it as a family record, you know."

"Right. Well, if you need a good probate lawyer I can recommend one."

"Oh. Well, if we need a lawyer, we may take you up on that offer."

"All right, then. It was nice meeting you. Enjoy your stay here in Palo Pinto."

"We will. Thank you."

The Sheriff went over to the clerk who had just helped Romas and Celius and had a discussion with her. While they were talking, he glanced over at them and the clerk did likewise. Celius squirmed in her chair.

"Do you think he is suspicious?" Celius asked.

Romas shrugged. "I don't know."

Finally, the Sheriff turned and walked away. A moment later the clerk came over and gave them the copy of the death certificate they were waiting for. For the first time, Romas noticed the name tag on the woman's blouse. It read: Evelyn Wilkins.

"Thank you," Romas said with a grin. "Are you related to the Sheriff?"

She smiled. "Why yes, Wade is my father."

"Oh. So, you get to see him a lot working here in the courthouse."

"Yes. That's one of the perks of the job."

"Has he been Sheriff long?"

"This is his second term. He's been in office seven years now. It seems like forever."

"Yes, well it must be a difficult job."

"You don't know the half of it. He's got this big county to protect and not nearly the resources he needs to do the job right."

"Oh, how many enforcers does he have?"

"Enforcers? . . . You mean deputies?"

"Yeah. Right."

"Just twenty-one and four of them work in the jail so that leaves only seventeen to cover three shifts."

"Wow. That is stretching it thin."

"Yes, I worry if something major goes down he won't have the backup he needs."

"Well, hopefully, that won't happen."

"I hope not. How long are you folks in town?"

"We don't know yet. My aunt really liked living on the bluffs above the lake so we might stay a while to see if it might be a good place to settle down."

"Oh, yes I love those homes on the bluffs. Possum Kingdom is a very friendly community, too. I think you'd like it."

"Well, I'm sure we would. Thanks for your help," Romas said. "I guess we'll see you around."

They left the Clerk's office and then took the stairs to the Department of Motor Vehicles office in the basement. After they'd picked up a pamphlet on obtaining a driver's license, they went outside where they saw the school bus that had brought them to Palo Pinto had returned. They walked over to it and asked the driver how much time they had before it would be leaving. He said he was leaving at 4:00 p.m. which gave them about thirty minutes to kill.

"Anything else you want to see before we have to leave?" Celius asked.

"There is one more thing we have to do," he replied.

"What's that?"

"We need to steal someone's wallet."

"What? With the Sheriff lurking about? Are you crazy?"

"We need an actual driver's license and social security card as a model, so we can replicate them back at the shuttle."

"What if we get caught?"

"That can't happen. We must be very careful."

"So, how are we going to do it?" Celius asked warily.

"I saw a pickpocket in a movie, but I think stealing a wallet out of a purse will be easier than a man's pocket.

Why don't I create a distraction, and you can take the wallet out of one of those women's purses at the playground?"

Celius looked over at the playground in the park across the street from the Courthouse. There were several mothers watching their children play with their purses on the ground beside them. She took a deep breath.

"Okay. What kind of a distraction are you going to create?"

"I'm not sure. Just go stand by the women, and when it happens, steal one of their wallets, and then go directly to the bus and get on board."

Celius looked at Romas nervously. "Okay. Make it a good diversion."

Romas smiled and started walking across the street toward the playground. When he got to the sidewalk, he turned right as if he was going to walk right past it. As he walked, he carefully removed his memory gun and held it out of sight of the parents who were watching but aimed it directly at a group of children. When he pulled the trigger, the blue light swept over the children and they immediately collapsed. He quickly put the gun away, and then rushed over to the children as if he were going to help them. One of the mothers screamed and started running toward her child. The others followed. Celius bent down, took one of the wallets out of an unattended purse, and immediately started walking toward the bus.

"What happened?" Romas said to one of the women who was rushing up.

"I don't know. They all just seemed to collapse all at once. I've never seen anything like it."

The children were already beginning to stir and soon were waking up from the low dose of the blue light from the memory gun. Romas knew he hadn't hurt them, yet he still felt a little guilty for what he had done.

"What happened, honey?" a mother asked her daughter as she helped her up.

"I don't know, Mommy. I just felt dizzy."

"It must be this heat," another mother said.

Romas started backing off slowly, and then turned and walked quickly back to the bus. The driver asked him what had happened to the children and he just shrugged. A few minutes later the bus left for its return trip to the shuttle, and Romas and Celius breathed a sigh of relief.

9
Homicide

Markis and Sarna Lai knew what their GOT assignments were going to be on this, their first day on Earth because they had discussed them in detail with Jox and Rama before they had landed. Their task was to find jobs for all 1731 Tarizonian visitors on board the shuttle. They were called visitors rather than immigrants because according to the official GOT plan they all would be going back to Tarizon once the atmosphere had cleared.

Their secret mission, to prepare the way for the eventual mass immigration of millions of Tarizonians to Earth, had been assigned to them by Petri Volk and Cornelius Bruda before Earth Shuttle 7 had taken off. They relished their GOT assignment because, since everyone needed a job, it gave them an excuse to contact and interact with each and every fellow passenger on board without anyone being suspicious. During these interviews they could assess, not only each visitor's job skills, loyalty to the GOT and personal expectations, but also have access to the GOT's extensive background file on each of them. In these files, there would likely be information that could be used as leverage to get individual passengers to join their secret mission.

When the buses pulled up to the barn covering the entrance to the tunnels to Cactus Island, Markis and Sarna took the bus with the ultimate destination of Palo Pinto County's largest city, Mineral Wells. They assumed this would be the most fertile ground for finding jobs for the shuttle's passengers. So, their task would be to see what jobs were available and what would be needed to apply for them. It was nearly noon when the bus pulled up in front of the Baker Hotel where Markis and Sarna would be staying for a few days while they did their research.

The Baker Hotel was famous for its illustrious guests who had been lured there by the world-famous mineral baths of Mineral Wells. After they checked in, they went up to their rooms and unpacked. They didn't have any money, so it was fortunate that they wouldn't have to pay their bill until they left. They had been assured by Jox that current American currency would be delivered to them by days' end.

"We can't even dine in that divine restaurant downstairs without cash," Sarna complained.

"You packed us a lunch, didn't you?" Markis asked.

"Yes, of course, but I really wanted something other than shuttle rations. All the good food was eaten last night at the celebration."

"Well, food is supposed to be plentiful on Earth, so the Captain didn't think there was any reason not to eat it."

"So, what are we going to do while we are waiting for someone to bring us cash?" Sarna asked.

"I saw a sign downstairs about a concierge who was available to answer any question guests might have."

"Any questions? How fortunate. Let's go see what information we can get out of him. Maybe he'll know where we can get some complimentary food."

Markis agreed, so they left their room and went to the elevator. They stepped inside and pushed the button. When the door opened up to the hotel lobby, Markis pointed to the sign he'd seen on the way in. They walked over to it. A well-dressed, middle-aged man was behind the counter writing something in a ledger. A name tag indicated his name was Hunter. He looked up and smiled.

"Ah. . . . Hi. Mr. Hunter, we understand you're the

one to answer all our questions," Markis said.

"Yes. Absolutely. What questions do you have? The best restaurant in town? How to book a mineral bath, perhaps?"

"No," Sarna replied. "We just moved here, and we need to find a job. How would we go about doing that?"

Hunter frowned. "A job? Huh. I don't get that question too often. Well, there is the Texas Employment Commission. They have an unemployment office across town. Employers post jobs there. You can just drive around too, and if businesses need workers they often will put out a sign."

"Oh, really?"

"Yes, just look around, you'll see them in windows, on marquees or posted on signs on the front of buildings."

"Okay, I guess we need to scour the city then."

"Right. And, of course, there are classified ads in the newspaper. That's probably your best bet. There will be a lot of job advertisements there."

"What do employers usually expect you to have when you apply for a job?" Sarna asked.

"Well, this isn't really my expertise. I deal mainly in amusement and guest services."

"I know, but anything you could tell us would be appreciated."

"Ah. Okay. Well, they usually expect you to have a resume."

"A resume?"

"Yes, it's a short paper listing your contact information, previous jobs, experience and expertise and what kind of job you are looking for. You can get sample resumes in books at the library."

"The library?"

"Yes, it's just three blocks south of here. In fact, there are people there who can answer just about any question you have or point you to a book with the answers you need."

"Thank you," Markis said. "You've been most helpful."

"Oh, one last question," Sarna said earnestly. "Is there anywhere around here we can get free food?"

Hunter started to laugh. "I guess you really do need a job."

"Yes, we do," Sarna agreed.

"Well, you can get a complimentary apple at the front desk, and there are complimentary coffee and rolls in the lobby each morning."

"Oh, really," Sarna said evenly. She glanced over at the front desk then frowned and turned to Hunter. "Ah, what is an apple?"

Hunter began to laugh again. Harder this time. "Oh, I see. You're pulling my leg, aren't you?"

Sarna stiffened. "No, I didn't touch you."

"Come on, Sarna," Markis said shaking his head apologetically to Hunter. "Don't mind her. She gets this way when she's tired."

Markis took Sarna's hand and escorted her to the front desk where they both grabbed an apple from a bowl and then went back to their room. Sarna looked at the apple carefully and then asked, "How do you eat it?"

Markis inspected his apple and said, "Don't you remember in one of the movies we watched a man feed an apple to a horse, and the horse took a bite out of it."

Sarna nodded and took a bite out of her apple. She smiled. "Hmm. It's quite tasty. I wonder if we can get another one later."

"I doubt anybody would care," Markis replied as he bit into his apple.

When they were done, they went back to the lobby and got directions to the library and the local office of the

Texas Employment Commission. It was a sunny and hot August day, but dark clouds were forming off to the west. Sarna looked at them warily.

"It looks like a storm is brewing," she observed. "I wonder how bad it will be."

Just then there was a crack of thunder that made Sarna jump. "Oh, my God! What was that?"

"I think I remember reading about Texas getting some pretty strong storms in the summertime. We better hurry to the library before it gets any worse."

There was another crack of thunder, so they quickened their pace toward the library which was still a block and a half away. When they got to the corner, they started to cross the street and just as they stepped onto the curb, there was a cloudburst. Rain pelted them as they raced the last fifty yards to the front door of the library.

"Oh, look at me," Sarna complained. "I'm soaked."

Markis laughed. "That was kind of fun, actually. I think I'm going to like it here in Texas."

They split up to go to the restrooms to dry off a little with paper towels. When each came out as dry as they were going to get, they went to the information desk where Hunter had promised them all their questions would be answered. A thin, white-haired lady escorted them to the reference section of the library and pulled out two books she said would tell them everything they needed to know about applying for a job. They thanked her and found a table where they could sit down and study the two books. An hour later they decided they had learned enough and headed to the office of Texas Employment Commission.

The rain had stopped, and it was a bit breezy. Sarna took a deep breath. "The air smells so good. The rain must have done that."

"Probably," Markis agreed. "Maybe it cleaned the air."

After they had walked a half hour in the direction the librarian had told them to go, they saw a white building which had a sign in front indicating it was the offices of the Texas Employment Commission. They went inside and stood at the end of a short line. There were signs posted on the walls giving instructions to visitors and a picture of a man in a suit.

"Who's that?" Sarna asked pointing to the picture.

Markis strained to read the caption. "Governor, Price Daniel."

"Governor?"

"Yes, that must be the man who runs Texas. Like our chancellor, I guess."

"Hmm."

The line moved, and soon Markis found himself staring at a short dark-haired woman with an irritated look on her face. "Can I help you?" the woman asked.

"Ah. Yes. We're looking for a job. I understand—"

The woman handed Markis two sets of forms. "Fill all of these out and bring them back to me when you're done. Next!"

Markis took the papers and handed one set to Sarna. "I guess we need to fill these out."

"I heard," Sarna said looking for a place to sit down. Spotting an area with some small empty desks they walked over and found seats.

"Okay. Name, okay. Address, no problem. Date of birth, yeah, social security number? What's a social security number?" Sarna asked.

"Oh, I read about that in the book at the library. It's how the federal government keeps track of everybody. We're all going to need one of those."

"Right. Let's see, previous employment, education, typing speed? What is typing?" Sarna asked.

"I don't know. We'll have to ask Hunter, I guess."

"Yeah. It looks like we have a lot of work to do before any of us will be able to get a job."

"I agree, but we've done all we can here for now. Let's go back to the hotel and see if our money has been delivered. I'm very hungry."

Markis nodded and they got up and left, taking the employment application packets with them. When they got back to the hotel they went to the front desk and asked if there had been any messages. The desk clerk went to find out and came back with a brown envelope. Sarna grabbed it from the clerk and walked away to where she could open it privately. Markis followed her expectantly. Inside there was a small stack of twenty-dollar bills. Sarna counted them.

"Twelve," she said looking at Markis.

"Okay. That's 20x12 or $240.00. The room is $25.00 per night so we have $165.00 to spend."

"Good. Let's go eat."

"Okay," Markis agreed, "but let's go upstairs and get rid of these job application packets and our notes. I don't want to accidentally lose them."

They went upstairs, dropped everything on the bed and then freshened up for dinner. They were both excited because this was going to be their first taste of American food. They wondered if they were going to like it. When they returned to the lobby they noticed Hunter was still on duty, so they went by to say hello and ask him a few more questions.

"Thank you for your help earlier," Sarna said. "We found the library and Texas Employment Commission."

"Good. Did you get all your questions answered?"

"Well, most of them. One thing we didn't understand was the question about our typing speed."

Hunter frowned, then asked, "Have you ever taken a typing test?"

Sarna swallowed hard. "No. What is typing?"

Hunter laughed. "What is typing? Are you serious?"

She nodded. "I'm sorry, we're just tourists. We don't know about your local customs."

"Ah. Well, typing is mechanically printing. Haven't you ever seen a typewriter?"

"No. I'm afraid not."

Hunter shook his head in dismay. "Okay. Well, come with me. I'll take you to the business center and show you a typewriter. That will make it easier to explain."

They followed Hunter down the hall to the business center and walked in. Inside there were banks of cubicles for guests to sit in and work. In one of the cubicles, there was a big Royal typewriter. Hunter went over to it.

"Here you go. This is a typewriter. It allows you to print manually on a piece of paper. They are used mainly in businesses to write letters, do reports, and complete forms. If you want a clerical job, you'll have to know how to type."

Sarna just stared at Hunter for a moment. She thought of Tarizon where they simply talked into their wrist array and a computer would print their words out in any format they wanted. They were astonished at America's lack of technology but couldn't complain about it out loud without giving themselves away.

"Okay. I understand now," Sarna said, looking wide-eyed at Markis.

"Good. So where are you going to eat?" Hunter asked.

"In the dining room here in the hotel."

"Oh, no!" Hunter exclaimed. "You can do better than that. What kind of food do you like? Italian? Mexican? Mediterranean?"

"Doesn't anybody have American?" Sarna asked.

Hunter laughed. "Sure, that's easy. Go out the front door, turn left and go five blocks to the Black Horse. They have great hamburgers, fried chicken, steaks and their pies are to die for."

Sarna smiled. "Great. That's where we will go then."

"Okay. Bon appetite."

"What?" Sarna asked.

"Ah. Have a great dinner."

"Thanks."

"Before you go, let me tell about another American custom you should know about."

"What's that?" Markis asked.

"Tipping. When someone serves you well, you should give them a tip. For instance, when your waitress at the Black Horse serves you, she will expect you to leave her a tip of at least 10% of the bill."

"Really?"

"Yes, and if they do a really great job, it's common to give as much as 20%."

A smile suddenly came over Markis's face. "Oh, you mean we should give you a tip?"

"Yes. Not that I'm asking, but I don't want you to be embarrassed. If you don't give a tip to your waiter or bellhop they might get angry with you."

"Okay, but what if there is no bill? How do you know how to tip?"

"Anything that seems reasonable to you depending on what service was provided."

Sarna pulled out the envelope full of twenty-dollar-bills, took one out and handed it to Hunter.

"Would this be appropriate?" she asked.

Hunter's eyes widened. "Well, that would be quite generous. Ah. Let me give you a ten-spot back. I think that would be fair."

Hunter found a ten-dollar-bill in his wallet and gave it to Sarna. "Thanks. Have a good evening."

When they stepped outside and started walking

toward the Black Horse Café they noticed it had cooled down considerably and was quite pleasant. Sarna took Markis's hand, squeezed it and smiled at him.

"This has been quite an enjoyable day. I'm so glad we decided to come to Earth."

"Even as backward as they are here?"

"Yeah. There is something about it here. The people are very friendly, and it just seems very safe. You know what I mean?"

"Yes. America is not at war with anyone although I heard talk of one going on in a place called Vietnam. Luckily, it is a country far away, so it is still quite tranquil here."

The light in front of them turned red but Sarna and Markis didn't realize what that meant, so they continued on across the street. Suddenly, a car came barreling down the street right at them. Markis saw it and stepped back. He tried to pull Sarna with him, but she resisted, and the car struck her tossing her into the air like a rag doll. She came down with a dull thud. Markis ran over to her and lifted her head off the hard pavement.

"Sarna, are you okay?"

Sarna looked up at Markis for just a second and then her eyes closed. He tried to wake her, but she did not respond. People on the street began to gather around them. The driver of the car came over obviously upset.

"Didn't you see the light was red?" he complained. "Is she okay?"

"No. She's not okay," Markis replied angrily. "Why didn't you stop when you saw her?"

"Someone should call an ambulance," a passerby said. "She needs to go to the hospital."

Markis stiffened. "No! No! No hospitals," he said. "She'll be okay."

Markis knew if she were taken to a hospital they

might discover that she wasn't like the humans here on Earth, and that discovery could jeopardize their entire mission.

"Hey man," the driver said, "the light was green. I had the right-of-way."

"You skutz! You saw her, you could have stopped!"

"Screw you! I had a green light. You better have insurance. There's some serious damage to my car."

"My mate is dying and you're worried about that piece of junk."

"She should have paid attention to the traffic lights. Take her to the hospital, she'll be fine."

"No. I said no hospitals."

"Then if she dies you can't blame it on me."

"I do blame it on you, and if she dies you're going to die too!"

"Ah! That's outrageous. I'm going to tell the police you threatened to kill me."

"No, you're not!"

Markis reached back and pulled out his laser gun from an ankle holster and pointed it at the driver. "You're not going to talk to anyone about this," he said and pulled the trigger. The laser burst hit the man in the stomach and he immediately collapsed. Seeing what had happened, a woman screamed. Markis turned and pointed the laser at the woman, but then thought better of it. He holstered the laser, pulled out his memory gun and fired, first at the woman and then at the crowd of spectators that had gathered on the sidewalk. They all collapsed. "Skutz!" he screamed immediately regretting what he'd done.

He knew he'd acted rashly out of anger, frustration, and concern for Sarna. If he got caught, the mission would be compromised. Now, what am I going to do? Skutz! Then he remembered there was supposed to be emergency help close by at all times.

Looking down at his wrist array, he punched in the emergency code. He knew help would be dispatched immediately, but how long would it take them to get there? And would they get Sarna back to the ship in time to save her life? The memory gun would only give him a five or ten-minute head-start at best, but what would he do if that wasn't enough time?

10
Emergency Alert

Romas and Celius sat quietly on the bus as it lumbered along toward Possum Kingdom Lake. Their day's mission had been a success, but it had mentally drained them. It was always risky using the memory gun because there could always be someone in the distance who observed the use of the gun but wasn't close enough to have his or her memory erased. Romas wished he hadn't used it.

As they were driving, Romas became curious about the driver. How had he learned to drive? Where had they gotten the school buses? His curiosity getting the better of him, he got up and moved to a seat directly behind the driver.

"Hey. You're one of the crew members, right?"

The driver looked over his shoulder and gave Romas a once over. "That's right, Artek."

"So, Artek, where did you learn to drive?"

"On our last trip two cycles ago. I went to a local driving school. It wasn't too difficult."

"Huh. Where did you find these buses?"

"When we were here the last time, we picked them up at an auction. They were old models and in poor condition, so we got them cheap. The ship's engineer restored them to perfect condition and we left them in the barn for when we returned."

Romas' wrist array beeped. He looked down at it and saw it was a rescue request. "Oh, no. Markis is in trouble. We need to go to him now."

"My orders are to take everyone back to the ship."

"I know, but someone has to go help Markis now. He's in Mineral Wells and he wouldn't be sounding an alarm unless it was critical to the mission."

"Okay. We can turn around and go to the shop."

"What shop?"

"Parr Heating & Air. Jox bought the business this morning. You and I can take one of the vans and go help Markis."

"Perfect. Thanks."

Artek slowed the bus and then did a U-turn at the next intersection. They had driven for about twenty minutes when they got to the outskirts of Mineral Wells. Artek slowed and turned into a driveway next to a warehouse building with a sign on the front indicating it was the home of Parr Heating & Air. They drove the bus behind the warehouse where it could not be seen and got out.

Artek had told the passengers there was going to be a delay getting back to the ship while they responded to a distress call, and that they could stay on the bus or mingle around outside but not to stray too far. Then Romas, Celius, and Artek climbed into one of the panel vans and drove into Mineral Wells.

✝✝✝✝✝

When people started to wake up from the memory gun, Markis was in a panic. He could shoot them again, but a second shot would likely give them brain damage. Besides, more people were gathering now wondering why dozens of people were lying unconscious on the sidewalk. Suddenly, there was a siren. He knew that meant the police were coming. He had no choice but to run and hide. Bending over Sarna, he picked her up and began walking quickly away, down a side street, and into an alley, as far away from the crowd as he could get.

After he had walked half a mile, he felt exhausted and knew he'd need to rest soon. Looking around, he realized that some of the buildings in the area were abandoned. He went to the closest one, kicked in the back door, and entered. Inside, he found an old mattress against a wall, so he sat Sarna down and collapsed beside her. He heard more sirens, but they seemed far away.

†††††

When the Parr Heating & Air van arrived at the corner where the accident had occurred, there were two police cars with their lights flashing and a crowd of spectators on the sidewalk adjacent to them. Romas and Celius rushed over expecting to see Markis and Sarna but they were nowhere to be found.

"What happened?" Romas asked the first spectator he encountered.

"A woman got run over, and then I don't know what happened. I must have passed out. When I awoke, the driver who hit the woman was dead and the woman who had been hit had vanished."

"How did the driver die?" Romas asked tentatively.

"I don't know. It must have happened while I was passed out."

"So, was there anyone with the woman when she was hit?"

"Yes, a man was with her. He managed to dodge the car but the woman was too slow."

"What happened to the man?"

He shrugged. "As I said, he was gone when I woke up."

They stepped away from the man and Romas scanned the area worriedly.

"Why is the man dead?" Celius asked. "I didn't think the memory gun was lethal."

"It's not. Markis must have had a laser. I've seen one

103

on his ankle before, I just don't understand why he felt compelled to kill someone."

"He must have been very angry."

"Apparently."

"I wonder which way they went," Celius said.

"Good question," Romas replied.

Romas looked over at the accident scene and saw a white sheet pulled over the dead man's body. He desperately wanted to go over and examine it but knew that would attract attention, and that was something he didn't want. He looked around to try to figure out which way Markis would have fled. After a moment of consideration, he went back to the van and told Artek to drive slowly down the side street away from the main boulevard.

Romas looked down at his wrist array, but it was quiet. He knew the only way he could find Markis would be if he called for help again. Each time an alarm was made the wrist array would send out the sender's position as well. When they got to the second cross street, they slowed and Romas looked both ways. After a few seconds, he decided going right looked like the best option. The quality of the neighborhood was declining this way and that usually meant more places to hide and less scrutiny from the local residents.

Finally, his wrist array buzzed. Markis had sent another alarm. He checked the coordinates and realized it was only a few blocks away. They accelerated and soon were in front of a dilapidated white-framed house where Markis and Sarna were hiding out. They approached the back door carefully and announced their presence.

"In here," Markis yelled. "Hurry, Sarna's barely breathing."

They rushed in and saw Markis holding Sarna's head desperately. She was unconscious, her breathing labored, and she barely had a pulse.

Sirens could be heard in the distance. Celius looked up nervously.

"Let's get her back to the shuttle," Romas said. "There's nothing we can do for her here."

Between the three of them, they loaded her clumsily into the back of the van and then got in front to leave. The sirens now were getting louder, so Artek gunned the engine, and they raced away in the opposite direction from the approaching police cars. Soon they were clear and breathed a sigh of relief, but they couldn't help but look back frequently at Sarna, fearing the worst. When they had made it back to Parr Heating & Air, Artek stopped and let Celius off to explain to the others what had happened, and to advise them they would have to stay there a few more hours before they'd be taken back to the shuttle.

An hour later, when they'd made it to the shuttle and Sarna had been taken to the ship's doctor, Romas began quizzing Markis about the incident and the death of the Earth-citizen. Markis ran through the events as best he could recollect but didn't mention how the driver ended up dead.

"So, how did the driver die? Was it from injuries sustained in the accident?"

Markis shook his head solemnly. "No. I killed him with my laser."

"You did what?" Romas said. "You weren't authorized to kill anyone. You weren't even supposed to have your laser with you."

"I thought he'd intentionally hit Sarna. He made no effort to avoid her and he showed no remorse after it happened. All he did was complain about the damage done to his car and the time he'd lose dealing with the accident. I told him to shut up, but he just kept complaining and moaning about what an inconvenience he had suffered. He didn't care about what he'd done to Sarna. So, I lost my temper. Before I knew it, I had the laser out. Seeing the gun didn't faze him at all. He just kept yelling at me and threatening to have me arrested, so I pulled the trigger to shut him up."

"Oh, Pelgrem, save me! What were you thinking?" Romas said angrily. "Now you've compromised the mission for sure. The police will be searching the entire county for the killer. That will make it impossible for us to quietly blend into the populace."

"I know, but I had no other choice."

"Sure, you did," Romas replied sternly. "You could have left the gun on the ship. You disobeyed express orders."

"I'm supposed to go out into a strange world without a weapon?"

"Yes. These Americans are peaceful. You weren't in danger."

"Yeah. Tell that to Sarna."

Romas sighed deeply. "That was an accident and it was probably your fault anyway. Didn't you study your assimilation manual? Traffic signals were a covered topic."

"I read it," Markis replied defiantly.

"Then why did this happen?"

Markis didn't respond.

"All right," Romas said. "Go see how Sarna is doing. I will meet with the Captain and the leadership about this catastrophe. They are going to be livid!"

11
Criminal Enterprise

Although Mineral Wells had a police department, the Sheriff's Office handled all homicide investigations, so Sheriff Wilkins had been called in after the strange accident in downtown Mineral Wells.

"So, what was the motive, you think?" Sheriff Wilkins asked Walt Winters, the County Medical Examiner.

Walt looked up at the Sheriff who was slowly working a mouthful of chewing tobacco. "Anger, I guess. Someone he cared for was brutally injured right before his eyes," Walt said and then turned back to continue his examination of the body.

"So, you think the perp just snapped?"

Walt took a deep breath. "It could be. From what I can determine, the driver had a green light and the right of way. So, when the shooter and the victim stepped out in front of him he either wasn't paying attention or was pissed off enough not to stop. From what the witnesses are saying he could have stopped had he wanted to. But he didn't stop or even brake for that matter. There are no skid marks."

"Maybe he thought they'd both make it out of his way," the Sheriff speculated.

"Maybe so, but he obviously miscalculated. The woman was knocked out and apparently unresponsive after she was hit. We don't know the extent of her injuries or if she even survived since she left or was taken from the accident scene."

"Where do you think they went?" the Sheriff asked. "They were on foot. They couldn't have gone far."

"I don't know. There are patrol cars searching for them now."

"So, if the shooter thought the driver had been reckless or hadn't shown sufficient remorse for what he had done, it could have set him off."

"That would be my guess," Walt said, "but that doesn't explain the wounds on the body. Take a look."

The Sheriff pulled the sheet up to get a good look at the victim. He frowned when he saw the charred clothing and burns all over the body.

"Where are the bullet wounds?" the Sheriff asked.

"There aren't any," Walt replied. "I have thoroughly examined the body, and there are no entry or exit wounds."

"I thought one of the witnesses said the driver was shot?"

"Yes. One of them did. A man down the street said he saw the assailant pull out a gun, point it at the victim and shoot. The odd thing is he didn't hear a gunshot although he did see a muzzle flash."

"He used a silencer?"

"I don't know. Possibly."

"What about the other witnesses?"

"No one else saw the victim take the shot."

"What? How is that possible?" the Sheriff questioned. "They were all within spitting distance."

"I know, but for some reason, they all passed out about the time this happened."

"Passed out? You mean, like in Palo Pinto earlier today?"

"Yes. That's right."

"So, a bunch of children suddenly pass out on a playground and when they wake up they can't remember anything, and on the same day a group of accident witnesses all pass out just before someone is shot and none of them remember a thing?"

"Quite a coincidence," Walt said.

"It couldn't be a coincidence," the Sheriff argued, "not something as odd as this. The owner of this weapon, whatever it was, obviously was at both crime scenes."

"Right. But it wasn't a conventional gun. It was shaped like a gun but discharged a flame or electric charge."

"I have never heard of such a weapon. Have you?" the Sheriff asked.

"Well, I saw plenty of flamethrowers in the war but never the size of a revolver. I'll reach out to my contacts in the Army and see if they know of any weapons like this."

"Good. Let me know what you find out. In the meantime, I'm going to work on identifying everyone at the Palo Pinto crime scene. One of them has to be our killer or at least knows who the killer is."

A sheriff's deputy walked up and tipped his hat to the Sheriff. "Sir, the police haven't had any luck. They've covered a mile in each direction."

"Okay," the Sheriff said dejectedly. "They've obviously gotten away. Call off the search but go on over to the County Hospital and have them alert all doctors in the county to be on the lookout for a woman seeking treatment who has injuries consistent with being hit by a car."

"Yes, sir," the deputy said and walked away.

The Sheriff thought about the scene at the park in Palo Pinto and started making mental notes of who was there. He knew most of the kids at the playground were from New Horizon's Day Care Center used mainly by the county employees at the Courthouse. Then he remembered the school bus. *Why would there be a school bus in front of the Courthouse on a weekday or any day for that matter?* He hadn't remembered seeing any children around the bus but did remember several adults climbing aboard. *Why were adults riding the bus? Who were they and why were they at the Courthouse?*

"All right," the Sheriff said. "I've got to go check some things out over in Palo Pinto. Keep me posted if the autopsy provides any evidence as to the nature of the weapon used on the victim or if the military weighs in on what it might be."

"Will do," Walt said.

The Sheriff got back in his cruiser and drove down the street in the direction the two pedestrians had made their escape. He knew in his heart there was more to this incident than a simple case of anger or retaliation. These people were hiding something, some kind of criminal enterprise going on in his county, and he was going to get to the bottom of it.

†††††

Romas took his seat in the Captain's Conference Room aboard Earth Shuttle 7. The big conference table had twenty chairs, enough for the Captain and three of his executive officers, Jox, Rama, Romas, Celius and several other GOT staff members. The mood was solemn.

Romas addressed the group. "As you know, there was an incident in Mineral Wells this afternoon. Markis and Sarna had concluded their initial research at the local library and office of the Texas Employment Commission and were on their way to have dinner at a local restaurant when it happened. Apparently, they stepped off a curb and were about to walk across a street when a motorist driving recklessly came at them. Markis saw the vehicle coming, stepped back and tried to pull Sarna back as well, but the car struck her anyway."

There was a gasp from those sitting at the table. "How badly was she injured?" Rama asked.

"A broken hip, bruised ribs, and punctured lung. She lost a lot of blood because Markis had to carry her away from the crowd and hide her until we could pick them up.

110

She's going to be alright, that's not the problem."

"Go on," the Captain said.

"So, apparently Markis was angered by what he perceived to be the reckless injury to his mate, particularly when the driver showed no remorse and complained bitterly to him about their walking on a red light. He wasn't sure if she'd survive and when the driver's belligerence persisted, took out his laser and shot the man."

There were more gasps from the group. "Skutz," Jox said. "Markis has always had a hot temper. Does he realize he may have jeopardized our mission?"

"He didn't at the time, I'm sure, but he does now. I have made it abundantly clear to him."

"This is going to complicate our efforts to settle here," the Captain said. "There will be a criminal investigation and you can be sure we will come under considerable scrutiny. The citizens in this county will be on the lookout for anything unusual."

"Yes, the laser burns on the driver will surely seem unusual to them," Romas added.

"What options do we have?" Jox asked. "Can we move to another county?"

"We could but I'm hesitant to risk a take-off being detected when law enforcement is in a heightened state of alertness," the Captain said. "Plus, our alternative landing site is not nearly as well concealed as this one."

"Where is the alternative site?" Romas asked.

"It's farther east near a lake called Tawakoni," the Captain replied. "It's also in a sparsely populated area, but not on an island. There would always be a risk that someone would stumble across us."

"Okay. So, we will have to stay and deal with the situation unless things get unbearable. But the immediate question is how we should punish Markis for his actions," Romas noted.

Jox shook his head. "I'd say, strip him of all rank and responsibility and make him a common laborer, that's what he deserves, but we need his talents too much for that."

"But his actions were irresponsible, and we can't afford to have a man in charge of our security who can't control his own temper."

"His mate was nearly killed," Celius interjected. "What one of you could control your outrage under those circumstances?"

"Yes, of course. But they were both acting negligently by crossing a street on a red light," Jox replied. "There is no excuse for ignorance of local laws and customs. That is something we've drilled into everyone. He has to be punished in some fashion."

"I think a public reprimand would be sufficient," Romas said. "He's a proud man. A public reprimand will cause him much embarrassment as well as being instructive to others about the perils we face every day here on Earth."

"I agree," the Captain said. "Is there agreement on this, or does someone else have an idea?"

Everyone looked around at each other, but no one spoke up, so the Captain said. "Then so be it. Tonight, after dinner we will announce the public reprimand over the shuttle's com-system."

"All right," Jox said. "Is there any action we need to take to protect ourselves from the criminal investigation that is underway?"

Romas shook his head. "I don't think so. We don't know that the investigation will ever reach us. Any reaction on our part could actually attract attention. For now, we should just keep our eyes and ears open for any hint of trouble. We can formulate a response to a specific threat when and if it presents itself."

"I agree," the Captain said. "It's no time to panic. We should just move ahead as planned."

Romas breathed a sigh of relief when the meeting was over. He had feared that the leadership would overreact to what had happened. If they took drastic measures against Markis, he might leave their group with his family and take as many others as he could persuade to follow him. That would definitely jeopardize the mission. He was glad the Captain had supported his call for restraint. Although Romas wasn't sure that Markis was the right man to be head of security for the mission, there wasn't anyone aboard who had his experience and knowledge, so he just prayed he'd learned his lesson and would carry out his duties responsibly in the future.

12
Investigation

When Sheriff Wilkins got to the Palo Pinto Courthouse, he went straight to the County Clerk's office. When he walked through the door his daughter Evelyn went over to him. "What's going on in Mineral Wells? Someone said there was a shooting."

The Sheriff spat tobacco into a Dairy Queen cup he was holding in his left hand. "That's right. A woman was hit crossing the street and her husband or boyfriend killed the driver who was responsible."

"Oh, my God! Did you bring him in?"

"No. He's still on the loose."

"What are you doing here? Shouldn't you be out looking for him?"

"He vanished, and all the witnesses passed out. No one has any memory of what happened or even which way he and the woman escaped."

"You mean—"

"Yes. Just like yesterday. I came back here because of the incident at New Horizon. The same weapon was used at both crime scenes, so the shooter must have been here yesterday."

"Right. That would make sense."

"Do you remember seeing a school bus parked outside yesterday?"

Evelyn grimaced. "A school bus? . . . Ah, yeah, now that you mention it. I saw it out there at lunch."

"Were there any field trips to the courthouse yesterday?"

"There weren't any school kids around here that I saw. You should go talk to Betsy Reynolds. She's New Horizon's director. Their building is right across the street from the lot where the bus was parked. She would have been curious, I'm sure and must have checked it out."

The Sheriff nodded. "Thanks. I will do that," he said and then rushed out hoping and praying that Betsy Reynolds would know something. As he crossed the street to the daycare center, he saw a line of cars parked with parents impatiently waiting for their children to be released. As he approached the front door it swung open and children began running out. He stopped and waited for the children to pass and then went inside. A dark-haired woman with thick-rimmed glasses was reprimanding a teacher about something, so he figured she must be Betsy Reynolds. He walked over to her and waited until the teacher walked off.

"Mrs. Reynolds?"

The woman turned and gave the Sheriff a once-over. "Sheriff Wilkins?"

"Yes."

She grimaced. "What are you doing here? I have already told your deputies everything I know."

"Yes, but there's been a new development."

"Oh really?"

"Yes. In Mineral Wells today I was called to the scene of an accident and found a crowd of people who had all passed out just like the children in your playground yesterday."

"Oh my God! Are you serious?"

"Yes. It was very unusual. There's got to be a connection between these two incidents."

"A connection?" Betsy repeated.

"Yes. Some sort of weapon caused a lot of people at both crime scenes to lose consciousness. And it's not a weapon I have ever seen or even heard about, so I'm fairly certain we are looking for one shooter who used the weapon at both crime scenes."

Betsy nodded. "I don't remember seeing any weapons. All I remember is standing outside watching the children play, and then suddenly a group of them fainted all at once like they were machines and the power had been turned off."

"You don't remember seeing anyone who didn't belong hanging around?"

"No. I don't think so," Betsy replied thoughtfully. "Wait a minute. Now that you mention it, there was a man on the sidewalk. He'd just walked by when it happened."

"Was he carrying anything in his hands?"

"I don't know. I wasn't paying much attention to him. I do remember he came over after the children fainted and offered his help. He didn't have anything in his hands then."

"What did he look like?" the Sheriff asked.

"Middle-aged, medium height, white shirt and pants, and a very pale complexion. He obviously didn't get much sun."

"What did you say to him?"

"I thanked him but said there was no need. Everyone seemed to be okay."

"Did you see where he went when he left?"

"Hmm. Now that you mention it, he went the wrong way. He had been walking west when the kids started fainting, but when he left he went in the opposite direction."

"That is telling. He may have used a weapon on the children, but why? What did it accomplish by knocking them out for a few minutes? They weren't hurt as I understand it."

Betsy shrugged. "You got me, Sheriff. It makes no sense."

"Did you see a school bus?"

"School bus?"

"Yes. Apparently, there was a school bus in the courthouse parking lot yesterday. That may have been how the man got here and why he left in that direction after the incident."

"Right. I did see an old school bus leave the parking lot shortly thereafter. It seemed a little strange at the time, but I was too busy to give it much thought."

"An old school bus; not one of the regular buses in operation now?"

"No. One of the ones that were retired a few years back."

"Huh," the Sheriff said. "I did see a couple of tourists at Dave's this morning, a husband and wife. The husband fits your description of the man who walked by the children," the Sheriff said. "I saw him later at the County Clerk's office. He said his aunt used to live in Palo Pinto and he was thinking of moving here."

"Really. Did he tell you his aunt's name?" Betsy asked.

"No, but I can find out. He got a copy of her death certificate. There will be a receipt."

"Well, there you go, a solid lead."

"Yes, indeed. Thanks for your help," the Sheriff said. "If you think of anything else, let me know."

The Sheriff turned and headed back across the street to the courthouse. After a few steps, he adjusted his course and headed to Dave's Diner to see Belinda. He figured she had served the mystery couple when he came in the diner and might have learned something about them. A bell rang as he opened the door. There were only a few patrons in the diner as it was only 4:30 p.m. Belinda was at the cash register counting the day's cash.

"Belinda, I need to talk to you," the Sheriff said.

"Hi, Sheriff. What's up?"

"You remember the man and woman who came in here yesterday morning while Curt and I were here?"

"Sure. They were a strange pair."

"How so?"

"The man was dumb as a doornail," she said with a chuckle. "Didn't even know how to buy a newspaper or make change."

"Yeah. They said they were tourists, didn't they?"

"Right. From Hungary they claimed."

"Ah. Did you see how they got here? Did they have a car?"

"No, but I know they'd been at the pawn shop before they came here."

"How do you know that?"

"Because Ben told me when he came in for lunch. Said they sold him a diamond and he made a killing."

"Really. That's odd. I hope it wasn't stolen for Ben's sake."

"You couldn't prove that it was or wasn't, could ya?"

"It wouldn't be easy," the Sheriff admitted thoughtfully. "I guess I better go have a conversation with Ben."

"Probably should," Belinda agreed.

The Sheriff nodded. "Thanks. See you in the morning."

"I'll have the coffee ready bright and early."

The Sheriff stepped out into the hot afternoon. A big thermometer on the wall said it was 102°. The heat was particularly stifling with his uniform on. Perspiration trickled down his forehead and into his eyes as he walked. He wiped it away with his sleeve. When he got to Big Tex

Pawn he stepped inside and welcomed the cool relief of the big ceiling fans.

Ben looked up and smiled, "Hi, Sheriff."

The Sheriff took off his hat and held it in his hand. "Hi, Ben. How you been?"

"Fine. What's going on?"

"I heard you did some business with some tourists yesterday."

"Who told you that?"

"Belinda. She said you bought a diamond off them."

"Yes, I did. It was a nice one, and I got it cheap."

"Where did they say they got it?"

"Why? You don't think it was stolen, do you?"

"I don't know, but it seems a bit suspicious. A tourist walking in and selling you a big diamond."

"I guess, but strange things like that happen all the time in pawn shops. People get desperate, you know."

"I do, but if it turns out it was stolen, or somebody was laundering money you could be in a world of hurt."

Ben sighed. "They seemed like really nice people, but now that you mention it they were pretty nervous."

"If you see them again, you call me immediately, okay? They may have been involved in an incident over in Mineral Wells. I really need to talk to them."

"Will do, Sheriff. If they come in again, you'll be the first to know."

"Good. See you later."

The Sheriff went back to his office and worked for a while. Then he and Curt Gibbons, his chief deputy, went to Possum Kingdom Lake to see if they could find the two tourists. Curt was young, just out of junior college. He'd been a high school football star, tall, lean and handsome enough to get any girl he wanted but hadn't been quite good enough to get a college scholarship. So, he ended up in junior college and got a degree in criminal justice. The

Sheriff really liked him and was grooming him to take over his job when he retired.

They went to two local motels, the state park campground, several diners, a popular convenience store, and bait shop, but nobody had seen the strange couple.

It was nearly 8:00 p.m. and they were about to give up and call it a day when they drove by a warehouse by the lake. Curt glanced at the metal structure wondering what was stored in it when he spotted a school bus parked in the rear. Curt looked at the Sheriff and asked, "Could that be the school bus you're looking for?"

The Sheriff slammed on the brakes and looked over where Curt was pointing. "Yeah. That could be it," he said as he shifted the patrol car into reverse, backed up, and pulled into the parking lot. After driving around to the back, they found not one but three old school buses parked in a row.

"You know who owns this warehouse?" the Sheriff asked as he got out of the patrol car.

"No," Curt replied, slamming his door as he got out on the passenger side. "I've never seen anyone here. I thought this place was abandoned."

"Obviously, it is not."

The Sheriff walked over and put his hand on the hood of the bus. "Still warm. It's been driven today. Take down the VIN and license plate numbers so we can find out who owns it."

Curt took out a notebook and wrote down the information. Then he looked over at the warehouse. "I wonder what they have stored here. I don't see any windows."

"Could be a boat, but I don't see a ramp or a dock. We should take a look inside."

"Should we get a warrant?" Curt asked.

"Probably, but I doubt the judge would give us one

with as little evidence as we have. Let's come by here early tomorrow morning and see if anyone shows up. If nobody does, then we'll try to get a warrant. But if they do, maybe they'll show us around and answer some questions."

"You want me to watch this place tonight in case somebody comes in the night?"

"Nah. We just need to be here before sunrise. It's not likely there'll be any action before then."

"Right," Curt agreed.

When the Sheriff got home, Evelyn was reading a book. She got up as he walked in the door.

"Finally," she complained. "Where have you been?"

"Out trying to find those two tourists. I think they must be involved in the murder in Mineral Wells somehow."

"Really? Huh. I'll warm up your supper."

"Thanks. We found some old school buses. One of them was probably the one that was seen up at the Courthouse."

"That's great, Dad," Evelyn said. "Good work."

"I need to find out who these people are? I wish I would have asked them their names. Didn't you write out a receipt to one of them?"

"Yes. I did give one to the woman. I'll find our copy of the receipt and tell you her name first thing in the morning."

"Good. We've got to find them and figure out what they are up to before somebody else turns up dead."

Evelyn sighed. "Yes, but you need to be careful. You don't know anything about this weapon they have. They could ambush you with it at any time."

"I know. I am always careful. You know that."

Evelyn nodded warily. "I know, but I have a bad feeling about this weapon that kills without bullets. I know you have to find it and make sure nobody else was hurt by it, but please be careful and call for backup if you find them. Don't try to be a hero."

The Sheriff nodded absently. He was a cautious man, but he had no clue how to protect himself from a weapon he knew nothing about. They could wear vests, but he wasn't sure they'd do any good. He finally decided they'd just have to be wary, and if things started to go sideways, they'd shoot first and ask questions later.

"I will," the Sheriff said. "Don't worry. Now, where's that supper you had for me?"

Evelyn smiled. "I'll heat it up. Go wash up and it will be ready by the time you're done."

13

Confrontation

It was already 85° at 6 a.m. when Romas and Artek stepped out of the warehouse on the shore of Possum Kingdom Lake. Romas looked out at the high bluffs of Cactus Island in the distance to see if anyone was lurking about but saw no one. The island was so infested with cacti that few ever tried to land on it, and those who did usually regretted it.

From the air, the island appeared flat with a smooth surface like it had been excavated for a football field or a parking lot. Earlier, the Tarizon visitors had spread a rumor that a recluse had bought the island to build a home completely isolated from the world but had died just as construction was beginning. As the story was told the recluse's heirs had no interest in completing the house, which would have only been accessible by helicopter, so the project was halted. Had anyone not believed the rumor and dug just five feet below the surface of Cactus Island, they would have been quite shocked to find the hull of a spaceship. Romas thanked Pelgrem that nobody had done that, at least not while an Earth shuttle was deployed there.

Romas watched Artek as he got inside one of the school buses and started the engine. On his instructions, Artek had refueled them the night before so they could get an early start. If he'd learned anything on the first day on Earth it was that quiet assimilation into the local community was going to be a daunting task, so they needed to be focused and diligent in all their efforts. Any delay could jeopardize the mission.

Romas heard conversation coming from the warehouse. He looked over and saw Celius emerge followed by many others who were going into Mineral Wells that day. He had already given them freshly printed social security cards, individualized resumes, and drivers' licenses modeled after the one Celius had stolen. In an early briefing, a group of the visitors had been told to go register at the Texas Employment Commission to see what jobs were available and then apply for as many as possible. Others were going to look for jobs listed in the newspaper or posted outside various businesses around town.

When Artek had the bus ready, he signaled for everyone to come aboard, but before they made it to the bus a Sheriff's patrol car screeched around the corner and sped quickly into the parking lot. When the car came to a halt, Sheriff Wilkinson and his deputy stepped out. While the Sheriff was taking in the strange scene, he spotted Romas and walked over to him.

"Good morning," the Sheriff said evenly.

"Hi, Sheriff," Romas replied courteously. "What's going on?"

"You're not an easy man to find."

Romas shrugged. "Well, that's not surprising since we don't live here. Why are you looking for me?"

The Sheriff ignored Romas' question and asked, "What is this place?"

"A garage, I believe," Romas replied. He pointed toward the bus. "Our driver keeps his buses here."

"Why do you need buses?"

Romas frowned. "Ah. Well, as you can see there are a number of us traveling together, so it's cheaper to be driven around in a bus rather than renting cars."

"How many are traveling with you?"

"Quite a few," Romas replied warily.

"How did you all get here this morning?"

"Oh, we stayed here last night. Mr. Artek lets us stay in bunks. It's much cheaper than a motel."

The Sheriff looked at Romas and the others skeptically, then said, "Well, I'm not sure that's legal, but that's another matter. I'm going to have to take you and your wife back to Palo Pinto right now. I have some questions for you."

"Questions about what?" Romas asked feigning surprise.

"Ah. I don't want to talk about it here. Just come back with me to my office and we'll sort it out."

Romas considered the request a few seconds and then shrugged. "Sure. We'll be happy to help you out in any way we can."

There was a flash of blue light and the Sheriff and his deputy collapsed. Romas turned to see who had used the blue light on them and saw Markis holding the weapon. Romas shook his head angrily. "Why did you do that? We could have gone with them to answer their questions. The memory gun wasn't necessary."

"What are you talking about?" Markis replied. "What if they had gone into the warehouse. They would have seen our cave. I'm head of security. I couldn't let that happen."

"They didn't ask to go in the warehous? You overreacted and now we have a mess on our hands."

"Don't worry. I gave them a hard dose. They'll be out for hours and won't remember what they ate for breakfast."

"A hard dose! Are you crazy? What if there is brain damage?"

"Who cares? Just kill them and dump their bodies somewhere."

"No. That will just make matters worse," Romas

spat. "Let me think a minute." He looked at the squad car and then in the direction they had come. "Okay, here is what we are going to do. He took Artek aside and told him.

"Yes, sir," Artek replied.

"When they wake up they will remember nothing," Romas promised.

"Good thinking," Celius said smiling. "I was worried there for a moment. What about these skid marks they made when they drove up?"

"Right. We will have to quickly remove any evidence that any of this happened. Get a couple crew members on that."

"I will," Celius replied and walked off.

"See, the memory gun was a good response," Markis argued. "Problem solved."

"Maybe," Romas replied. "But then again, you may have just exacerbated the problem. One memory gun incident may be forgotten, two could be troublesome but three could be our undoing."

Markis shook his head. "No, this will all blow over. I promise you."

"Right. Well, if you hadn't killed someone, that might have been the case."

Markis shook his head and then walked over to help Artek put the bodies back in the squad car. Twenty minutes later they all got onto the bus and drove off. As they drove by the patrol car, where the Sheriff and his deputy lie unconscious, Romas worried that the Sheriff or his deputy might wake up with brain damage, or not wake up at all. If that happened the federal government or even the military might be called in—so much for their quiet assimilation into the local community.

After they'd left off the job seekers at the TEC, Artek drove Romas and Celius to a real estate office they had been told specialized in ranch property. It had occurred to them that a ranch would be a place a lot of people could live unnoticed. The name of the firm, according to the sign out front, was Wells Realty. A woman looked up as they stepped inside the reception area.

"Hello. Welcome to Wells Realty," the receptionist said with a bright smile.

"Hi," Celius said. "We heard you all handle ranch property."

The woman nodded. "Yes. We have a number of ranch listings. Let me see if Paul is busy. Hang on."

She got up and went into a back office. A moment letter, a small, slightly overweight man with red hair came out smiling. "Hi. I'm Paul Wells. I understand you're looking for some property."

"Yes," Celius said.

"Good. Come on back and I'll show you what we have available. About how many acres are you looking for?"

"We're not sure," Celius replied. "We are immigrating from Hungary with several other families and need something large enough for everyone."

Paul motioned for them to sit in two side chairs across from his desk while he fumbled through a stack of files. After a minute, he opened a file in front of them. "Here is a brand new listing for a 152 acre ranch. The owner died, and his wife is moving to town. It's a small ranch. Are you going to raise cattle?"

"Possibly," Romas said. "We don't have any ranching experience though."

"Oh, well maybe I can find you a seller who would be willing to provide training. That happens sometimes. The old owner stays on for a year or so as a consultant."

"That would be helpful," Romas replied. "We have plenty of labor. There will be over a hundred of us and many more to come."

"Hmm. I've noticed there's been a lot of immigration

into the county these past few years. Luckily there is plenty of cheap land available right now."

"Good. We don't have unlimited resources."

Paul looked up suddenly and smiled. "You know, there's an 800-acre ranch up for foreclosure. You could probably get it cheap if you could pay cash at the courthouse steps."

"How cheap?"

"The bank is owed $48,000, so they will stop bidding when it gets to that price. I bet you can get it for less than $50,000, and I know the owner will be looking for a job once the sale is complete."

"Excellent. What do they call the place?"

"The Timber Creek Ranch. It's even got a couple of oil wells on it. They're only pumping about ten barrels a day, but you'd still get a nice little royalty that's almost enough to pay your property taxes."

Can we take a look at it?"

"Sure. Let me call the owner and see if he is up for visitors."

Romas nodded and looked encouragingly at Celius. Paul dialed a number on his rotary phone and waited. After a moment, he got through and asked if he could bring by some prospective buyers. He smiled and hung up the phone.

"Yes. Mr. Briggs said to come on over," Paul reported as he stood up. "Let me get my coat, and I will drive you over there."

"Great!" Romas replied.

A few minutes later they were packed into the front seat of Paul's pickup and driving north on State Highway 281. About twenty miles out of town Paul turned left onto a dirt road. They traveled another two or three miles when they came upon a stand of trees sheltering a large house and yard. Beyond the house were several structures including a barn, bunkhouse and a large metal building.

Paul slowed and pointed to a yellow sign. "The school bus picks up kids here at 7:30 a.m. every school day. Do you have children?" he asked.

"Yes, we have quite a lot of them, actually."

"The bus takes them to Mineral Wells where there is an elementary school, a middle school, and a high school."

"Oh. Okay."

"I have the phone number for the administration office if you need it to get them enrolled."

"Yes, that might come in handy if we decide to let them go."

"Well, I don't know what the law is in Hungary, but here in Texas school is mandatory."

Paul pulled the truck up into the driveway and killed the engine. "This is it," he advised as he got out of the truck.

As Romas and Celius climbed out, a tall, grey-haired man in overalls came out of the house and approached them. "Hello. Welcome to Timber Creek Ranch," Jamie Briggs said, extending his hand exuberantly. Romas shook it and smiled. Celius nodded.

"Jamie, this could be a good deal for you," Paul said.

"How's that?" Jamie asked.

"If these folks buy your property at foreclosure they might be interested in keeping you on to teach them the business."

Jamie raised his eyebrows. "Really?"

"Sure, they don't know anything about farming and ranching. It could be the perfect deal for you."

Jamie nodded. "Yeah. Sounds interesting. I was planning to go to Dallas and stay with my brother, but I hate the city."

"Maybe you could stay in the bunkhouse?" Paul suggested.

"Well, we'd want you close by if you were going to

teach us the business. I'm sure we could work something out."

"Good," Paul said. "I'll start working on the paperwork while Jamie shows you around."

"Okay," Jamie said. "Ah. Let's start with the house."

Jaime led them up the walkway to the front porch. Romas noted that the exterior was in desperate need of painting and was in general disrepair. That didn't concern him though as the place would have to be completely redone to accommodate their needs anyway. The wooden porch creaked as they stepped on it and approached the front door. Paul pushed the door open and then stepped away so they could enter.

After seeing the house, they went to the barn where several horses and milking cows resided. Behind the barn, there were a chicken shed and pigpen. The metal building, they discovered, housed assorted tractors and other farming equipment. Romas was getting excited as he imagined their first enterprise getting underway.

When they got back to Paul's pickup, he had a contract put together and handed it to them to look at.

"This looks good," Romas said, "but I will have to consult with the others before we make a commitment."

"Sure," Paul said. "The foreclosure sale isn't until next Tuesday, so you have a few days."

"How does it look to you, Jamie?"

Jamie looked up from the contract and smiled. "Fine. I guess it all hinges on you folks being the successful bidders at the foreclosure sale."

Paul nodded. "Right. But I don't know of anybody planning to bid. The Bank's note is a little steep for most people."

"Is the price going to be okay with you?" Jamie asked Romas.

"Ah. Yes. It shouldn't be a problem if we decide to go

through with it."

"Good. Let me know just as soon as you make up your minds; there's some spraying that needs to be done here pretty soon to prevent insect damage to the crops."

"Sure, just give me a day or two."

Paul drove Romas and Celius back to his office, and while they waited for the bus they discussed the school situation.

"This mandatory education law is going to be a problem," Celius complained. "We can't let our six-year-olds and under go to a public school. They could easily compromise our situation."

"Yes. We need to see what this home-schooling is all about. If that means we teach our children, that would be perfect."

"That must be what it means, but I'm sure there will be rules and paperwork to be done."

Romas nodded. "When the children are older, it would probably be good to let them go to school. They need to learn as much about Earth and America as they can. There is no telling how long we will have to stay here."

Romas wondered how all their children would do in school. The work would be easy enough. On Tarizon children were finished with school by age twelve. But how would they interact with these American children? Would they fit in, or were they so different that they would be ridiculed and bullied by the American children? But, most importantly, could they be trusted to keep their true identities secret? That wouldn't be easy. Romas prayed it would all work out.

14
The Accident

The Sheriff's eyes opened to a smoky haze. He felt hot and disoriented. Glancing ahead he noticed the windshield was shattered. "What the hell!" he mumbled. To his right, he saw Curt slumped over in his seat. He grabbed Curt's shoulder frantically. "Curt! You okay? You okay? Wake up!"

Curt stirred, and his eyes opened. He sat up and looked around curiously. "What's going on?"

"I think we've been in an accident," the Sheriff replied looking around wide-eyed. "Where the hell are we?"

Curt glanced from side to side and moaned. "I don't know. All I can see is dirt."

The Sheriff opened his door and got out of the patrol car but immediately stumbled. He grabbed the door to keep from falling. Curt followed suit and tried to stand up but ended up on his knees. "Damn it! I can't even stand up."

The Sheriff came around and helped Curt to his feet. He stood up and leaned heavily against the door. For the first time, they inspected the front of the patrol car and saw it had been crushed like an accordion against a tree.

"You going to be okay?" the Sheriff asked as Curt tried to walk.

"I'm not sure," Curt admitted. "My head is killing me, my hand is bleeding, and I think I've cracked a few ribs."

"Hmm. I feel the same way. We better get some medical attention. I can't even find the radio. Let me see if

I can figure out where we are. There may be a house or filling station close by with a telephone where we can call in for help."

The Sheriff stood up straight and took several deep breaths. "I'm really dizzy. I'm not sure I'll be able to walk. I must have cracked my head on the windshield."

"Me too. My forehead is swollen."

The Sheriff started moving slowly out of the ditch and up onto a narrow county road. Looking around he searched for a landmark or something familiar that might help him get his bearings but saw nothing. A few moments later, Curt joined him and frowned.

"This looks like the road to Jasper Ranch. I was here a few weeks ago."

The Sheriff nodded, "If that's true, the ranch house should be less than a mile up the road."

"That's right. Let's go," Curt said.

They started slowly stumbling north toward the ranch. The sun beat down on them relentlessly, and they were soon desperate for water. Unfortunately, what water they had was back in the patrol car, and neither had the strength to go back for it.

After nearly an hour walking in the triple-digit heat, they came to the crest of a hill and saw the ranch house in the distance. Relieved by the sight, they began walking faster and faster until they finally reached the front yard. Noticing a hose attached to a water faucet the Sheriff headed over to it and turned it on. Water began gushing out of the hose, and the Sheriff held it up for Curt to take a drink. Curt got his fill, and then passed the hose back to the Sheriff.

"Knock on the door, and see if anyone is home," the Sheriff said.

Curt walked up onto the porch and began knocking on the door. After a minute, an old woman opened the door and looked out at them curiously.

"Can I help you?"

"We've been in an accident. We need to use your phone."

"Oh, my Lord. Come in!" the woman exclaimed as she opened the door for them.

The Sheriff stumbled by her and looked around for a phone.

"In the kitchen," the woman said pointing to the rear of the house.

The Sheriff found the phone, picked it up, and dialed.

"Sheriff's office," the dispatcher said.

"Jane, this is the Sheriff."

"Thank God! Where have you been? Everyone's been worried sick about you."

"I don't know. We were in an accident and apparently have been unconscious for a while."

"A while? How about 12 hours! You didn't come back last night after your shift."

The Sheriff felt like he'd been gut-punched when he realized they'd been unconscious for over 12 hours. He closed his eyes trying to remember anything, but his mind was a blank. "Did you say 12 hours?"

"Yes. Sheriff, I have been calling you every 15 minutes since yesterday afternoon. Where the blazes are you anyway?"

"Ah. Up at Jasper Ranch."

"What were you doing up there?"

"I have no idea."

"Jesus almighty! Everyone's been searching for you. We were about to call in the Texas Rangers."

"You didn't, I hope. We're okay, but we need to go by the hospital to get checked out. Neither of us is feeling too well. You'll need to get a wrecker out here too."

"Okay. I'll get an ambulance and wrecker out there and call your daughter too. She was very upset when you didn't show up last night."

"My daughter?"

"Yeah, Evelyn. You know."

"Right. Sure. She was worried?"

"Yes. Of course, she was."

Forty minutes later, a Sheriff's patrol car and an ambulance pulled up in front of the main house at Jasper Ranch. A deputy ran up to the front door and knocked. The door opened, and the Sheriff let him in.

"Hey, thanks for coming to get us," the Sheriff said.

"Of course. We've been so worried about you two."

The Sheriff grimaced in pain. "Curt's lying on the sofa. You'll need to help him into the ambulance."

"The drivers will take care of him. Let me help you. Can you ride in my patrol car?"

"Yes. I think so. Did you find the wreck?"

"Yeah. It was hard to miss. You must have been going pretty fast to crush the hood the way you did. What happened anyway?"

"I don't know. Neither Curt nor I have any memory of what happened."

Rich frowned. "How could that be? You must remember something."

The Sheriff shook his head. "No, nothing since breakfast yesterday, and I barely remember that."

"You must have suffered a concussion, I guess. That would explain it."

The Sheriff sighed. "I guess. I really don't know."

"Ah. Were you two out partying? There was a bunch of empty beer cans in the back seat."

The Sheriff stiffened and looked at Rich. "What! No, we . . . well . . . I don't remember, but clearly, we wouldn't have been drinking and driving."

"Yeah, well don't worry about it, I threw the cans in my trunk. I'll toss them in the first trash can I see."

The Sheriff's face had turned white. He was mortified by the fact that empty beer cans had been found in his patrol car. He knew there had to be an explanation, but his mind was a blank. What is going on? When they arrived at the hospital in Mineral Wells, Evelyn was in the waiting room pacing. She ran over to her father when she saw him come through the front door.

"Dad! Are you okay?"

"Just shaken up a bit," the Sheriff replied. "I'll be okay."

Evelyn gave him a hard look. "You look terrible. They say you hit a tree?"

"Apparently. I don't remember anything."

"I bet you got a head injury. What were you doing out there? Why didn't you call in?"

"I told you. I don't remember," the Sheriff replied irritably.

An orderly took the Sheriff by his arm and pushed him down the hall toward an examining room. "Let's let the doctor check him out, Evelyn," he said. "He'll figure out the extent of his injuries and let us know. I'll come and get you just as soon as he finishes his examination."

Evelyn reluctantly turned and went back to the waiting room. Her mind was a muddle of confusion and worry. Her father had always been a rock, and his sudden disappearance and loss of memory scared her. When she made it back to the waiting room, she found a cluster of friends and well-wishers gathered. They had lots of questions, but she had no answers, so she retreated to the chapel where she could be alone to think and pray.

Forty minutes later she was summoned to the treatment room where she found Dr. Ben Sanders standing next to her father who was sitting on the edge of the examining table. Her father had on a hospital gown which she knew meant he was being admitted.

"Your father has suffered a serious head trauma and he needs to stay here a day or two, so we can keep a close eye on him."

"Yes, of course. How bad is it?"

"I'm okay," the Sheriff assured her.

"We don't know how long he and Curt were unconscious, but it was at least several hours. That suggests a serious injury. We'll do some testing tomorrow to try to determine the extent of it."

"Oh, Dad. I'm so worried."

"Don't be. I'll be fine."

"You don't remember anything? Where you were going? Who you went to see?"

"Nothing. Did I tell you anything before I left home yesterday?"

"You were going to try to locate those tourists who were riding around in a school bus. You called in a license plate number to Jane."

"I did? What tourists?"

"You know, the ones that came by the Courthouse looking for their aunt's death certificate. They were riding around in a school bus with some other tourists."

The Sheriff looked at her blankly.

"Anyway, I called in the number and apparently the buses were sold for scrap several years ago. So, that was a dead end."

"Huh," the Sheriff replied. "I wonder where we saw the buses. I don't remember anything."

"Well, you should go home, Evelyn," the doctor said. "There's nothing you can do here tonight. Let your father rest and you can visit him tomorrow afternoon after we've completed his testing."

Evelyn nodded and reluctantly left to drive home.

She had a bad feeling about her father's mysterious accident and loss of memory. She hadn't said anything but thought it a strange coincidence that her father and Curt were both experiencing a memory loss at the same time they were investigating the exact same phenomenon. A memory loss was a common injury in an auto accident, but still, she wondered if there wasn't a connection to the memory losses her father and Curt had been investigating.

She was worried too about her father's condition. She knew her father, and despite his assurances that he was okay, she knew he wasn't. And it wasn't just his injury that she was worried about but also the bizarre circumstances surrounding it. The unknown was always frightening and there were so many unanswered questions. What she feared and what terrified her the most, was her gut feeling that the worst was yet to come.

15
Timber Creek Ranch

By the end of the week, things were looking up for the visitors. Paul Wells managed to negotiate a deal for the purchase of Timber Creek Ranch, and over a dozen of the Tarizonians had found jobs in Mineral Wells. Paul had even got the bank's agreement that the buyers could move into the property the moment the $52,000 purchase price had been put in escrow.

Romas knew that converting diamonds into cash was going to be a challenge. A large transaction like that was likely to be noticed, and that was the last thing the visitors wanted particularly since they were already on the Sheriff's radar.

After discussing the situation with the Captain and the Board, it was decided they would need to go to a big city like Ft. Worth where there would be a dozen or more pawn shops to choose from. So, they agreed they'd go to six pawn shops to get the necessary money.

While Romas and Celius were in Ft. Worth the shuttle's engineers went out to the ranch to plan how best to use it. After a careful inspection and much discussion, the engineers decided they could build living quarters under the metal building, the barn, and outbuildings that could temporarily house all of the visitors and permanently keep about half of them. This was obviously the right move to get the visitors off the Earth shuttle and safely hidden away, so the Board unanimously approved the plan.

The only tricky part of the plan was keeping the previous owner Jamie Briggs, who would be teaching them the farm and ranch operations, from discovering that over 1,700 people would be soon occupying his ranch. So, they agreed he would be told that they were going to renovate the buildings so they could hold more equipment, supplies and house more ranch hands as they were needed.

Romas and Celius were not completely convinced Briggs would buy the story, but even if he didn't it was unlikely he'd figure out what was really going on, particularly if they kept him busy and paid him well for his services.

Of a greater concern was the Sheriff's murder investigation. They weren't sure it had been permanently derailed. The Sheriff and his deputy had been sidetracked for now, but there was no guarantee that would last. In fact, Romas was pretty sure the Sheriff would be hot on his trail once he had fully recovered.

✝✝✝✝✝

After a few days in the hospital, Sheriff Wilkins insisted on going home even though his doctor had refused to release him. Reluctantly, Evelyn brought him home but took a week's vacation to keep an eye on him. He still had no memory of what had happened which was very unsettling to her. When she was satisfied he was back to his normal self, she told him her suspicions.

"I'm worried about you going back to work?"

"Why?" the Sheriff asked.

"I know you are going to resume your search for the tourists with the strange gun. I'm worried that this time they will kill you."

"Nonsense, I'll be more careful this time."

"How? You have no idea what you're dealing with here. Neither the military or the FBI have ever seen such a weapon."

144

The Sheriff sighed. "Well, that's true, but we'll figure it out."

"Maybe, maybe not. I don't want to lose you."

"So, what would you have me do? Ignore the worst threat that has ever come to Palo Pinto County?"

"No. You need to be smarter than them."

"But how do I do that?"

"Resign as Sheriff. Make them think they have beaten you. Then we'll keep a close eye on them. Eventually, they will make a mistake and you can nail them then."

"We?"

"Yes. I'm going to get involved. They tried to kill you. It's personal now."

"No. You're a civilian. You're not trained for this type of thing."

"I don't need any training. All I'm going to do is keep my eyes and ears open and when they resurface, I'll be friendly and try to get close to them."

The Sheriff shook his head. "So, you want me to actually resign?"

"Publicly, yes, but it will be an undercover sting operation. You can coordinate it with the Texas Rangers or the FBI, but nobody in Palo Pinto County can know the truth. I'll tell everyone it was because of the accident."

The Sheriff nodded, and Evelyn smiled. She couldn't wait to nail the bastards who had nearly killed her father.

16
The Bruda Arms Empire

After Sandee's media conference and subsequent attendance at the peace conference with Chancellor Dosimo and Ambassador Talvihn, his remarkable story quickly spread across Lyon and Serie. Growing crowds as well as a contingent of reporters from as far as Lower Serie began following him wherever he went.

Convinced that Sandee's claim to have been assigned by Pelgrem to save Tarizon was true, Ambassador Talvihn lent him Salina to assist him in his mission. This pleased both Sandee and Salina as they had hit it off well from the beginning and had been growing closer each day.

Salina believed most citizens of Tarizon, having suffered dearly during a century of war, would be excited, if not thrilled, by the idea that Pelgrem had appeared to Sandee and given this young orphan the mission to bring peace to the world.

Many were skeptical of this claim, she knew, but they would still listen to what he had to say because his message was compelling. If peace didn't come soon to Tarizon, the planet would never recover from mankind's abuse and all life on Tarizon would be extinguished.

So, for the next five cycles Sandee, with Salina at his side, traveled across the globe to all the nations of Azollo, Lemaine Shane, Ock Mezan and Turvin preaching about Pelgrem's warnings and the necessity to bring about peace.

With Salina's help and guidance, his confidence and

skill increased daily resulting in more compelling sermons and speeches. Each day the crowds following him grew larger as well as the press corps following him. This energized Sandee and encouraged him. He envisioned that one day soon there would be such an overwhelming groundswell of support for peace that the nations of the world would have no choice but to cease hostilities and commence peace negotiations. But along with the growing support for Sandee's peace movement, there was also growing concern amongst the rich and powerful war profiteers. One of them was Cornelius Bruda.

Cornelius Bruda grew up on a large ranch near the headwaters of the Pollo River in the White Mountains of Northern Tributon. It was no longer a working ranch due to water and air pollution from decades of war, but it still was a pleasant place to live far away from the turmoil of the domed cities and the injured, sick and dying humans who wandered aimlessly throughout the countryside.

The eldest of eleven children, Cornelius was raised almost entirely by his mother since his father had interests in a variety of defense companies all over Tarizon that required his constant attention. Being the eldest male actually living on the ranch on a daily basis, Bruda was forced to take on a lot of his father's responsibilities including being the male role model for his younger brothers and sisters.

One of his father's most lucrative businesses interests was in Areon Armaments which manufactured weapons of all sorts as well as hover tanks and military transport vehicles. As a youngster, Cornelius loved visiting the Areon plant and made it clear that was where he wanted to work when he grew up.

Cornelius' father told him that he would be welcome at Areon but only after he had served a twelve-cycle tour of duty in Tributon's National Army. Serving in the TNA was a prerequisite to his employment, his father explained because to be successful in the armaments business it was important to understand its customers as well as develop strong relationships within the military command staff that he could exploit in later cycles. This was sometimes referred to as the MIA or Military Industrial Alliance. It was not a formal organization but existed behind the scenes out of view of the public and the press.

A child's education on Tarizon was complete at age twelve because of its advanced educational techniques. So, when Cornelius was just thirteen he signed up for his first six-cycle enlistment with the TNA. Because of his father's connections, he entered as an officer candidate and soon made staff lieutenant. Having grown up around weapons of all sorts, both traditional and experimental, he knew more about them than most of his instructors. Because of this he quickly became a very well respected officer and leader in the TNA. By the end of his second six-cycle enlistment, Cornelius had made it to the rank of Colonel, a feat that had never before been accomplished by anyone in the TNA by such a young age.

Upon discharge Cornelius immediately reported to work at the Areon Munitions plant twenty kylods south of Vaceen. Being a quick study and the eldest of the Bruda children, he moved up the ranks of the company quickly. At the age of thirty, he found himself at the helm of this lucrative division of Bruda Industries. Of course, with war raging all over Tarizon the armaments business was booming and Areon was doing quite well. But now in his fifth cycle at the helm Cornelius was worried. Recently there had been a lot of disturbing talk of peace. Peace would be a disaster for Areon and Bruda Industries. He couldn't let that happen, particularly since his father would be retiring soon and he would be ascending to the helm of the Bruda Empire.

It was late one afternoon, during a meeting with General Tulh Bakker of the TNA's Central Command, that the topic of Sandee Brahn and the peace movement came up.

Bruda had served under General Bakker in the TNA and had developed a strong relationship with him since Bakker made the final decision on all TNA's procurements. When Bruda left the military and went to Areon, one of his first acts was to put Bakker on the company's goodwill payroll. The fat, bald-headed General enjoyed the enhanced lifestyle this extra MIA income provided and would do anything for Bruda to ensure it continued.

General Bakker told Bruda he'd just returned from Pompelus, the capital of Vada, where he had been meeting with Lyon's Defense Minister. The two countries were allies and there had been reports of troop concentrations near Darkland's northern border.

"Lyon's leaders were nervous and wanted assurances Tributon would honor their mutual defense treaty," General Bakker explained.

"Did you give it to them?"

"Of course, but I'm not so sure I could deliver if an actual invasion took place."

"Really?"

"Yes, we're spread pretty thin already trying to deal with all the refugees from Quori crossing our southern border."

"Yes, I've been following that. It's a dangerous situation indeed," Bruda said.

"Did you hear that some of Sandee Brahn's followers are urging him to run for a seat in Lyon's General Assembly?"

"What? They want him to go into politics?" Bruda said, incredulous.

"Yes. I was surprised too. You'd think politics would

be beneath a holy man."

Bruda frowned. "You'd think, but it would give him a platform for his peace rhetoric."

"Right. And the media will pay more attention to him if he actually has a recognized constituency."

"What does Sandee say about it?" Bruda asked.

"He hasn't committed to the idea yet, but he is getting frustrated with the governments around the world ignoring him."

"What is your assessment of his chances, if elected, of swaying the Assembly to his point of view?"

"I don't know. Everyone is weary of war," General Bakker said. "And, of course, Ambassador Talvihn is Sandee Brahn's biggest supporter. It wouldn't surprise me if it wasn't his idea for Brahn to run for the Assembly."

"What about Chancellor Linzcot. He's not changing his stance, is he?"

"No. Not yet. But he senses the mood of the public and he's a politician. He'll do whatever it takes to get reelected."

"Then we must end this peace movement now before it gets any stronger," Bruda said.

"Right. But, how do we do that?"

"Get rid of Brahn. Without him, there is no peace movement."

"But he's under the protection of Ambassador Talvihn's security team, not to mention a pack of rhutz."

"True," Bruda agreed. "We'll have to kill the rhutz at the same time."

"It won't be easy to kill a pack of rhutz. Aren't they telepathic?"

"Yes, and rhutz also have the gift of telekinesis. But don't worry, I know how to deal with the rhutz. My father and I used to hunt them out on the ranch. Back when we actually had livestock, a rhutz would often come at night and kill one or two of them and then the pack would feed on them until daylight. Of course, my father couldn't tolerate that, so he and I would hunt down the rhutz responsible and kill them."

"Wasn't that rather difficult and a bit dangerous?" General Bakker asked.

"Very dangerous. If the rhutz saw or smelled us coming they could disarm us with their invisible hand. It was a perilous venture indeed."

"And yet you still hunted them?"

"Yes, and we killed plenty of them. The trick was to stay upwind and bring a long range sniper rifle. The rhutz were telekinetic but they couldn't stop something they couldn't see."

"So, your plan is a sniper attack?"

"Precisely. So, we will have to have someone watch them and study their habits so we can pick the right time and place for the attack."

"I've got a man I can put on it," General Bakker said.

"Good. This needs to be done soon. We both have a lot to lose if this peace movement spreads."

"Don't worry. I'll get right on it."

"Okay. Just be sure it gets done. We can't afford another fiasco like the GOT evacuation."

Another threat to the Bruda empire was the Group of Twenty's apparent abandonment of Tarizon. Bruda Industries was a member of the GOT, but it had opposed the evacuation since it was enjoying huge profits from the global wars. The GOT was critical to all of Tarizon's 31 nation-states because it backed the only currency worth anything, the Soni Credit. There was no hard currency anymore, just the pledge of each member of the GOT that they would accept Soni Credits for the purchase of goods and services without question. To administer this currency the GOT had set up the World Bank which was simply a data center that kept track of everyone's credits.

The system worked well because every transaction was instantaneous and completely secure. There were no bad debts because there were no banks to lend individuals money. Businesses were issued mobile devices called registers that allowed them to handle financial transactions and communicate with the World Bank. Every trade association on Tarizon adopted and supported this system to prevent a total collapse of the world's economy. But, with the GOT gone, the world's economy was now again in danger.

General Bakker sighed and shook his head. "Well, that was unfortunate. I sent a response team the moment you called me, but Earth Shuttle 7 had already taken off when it arrived."

"I know. It wasn't entirely your fault. They did a good job of concealing their timetable. Only the people who signed up to go were kept informed and even they didn't know exactly when they would leave. I thought we had more time. I'm really surprised they'd just drop everything and leave the planet."

"What happens to all their property?" General Bakker asked.

"As I understand it they left it in the hands of caretakers whose job it is to preserve it for them until they get back."

"They are pretty naive to think there will be anything left when they return."

Bruda chuckled. "Yes, a very stupid move for them but a great opportunity for us."

"So, how should we procee?"

"The first thing we must do is make sure the World Bank is not compromised. If it collapses anarchy and chaos will ensue and value of Bruda Industries will plummet. We can't let that happen."

"No."

"You should send a security force to Shini, and station them outside the World Bank to deter anyone from trying to interfere with its operation. It has to be business, as usual, no matter what else happens."

"I will take care of it immediately," General Bakker promised. "I have a friend in the Rigimol militia who owes me a favor."

Rigimol was the nation that bordered Tributon to the northwest. Tributon was allied with Tuht and Synclare on the continent of Turvin and, Lortec, Serie and Lyon on the continent of Azollo. The members of the North Sea Alliance, or NSA as it was called, had robust economies making it a formidable force both economically and militarily. The leaders of the North Sea Alliance believed and fought for human rights, justice, and equality for not only humans but all life-forms on Tarizon.

Soni, Rour, Quori, Lower Serie, Vada, Allso, Ock Mezan, and Darkland made up the Dark Sea Alliance or DSA. They were not as prosperous as the North Sea Alliance, but they were a formidable adversary because they were ruthless, cunning and lacked any moral constraints. They believed in slavery, the superiority of a pure human race, and a strong central government controlled by an enlightened few.

Only the continent of Lower Azollo and its nations of Morissee, Ledium, and Queenland had avoided the world wars and managed to remain peaceful. This was probably for two reasons. First, it was situated very distant from the other continents and, secondly, being primarily a farming and ranching region, it produced 80 percent of Tarizon's food supply. Mess with Lower Azollo and the people of Tarizon would starve.

Bruda Industries over the cycles hadn't officially taken sides in the many wars between Tarizon's nation-states. That would have been bad business since they sold huge amounts of armaments to any nation that had the money to buy them. But if the day ever came where they were forced to take sides, everyone knew they'd stand with the DSA.

Bruda stood up. "Alright then. I've got another meeting. Keep me apprised of your progress and any new developments."

General Bakker stood, gathered his things and left. Bruda went back to his office and entered his communications room. One entire wall was a huge, 3D video communicator that displayed the objects being viewed almost as if you were actually there. Two banks of theater seats were situated in the center of the room, and on both sides were workstations equipped with an assortment of computers, monitors, radars, sensors, telescopes and other state-of-the-art equipment which allowed him to monitor significant activity across all of Tarizon.

Bruda had a few loons before his next appointment, so he called up the latest news on Sandee Brahn. The big video screen lit up and the news clip began. An attractive reporter stood stiffly before a sports arena where throngs of people were pouring out of the exits. She tossed her dark brown hair aside and smiled into the camera.

"This is Veile Shante, on assignment for the Lyon News Agency, outside the Dalo Championship Arena where the self-proclaimed prophet, Sandee Brahn, has just spoken. A capacity crowd of some 30,000 citizens listened for nearly a kyloon as Sandee warned of the perilous consequences if the governments of Tarizon continued to wage war cycle after cycle. Let's listen for a moment."

The scene changed to the center of the arena where a podium had been set up. Sandee Brahn, dressed in a plain white shirt and pants and brown sandals, stood before the crowd. Whisper sat at his side and three other rhutz stood behind them eyeing the crowd. He raised his hands toward the sky.

"*Citizens of Dalo, I come before you by the command of the God of Pharidon, of Tarizon, of Earth and the multiverse, the Almighty Pelgrem. He came to me on the night that my parents and family had been senselessly murdered. Murdered by deserters from the Lecton Army who had gone on a rampage across their own homeland. These were madmen who had been driven insane by the greed and selfishness of their chancellor and generals who cared nothing for the welfare of the people.*

"*But I am not here to mourn the loss of my family or to seek vengeance for their murders. I am here to mourn the loss of our planet, our beloved Tarizon, that was given to us by our God, Pelgrem. I am here to tell each and every one of you that we all must turn away from war and violence and instead seek peace and reconciliation.*

"*It is no secret, our planet is dying. Our bombs and weapons, besides killing billions of citizens and destroying the world's infrastructure, have polluted our water, laid barren millions of acres of prime agricultural land, and dumped millions of barrels of toxins into the atmosphere. Our scientists tell us that these pollutants now filter out 30% of the sun's rays, and if we continue down this perilous road our planet will go dark within 50 cycles.*"

The crowd stirred. Someone shouted, "*What can we do?*"

Another joined in, "*Sandee, show us the way!*"

"*Tell us what to do!*" Another screamed.

Sandee raised a fist. "*You must tell your citiheads, your assemblymen and your chancellor that you are tired of war, you have seen enough hostility, anger, and animosity. It is time to forgive, to seek reconciliation, to find justice in compromise and to work together to bring peace.*

"If we begin now, it is not too late to save our planet. All we need to do is withdraw the blade that threatens our world. If we do it now, the atmosphere will slowly recover, we can begin to heal our sick, rebuild our cities, and restore Tarizon to its original majesty. But time is short. Soon, it will be too late."

The screen returned to the reporter who summed up the scene,

"Sandee went on for some time warning his followers that action must be taken immediately to bring about peace or all would be lost. It was his familiar sermon, a message that no one disputes, but one that few governments are listening to as wars continue to rage all across Tarizon. This is Veile Shante reporting from Dalo far away in the beautiful Emerald Ocean."

The screen went blank and a smile crept over Bruda's face. *Yes, Sandee Brahn, I'm sure you are a fraud, but I can't take a chance on anyone important starting to listen to all this peace nonsense. Enjoy all this attention now, because your days are numbered. I promise you.*

17
Truancy

It was late fall in Palo Pinto County, nearly a year after the settlers had arrived on Earth, and the weather was a balmy 82°. As usual, the Timber Creek Ranch was a bustle of activity. Today the children were playing baseball as part of their assimilation training. Two teams in the midst of play on a makeshift field with many watching with great interest and enthusiasm.

Dust could be seen in the distance from a vehicle approaching at a high rate of speed from the main road onto the ranch. Romas, who had been sitting on a rocking chair on the front porch, got up and yelled to someone inside the house. Rama Sloken came out and stood next to Romas.

"Who could that be?" Rama asked.

"Don't know," Romas replied, "but it can't be anything good."

The two men stepped off the porch and headed out to meet the vehicle as it came up to the house. The game stopped, and the children watched warily as the two uniformed men got out of a white and tan patrol car. Letters on the car's door read, "CONSTABLE," and a bar of red and blue lights had been mounted on the vehicle's roof.

"Can I help you?" Romas asked them as they got out of their vehicle.

"I'm Constable Harris," he replied and showed them his badge. "You in charge here?"

"Yes, one of those in charge. I'm Romas Garciah."

The Constable took out a notepad, opened it and

wrote something down. He looked up and said, "Who do these children belong to?"

"Ah. Some belong to me, others to Rama here and the rest to workers here on the ranch."

Harris looked at Rama and asked, "And your full name, sir?"

"Rama Sloken. I'm the ranch foreman."

"Where do these kids go to school?"

"School?" Rama repeated.

"Yes, you know school is compulsory in Texas."

"Ah, yes," Romas replied with a smile. "Well, many of the children have completed their education. For the others, we conduct our own classes."

"Is your school accredited?"

"Accredited? Ah... No, I guess not."

"Then these kids need to go to a public school."

"But—" Rama protested.

"No buts about it. You either show me a high school diploma from an accredited high school or proof they are enrolled in an accredited public or private school, or I'll arrest every parent out here and haul them in to see the Justice of the Peace."

"Yes, sir," Romas said. "Of course. That won't be necessary. We'll get them enrolled right away."

Constable Harris nodded. "Good. I'll be back next week to make sure you've kept your promise."

Romas swallowed hard. "Sure, no problem."

"Good day, then," Constable Harris said, tipping his hat.

The two men went back to their patrol car, got in, and left in a cloud of dust. Romas looked out at the children, staring at them. He smiled and said, "Nothing to worry about. Carry on."

The children unenthusiastically returned to their game, while Romas and Rama returned to the house. They went inside and told their mates what Constable Harris had told them.

"What are we going to do?" Celius asked worriedly. "We can't let them go to school."

"We'll have to," Romas replied. "We can't afford any scrutiny from the Constable or Justice of the Peace."

"But our children will be terrified being thrown into classes with strangers. What if one of them inadvertently reveals our secret?"

"We'll just have to make sure that doesn't happen," Romas replied.

"What about the ones who are part Seafolken," Lill Sloken asked. "In high school, don't students have to take showers together after recreation? The kids would notice their gills and see their hands and feet swell in water."

"That's true," Romas agreed. "How many children with Seafolken blood do we have?"

"Nineteen or twenty," Rama replied. "Nine boys and ten girls, I think."

"Can they be excused for any reason?" Lill asked.

"For a brief period, I'm sure," Romas replied, "but not indefinitely. We'll have to hide the Seafolken children. The rest will have to go to school."

"But what if they are examined by the school nurse or sent to a doctor? There are differences between Earth-humans and our people," Lill objected. "Some of our boys don't have nipples and most don't have an appendix, to name just the two most obvious."

"That's not likely to happen," Rama replied. "If our children get sick, we'll keep them home. We'll just have to monitor their physical condition on a daily basis."

"Perhaps our surgeons can add artificial nipples on the boys," Celius interjected.

"Really?" Lill questioned, irritably. "There's got to be another way."

"Why don't you ask Jamie about it? He had children. They've all grown up, but he'd know if there were any exceptions."

They summoned Jamie Briggs to the house and told him about the Constable's visit.

"We don't want our kids to go to public school, but I guess we don't have any choice in the matter."

"No. School is compulsory," Jamie said.

"What about physical education? We don't want our children dressing in front of their schoolmates."

"I don't know of any way out of that, except physical injury or disability. You'd have to have a doctor's note."

"What about having to see school nurses or doctors? We have our own doctors here. There's no need for our children to be subjected to unnecessary medical treatment."

"Ah. Well, the only exception that I have heard about is for religious reasons."

"Tell us about that," Lill said.

"Well, I know Christian Scientist don't have to see doctors or nurses and they are excused from health class. They don't believe in doctors."

"And they get away with that?" Romas asked.

"Yes. Religious freedom is guaranteed by the Constitution."

"So, how do we join this religion?"

"There is a church in town. I'm sure they'd love you to join them."

Romas thanked Jamie, and he left. Jamie hadn't solved all their problems, but he had given them some good ideas. The next day Celius called the school administrator and got instructions on how to enroll all their children in school. Before that happened, however, they had lots to do. Many of the male children would need minor surgery to add nipples to their torso, and they'd all have to become Christian Scientists to avoid being subjected to medical treatment at school. But the worst task would be breaking the news to the children that they'd have to enroll in school, most of whom thought their education was behind them.

"We have to go to high school?" Ritz complained. "That's ridiculous."

"From our perspective, perhaps, but we are on Earth now, and children here are expected to go to school. If we try to fight it, we'll draw unwanted attention to the ranch and our people."

"I've already finished what amounts to college here on Earth," Bellah noted.

"True, but there will be subjects you know nothing about like history and geography," Celius pointed out.

"I've already met some kids from Mineral Wells High School," Ritz said. "They are all idiots."

"Well, you haven't met all of them. I'm sure many of them are smart and talented," Rama replied. "Plus, it would be good for you to make some friends. Friendships can be useful at times."

"Okay, whatever. Can we go to Dairy Queen for milkshakes? It's where the kids here on Earth hang out. We better do some research so we won't stand out when we start classes next week."

Rama looked at Romas. Romas nodded. "Go ahead, but be back by 10:00 p.m.," Rama said.

Rammel, Eroh, Blinh, Ritz, and Bellah got up and left the room. They went outside and got in the old Ford station wagon that their parents had purchased for them to share as transportation. The old Ford didn't look like much, but the shuttle engineers had reconditioned its engine, so it ran like it was fresh off the assembly line. When they got to the Dairy Queen on the outskirts of Mineral Wells, the parking lot was nearly full as it was Friday and there had been a high school football game earlier in the evening. They went inside and took in the scene. Every booth was teeming with teenagers and there was a line of customers waiting to order their food.

"What should we order?" Bellah asked.

"Everyone seems to like milkshakes and French fries," Rammel noted.

"I've tried French fries," Eroh advised. "I like them."

"Me too," Bellah agreed. "Order that for me with a chocolate milkshake."

"Same for me," Ritz said. "I'll go find us a table."

Ritz walked into the main dining room and looked around. Every booth was taken, and no one seemed close to being finished. Having the gift of telepathy and being spoiled all his life, Ritz always got what he wanted, and had little patience when things didn't go his way. He wasn't going to wait around for a booth to become available, he'd make it happen.

After determining the most desirable booth, he focused on one of its occupants. He knew the girl he'd targeted was a cheerleader because she wore a uniform that matched several other girls he'd seen earlier. Their eyes met, and he reached into her mind without resistance. Her name was Molly Moore and she was a junior at Mineral Wells High School. Her companion that night and best friend was Monique Snyder. Ritz withdrew from Molly's mind and focused on a point on her forearm and then pinched it hard with the fingers of his third hand. The girl screamed and grabbed at her arm.

"What's wrong?" Monique asked worriedly.

"Something bit me," Molly muttered. "It hurt like hell."

Monique gave her a confused look and then replied, "It must have been a horse fly. I've seen them around here before."

Ritz pinched her again. Molly recoiled and rubbed her arm. Her eyes darted around the room suspiciously. "It did it again! Did you see it?"

"No. I didn't see anything."

Grinning, Ritz pinched her a third time, and Molly slid out of the booth and stood a few feet away shaking noticeably. "Let's get out of here. This place needs to be fumigated."

Monique reluctantly stood up. "I didn't see anything. We're supposed to wait for Al and Burt."

"I don't care. I'm leaving," Molly said. "Stay if you want, but I'm not hanging around and be eaten alive by a rabid horsefly."

"Okay. Okay. I'll come with you, but I think you are overreacting."

After the girls had left, Ritz went over and sat in the empty booth. Bellah sat next to him and chuckled. "That was mean."

Ritz shrugged. "It's no big deal. They were just a couple of empty-headed teenagers."

"Why do you say that?" Bellah asked.

"I've watched them and scanned their minds. All they care about are their looks and what football player has a crush on them. They have no appreciation for their parents or the peaceful and prosperous lives they lead here on Earth."

"Right," Bellah replied. "They should live a day amongst the mutants on Tarizon."

"They wouldn't last a day," Ritz replied.

A few moments later, Rammel, Blinh, and Eroh showed up with their orders. After placing everything on the table, Rammel and Blinh slid into the other side of the booth and Eroh got a spare chair and sat on the end.

"So, football seems to be pretty popular here on Earth," Rammel noted.

"Yeah. There was a big game tonight," Eroh said. "The Rams beat Lake Worth 21 to 7."

"What's a Ram?" Bellah asked.

"It's their mascot," Eroh replied. "Every school is assigned a unique animal that is supposed to represent the characteristics of their football team."

"Are you kidding?" Bellah asked. "That is so silly."

"Tell me about it," Ritz agreed. "These kids don't really care much about learning. All they want to do is party and get drunk."

"What? You don't like to party?" Bellah asked jokingly.

"Sure, I do, but I'm not obsessed with it like most of these kids."

"Do you think high school will be difficult?" Eroh asked. "I'm kind of worried about it."

"It will be a breeze," Ritz replied. "We already know way more than any high school student going to Mineral Wells High, I promise. I'm just worried about dying from boredom."

"I won't be bored," Rammel advised. "There's a lot I don't know about Earth's history and geography, and I know nothing about America's government or its economy. I'm excited to get the opportunity to study it."

Ritz shook his head. "Take notes for me, would you?"

Blinh and Bellah laughed.

"Sorry, I don't take notes," Rammel said with a grin. "I've developed this system for learning that allows me to remember everything important. You should try it sometime. It is often referred to as listening and other times as paying attention."

Eroh chuckled and Bellah smiled. Ritz said evenly, "No, listening is no fun. I'd rather plunge deep into people's minds and dig out all their secrets."

"Why would you want to do that?" Blinh asked. "You plan to blackmail them?"

"Maybe," Ritz replied. "We might need them to do

something for us down the road. It's always good to have leverage."

"That's true," Blinh agreed. "I wish I had the gift."

Ritz shrugged. "Are you sure you don't have it? Sometimes people do but never learn how to use it."

"No. My parents had me checked," Blinh replied. "They were very disappointed when they found out I didn't have it. They both have it and Bellah has it, so they thought I would."

"Skutz," Ritz said glancing at Bellah. "Tough luck."

Ritz turned to Rammel and asked, "How about you, Rammel? You got the gift?"

"I'm afraid not," Rammel replied. "It doesn't run in my family."

"Too bad. You'll just have to listen to the teachers while I have all the fun."

Everyone but Rammel laughed.

"What I'm worried about the most is PE class," Eroh said. "I don't know any of the sports here on Earth, and I'm not anxious to take a shower with other guys. They are all so hairy."

"Don't worry about it, just tell them in Hungary it's customary to shave everywhere," Rammel said. "I doubt they will give it a second thought."

Eroh frowned, not convinced that would be the case. Bellah was concerned as well. She knew girls would notice her differences and they'd gossip about it. She dreaded the thought of going to school and wished there was a way she could get out of it.

The following Sunday Celius and Sarna took all of them to the First Church of Christ Scientists where they all enrolled as members of the church. After they sat through their first church service on Earth, they each were given copies of the Science and Health, which contained the church's doctrine. Celius instructed them to keep the book in their lockers to make it appear they read from the book daily.

On Monday the new students all drove to Mineral Wells High School for their first day of class. They parked the Ford station wagon in the school parking lot and reported to the school secretaries' office to get their schedules and a parking pass for their car. They also had a note from their parents advising the school that they were Christian Scientists and did not want their children exposed to doctors, nurses, or any public health instruction, as they believed only God could heal the sick and knowing the truth would ensure their good health. The school secretary let out an audible laugh after reading the note but didn't say anything.

"Ritz and Eroh, you have physical education first period."

Eroh instinctively felt one of his breasts where he now had a nipple like most American men. The others smiled.

"Where do we go?" Eroh asked.

"Go to the gym. Out the door you came in and take a left. Go all the way to the end and you'll see a sign." She handed them each their schedules.

"Okay," Eroh said and left with Ritz right behind him.

The school secretary looked at the remaining schedules and said, "Rammel and Blinh, you two have English class first period. Go out the door you came in, turn right and go until you get to Room 22. Ms. Elaine Meadows will be your instructor."

After taking their schedules Rammel and Blinh left leaving Bellah behind. She watched them leave nervously.

"Bellah Lai. That's a pretty name," the school secretary noted. "What nationality is that?"

"Hungarian," Bellah replied.

"Really, my mother was from Hungary. I thought I knew most of the common Hungarian names, but I guess not."

"It means pretty."

"Oh, well, it definitely suits you."

Bellah smiled. "Thank you."

As they were talking a tall, handsome, muscular boy walked in and smiled at them.

The secretary smiled warmly at the boy and said, "Tom. What do you need?"

"Oh. I have a note from my father about why I missed class on Friday."

"Okay, put it on my desk."

Tom put the note on the desk and was about to leave when the secretary's face lit up.

"Oh, Tom. This is Bellah. This is her first day and she's going to have a history class first period with you. Do you mind showing her the way and introducing her to Mr. Reynolds?"

Tom smiled at Bellah. "No. I would love to."

Bellah smiled back and looked expectantly at Ruth. Ruth handed the schedule to her and said, "All right. Hurry off now. There are only two minutes until the bell."

Tom and Bellah turned and left the office. Tom pointed the way down the hall and they walked briskly toward first period history class.

"So, where are you from?" Tom asked.

"Hungary."

"Really. You don't have an accent."

"I don't?"

"No. You sound pretty American."

"Well, our English instructors worked us very hard and we watched a lot of American movies. I guess that helped."

"Oh. You like movies?"

"Yes. Very much."

"Great. Ah, maybe I could take you out some time, to the movies, I mean?"

Bellah hesitated and then asked. "What do you mean?"

"Ah, the movie theater downtown. I would like to take you there sometime. I'm not sure what's playing right now, but I'll check the afternoon paper and find out. What kind of movies do you like?"

The bell rang as they stood talking outside class.

"Shoot," Tom said. "We better get inside quick. You don't want to get a tardy on your first day."

Bellah smiled and followed Tom inside. Tom directed Bellah to an empty seat across from him. Bellah wondered if she would be allowed to date an American boy. She doubted the leadership would want that to happen. They wanted the Tarizonian presence to be kept secret at all costs. Her parents, of course, had a different view about interacting with Americans as they secretly intended to stay on Earth. In light of that, they argued it would be more dangerous to try to remain segregated. People would be suspicious if they didn't mingle with the rest of the community.

She hoped her parents' view would prevail. She liked Tom and wanted to accept his invitation to go to the movies. *What kind of movies do I like? I like them all, but obviously, that's not a good answer. Maybe the Captain will know how to answer that question?* Her thoughts were interrupted by Mr. Reynolds calling the class to order. She took a deep breath and tried to compose herself. Relax, everything will be fine, she kept telling herself.

Mr. Reynolds handed out textbooks, an outline of the course and a reading list from which everyone had to select three books to read during the semester. After explaining his rules for the class, he told them the story of the Boston

Tea Party. Although it didn't seem terribly relevant to her life on Earth, Bellah did find it somewhat interesting. Before she knew it, the bell was ringing for second period. Everyone got up and scurried outside.

"Come on," Tom said. "You only have five minutes between classes. What's next on your schedule?"

Bellah looked down at her schedule and sighed. "Oh. PE."

"Good. Me too, although you'll be in the girls' class. Come on. Follow me."

They went to the end of the hall and stepped outside. Across the courtyard was the gymnasium. Tom pointed to the girls' entrance. "Go right over there and go inside. Just follow the girls coming in. They'll be going to class."

Bellah nodded and rushed over to the door where another girl was going inside. She held the door for Bellah.

"Oh, thank you," Bellah said as she went through the door.

"You new?" the girl asked. The door closed behind them.

Bellah smiled. "Yes. I'm afraid so."

"Not to worry. I'll get you up to speed," the girl said leading the way. "Come on. The locker room is just down the hall. I'm Liz by the way."

"Oh, a pleasure to meet you. I'm Bellah."

"Do you know Tom? I saw you two walking down the hall together."

"Ah, not really. The school secretary asked him to guide me through my schedule today."

"Oh. Lucky you. I think he likes you."

Bellah laughed. "Why do you say that?"

"I know him pretty well, and I could tell he was enjoying his assignment."

Bellah blushed.

"He's a big man on campus, you know."

"Really. How so?"

"His father's a state senator and very rich. And, of course, he's a tight end on the varsity football team."

"Are you two friends?" Bellah asked.

"Yes. I guess we are still friends. I went with him for a while last year, but we broke up."

"Went with him?"

"Yeah, we were a thing, so to speak. But Tom doesn't stick with one girl too long. He's got wandering eyes. The grass is always greener, you know."

Bellah didn't totally understand but she got the message that Tom wasn't to be trusted in matters of romance. She thought about his offer to take her to the movies.

Liz opened the door and nodded for Bellah to enter. Inside the locker room was a buzz of activity as dozens of girls were changing into their gym outfits.

Liz frowned. "Did you bring gym clothes?"

Bellah's face dropped. "No. Was I supposed to? Nobody mentioned gym clothes, although it makes sense. Skutz. Now, what am I going to do?"

"Yeah, but no worry. You are about my size. You can use my spare set today."

"Oh, my God! Thank you, so much," Bellah said shocked that Liz was being so nice. Ritz had told them that he looked into the minds of many of the high school girls and found them to be shallow and self-centered, but she didn't think Liz fit into that mold.

"Here you go," Liz said as she handed her a plastic bag containing navy blue shorts, a white T-top, socks, and sneakers. "Find an empty locker and I will go get you a padlock."

"A padlock?" Bellah asked.

"Yeah. The girls will go through your locker if it isn't locked. They will take anything that they like, and there's no telling what foreign objects they might put in there if you give them the chance. Trust me. You want a padlock."

"Yes. Get me one. Thanks," Bellah said, taking the bag. She looked around and found an empty locker at the end of the row. She rushed over and began changing. When she was nearly done, Liz showed up with a padlock.

Liz looked up at the clock. "Okay, we have two minutes to be lined up outside."

As the bell rang Liz and Bellah stood in a long line of girls. A moment later, their PE teacher came out holding a clipboard, surveyed the group and then took roll. When she was done, Liz said, "Ah. Ms. Jones. We have a new student, Bellah Lai."

"Oh, okay. Hi, Bellah. Welcome to Mineral Wells High School. We are learning volleyball this semester. Are you familiar with the game?"

"No. Sorry, I'm not."

"That's okay. It's a pretty simple game. Liz will explain things as we go."

There were two volleyball nets, so girls were split into four teams and the games began. Bellah was in good physical shape as everyone on the ship was expected to stay in top physical condition in case anything went wrong, and they were forced to fight or retreat to their ship. With Liz's assistance, it didn't take her long to master the fundamentals of the game. Soon, she was carrying her own weight and her teammates were obviously impressed.

When the games were over, they went inside to shower and change back into their street clothes. Bellah was in a good mood as several of Liz's friends came over to meet her. For the first time, she was starting to feel good about attending high school. She took off her clothes, grabbed a towel and then hit the showers. Bellah turned on the shower and closed her eyes as the hot water ran over her. It felt so good. All the girls around her were talking excitedly about volleyball, school, their boyfriends and football, of course. Then it suddenly turned quiet.

Bellah opened her eyes wondering why it was so quiet. Then she noticed everyone was staring at her. She looked at all the naked girls around her and immediately saw the problem. They all had hair in a place she'd never seen it before. Skutz! Now, what am I going to do? Damn it.

"That's the new craze in New York, isn't it?" Liz said. "Shaving down there where the sun doesn't shine. It hasn't made it to Texas yet."

"Until now, anyway," the girl next to her said. "I like it. We should all do it."

"Yeah," Liz agreed. "That way the teachers will have to let us do it. They can't suspend all of us."

Bellah laughed. "Thank you, but I don't want to get anyone in trouble."

"Nonsense," Liz replied. "Thank you for showing a little courage. I can tell you're going to be an inspiration for all of us."

After class Tom was waiting for Bellah to escort her to the next class. Bellah wanted to go out with Tom now more than ever. He was handsome, athletic and had a rich and powerful father. He'd be just the right guy for her. With his family's power and money, she'd be in the perfect position to fulfill her secret mission on Earth. The mission that really mattered. To groom Earth for its eventual domination by the highly advanced and superior humans from Tarizon. She couldn't wait for their first date. Her father would be so proud.

18
Football

Eroh and Ritz left the school secretary's office and went to the end of the hall as instructed. A sign by the door indicated the gym was in the next building. They exited the classrooms and saw the gymnasium ahead. Students were pouring in and out of it, so they got in line with those going inside. A man with a clipboard was standing by the door so they went up to him.

"We're new students. Where should we go?"

The man looked down at them and gave them a once-over. "Have you ever played football?" the man asked.

Ritz smiled. "No, but I'd like to learn. It seems like that's all the cute girls are talking about."

"You've never played football?" the man asked again.

Ritz grinned again. "No, sorry. We're from Hungary."

"Well, Coach Lawson's rule is that every new student has to be evaluated for his football potential. I'm Assistant Coach Brian Cobb. Come with me, boys."

Ritz looked at Eroh. Eroh shrugged, and they both followed Coach Cobb. He led them into the locker room and pointed to a pile of freshly laundered gym clothes.

"Put on some shorts and a T-shirt. If you look around you can probably find some sneakers too. Meet me outside on the practice field in ten minutes."

They nodded and watched the Coach as he left and went into his office. "Okay. Do you have any idea how to play football?" Eroh asked.

"Not really. I did watch a couple of games before we

landed, so I've got a general idea."

"Well. This should be interesting."

They quickly got dressed and rushed out to the practice field. The gym class was already engaged in a flag football game. Ritz and Eroh went to the sideline and watched. A moment later Coach Cobb joined them.

"Okay, boys. Let's go over to the track. I want to see how fast you are first."

They followed him out to the track that went around the practice field. He told them to stand on a spot that was marked in chalk. "Stand here. I'm going to walk down to the 100-yard marker, and when I blow my whistle I want you to run as fast as you can toward me. Okay?"

"Yes, Sir," Eroh said.

Ritz nodded.

The Coach walked to his position, got out his stopwatch, and then reached for his whistle which was hanging around his neck. Ritz and Eroh bent down in the ready position. The Coach blew his whistle. Eroh lunged forward with Ritz on his heels. Midway, Eroh had increased his lead and finished well ahead of Ritz. The Coach looked down at his stopwatch and stared at it for a long time. Finally, he looked up at them.

"Huh. That was pretty fast. Were you two on the track team back in Hungary?"

"No. We didn't have time for games," Eroh said. This was one of the stock answers they'd been taught before they landed. The people of rural Hungary were poor and had to work hard every day just to survive.

"Why don't you try it again?" Coach Cobb suggested. "I want to make sure my stopwatch was working properly."

Eroh and Ritz looked at each other, and then trotted back to the starting point. Coach Cobb again set his stopwatch, took hold of his whistle and blew it. Eroh and Ritz took off again. This time Ritz got the jump on Eroh but had lost the lead at the midpoint and again finished two steps behind Eroh. The Coach again stared at his watch for a long time. Finally, he shook his head and smiled. "Well, that's the best time I've seen all year. Let's see how far you can throw a football."

Eroh and Ritz smiled at each other, and then followed the Coach to a large laundry basket full of footballs. He picked out two of them and gave one to each. He told two of the players waiting on the sideline to go downfield fifty yards to field the throws. They took off obediently, and when they were downfield he looked at Eroh.

"Let's see what kind of an arm you have," Coach Cobb said. "Throw the ball as far as you can."

Eroh looked at his ball curiously, not sure how to throw it. Coach Cobb let out a frustrated sigh, and then took the ball and showed them the mechanics of throwing a football. Figuring they needed a little practice time, he called back the two players waiting downfield and told them to play catch with Eroh and Ritz and give them pointers on how to throw a football. The two players rolled their eyes at the assignment but knew better than to question their coach.

It didn't take Eroh and Ritz too long to get the hang of it and they were ready for the test when Coach Cobb came back ten minutes later.

"Okay, Eroh. You go first."

Eroh looked hard at the boy standing fifty yards away, took a few steps and threw the ball right into his outstretched arms. The Coach smiled.

"Not bad for your first toss. Okay, let's see what you can do, Ritz."

Ritz didn't hesitate. He took his ball and launched it toward his receiver. The ball sailed over his head and landed ten yards beyond. The Coach's mouth dropped. Then he looked over at Ritz and shook his head.

"Wow! I need to introduce you two to Coach Lawson. He's going to be thrilled to meet you."

†††††

Rammel and Blinh entered their classroom, stepped to one side and surveyed the situation. Students were coming in steadily, taking their seats, chatting with neighbors and slowly getting ready for class. At the front of the room, a trim, pleasant-looking, redheaded-woman sat at a desk going through her notes. When she looked up, Rammel smiled. She motioned for them to come to her. They walked over to her.

"Hi. Are you my new students?" Ms. Meadows asked.

"Yes, I believe so," Rammel said. "I'm Rammel Garciah and this is Blinh Lai."

"Nice to meet both of you. I think there are two empty seats in the back. After the bell rings you should be able to find them. After class, we can talk about how you're going to catch up since you are enrolling midway into the semester."

Rammel and Blinh nodded and moved out of the way so Ms. Meadows could start class. When the bell finally rang, they found their seats and waited for class to begin.

The class was discussing Herzog by Saul Bellow, a novel they had just finished reading. Rammel and Blinh listened intently but the discussion meant nothing to them. When class was over, they went back to Ms. Meadows as instructed.

She looked at them thoughtfully and said, "The semester is half finished, and I'm sure you don't want to repeat it, right?"

They both nodded.

"So, I'm going to need to give you some extra credit work to do, so I'll have something to grade and replace for the five weeks you have missed. It will require about an hour a day after school."

"Thank you," Rammel said. "What do we need to do?"

"You can join the debate team or participate in Moot Court."

Blinh frowned. "Debate? You mean, argue about different topics?"

"Yes. Something like that. Each year there is a topic assigned, and the teams debate the topic pro and con."

"Oh. Okay," Blinh said. "What about Moot Court?"

"That's where you become a prosecutor or an advocate for a person charged with a crime? It's for those interested in the legal profession or politics."

"I'll do the Moot Court," Rammel said. "My father was a judge back home. It's what I think I want to do as well."

"Perfect," Ms. Meadows said making a note. She looked up at Blinh and smiled. "And what about you, Blinh?"

Blinh thought a moment and then replied, "Debate sounds good. My mother is always complaining about how much I like to argue."

Ms. Meadows laughed. "Good, then. I'll inform the sponsors and let them know to expect you, starting tomorrow after class."

She gave them instructions on where to go and then walked with them to the cafeteria where lunch was just beginning. She excused herself and went into the teacher's dining room. They looked around for their friends.

"There they are," Blinh said pointing to a table in the distance where Bellah, Ritz, and Eroh were already eating. After getting in line, and getting their food, they joined them.

"Hey, there you are," Bellah said. "We wondered what happened to you two."

"We had to meet with our teacher after class," Blinh

complained. "She's making me join the debate team and Rammel has to do Moot Court."

"Seriously? Why?"

"If we don't, we won't get credit for English class since we haven't been here all semester."

Bellah shook her head. "That stinks."

"Yeah, it does. It's another hour wasted each day, and we have tournaments on the weekends."

"Well, it's even worse for Eroh and me," Ritz replied. "We've been recruited for the football team if you can believe that."

"What?" Bellah asked excitedly. "How did that happen?"

"Apparently Eroh is very fast, and I've got a strong arm," Ritz replied, "at least compared to the other students. We figure it's due to the fact that Tarizon is much larger than Earth and has 1.2 Earth gravity. Our muscles have been more fully developed."

"That's right," Rammel agreed. "I hadn't thought of that."

"So, we have to stay after class every day for football practice and there are games every Friday night."

"Wow! That means all those cute, empty-headed cheerleaders will be following you around like little puppy dogs," Bellah teased. "You must be thrilled."

"Not really," Ritz replied. "We've got more important things to be doing. It's going to be a major distraction."

"Talking about distractions. I've already got a date," Bellah bragged. "His name is Tom and he's tall, rich and handsome, not to mention he's the son of a state senator. He wants to take me to see a movie."

"Boy, you work fast," Eroh said. "You haven't been here half a day yet."

"It sounds like we're all doing okay," Bellah replied. "Now, if you don't mind. I'm starving."

Bellah began eating earnestly and the others soon turned their attention to the less-than-spectacular-cuisine before them. When they were done, they split up and headed off to their next class wondering if the last half of the day would be as interesting as the first had been.

19
Salina

Even as the crowds following Sandee grew larger and larger, and his fame grew throughout the world, it didn't seem to him that Tarizon was any closer to peace than it had been the day Pelgrem had come to him. After a sermon at the Black Hill Cathedral at the fork of the Mulga River in Darkland, Sandee complained of this to Salina.

"That was your best sermon yet," Salina said. "You had the worshipers spellbound."

"You think so? I felt good. It seemed like I was really connecting with them, but—"

"But what?"

"But, it's nothing but talk. Nobody in the government seems to care much about what the wars are doing to the planet, and they sure don't care about how it's affecting the people."

"Well, that's true," Salina admitted. "There are so many war profiteers who have their tentacles in every branch of government. The politicians are getting fat off of them for sure. But eventually, the people will rise up and force the governments to sue for peace."

Sandee shook his head. "I don't think we have time to wait for that to happen. We need to speed up the peace process somehow."

Salina nodded. "You're right. I'll talk to my father and see if he has any ideas."

While Salina and her father were trying to come up

with new strategies for their peace movement, Sandee was growing more and more pessimistic about his crusade for peace and fell into a deep depression. He began to doubt that he could ever stop the senseless warfare and started to wonder again if Pelgrem really existed or had He been but a figment of Sandee's imagination. The only thing that kept Sandee from succumbing to these doubts was Whisper's constant assurances that his peace mission was indeed ordered by the God Pelgrem. No matter how hard he tried, Sandee could not explain why a rhutz would leave his pack to wander the globe with a human unless ordered to do so by a god.

Later that fall, Sandee was returning by steamship from Dalo in the Emerald Ocean. It was a cold and foggy day, and Sandee was exhausted from his trip. Salina had left him a week earlier to confer with her father so he had been lonely as well. Sandee and his entourage docked on the east coast of Lyon at Ya Lat, the capital city, and were met by Salina, Ambassador Talvihn, and a security force hired to deal with the huge crowds he was now drawing.

Sandee had missed Salina terribly and was happy to see her again. Even though Sandee was always surrounded by people who loved and adored him, he didn't know many of them that well and often felt alone and a bit uneasy. Only when Salina was at his side did he feel happy, confident and optimistic about the eventual success of his mission. When he saw her standing on the dock he rushed over and embraced her.

"Salina, it is so good to see you. I've missed you," he said as he held her tightly. After a moment he reluctantly let her go and looked into her eyes.

She smiled up at him. "It is good to see you again, too. How did you do in Dalo?"

"Not so good, I'm afraid," he said bitterly.

She frowned. "Weren't the people receptive to your

message?"

"Oh, yes, I have won over the people, there is no doubt, but the government has no interest in doing what's right for them and Tarizon."

Salina sighed. "Yes, it is frustrating to witness such stubbornness and stupidity. The Ambassador and I have been discussing other options."

"Good. I'm anxious to hear them."

Salina took Sandee's arm and they began walking away from the docks and toward the street where several vehicles were waiting for them. Whisper and his pack followed them. A security guard dressed in a black suit opened the rear door for them.

As they drove inland, the fog gave way to the familiar burnt yellow haze prevalent outside the domed cities. The haze not only smelled bad but also caused a plethora of respiratory ailments and diseases that plagued the unprotected population.

On a good day, people struggled to breathe on their own, on a bad day they were forced to wear a cumbersome filtering apparatus called a breather in order to survive outdoors. Some homes and personal transporters had filtering systems, but most did not as they were in short supply and expensive.

They traveled to a local inn called the Coral Reef Inn where Sandee and his entourage were to stay the night. It was a small tavern off the main road that Salina hoped would give them privacy. If anyone recognized Sandee the place would immediately be mobbed with followers and the press. Having just returned from a long journey he needed rest and she was going to be sure he got it.

At dinner that night when Sandee complained again of the lack of progress in bringing peace to Tarizon, Salina suggested that Sandee run for the General Assembly. He was skeptical of the idea at first. He had always imagined that peace would be fueled by an outpouring of support from the people, not by a hall full of politicians.

"Each cycle 30 seats in the General Assembly are up for re-election to a six cycle term," Salina explained. "You'd have no trouble winning a seat. Then you could address your concerns to the members of the General Assembly and get them behind your peace movement."

"Yes, but Lyon is but one of 31 governments."

"You forget about Lyon's allies, Tributon, Rigimol, and Tuht. They would most likely follow you if you convinced Lyon to push for peace. And these nations are the richest of all of Tarizon."

"I wish I could talk to Pelgrem about it. It sounds like a good idea, but He never said I should become a politician. Aren't politicians the problem? They are selfish and think only of how to stay in power."

"That is true for many, but there are good, honest citizens in the General Assembly too. I know of many and I could introduce you to some of them."

"Well, I would certainly like to meet an honest politician."

Salina laughed. "Good. Actually, you may have hit on the answer we've been looking for. We have to convince the members of the General Assembly that their reelections will be jeopardized if they don't back your peace efforts."

"Do you think my followers would do that? I mean, if I told them not to vote for anyone who supported the war, would they follow my advice?" Sandee asked.

"Yes, I think they would," Salina said. "And I think that it should be part of your sermons in the future. Point out the Assemblymen who are supporting the war and tell your followers not to vote for them."

Sandee nodded. "Yes. That sounds like sound advice. Can you get me a list of the supporters of the war in the General Assembly?"

Salina smiled. "Sure, I will send you a list of their names. I know them well."

"When can I meet with some of these honest politicians? I should like to hear their advice."

"Tomorrow. I will set something up for after lunch."

The waiter showed up with two bottles of Tekari to go with their dessert. It was a strong drink and left them feeling slightly buzzed and light headed. Sandee suddenly felt a strong urge to take Salina to his room. Salina had refused to have a romantic relationship with Sandee thus far, but it was getting harder and harder for her to resist him as he got older. They loved each other and now that Sandee was seventeen there was no legal or ethical reason for them not to be lovers.

"Shall we take this discussion to my room?" Sandee suggested with a broad smile.

Salina eyed him warily. The Ambassador had warned her not to go to bed with him due to their age difference and the fact that it might be a distraction from his mission of peace. He argued such a relationship could taint Sandee's image of purity as well, but that made no sense to her. Pelgrem hadn't asked Sandee to give a pledge of sexual abstinence. *So what difference would it make if they were lovers? Besides, he needs me now. He's depressed and lonely. Perhaps I can help renew his spirit and give him the strength to see his mission through.* Finally, she heard herself say, "Sure, I'd like that."

20
A Change of Strategy

The next day Salina took Sandee to the offices of Assemblyman Renh Renno where he met with five of the Ass\emblymen she had told him about. Renno's offices were adjacent to the Capitol Building in downtown Ya Lat. It wasn't the first time Sandee had been to Ya Lat. He'd given sermons in several of the churches there but he'd never been to the Capitol Building. As they drove by its three cylindrical towers that surrounded the general assembly hall, he wondered if he were making a mistake getting into politics. It was a complicated game that he knew nothing about.

Whisper sensed his concern and reached out. *"Don't worry, my friend. You cannot make a mistake. Pelgrem is guiding you on this journey."*

"I know," Sandee thought. *"But it's just so frustrating. I didn't think it would be so hard. We have been working day and night for five cycles and have accomplished nothing."*

"We have accomplished a lot. We have been planting seeds and now they are beginning to grow."

"So, you think a change in strategy is a good idea?" Sandee asked.

"You should trust your friend. She is a bright light and her heart is true. She would never do anything to hurt you."

"You can tell that about her?"

"I have searched her mind and found nothing but love for you and a yearning for peace."

Tears welled in Sandee's eyes at Whisper's words. He wiped them away with the back of his hand. *"How is it that you can read her mind but I cannot?"*

"She guards her mind when she looks at you because she cares about you and doesn't want you to know what she is thinking. But it doesn't occur to her that she should guard her mind around me as well."

"Ah. Well, good. Now I will expect daily reports."

"No. I will not be a spy for you. I am here by the will of Pelgrem to protect you and guide you on your quest for peace."

"Okay. Okay. I wasn't being serious. So, why did you tell me she loved me?"

"I'm not telling you anything you didn't already know in your heart. Now quit worrying about Salina and get on with the tasks ahead."

When they arrived at Renno's office he led them to the conference room where his fellow Assemblymen were waiting. Salina introduced everyone and an aide served sankee, a popular drink at business meetings. Whisper circled the conference room a few times and then settled down where he had a clear sight of the door. Renno and the other Assemblymen eyed him warily.

"Okay. Thank you all for agreeing to meet," Salina said. "As I told you over the communicator, Sandee is dissatisfied with his efforts to bring about peace to Tarizon. His following is growing every day and public support of his peace mission is strong, but the wars still rage on and nothing has really changed."

"That's because war is profitable," Assemblyman Renno noted. "The government spends billions of credits on guns, munitions, vehicles, food, uniforms, and supplies. To keep the credits flowing, the defense industry makes huge campaign contributions to those Assemblymen who support the war effort."

"Right. So, what if Sandee were to tell his followers not to vote for those Assemblymen who supported the war?" Salina asked. "Do you think they might change their stance?"

Renno shook his head. "Not necessarily. They are used to getting the lobbying money from the defense industry and rely on it. Unless they could get their campaign financing from another source, I doubt they would respond to your threat to turn their constituents against them. Besides, you would have to put up a slate of candidates to oppose those Assemblymen who didn't respond and that would be a tremendous undertaking."

Sandee frowned. "So, what can I do to bring about peace? We must stop the war soon or it will be too late."

"Why don't you run for the Assembly or maybe even for Chancellor? If you were elected you would be in a position to really advance your peace movement."

"Sandee and I have talked about his running for the Assembly," Salina said. " I think it's a good idea. It would be much harder to get elected Chancellor, and he can't afford to lose. But I'm sure he could easily get elected to the Assembly where he could continue to work on the outside as he does now but also push for peace in the General Assembly."

"But how could I get elected to the Assembly? I don't live in Lyon and I am not a citizen. I travel all over the world and live in a tent or under the invisible stars most of the time."

"That's not a serious problem," Renno replied. "You'd simply have to rent a compartment here, declare Lyon to be your place of residence and apply for citizenship."

"That's it?"

"Well, you would have to cut back on your traveling once you were elected. You'd have to attend the legislative sessions which are held daily all spring and into the summer."

"I'd also have to campaign which takes more time. Plus, I'd need credits and an organization, right?"

"Yes," Salina agreed. "But you already have an organization and many followers who would be anxious to contribute to your campaign. I think this idea is quite feasible."

"What about Whisper? Do they allow wild animals in the Assembly Hall?"

They all laughed. Whisper raised his head realizing they were talking about him.

Renno said. "No, but you can say he's an aide and get credentials issued. I doubt there are any rules that prohibit you from hiring a rhutz."

They all laughed again. The meeting continued for several kyloons. When all his questions had been answered, he nodded and said, "Okay. I'm halfway convinced. Let me think about it for a while and discuss it with Whisper. It is a major change in strategy. I will let you know of my decision soon. Thank you for your help."

They left Renno's office and drove back to the Coral Reef Inn. It was early afternoon and they hadn't eaten lunch, so Salina suggested they freshen up and then meet in the dining hall. Sandee didn't really need to do any freshening up, so he and Whisper decided to get a little exercise by walking to the waterfront and back. The security detail thinking Sandee was safely in his room took a break.

Sandee and Whisper stepped out of the Inn and started walking down the sidewalk toward the waterfront. A strong ocean breeze ruffled Sandee's long golden brown hair. A shot rang out. Sandee felt a sharp pain in his shoulder. He put one hand over the wound and watched in disbelief as blood soaked through his bright-white shirt. Cringing in pain, he fell to one knee. Whisper moved quickly in front of Sandee and looked in the direction of the shot. A second shot rang out and Whisper's left front leg shot out from under him. He stumbled and fell onto his side.

"Oh no!" Sandee moaned as he crawled over to him. "What have they done to you?"

Members of the security team started rushing out of the Inn and fanning out around Sandee and Whisper. A tik later Salina rushed out with fear and concern in her eyes. When she saw Sandee she went to his side.

"Oh, my God! Sandee! How badly are you hurt?" she asked taking him in her arms.

Sandee cringed as she put pressure on his oozing wound. He tried to speak but nothing came out of his mouth. Then he went limp in her arms. Tears flowed from Salina's eyes and Whisper whimpered as he licked his wound.

"I have failed Pelgrem," Whisper thought. *"It was my job to protect Sandee until he completed his mission."*

Suddenly three rhutz sprang out of the bushes and took up guard duty around Sandee, Salina, and Whisper. One of them took over the licking of Whisper's leg. *"We are here, brother. We will protect you and Sandee from those who want him dead. It is not just your duty but the duty of all rhutz on Tarizon."*

A public enforcer and a member of the security detail ran over to them. The rhutz growled at them so they stopped a few strides away. "We've called a meditaxi," the PE said. "It should be here in five loons."

Salina nodded.

"My men have set up a perimeter. The assassin will not get away."

There was gunfire in the distance. Salina looked over in the direction of the shooting. "What's happening?" she asked nervously.

The PE listened to a report coming over on his communicator. A smile came over his face. "They've caught the assassin. He's down."

"Thank God," Salina said, then turned her attention back to her beloved Sandee. "Please don't die! You can't die, my love. You have so much work to do. Tarizon needs you, and I can't live without you."

The PE looked over at Sandee worriedly. "Is that really Sandee Brahn?"

"Yes, it is," Salina moaned. "They've shot Sandee Brahn! Someone has shot our Savior!"

There was a whirring sound above as a meditaxi arrived and settled down fifty strides away. A crew sprang out of the craft and rushed over to Sandee and started administering first aid. They took his vitals and put a dressing over the wound to stop the bleeding. They tried to talk to him but he was unresponsive.

Soon they had him stable and on a stretcher to be airlifted to the local casualty center. When two of the rhutz followed Salina into the meditaxi a crew member started to object until the rhutz let out a menacing growl. He raised his hands and meekly let them pass. A few tiks later the meditaxi took off and disappeared over the rooftops.

Several of the security detail turned their attention to Whisper. The rhutz protecting him growled at them when they approached to carry him to a Grinden for transport to the local animal hospital. Fortunately, Whisper understood what they were trying to do, and started hobbling toward them. They opened the door, Whisper and two of his pack got in, and they drove off in a rush.

As the PE was securing the crime scene, a reporter and cameraman rushed over. "What happened here?" the reporter asked. "Is it true Sandee Brahn is dead?"

The officer shook his head. "No, he was alive when they took him away."

"How serious were his injuries?"

"I am not a doctor, sorry."

"If he dies, do you think his peace movement will die with him?"

"I don't know, but I hope not," the PE replied. "I think he was on the right path. We need peace, not war, and we need it now!"

21
The Intergalactic Fleet

Cornelius Bruda excused himself from a meeting and rushed to his office. General Bakker had told him when the assassination attempt was to take place and he was anxious to see how it would play out. He sat down and turned on the VC to his favorite news station. A reporter was in the middle of giving a report on Vaceen's dwindling water supply and what the Vaceen City Council was going to do about it when the reporter was cut off by a news bulletin.

"Hello. I'm Tone Wajh. Sorry to break in on our programming, but we've got developing news in Lyon. The screen flipped to the front of the Municipal Casualty Center near the Capitol Building.

"Veile Shante is in Ya Lat with the story. Veile."

"Yes Tone, there has been an assassination attempt on the life of the self-proclaimed prophet Sandee Brahn. The attack took place in front of the Coral Reef Inn in East Ya Lat where Sandee was staying while he was in the Capitol. There is no word on the extent of Sandee Brahn's injuries other than a statement from a casualty department spokesperson indicating that Brahn was in surgery and his condition was critical.

"Sandee's constant companion, Whisper the rhutz, who was also shot, may have saved his life, according to witnesses on the scene. Apparently, after the first bullet hit Sandee, Whisper got in front of him and shielded him from

the second bullet. Whisper is undergoing treatment at this time. His injuries are not reported to be life-threatening.

Shante turned slightly and the camera swept over a growing crowd of obviously anxious citizens. They were chanting. Peace, not war! . . . Peace, not war! . . . Peace, not war! . . . Peace, not war!

"As you can see a large crowd has gathered in front of the Municipal Casualty Center here in Ya Lat. They are stunned, saddened and angry over what has happened here today. As you can hear some are chanting 'Peace, not war!' This passion is something new for Sandee's followers. Prior to today, they were very quiet and peaceful, but this assassination attempt has angered them.

"Just after the assassination attempt today, a local Public Enforcer was asked by a reporter on the scene if he thought Sandee's peace movement would survive Sandee's death. The PE's response was he hoped so because Tarizon needed peace, not war. As you can see the new slogan has caught on. And it is fitting because this is what Sandee Brahn stood for all along. Rumors are that he was in Ya Lat today to consider a new strategy for bringing peace to Tarizon. Apparently, he will be seeking a seat in the Lyon General Assembly."

Tone Wajh interrupted, "Shante, what about the shooter? Do we know who that was yet?"

"Yes, actually there were two of them. After the shooting, the security team that had been traveling with Sandee chased after the assassins, and with a local PE's assistance, were able to corner them in an alley about a kyloon from the inn. A gun battle ensued and both assassins were killed. A spokesman for the Public Enforcer's office has informed me that neither of the men had identification nor were they in the PE's fingerprint or facial recognition databases."

Bruda shook his head in disgust and turned off the VC. He picked up his global communicator and punched in the code for General Bakker.

"Bakker," he said evenly.

"What happened? Sandee is still alive."

General Bakker recognized Bruda's voice and stiffened. He'd been expecting the call. "Ah. . . . right. So, I have heard," the General replied calmly. "Don't worry, he's not going to survive."

"How do you know?"

"He was hit with a bullet-bomb. It exploded six inches from his heart."

"Then why is he still alive?" Bruda asked irritably.

"I don't know. He should have died at the scene. But it doesn't matter. I have a contingency plan, one of my men infiltrated his security team. He'll make sure Sandee doesn't make it through the night."

Bruda softened his tone a bit and said, "Alright. Just make sure he doesn't."

"Don't worry. I have it under control."

"What about the assassins? They can't be traced back to you, can they?"

"No. Not a chance. They were deep cover operatives, totally off the grid."

"Okay, the next time I turn on the VC I better hear that Sandee Brahn is dead and his peace movement is history!"

"Not a problem," General Bakker assured him nervously.

Bruda disconnected, and then dialed the number of his friend Joh Crille at the Ya Lat Public Inquisitors' Office. They had met at a military conference cycles earlier where Bruda recruited him to provide local intelligence. He received a credit bonus each month for his trouble. After a few beeps, a gruff voice came on the line. "Crille."

"Bruda here."

"Yes, sir. What can I do for you?"

"I just saw on the VC that Sandee Brahn was shot."

"Yes. That's right. It's a madhouse around here."

"So, what's his condition? The reporter on the VC was pretty vague."

"Yeah. Well, it was a pretty gruesome sight. His shoulder was nearly blown off."

"Is he going to make it?"

"From what I hear the doctors are amazed he's still alive, but they say right now he's stable."

"Let me know if there is any change, okay?"

"Sure, no problem."

Bruda disconnected and took a deep breath. He couldn't believe Sandee Brahn was still alive. He scrolled through his directory and selected the number of his close friend Petri Volk at Menges Mining. Menges Mining was a major supplier to Bruda Industries and another member of the GOT. Petri and Bruda were both on the governing board of the World Bank and worked together on a lot of projects of mutual interest.

"Petri. This is Cornelius."

"Hi. How are you, my friend?"

"Not so well, actually. Did you see the news?"

"Yes. Why is Sandee Brahn still alive?"

"I asked General Bakker the same thing."

"Maybe Pelgrem is watching over him after all," Petri suggested.

"Nonsense. We both know Pelgrem is a myth."

"True, but not everybody believes that. Have you seen the crowds gathering at the casualty center?"

"I have, but don't worry. Sandee will be dead soon, one way or another."

"Glad to hear it. So, what did you call about?"

"Have you heard anything about the GOT

evacuation?"

"Yes, my brother-in-law called from Earth Shuttle 7 before they went FTL. He said everything was fine. The missiles didn't do any serious damage."

"So, is he on board with our plan? Can we trust him?"

"Absolutely," Petri said. "He's always wanted to visit Earth and he is really excited about spying for us and setting up an intelligence network. Sarna is smart and an excellent organizer too, so between them, they will get the job done."

Whereas Markis knew production, Sarna Volk knew numbers and how to manage people. So this tall, sassy redhead ran the accounting and personnel side of the mining operation and Markis made sure all production quotas were exceeded. Together as a team they had been a dynamic force and ran a highly lucrative operation.

"Good," Bruda said. "This network will be quite invaluable when the idiot-generals and greedy politicians finally destroy Tarizon and force us to leave."

"How long do you think it will be before that happens?" Petri asked.

"Not long, unless Sandee Brahn manages to live through the night."

"It's too bad we can't leave right now."

"I know, but we're not ready."

"Right. We have to build the Intergalactic Fleet."

"That's right. If we leave Tarizon, Earth is the only habitable planet we could go to, and we won't be welcome there. So, we better show up with an overwhelming military force."

Petri nodded. "And spaceships are expensive."

"Exactly."

"So, any word yet on when production will begin?"

"The assembly plant on Clarion should be up and

running by the end of the cycle."

The assembly plant was being built on the back side of Clarion so that it could not be observed by telescope. Near zero gravity was ideal for manufacturing spacecraft, allowing for much greater precision and accuracy in production. But it was costly supplying the facility and maintaining an artificial environment for the engineers and workers stationed there. Bruda Industries led this undertaking but had many partners. Each diverted most of their profits to the venture. There were also many admirals, generals, and other high ranking military officers from several different armies around the globe involved in the project. They had set aside their animosities and national allegiances for the promise of future wealth and power. These officers provided additional guidance and expertise and, in the end, were promised command of the Intergalactic Fleet on its mission to Earth.

"I'd like to see the facility," Petri said, "since I am investing so much in it."

"Of course, I will call General Bakker to arrange a visit soon."

Bruda disconnected and leaned back in his chair. The Intergalactic Fleet was a monumental undertaking and would require a huge capital investment, yet it was critical that the project be kept completely secret. He couldn't afford to alarm the politicians and generals who, unbeknownst to them, would be financing the project.

22
Media Conference

Salina, along with several aides and a security officer named Salh Pallos, waited impatiently while Sandee was in surgery. The doctors had not been particularly communicative about Sandee's condition. They had simply indicated that he was in surgery, that there had been a catastrophic injury to his left shoulder and shrapnel had penetrated his heart and lungs. While they were sitting in the waiting room anxiously, a public enforcer and a public interrogator came by to take their statements. They introduced themselves as PI Ren Baldor and PE Sine Cranz. Baldor asked Salina about the events leading up to the attack.

"We had just returned from a morning meeting in the Capitol Building complex," Salina recalled. "We pulled up in front of the Coral Reef Inn and agreed to take a break and then meet for lunch in a kyloon. I went to my room and I assumed Sandee and Whisper would go to their room, but they apparently decided to take a walk."

"Why wasn't there any security with Sandee and Whisper when they took their walk?" Baldor asked.

Everyone looked over at Salh. He shrugged. "Ah. Well, as Salina said. We thought he was safe in his room. I told my men to take their lunch break and meet back in half a kyloon. He didn't tell anyone that he was planning to take a walk."

"But isn't it your policy to have eyes on your client at

all times?" Baldor asked.

"No. We are not allowed in his room."

"But you should have had someone posted at his door, right? Then you would have known if he had left and could have followed him."

"Maybe," Salh agreed, "but he had Whisper and three other rhutz. We didn't think anyone had a chance at getting to him."

"Have there been any threats on his life recently?" Baldor asked.

Salina shook her head. "No, nothing significant. There are always a few hecklers in the crowd, but I don't think Sandee has ever felt threatened."

"Who opposes your peace movement?" Baldor asked.

"The military, most of the central governments on Tarizon, and of course those who sell to the military and benefit economically from the war," Salina replied.

"That's a pretty long list. Are there any particular individuals in those groups who have threatened or verbally attacked Sandee in any way?"

"No. Unfortunately, we haven't been much of a threat, so far. Sandee gets good crowds but the governments of the world pretty much ignore him."

"Really? That's surprising. He gets good media coverage here in Lyon. And, of course, after this assassination attempt, his media exposure is going to skyrocket."

"That's true," Salina agreed, "unless he dies or is too crippled to continue his peace mission."

Baldor nodded. "Well, I'll pray for his full recovery."

"Thank you," Salina said.

The two officers left and Salh excused himself to go get Sankee for everyone. While he was gone, the surgeon who had been working on Sandee came out to speak to her.

"He's out of surgery and in recovery now," the

surgeon said. "I had to rebuild his shoulder and remove shrapnel from his heart and lungs. His heart stopped two times during the surgery but somehow we got him back each time."

"Oh, no. Is he conscious?"

"No. He hasn't woken up yet, and I must warn you there were a few tiks where his brain wasn't getting oxygen. There could be brain damage."

Salina gasped. "Oh, no."

"But let's assume for now that he will fully recover. There's no reason to be pessimistic at this point."

"Thank you, doctor," Salina said dejectedly.

The doctor left, and Salina sunk into a chair and began to weep. One of the rhutz walked over and looked into her eyes. She felt a warm feeling in her mind. "Don't worry, Salina. Pelgrem will look after Sandee. He won't let him die."

Startled, Salina stiffened. She'd never experienced mental telepathy before. But after a moment, she smiled. "Thank you. That's good to hear," she said out loud.

An alarm began sounding and medical personnel began rushing toward the surgical suites. Salina stood up nervously. She looked around for Salh, but he hadn't returned with their Sankee. Fearing that the alarm was somehow connected to Sandee, she began running down the corridor toward the recovery room. The three rhutz followed her. There was a crowd of doctors and nurses around the doorway. Suddenly they rolled Sandee out of the room and past Salina.

"What's happening?" she asked. "Where are you taking him?"

"Back to surgery," a nurse said. "He's been poisoned and we have to pump out his stomach."

"Poisoned! . . . What?"

Salina just stood there stunned for a moment. Then

she thought of Salh. Right after he left Sandee was poisoned. Could it be a coincidence? The rhutz read her mind. They looked at each other.

"Salh has betrayed Sandee," Snowflake thought.

"One of us should prevent his escape," Autumn replied.

"I'll go," Midnight said and started running back down the hall.

"I'll stay with Salina," Snowflake thought.

"Then I'll guard Sandee," Autumn said and rushed after the medical staff.

†††††

Midnight went back to where Salh had been sitting in the waiting room. He sniffed his chair until he found Salh's scent, and then sped off down the hall. The scent led him to the recovery room where Sandee had been poisoned. The smell of the poison permeated the room. Midnight held back an urge to vomit. He walked slowly out of the room, and then picked up Salh's scent again. It led him toward a stairwell. He opened the door with his third hand and rushed down the stairs to where a door led to the first-floor lobby, then made the door open and stepped out.

The scent was much weaker now, immersed with many other scents of humans, medicine, machines and others he couldn't identify. He took a deep breath and caught Salh's scent again. It was going down the hall to the Emergency Room. Following the scent, he ran out of the Emergency Room into a parking lot. The scent was a bit stronger so he quickened his pace. Then he saw Salh getting into his patrol vehicle.

As Midnight approached, the vehicle's engine came to life and it lurched backward out of the parking space. Midnight reached out with his third hand and tugged on a wire under the car's hood. He knew if a few wires were loosened the vehicle would be temporarily disabled. The first wire did nothing when it came loose but cause the car to sputter a bit, but pulling the second wire caused a deep sucking sound and the engine came to a halt.

Salh tried to restart the engine but it was dead, so he opened the door and got out. Midnight rushed toward him. Salh raised his laser gun, but before he could pull the trigger the gun shot out of his hand and landed twenty feet away. Salh ran after it, but before he reached it Midnight was on him. They rolled over and Salh tried to grab Midnight's neck, but couldn't get a good grip. For an instant, they made eye contact, and Midnight dug into Salh's thoughts to find out who had hired him. Once he had the information he wanted, Midnight sunk his teeth into Salh's throat and bit down with lethal force. Blood gushed out and within a few tiks, Salh was dead.

Midnight, satisfied Salh was dead, looked up with blood dripping from his mouth. Several people in the parking lot who had seen the attack began to scream. Most began to run as Midnight pondered what he should do. Instinct told him to run for the woods. He knew that the humans would want to kill him when they found out he had killed one of their kind, no matter if the human was an assassin or not. In the woods, there would be more rhutz who would help him hide until he could figure out what to do. He took off in that direction.

✝✝✝✝✝

Autumn rushed down the hall right behind the medical team taking Sandee to the surgical room. A nurse tried to keep her out of the room but Autumn ignored her and rushed in. She sniffed all around the room for signs of trouble. When she was satisfied there was no danger she found a place in the corner and sat.

"We can't have a rhutz in the room while we treat the patient," a nurse complained.

"He's losing color and he's stopped breathing,"

207

another nurse said anxiously.

"Forget the rhutz," the doctor said. "Let's get those toxins out of his system."

The team worked on Sandee for twenty loons, flushing out his stomach and treating him with a variety of anti-inflammatory medicines. When they had done all they could, he was stable, but still could not breathe on his own.

Suddenly Autumn stood up. Everyone turned and stared at her. She had felt Midnight's anguish from his altercation with Salh. Her instinct was to go to her brother's aid, but her duty was to protect Sandee. She saw in her mind's eye that Midnight was safe and seeking shelter in the woods. She sat back down. Everyone turned back to their patient.

When they finally took him to an intensive care room, Autumn followed right behind and settled down at his side when the nurses had finished with him.

A few tiks later the nurses left, and Salina walked in the room with Snowflake at her side. She was weeping and the two rhutz felt her pain. Autumn and Snowflake exchanged thoughts about Midnight but agreed he was not in any immediate danger. Salina began to talk to her fallen lover.

"Oh, Sandee. You cannot die on me. I love you and cannot live without you."

Sandee didn't move. The breathing machine forced air into his lungs and his chest rose and fell as if he were sleeping deeply. His color was pale and his skin was cold. Salina found another blanket and put it over him. She sat on the side of his bed and wept.

Suddenly the door flew open and two Public Enforcers brandishing laser pistols stormed into the room. Autumn and Snowflake stood up and growled. Shots were fired and Autumn and Snowflake fell to the ground. Salina stood up as the two rhutz wriggled and whimpered in agony.

"What have you done!" she screamed. "They were our protectors."

"There were three of them, right?" the officer asked.

"Yes," Salina replied, her eyes fixed on Autumn and Snowflake who had become still.

"There were three, right?" the officer repeated angrily.

Salina jumped. "Yes. Midnight ran after the man who poisoned Sandee."

"Well, he caught up with him and killed him. Then he took off into the woods. I have orders to detain these two rhutz until we can sort things out. You better hope the man the rhutz killed was responsible for the poisoning. If not, we may have to put-down all three of these beasts."

Salina looked back at the fallen rhutz. "But you've killed them already."

"No. Our lasers were on the stun setting. They'll be okay in a few loons."

"Oh, thank God," Salina said as she began to cry.

Two other PEs put collars and muzzles on the two rhutz and dragged them out of the room. Salina just stood there in shock as the door closed and she was alone again with Sandee. He hadn't stirred during the altercation with the public enforcers. She looked down at him and wondered if he'd ever regain consciousness. *Surely, Pelgrem won't let you die. Unless he's given up on you. Could that be possible? She sighed. No, this must be part of his plan. It has to be part of his plan.*

The door opened and Ambassador Talvihn and his mate Sela walked in. "Salina, we heard what happened and rushed right over." He looked down at Sandee. "How is he? He looks terrible."

"I don't know. They pumped out his stomach and gave him medication to counteract the poison."

"Poison? I thought he'd been shot?"

"Oh, you haven't heard. After they reconstructed his shoulder and took shrapnel out of his heart and lungs, he was poisoned."

"Oh, my God!" Sela exclaimed. "I'm so sorry."

"It's a miracle he's still alive."

"Why did they kill your two rhutz?" the Ambassador asked. "We just saw them dragging them away."

"They claim they're not dead," Salina replied. She explained what had happened and then asked, "Do they have any leads on who is behind this?"

The Ambassador shook his head. "Not really. There has been a lot of speculation, but no real evidence linking anyone to the crime."

"So, if he does survive, how are we going to keep him safe in the future? Obviously, we can't depend on private security anymore."

"If he is elected to the General Assembly he'll have government security, and I will make sure special attention is given to the selection of his security team."

As they were talking a nurse came in. "I'm sorry, but you'll all have to leave. The doctor wants to come in and do some more tests."

"Why don't we get some dinner?" Sela suggested. "I bet you haven't eaten."

Selina thought for a moment. "No. Not since breakfast."

"Come on then. I know a place not too far from here."

When they left the hospital, they were shocked to see thousands of people standing around waiting for word of Sandee's condition. When a reporter saw them, he rushed over followed by many others.

"Mr. Ambassador. Any word on Sandee's condition?"

"Ah. You should ask his doctors," he said without stopping.

Another reporter asked, "Is it true he was attacked again while in the hospital?"

"Yes. He was poisoned," Salina replied. "Someone tried to kill him twice today. It's an outrage!"

"But he's still alive?" the reporter pressed.

Salina pushed her way through two reporters that had stepped in front of her. "Yes, barely," she replied.

"Do you know who the rhutz killed?" a third reporter asked.

"Midnight killed one of the assassins, I assume," Salina replied.

"That's all," the Ambassador said angrily. "No more questions."

Their Grinden pulled up to the curb and they quickly got in and drove away.

✝✝✝✝✝

Bruda paced back and forth anxiously in his large 27th-floor office at Bruda Industries' headquarters in downtown Vaceen. He looked at his wrist array for the time and saw it was early morning across the globe in Ya Lat. There had been no official word as to Sandee's condition after the second assassination attempt. He scrolled down the menu of his GC and selected the number of his friend Joh Crille at the Ya Lat Public Inquisitors' Office and waited. A few tiks later the dispatcher answered, reported that Crille was out in the field but that she would connect him. A tik later Crille's image and a voice came up.

"Yes," Crille said.

"Jon."

"Oh, Cornelius. Hello. What can I do for you?"

"What's the latest on Sandee Brahn's condition?"

Crille swallowed hard. He wasn't in Bruda's inner circle, but he was smart enough to know that Bruda wanted Sandee Brahn dead. "Ah . . . well, he's still alive, I'm afraid. The doctors seem to be optimistic. They said the first few kyloons were the most critical and obviously those have passed."

Bruda struggled to keep his anger in check. "I see. Do they know the identity of the assassin?"

"Ah. . . . Well, actually they do. The first two assassins were killed by a PE. The second was cornered by one of Sandee's rhutz who provides security. Midnight, I think, is his name. But the assassin didn't survive the encounter."

"The rhutz killed him?"

"Yes and then he fled into the woods."

"Is anybody looking for him?"

"Yes, the public enforcer sent in a search team but they haven't found him yet."

Bruda took a deep breath and then let it out slowly. "Okay. They've got to find the rhutz and kill him. Do you understand?"

"Actually, their orders are to capture him, if possible."

"No. That's too dangerous. You don't want to mess with a rhutz, particularly when he is being protected by a pack."

"Then maybe they should just let him go," Crille suggested.

"No. We can't let a rhutz get away with murder."

"Even if the victim was Sandee Brahn's assassin?"

"That doesn't matter. The rhutz have no authority to kill humans. It's a bad precedent to let them get away with it no matter what the circumstance. No one can be the prosecutor, judge, and executioner."

"That makes sense. I'll talk to the Captain about it and warn him against trying to capture the beast alive."

"Put out a reward, 25,000 credits to the officer or citizen who kills him," Bruda said. "Bruda Industries will cover it."

"Yes, sir. I'll get right on it."

"And keep me posted on Sandee's condition."

"Will do."

Bruda disconnected and resumed pacing back and forth. He knew rhutz had telepathic abilities and even if Salh didn't say a word, a rhutz could read his mind and get a lot of dangerous information. There was no option but to make sure Midnight was killed.

✝✝✝✝✝

When Salina, Sela and the Ambassador returned to the Casualty Center they were shocked to see Sandee sitting up and drinking some water from a cup. His color had returned, and when Salina took his hand, it was warm again.

"Oh, my God! You're awake," Salina said happily. "I can't believe it."

"Nor can I," the Ambassador agreed. "A kyloon ago I wondered if you were going to make it. Did Pelgrem come to see you again?"

Sandee smiled. "No. Not that I can remember. I just woke up feeling very hungry."

"Have they fed you?" Sela asked.

"No, they say my stomach is in no condition to digest food right now. My dinner is going directly into my veins."

Sela frowned. "Oh, well. At least you'll be around to feast another day."

"What about your shoulder?" Salina asked.

"It's a little sore. They have me on some strong pain meds, so if I seem a little incoherent, don't be surprised."

"Did you know there are 10,000 people camped out front worried sick about you?"

"So, I heard. I wish I could go out and thank them for coming."

"Not a chance," the Ambassador said. "If someone tried to kill you twice, let's not give them a third

213

opportunity."

"They can't kill me," Sandee reminded him. "Pelgrem won't let them. Not until there is peace on Tarizon."

"Don't push your luck," Salina said. "You're still a mortal."

"Where's Whisper?" Sandee asked. "He saved my life and I haven't had a chance to thank him."

Salina sighed. "He's okay. He's recovering at an animal hospital not too far from here. But Snowflake and Autumn have been taken into custody."

Sandee stiffened. "Into custody? Why?"

Salina explained what happened.

"We have to find Midnight before the public enforcer does," Sandee said anxiously. "They'll kill him if they find him."

"No," the Ambassador cautioned. "You have to let the authorities handle it. You don't want to be accused of aiding and abetting a fugitive."

Sandee started to get out of bed. "No," Salina said. "What do you think you're going to do? You don't know where he is."

Sandee looked up at Salina. "There must be something we can do. Whisper will never forgive me if I don't do something."

"He's with a local pack. They will protect him."

The door opened and PI Baldor and PE Cranz walked in with somber faces. Baldor cleared his throat. "It's good to see you are awake and looking better, Your Holiness."

"Thank you," Sandee replied, "but just call me Sandee."

"Ah, of course, Sandee. We just came to tell you that they tracked down your rhutz, Midnight and things didn't go so well."

"What do you mean?" Sandee asked anxiously.

"What happened?"

"They sent out a tactical squad to try to capture him but when they found him and tried to tranquilize him, the squad was attacked by a pack of rhutz. It was a bloodbath."

"Midnight is dead?" Sandee asked.

"Yes, along with seven other rhutz and two of our squad members were bitten pretty badly."

"Oh, my God!" Salina gasped.

"You should have let us handle Midnight," the Ambassador said irritably. "This all could have been avoided."

"We had no choice. We had to follow protocol," Baldor replied. "Anyway, you can pick up your other two rhutz and Whisper tomorrow."

The Ambassador nodded. "Okay, thanks for coming by and letting us know."

Baldor and Cranz left leaving everyone shaken.

"Poor Midnight," Salina said. "He catches the assassin and instead of being a hero, he's treated like a dangerous fugitive."

"So, what now?" Sandee asked. "What do I do now? My peace movement is falling apart."

"No, not really," the Ambassador replied. "It's stronger than it has ever been."

Sandee just stared at the Ambassador. "How can you say that? Whisper and I almost died."

"But you didn't, so now you have the attention of everyone on Tarizon. When you speak now, they will listen."

"So, you think I should just resume my preaching?"

"No. You have the people behind you. That's pretty clear by the crowd out front. As we previously discussed, I think you should run for the General Assembly and win a seat. It makes sense now to move the peace debate to the halls of government. Once you convince Lyon's General Assembly that it is time for peace, then you can travel to the other nations of the world and convince their governments that they should join the cause of peace too."

"What do you think, Salina?" Sandee asked.

Salina thought a moment. "I agree with the Ambassador. You should stay here in Lyon for now and run for the General Assembly. And since you have a big crowd outside praying for you, you have the perfect platform for making your announcement."

Sandee nodded. "Okay. Let me talk to Whisper about it and, if he agrees, I'll make the announcement tomorrow."

††††††

Bruda woke up with a start when his GC beeped. He had fallen asleep in his chair after he had talked to PI Crille in the middle of the night. He saw it was Crille again.

"Yes, what did you find out?"

"You can rest easy. Midnight is dead. They tried to capture him alive, but when the pack that was protecting him attacked there was chaos."

"Good. So, did any of the rhutz get away?"

"Yes, about half of them retreated once shots were fired."

"Alright. I guess we can't worry about them. What time is it there."

"Morning, 800 kyloons."

"Okay. Thanks for the update."

Bruda disconnected, then stood up and yawned. He heard noises in the next office so he walked out into the hall and looked to see who was there. It was his secretary, so he asked her to get him some Sankee. He went back into his office, turned on the VC and requested the latest news. He scrolled down to a story on Sandee Brahn.

The screen opened to the front of the Municipal Casualty Center in Ya Lat where Veile Shante was again reporting.

"A spokesman for the MCC reported that Sandee

Brahn's condition has been upgraded from critical to fair. Rumors have it that Brahn is recovering quickly and may be released in a few days.

"Just moments ago a spokesman for Ambassador Talvihn, who is a close friend of Sandee Brahn, announced that there would be a news conference at 1100 kyloons to report on Sandee Brahn's condition and to reveal his plans for the future."

Bruda looked at his wrist array and saw it was 1057, so he sat and waited for the news conference to begin.

"We are told that Whisper the rhutz has been released from the animal hospital and will be here today at Sandee Brahn's side. The crowd in front of the MCC, which has been steadily growing since Sandee's first admittance, is in a festive mood now that the word is out that Sandee is recovering nicely."

A front door to the MCC opened and two security guards walked out and surveyed the crowd. The PEs had the crowd cordoned off across the street. The fifty or so members of the press were directly in front of the MCC where a podium and cluster of microphones were set up. Selina, the Ambassador, and Assemblyman Renno next came through the door followed by Snowflake, Autumn and Whisper. Finally, Sandee was wheeled up in a wheelchair by a nurse.

The Ambassador went to the podium. *"Citizens of Lyon, members of the press, I am Ambassador Mill Talvihn and, I am proud to say, a good friend of Sandee Brahn who just a few days ago was shot by a would-be assassin. The assassin, no doubt, was hired by a coward and war profiteer who cares nothing for the people of Tarizon or the planet itself which is in crisis."*

The crowd stirred and a few chanted, *"Peace, not war! Peace, not war!"*

"When he learned he'd been unsuccessful, he sent a second assassin, this time to poison Sandee Brahn. Fortunately, neither assassin was successful."

The crowd cheered and then began chanting again. *"Peace, not war! Peace, not war!"*

The Ambassador raised his hand to quiet the crowd. *"Yes, I am happy to report that Sandee Brahn survived and that his assassins did not."*

There was laughter and more cheers.

"Sandee Brahn is alive today by the grace of Pelgrem and the skill of the fine physicians and nurses here at the MCC, for which all of us will be eternally grateful."

There was a rousing round of applause followed by more chants of *"Peace, not war! . . . Peace, not war!"*

"At this time I would like to introduce Assemblyman Renh Renno, who, as you know, is a member of the Lyon General Assembly. He will speak about Sandee's plans for the future."

Assemblyman Renno went to the podium, *"Citizens, members of the press. Sandee is out here today against the advice of his physicians. He's recovering nicely as you can see, but he's too weak to be giving speeches right now, so the Ambassador and I volunteered to stand in for him.*

"What he wanted to tell you is that our peace movement will be moving into a new phase. The time for education and awareness is over. Now is the time for action."

There was applause and the chanting began anew. *"Peace, not war! . . . Peace, not war!"*

Assemblyman Renno continued, *"So, we are proud to announce that Sandee Brahn is filing today for a seat in the Lyon General Assembly."*

The crowd and press broke out in excited chatter.

"To get Sandee off to a fast start, I will be loaning my campaign staff to him, and I hope all of you will quickly get

behind him as well."

There were cheers and applause.

"Now, I think Sandee has a brief statement."

Sandee stood up slowly, walked to the podium and smiled. *"My friends and Citizens of Lyon, thank you so much for coming out and standing up for me and Tarizon today. I am overwhelmed by all of your support and good wishes."*

There were cheers and applause.

"Five cycles ago when Pelgrem came to me and sent me on this peace mission, I felt completely overwhelmed. How could one boy bring peace to a world in madness and chaos? But first, he gave me Whisper who fed and protected me. And then he led me to the Ambassador and the arms of my beloved Salina. And now, I have all of you. Everywhere I go you follow me and give me strength and hope.

The crowd screamed their approval.

"When I heard the shot and felt my shoulder exploding before my eyes, I was afraid I was going to die," Sandee said, holding back his tears. *"It wasn't that I was afraid of death, because we will all die someday. No, it was because I hadn't completed my mission of peace. I needed more time to save our beloved Tarizon. So, I prayed to Pelgrem to give me more time and he granted my prayer letting Whisper take the second bullet."*

There was laughter.

Sandee looked over at Whisper. *"Thank you, my friend for saving my life, again."*

Whisper stood tall.

"The Ambassador, Assemblyman Renno, and Salina have convinced me that we need to move into this second phase of our peace mission. From now on we will be focusing on convincing the leaders of Tarizon that peace is in their best interests and the best interests of the people. With all of your support, they will have to listen to us.

"Thank you all for being here today and pray that one day soon the sky will be clear, the water will be cleansed, and our sun will once again shine brightly over our beloved Tarizon. Peace, not war!"

The crowd cheered and began chanting again. "Peace, not war! . . . "Peace, not war!"

Bruda shut off the VC angrily. He was livid with General Bakker for letting Sandee Brahn live another day. But he couldn't afford to display any anger toward him since the General controlled an army and his government was one of his best customers. He made a mental note not to rely on the General again. He'd build his own private security team, a team that would be highly competent and fiercely loyal to him. There could be no mistakes in the future. He had to stomp out this peace movement at the very next opportunity.

✝✝✝✝✝

Several days later, Sandee, Salina, the Ambassador and many others in the peace movement attended Midnight's funeral ceremony. The road into the dense forest was narrow and winding and it took some time for them to get to the clearing where the ceremony was to take place. As they got out of their transporter vehicles, they saw hundreds of rhutz on the far side of the clearing. In front of them was a huge mound of black dirt with no vegetation of any kind. Midnight's body had been placed on a shroud at the base of the mound.

Sandee began walking across the clearing and the rest of the mourners followed. They formed a semicircle in front of Midnight's limp body. Sandee turned and addressed them.

"We are brought together here today to celebrate the life of the rhutz called Midnight," Sandee began. "Midnight was a volunteer in the peace movement recruited by

220

Whisper to assist my security team. He served tirelessly and without any compensation for our cause and has now made the ultimate sacrifice to bring about peace to Tarizon.

"Midnight had a mate and many offspring who now must live without him. We will all miss him, and I wish I could promise you he would be the last life sacrificed for our cause, but we all know that would be a lie. Many more will die before peace comes to Tarizon.

"There is nothing I could say to make Midnight's death right. "All I can hope is that all who have, or will, perish in this great endeavor won't have done so in vain."

Sandee lifted his hand into the air and pointed to the heavens. "Mighty Pelgrem! Accept the rhutz known as Midnight into the next life."

The crowd stirred and there was hushed conversation until all the living rhutz in attendance began to howl in unison. The crowd quieted immediately. A tik later thousands of black spidery creatures called sligots swarmed out of their nest and crawled up and onto the shroud. They swarmed over Midnight's body and began consuming it. In just a few loons his body had disappeared, leaving only the blood-soaked shroud. Then the sligots retreated into their nest.

The rhutz howled in unison one more time, then turned and trotted away. The witnesses were deathly quiet, just staring in disbelief until one of them fainted. Quickly, they all fled back to their vehicles and soon were gone. Sandee and Salina remained at the sligot nest staring at the soiled shroud until they were finally persuaded to leave.

23
Austin

Markis Lai knew he had to split off from the GOT settlement in Palo Pinto County. He needed privacy to effectively implement his secret mission on Tarizon. As long as he and Sarna had the Board breathing down their necks they'd be distracted by worry that their unauthorized activities would be discovered and thwarted. So, they decided to move their operation to Austin, Texas.

They chose Austin because it was the capital of Texas and it would provide them with more opportunities to infiltrate the state and the federal government. This was essential for their grand plan to plant Tarizonians into key positions in government, the military, and business throughout the United States.

At a meeting of the GOT Board of Directors, Markis and Sarna Lai brought the matter up. "Sarna and I and some of our friends have been talking about our current situation and we think it is time to branch out from Palo Pinto. It's getting too crowded at the ranch and now that we have been forced to enroll our students in school, it's putting our whole operation in danger."

"How many are we talking about?" Romas asked.

"About 128," Markis advised.

"That many?" Jox asked.

"Yes. It will be most of our security and intelligence operations. We want to keep everyone together, so our effectiveness isn't compromised. It will also be good to branch out in case of discovery. If the Sheriff's investigation compromises our operations here in Palo Pinto it won't be a total disaster for the community."

"Where are you planning to go?" Romas asked.

"Austin."

"What about your children? They will have to change schools. That could be a problem," Paya argued.

"Yes. We'll leave them here until the school year is finished, then some will have graduated, and the rest will have the entire summer to transfer to local schools." Markis replied.

"Well, you are free to leave if you want," Romas said. "But how will you provide for our security from Austin?"

"It's not that far away. We've taken scouting trips down there and it's less than four hours one way. If we go at night when the state police are not monitoring the highways, we can make it in two hours. So, it will not hinder our operations in the least."

Romas nodded. "Well, this isn't unexpected. I can't say I'm in favor of it, but I have noticed a restless spirit in the community. I'm sure others will be wanting to branch out as well."

Romas suspected there was more to the move to Austin than Markis was letting on, but if he opposed it too strongly it might divide the community which would endanger their survival. Better to be flexible but vigilant, he thought.

"Yes. It's nothing to be alarmed about," Markis agreed. "It is just part of the natural evolution of our resettlement here on Earth."

"Where will you live?" Paya asked.

"We found a 120-unit apartment complex that has just been renovated. We plan to buy it and move in there. The units we don't need will be leased out to provide us with operating income."

"How will you finance it? You don't have any credit?"

"We've discovered a very useful way to finance things in America. It's called the limited partnership. We have found a broker who will get investors to put up the money and let us manage the property as the general partner. It's perfect when you don't have any cash."

"Won't they require monthly payback on their investment?"

"Not right away. They are making the investment for tax evasion purposes, so they don't care so much about getting paid back quickly. In fact, if we paid them back quickly it would just increase their tax liability and make them very unhappy."

They all laughed.

"Don't you love America," Jox said.

The debate continued but in the end, the move was approved. At subsequent meetings of the Board similar requests were made. Many young settlers left to go to various colleges and universities around the state. Even though the Board wanted to keep the Tarizonians together for an eventual return home, they were free citizens and had a right to come and go as they pleased. Many individual settlers had left without asking for permission. Some found love and ran off to get married, others got caught up in the American dream and left to seek their fortunes, and many just left when they found more interesting jobs in Mineral Wells, Fort Worth or other close-by cities.

In 1964 the Vietnam War broke out and the U.S. Army began drafting more and more young men for military service. The Board went to great lengths to keep the young men in their community out of the selective service process. No Tarizonians were allowed to register for the draft and plans were in place to quickly relocate and hide anyone who was drafted, but Markis Lai and his splinter group had different ideas. At their first meeting after relocating to Austin, the matter came up. The members still in Palo

Pinto County attended by video conferencing technology not yet invented on Earth but provided by the engineers aboard Earth Shuttle 7.

"As you are well aware we have been directed by the GOT Board not to allow our people to be drafted. However, this is one edict we cannot obey. To follow it would be to miss an opportunity to get Tarizonians into positions of influence in the United States military," Markis advised.

"But if we defy the GOT Board they will cut us off and may well punish us for our disobedience," Sarna Volk complained.

"If they did, it wouldn't be a disaster. We don't really need them anymore, but their support is useful, so we'll make sure it isn't traced back to us," Markis promised.

"So, what is your plan?" Sarna asked.

He explained his plan.

24
Inspection

Vaceen, Tributon
9 BU

It was a perfect day, like every other day under the Vaceen dome, when Bruda stepped out to the curb in front of the Bruda Industries' Building. The temperature was comfortable, the air was clean and calm, and, of course, rain wasn't a factor. It rained outside the dome but the water simply flowed off of its vast surface into water storage containers where it was piped to decontamination plants for processing before being put into the public water supply.

A black luxury transporter called a Grinden emerged from traffic and stopped. The driver stepped out and opened the door for Bruda. He got in and sat facing forward. He nodded at Petri Volk who was seated directly in front of him with his aide and constant companion, Cameela Bruns. Bruda couldn't resist giving Cameela a wide smile. She was a very attractive, dark-haired woman of 42 cycles. Her pale skin and big brown eyes were quite alluring. Bruda turned away. He knew that she was not only a shrewd businesswoman but also had the gift of telepathy. He had to be careful around her because, on more than one occasion, he had felt her probing his mind searching for information or secrets that would give her an advantage over him. Although on paper Petri owned his vast empire, Bruda knew Cameela controlled it, so Bruda always treated her with the utmost respect.

"This should be interesting," Cameela said. "I have never traveled in space before."

"Yes," Bruda replied. "It is an exciting ride and the view from above the atmosphere is incredible."

"Well, I could think of better things to do," Petri said. "I've done this trip many times, and Clarion is a pretty desolate and inhospitable place."

"Yes, I know you've taken this ride before. How many mining operations do you have on Clarion?"

"Eleven and two on Segalux."

Segalux was Tarizon's second moon. It was smaller than Clarion but still had rich mineral deposits that were critical to many industries on Tarizon.

"Well, I'm sorry to drag you along but I need your expertise in evaluating the progress that is being made on building the manufacturing facility for the Intergalactic Fleet. I don't trust General Bakker completely. Oh, I don't doubt his loyalty, God knows we pay him enough to guarantee that, but it is his competency I worry about."

"Don't worry. I'm sinking a lot of my money into this project too, so I'll make sure he doesn't do anything imprudent."

"I have asked around about his engineering staff," Cameela added, "and apparently, they are first-rate."

"Glad to hear that," Bruda said.

They drove in silence for a while until the Grinden stopped and General Bakker got in. He took a seat beside Bruda. The Grinden resumed its trip to the spaceport. General Bakker was dressed in his black and white TNA uniform. A cluster of colorful medals hung from his left pocket.

"Gentlemen, Madam Bruns," General Bakker said respectfully. "Is everyone ready for a great adventure? I love these inspection trips. They are always so exciting."

"Yes, I am," Cameela replied. "I haven't been up to Clarion yet, but I'm afraid this is all business for Mr. Bruda and my boss."

"It wouldn't be so bad if it didn't take so long to get there," Petri complained. "Two days to get there, a day for the inspection, then two days coming home. It kills an entire week."

"Well, you have to relax and enjoy yourself or what's the use of living, right?" the General replied.

Bruda glared at the General. "I would be enjoying life a lot more if Sandee Brahn were dead."

"Ah, yes. Well, maybe he does have Pelgrem protecting him after all. I've never had so much trouble with a simple assassination."

"I saw on the VC this morning that he is favored to win a seat on the Lyon General Assembly," Cameela said. "Do you think more people will listen to him as an assemblyman?"

The General shook his head. "No, I think running for the General Assembly was a big mistake for him, and a lucky break for us. He is going to be so busy trying to represent his district he's not going to have time to keep his peace movement going."

"You better be right," Bruda said. "I'd feel a lot better if he were dead."

"In retrospect," the General said, "I think killing him would have been a mistake. You didn't want him to become a martyr, did you?"

"No, I wanted him dead, buried and forgotten."

The big Grinden turned left onto the access road to the spaceport. They drove past the public terminal to a private airstrip owned by Bruda Industries. A Loring 20 Executive Transport Liner sat ready for takeoff on the runway. The L20 was a smaller version of the L22 Troop Transporter used by the Navy for shuttling crewmen back and forth from Tarizon and Clarion. There was also an L21 which had only limited space for a crew but lots of cargo space.

General Bakker invited everyone aboard and instructed them on how to prepare for takeoff. The L20 took off like an ordinary airplane but when it got into thin air its thrusters took over to provide enough force to get the ship out of Tarizon's atmosphere. The ship began to shake violently when the thrusters came on and Bruda felt his body become very heavy as the L20 shot upward. With some difficulty, he looked over at Cameela and saw she was in great distress. He smiled crookedly and said, "It will only be another loon. Relax! Don't fight it."

Cameela looked over at him and tried to smile, but couldn't manage it. "Okay. Sure. Whatever you say."

The ship jerked and shuddered a few loons and then suddenly the pressure began to ease off. Bruda saw Cameela take a deep breath. She smiled at him. "Well, that was exciting. But I'm glad it didn't last too long."

"No. Not long at all. But, I'm afraid that's about all the excitement there will be on this trip."

"I'm not so sure about that," Cameela said, pointing to the rear portal where Tarizon, shrouded in a dirty yellow haze, could be seen in the distance.

"Yes, you're right. That is a stunning sight. Have you seen pictures of Tarizon before the wars?" Bruda asked.

"Sure, it's a different planet now."

Bruda nodded. "Indeed. That's why this project is so important."

"Yes. I know. Someday we may have to leave Tarizon."

"Right, but not just a few thousand of us, like the GOT took with them. I'm talking about millions of hand-picked humans who will travel to Earth and settle there permanently."

"Petri has mentioned that, but he has never told me how you will hand-pick these settlers."

"They will be only humans, of course. We won't be bringing mutants, Seafolken, rhutz or any other inferior life forms."

"What about the inhabitants of Earth?" Cameela asked. "Will you co-exist with them?"

"Perhaps, the pureblood humans, if they do not oppose us. But if they try to stop us, then we will crush them and rule Earth only allowing to live those who will submit to our rule."

"You mean as slaves?"

"Not necessarily slaves," Bruda replied, "but as an inferior class whose primary purpose is to serve their masters. As long as they respect their place there is no reason they can't have fulfilling lives."

"I see."

"Do you not agree?" Bruda asked.

Cameela gave Bruda a thoughtful gaze. "Of course that would be ideal, but I fear it is not a realistic goal. There are hundreds of millions of inhabitants on Earth who will have strong objections to your plans. How could one million of us from Tarizon take control of Earth?"

"It won't be easy and it will take a long time to accomplish, but it can and will be done," Bruda replied confidently.

Cameela raised her eyebrows. "Well, I hope I live to see the day."

Clarion could now be seen through the plane's front portal. "We will be changing course now to enter into an orbit around Tarizon. Then in about six kyloons, we will fire our thrusters to put us in a trajectory to intercept Clarion," General Bakker said. "When we get to Clarion in about 54 kyloons, we will go into orbit around it, then when we get around to its back side, we will descend into its thin atmosphere and fly to the base."

Two days later, the ship lurched into a steep descent and glided downward toward Clarion's desolate surface. When the ship got to an altitude of 10,000 feet, it leveled off. After a few loons, the craft flew over a low mountain range and then dipped into a valley littered with red boulders the size of small houses. Finally, in the distance, a construction site could be seen with dozens of cranes and heavy equipment working diligently. The ship's reverse thrusters brought it to a stop in mid-air and then the Captain gently set it onto the ground causing a cloud of dust to rise slowly around the ship.

"Well, this is it," General Bakker said excitedly. "It doesn't look like much now, but wait until you see the plans and aircraft designs in the control room."

"Lead us on," Petri said. "I hope you've got food. I slept through breakfast this morning, so I'm famished."

"Of course," General Bakker said as they disembarked and began walking through a docking tube to the terminal. "The crew down here has to eat and we feed them well to keep morale high."

"Yes, I can imagine that would be a problem on a project like this. . . . Morale, I mean."

General Bakker nodded. "It is for the civilians. Our military personnel expects it, but the engineers and production workers aren't used to being isolated like this on a top secret project."

"So, there is no communication with Tarizon?" Cameela asked.

"No. We are on the back side of Clarion, so all communication must be by letter or audio clip. And, of course, anything that goes out is censored. We cannot let anyone on Tarizon find out what we are doing out here."

"What about vacations and leaves?"

"There are none. The workers must sign a

three-cycle contract with the stipulation that there are no vacations off Clarion. They can take time off but they must stay on base. Some of the more important workers are allowed to bring their families out here if they want, but they can't leave once they get here."

"So, why would anybody sign such a contract?" Cameela asked.

"Because the pay is very good, and they are guaranteed a ticket to Earth when the Intergalactic Fleet eventually leaves."

"So, everyone here will probably not return to Tarizon?"

"Yes, that's quite possible, unless dramatic changes occur on Tarizon."

"What kind of changes?" Cameela asked.

"If the right people were ruling Tarizon we might not have to leave," Bruda interjected.

Cameela looked at Bruda and nodded. "You mean if you and Petri were in charge?"

"Us, or people like us who knew how to run things properly."

"Well, that's not likely to happen." Cameela said bitterly.

"Probably not, so that's why we better make this project work."

Once inside the terminal, the General led them to a commissary where they dined and then prepared for a tour of the facility. While they ate the commanding officer, Admiral Rigg Malty, joined them. They started the tour in the construction office where a miniature version of the completed project was displayed.

"As you can see," Admiral Malty began, "the main construction facility will have three floors. One on the surface and two beneath it. The manufacturing will be done on Level 1, warehousing and administration will be conducted on Level 2 and the workers' quarters and common area will be on Level 3. A series of large freight elevators will provide easy access to the entire facility."

"Wouldn't it be cheaper to build everything on the surface?" Cameela asked.

"Yes, but it would be much more expensive to operate the facility. You see Clarion has a very thin atmosphere so the temperature on the surface can be below zero at night but 180 degrees during the day. But the temperature at 20 feet below the surface is almost always between 50 and 105 degrees and with the proper insulation the range can be narrowed to 60 to 80 degrees, completely within human tolerance."

"Now this is what I came to see," Petri said looking at the next display of ships to be built at the facility.

"Ah, yes," Admiral Rigg said. "The attack cruisers. Aren't they magnificent?"

"Wow," Cameela said. "They're going to be huge."

"Yes, that's another reason we are building the Intergalactic Fleet on Clarion, you see, the huge attack cruisers can be much bigger if they don't have to enter a planet's atmosphere. They're being built specifically for FTL travel, so we want all the thrust to be focused on speed not escaping a planet's gravitational pull."

"Makes sense," Petri said. "Will the crew stay awake during flight?"

"Yes, that's another reason the ship has to be so big. Not only do we need room for thousands of fighters, shuttles, ammunition, supplies, personnel but also the FTL drive, a complete hydroponics, and hydration complex to produce food and water for everyone for at least a full cycle."

Cameela shook her head. "That sounds like a monumental project. Are you sure it can be done?"

The Admiral nodded. "Oh, yes we have had the

technology to do it for some time, but until now no one has had the resources to make it happen."

"Yes," Bruda said. "If the idiot politicians and Generals on Tarizon only knew they were funding their own demise. . . . No offense to you General Bakker."

"None taken," General Bakker said. "I like to think I'm more enlightened than the others. I can see the big picture if you know what I mean."

"We do, General," Bruda said. "So, how long will it take before we have our first attack cruiser?"

General Bakker looked at the Admiral and shrugged. "What do you think? Six to eight cycles."

"At least," the Admiral said. "As you said. It's a tremendous undertaking."

"And after the first one is finished, how fast to produce the others?"

"Once we get the first one done, we can probably do another one in about a cycle."

Bruda nodded. "So, in eleven cycles you could produce six attack cruisers?"

"Yes, if all went well," the Admiral said.

"What about the fighters, shuttles, and transporters?"

"They can be done on Tarizon so that's not a problem."

Bruda looked at Petri and smiled. "I'm satisfied. How about you?"

Petri looked at Cameela. She gave him an approving smile. "Sure, it looks feasible. Let's do it."

Bruda turned to General Bakker and the Admiral and said sternly. "All right. Let's get this project underway immediately. And make sure it's done right. I don't want to hear about any obstacles or miscalculations, just make it happen."

"Yes, sir," General Bakker said.

Supreme Mandate

"Don't worry," the Admiral said. "The Intergalactic Fleet will be the most powerful military force ever built by mankind. It will be invincible."

"Good, let's name the first attack cruiser, Invincible."

"Done!" the Admiral replied.

<h1 style="text-align:center">25
First Minister of Lyon</h1>

7 BU

After surviving the two assassination attempts, Sandee Brahn went on to be elected to the Lyon General Assembly. Although he was easily elected his candidacy caused much upheaval and animosity. His appeal to his followers to only support candidates who endorsed his peace efforts caused much animosity and resentment. When he was finally elected, he was shunned by the leaders of the Assembly and denied many of the usual appointments and considerations given other members.

Although this angered Sandee, it did not deter him from his mission. In fact, since he'd been ignored by the leadership this gave him more time to travel and get out amongst the people to spread his message. And he wasn't afraid to talk about the Assembly leadership, and how they were mere puppets and pawns of the military generals and industrial barons who controlled most of the governments on Tarizon.

Sandee even encouraged others to run against these corrupt assemblymen and offered his help in organizing and raising campaign funds for them. By the time four cycles had rolled by and Sandee was up for re-election, there were a dozen new candidates from his newly formed Peace Party on the ballot.

This second campaign was bitter and there were

many threats against his life and the lives of the other candidates, but on election day, twelve of the thirteen Peace Party candidates were elected. Although the Peace Party was still in the minority, leadership had no choice but to treat Sandee and the new members with respect.

During his second term, with the help of the other Peace Party assemblymen, Sandee made considerable progress in convincing a majority of the members of the Lyon Assembly that they should get behind his peace movement. But the critical boost for the peace movement came when Chancellor Rikin Linzcot announced that, after much consideration and soul-searching, he now supported Sandee's peace initiative.

Before the end of his second term, Lyon's General Assembly passed a resolution calling for the cessation of all warfare on Tarizon in order to slow, and eventually stop the rapid deterioration of the planet's ecosystem. And when Chancellor Linzcot was elected for his third term as Chancellor of Lyon, he appointed Sandee Brahn as his First Minister, responsible for all of Lyon's foreign affairs.

This new position provided Sandee not only with the full support of Lyon's government for his peace movement but also the support of all Lyon's allies in the North Sea Alliance. Although this was huge progress for the movement, Sandee knew there was still substantial opposition to overcome. But for the first time, he began to believe that he would eventually be successful. It was in this spirit that he gave his first address to the Lyon Assembly after his appointment as First Minister.

"Mr. Chairman, fellow assemblymen.

"It is with great honor and humility that I stand before you today as your new First Minister. I want to thank the Chancellor for appointing me to this position where I can more effectively work to bring about peace for Tarizon.

"We live in difficult and tragic times. Decades of war have polluted our atmosphere, contaminated our rivers and lakes, and killed millions of our citizens. Many of those who have survived are sick, disabled and unable to work. Their lives are marked by hunger, pain, and despair. Until now the future offered them no hope of a better life.

"But today a ray of sunlight can be seen coming over the horizon. It is the beginning of a new day on Tarizon. The state of Lyon and its allies of the North Sea Alliance are now committed to peace! This is a wondrous day! A day that is long overdue. A day that will never be forgotten. It's the beginning of Tarizon's salvation.

"We haven't got there yet. There is still much work to be done to convince the rest of Tarizon that these wars must stop, but for the first time, we will have at our disposal the power and resources of the world's five most powerful states.

"Unfortunately, there are many who profit by war and who will do anything in their power to thwart our efforts. These people only care about themselves, accumulating personal wealth and preserving the status quo. These people have no morals and will do whatever it takes to defeat the peace movement, including the use of threats, intimidation, bribery, violence and even murder.

"As you all know, I have personally felt the sting of the opposition's wrath, but I will not let that dissuade me from fulfilling the task assigned to me by the Almighty Pelgrem. Our mission of peace is Tarizon's last hope, not just for a brighter future, but for the very survival of humanity and Tarizon's other wondrous life-forms.

"So, again. Thank you, Mr. Chancellor. I look forward now to completing Pelgrem's mission and bringing about a lasting peace to Tarizon."

The members all stood up and gave Sandee a standing ovation. Tears of joy welled in his eyes as he absorbed the enthusiasm and encouragement of his colleagues. He looked over at his beloved Salina, who was smiling proudly. Even Whisper and the other rhutz seemed energized and excited. He took a deep breath thinking that his peace movement was now an unstoppable wave that would wash over the planet, and finally bring a lasting peace to Tarizon. He felt exhilarated and optimistic about the future like he'd never felt before.

After the General Assembly session was over, Sandee went back to his office where his new staff and the other leaders in the peace movement had gathered for a planning and strategy session in light of these most fortunate turn of events. Sandee sat at the head of a long black marble table that accommodated twelve. Salina sat to his left and Ambassador Talvihn to his right. Whisper and Snowflake walked around the table warily, apparently unnerved by the revelry. After ten loons of jovial banter and congratulations all around, Sandee called for order and the meeting got serious.

"Now that we have taken such a big step toward peace, I don't want to let up," Sandee said. "We need to move quickly to keep up our momentum."

"Yes. You're absolutely right," Ambassador Talvihn agreed. "I think you should go to Rigimol and Tributon and solidify their support."

"No," Salina objected, "that would be a waste of time. They are already committed to peace. We need to go to places where the generals and munitions manufacturers have a stranglehold over the government. That's where Sandee can make the most difference by appealing directly to the people and urging them to support candidates from the Peace Party."

"That's a good point," the Ambassador admitted, "but we should still confer with the governments of the North Sea Alliance first. We need not only their official support but their financial assistance as well."

Sandee nodded. "Why don't you go to Rigimol and Tributon and Salina and I will go to Soni. You'll do much better with the politicians there than I could ever do."

"That's fine, but I'm not sure you should step into such hostile waters right away. Soni is one of the most belligerent states in the world. Almost every munitions manufacturer has its home office there."

"That's precisely why I need to go there. I have to help the people take back control of their government and their destiny."

The Ambassador swallowed hard. "You've got a lot more courage than I do."

Sandee shrugged, "It's not courage, it's faith in Pelgrem and all of you."

Whisper suddenly stood up and started to whine.

"What's the matter?" Sandee thought.

"There is someone watching us. I can feel it."

"Watching us from where? Outside?"

"Yes. I feel their presence and their evil intentions."

"We have security all around the building. Nobody can get in here."

"I'm going to check it out," Whisper thought.

"All right, but I can't see how we could be in danger here."

Whisper dashed out of the room to everyone's astonishment except Sandee. He gave them a worried look.

"Whisper is a little paranoid, I think. He's going to check out a threat he's worried about."

The meeting continued and went on for nearly a kyloon. Many objected to Sandee going to Soni and tried to dissuade him from that idea, but he was not to be deterred. When the meeting broke up Sandee got up to leave but Whisper hadn't returned.

"It's time to go, my friend," Sandee thought.

"I'm to take you home," Snowflake advised.

Sandee looked around the room full of his friends and supporters and frowned. *"Okay, but everything here looks fine to me."*

Sandee and Snowflake left to go back to Sandee's compartment to begin packing for his journey. Salina stayed back with the Ambassador and Sandee's staff to help make the necessary arrangements for both the Ambassador's and Sandee's trips.

"So, are you as pleased as I am with our progress?" Sandee thought.

"Yes, it appears people are finally starting to listen to your pleas," Snowflake thought. *"Humans are so selfish. They think only of their personal gain rather than the good of everyone."*

"Yes, I wish humans were more like the rhutz," Sandee thought. *"It would make this whole process so much easier."*

When they reached the front of the building, a Grinden was waiting for them but a crowd of well-wishers and reporters stood between them and the vehicle.

"First Minister," a reporter yelled, "where will you take your peace movement now?"

Sandee smiled. "I'm going to Shisk. It's time to stir up the people there, and encourage them to take back their country and their destiny."

"But isn't that rather dangerous?" the reporter asked. "There's no guarantee the Soni government will protect you."

"I'm not worried, Pelgrem will protect me."

Snowflake leaped forward and the crowd parted to let them through. The driver had the door opened for them when they emerged from the crowd, so they quickly climbed in and he shut the door.

✝✝✝✝✝

Whisper bounded out of the conference room and out into the First Minister's general offices. He went to a window and peered down onto the busy street. It was crowded with traffic, news vehicles, and public enforcers. He scanned the buildings across from the conference room and, for an instant, saw a man with vision scope watching the building. Without a second thought, Whisper ran out into the hall and down the stairs. When he got outside, he raced across the street, nearly getting hit by passing vehicles. Once safely across the street, he raced up and down the sidewalk looking for a way into the building. Finally, he saw someone come out of a locked door and used his invisible hand to hold the door open until he could scamper through it.

His nose picked up the scent immediately. He could feel the watcher's fear and smell the odor of adrenalin drifting off his body. When he reached his destination, there was another door between him and the watcher. He tried to open it with his invisible hand, but it was locked. Suddenly, there was an explosion and the building rocked violently knocking Whisper off his feet. A tik later the door in front of him flew open and the watcher stood before him holding a long rifle. Whisper tried to wrestle the rifle away from the man with his third hand, but the man held it with a heavy grip. As the man rushed by, he hit Whisper in the head with the butt of the rifle sending him hard up against the wall. The watcher continued on without looking back, and when he got to the first stairwell he made his escape. Whisper tried to get to his feet and follow but he was too dazed to stay upright.

†††††

Cornelius Bruda stood in front of the big screen in the Blue Room. Several staff members were milling around, and there were several guests watching the screen.

"Give me the latest report from the Lyon General

Assembly," Bruda ordered.

The screen lit up and displayed a view of Lyon's Capitol Building. The scene shifted to an office building across the street. A reporter was holding a microphone and looking into the camera.

"This is Veile Shante for the Lyon News Agency. We are across the street from the offices of Sandee Brahn, the newly appointed First Minister of Lyon. We have been told that Sandee and his staff are in a strategy session making plans for the future, now that he has the full support of the Chancellor and the government of Lyon for his peace mission."

A rhutz could be seen exiting the building and racing across the street. There were angry honks and sounds of screeching tires.

"If I'm not mistaken, it looks like Whisper just ran out of the offices. I hope he wasn't hurt.

"There are reports from sources inside Sandee's inner circle that he will soon be leaving for Shisk to meet with representatives of the Soni government, industry leaders as well as local members of his Peace Party. Soni is currently at war with Rohr and Synclare, and Sandee hopes to assist in getting peace talks started."

The building suddenly explodes and the concussion knocks Shante off her feet. The camera shakes as fire and smoke pour out of the building. The reporter staggers to her feet and tries to compose herself. Finally, she says, *"Oh, my God! As you can see there has been a powerful explosion and the building is on fire!"*

Shante shakes the debris and soot from her head. She is shaking noticeably as she inspects her body for injuries. Looking up at the camera, she continues.

"I think I'm okay. Forgive me, if I seem a bit shaken,

but that was quite a jolt. I don't know what caused the explosion, but it seems to have been centered near the new offices of Sandee Brahn."

Chaos ensues around the burning structure as people begin to stream out the exits, fire and casualty personnel begin to arrive on the scene and security forces attempt to secure the area.

"We don't know that this was a deliberate act of terror, but it is no secret that Sandee Brahn has been targeted for assassination before. This may very well be yet another attempt to silence him and stop the peace movement."

Shante frowns as she hears something in her earpiece. *"Okay, I have just been informed that there have been at least three fatalities in the blast, but the bodies are badly burned and have not yet been identified. Again, just a loon ago there was a massive explosion in the First Minister's office located in the Fourth Assembly Office Building. Security forces, as well as casualty personnel, are on the scene trying to sort out exactly what has happened."*

People are seen running excitedly back and forth in front of the camera, some bleeding, many crying and moaning from their injuries.

"I'm not sure where Whisper was going just before the blast but he seemed to be on the hunt. Perhaps he saw the person preparing for this attack if that's what it was. We don't know yet if that was an attack or just a freak accident. But buildings just don't usually explode of their own volition. There isn't anything, to my knowledge, in a building such as this that would explode on its own in this fashion."

††††††

Cornelius Bruda walked over to his three guests watching the story unfolding on the VC. They are smiling and obviously enjoying the tragic scene. He pauses the video.

"So, what do you think?" Bruda asked.

"Well, do you think we finally got the skutz?" Petri Volk asked.

"I'm certain of it. The bomb was in a case directly under the conference table where they were all meeting. It was powerful enough to take out the entire building. Nobody could have survived it."

"How did you manage to get a bomb in there? Don't they have security?"

"Of course, so we had the bomb built into the conference table. When they finished out Sandee's new office, it was part of the new furnishings."

"How did you manage that?" General Bakker asked, obviously impressed.

"The official public enforcer's report will show there was a break-in at the furniture manufacturer's plant, but nothing was taken. The report will state the identity of the intruders is unknown, but that they were likely teenagers out for a little fun. It will indicate that a few empty Tekari bottles were found just outside the perimeter of the facility where teenagers have often been seen loitering."

"Very creative," Cameela said. "Now, I just hope all of this talk of peace will stop."

"It will, once Sandee is dead and buried," General Bakker replied.

"But what if he survives? What if Pelgrem is protecting him and he can't be killed?"

"If he survives this attack," Bruda replied thoughtfully, "we may have to embrace the peace movement."

General Bakker stiffened. "What? Embrace the peace movement?"

"Yes," Bruda said nodding. "But that might not be

such a bad thing. To finally bring peace to Tarizon there would have to be a government strong enough to enforce it."

"You mean like one central government?" Volk replied.

"Yes, one central government that will need a large army to enforce the peace."

"Oh, I get it," General Bakker said as a smile crept across his face. "So, even with peace, there will still be plenty of business."

"Yes, and if we control that one central government, then we can make sure business is always good."

"That sounds promising," Cameela admitted, "but there is one problem. There is no guarantee we could get control of this new government."

"No," Bruda admitted, "but organizing a new world government will be a chaotic process and take much time. While the world is bickering over the details of such an endeavor, we will be planning how to seize control of it, once it becomes a reality."

"Brilliant," General Bakker said. "Now, I almost hope the skutz survives."

"Well, let's see if there is a report on Sandee's fate yet," Bruda said as he resumed the video feed.

Shante is listening to the voice in her earpiece. She turns pale and her face becomes solemn. *"I've just been told that one of the victims of the blast was a woman who has tentatively been identified as Salina Gill, Sandee Brahn's chief of staff and constant companion.* Shante is visibly shaken, and tears begin to well in her eyes. She wipes them away with the sleeve of her blouse. *"Excuse me, but I knew Salina well. I've been covering Sandee for some time, and I often travel with them. Salina was a wonderful woman, and I know Sandee will be devastated by her death if he somehow survives this latest attack on his life."*

The scene shifts to a high rise apartment complex in downtown Ya Lat. A Grinden rolls up and stops. Several people as well as a rhutz get out of the passenger's doors and hurry into the building.

"As you saw, it appears Sandee Brahn survived the attack or left before it happened, and just entered the building where he has a compartment. He had one of his rhutz with him, and neither of them appeared to be injured."

Bruda shrugged, trying to hide his disappointment. "Well, there is your answer. It looks like the skutz managed to survive again. We have no choice now but to shift our strategy. It is time for us to get behind this peace movement."

They all looked at Bruda warily, but no one challenged him right away. The idea of Tarizon having one central government was indeed intriguing and ripe with possibilities. They could see that now, and they had faith that Cornelius Bruda could figure out how to exploit this new development for their mutual profit.

"Still, we don't know what impact Salina's death will have on Sandee. He may no longer have the will to carry on," the General noted.

"That's true," Cameela agreed. "We shouldn't do anything rash right away."

"Fine," Bruda said. "But if the peace movement isn't dead soon, we will have no choice but to embrace it."

Everyone nodded their agreement.

26
In the Shadows

Evelyn Wilkins had lived and breathed law enforcement all her life. Her father had been Sheriff of Palo Pinto County most of her life, and her grandfather held the office before that. Evelyn liked the political side of her father's job as sheriff. She liked the campaigning, the parties, the strategy meetings and the drama of the elections. That's why she ran for County Clerk. It wasn't a job she wanted to do forever. It was a stepping stone to becoming a county commissioner, a state senator or even going to Congress. Now her life had been turned upside down with her father's suspicious accident. Everything had to go on hold until they figured it out. After all, their duty to protect and serve the public was paramount.

Her first task was to find the tourists from Hungary whom she had briefly met in her offices almost two years earlier. Was it a coincidence that on that very day a non-lethal gun had been fired at helpless school children across the street from her courthouse? The sheriff had gleaned that the device had been used to create a distraction for a common purse snatcher. She might have believed that had it not happened again in Mineral Wells, this time to confuse witnesses to a homicide. Now, finally, she'd caught a break. While attending the annual county fair she'd spotted the man and his wife strolling through one of the exhibit halls. She was shocked and elated at her good fortune as the FBI special agent assisting her in the investigation had been growing weary of their lack of progress, and she feared he was about to close their file and end the investigation. She called him as soon as she spotted Romas Garciah and his wife Celius. Walt and she met the next day at the FBI field office in Ft. Worth with Special Agents Glenn Johnson and Hal Bennett to discuss a strategy going forward.

"So, where are the suspects living?" Agent Johnson asked.

"I followed them to the Timber Creek Ranch up near Possum Kingdom Lake," Evelyn replied. "It's some kind of a commune. Hundreds of people are living and working there."

"Is it a religious cult?" Johnson asked.

"Maybe," Walt said. "Many of them claim to be Christian Scientists, but I think that's just so their children won't be examined by the school physicians."

"Why?" Agent Bennett asked.

Walt shrugged. "Who knows. They don't break any laws that we know about, so we leave them alone."

"Is someone watching the place?" Agent Bennett asked.

Walt nodded. "Yes. Curt Gibbons, who officially took retirement when I did, is out there now. He has identified the leadership and their children. Some of them attend Mineral Wells High School. A couple of them are football stars."

"Really?" Agent Johnson asked.

Evelyn nodded. "Yes. Ritz Slocum is a running back and Eroh Garciah is their starting quarterback. He has an arm like you've never seen before."

"So, how do you want to proceed?" Agent Johnson asked.

"I'd like to go in undercover," Evelyn advised.

Agent Johnson frowned. "How would that work?"

"I've met Eroh's father, Romas Garciah and his wife. So, I'd have to make contact with them and convince them that they are not suspects in an on-going investigation. Once I have gained their trust, I'll strike up a relationship with some of their teenagers. I'm only twenty-two so it won't seem unusual for me to want to hang out with them."

"But you're an elected official?" Agent Bennett protested.

"I know, but two of their students, Blinh Lai and Rammel Garciah are in debate and moot court. They're very interested in politics, so that will be our common interest."

Walt shook his head. "I've told her she's nuts even thinking about going undercover, but she won't listen," Walt complained. "Maybe you can talk some sense into her."

Agent Bennett shrugged. "Well, it's plausible enough. It might work."

Walt frowned. Evelyn smiled broadly.

"So, how can we help?" Agent Bennett asked.

They discussed the plan in more detail over the next few hours, and then Walt and Evelyn returned to Mineral Wells. The next day Evelyn called her old high school English teacher Elaine Meadows.

"Ms. Meadows. This is Evelyn Wilkins. How are you?"

"Fine. It's been a few years since you were in my class. You've certainly done well for yourself."

"Thank you. I just wish my father hadn't had to retire."

"Oh. Yes. I read about that. Such a tragedy."

"Yeah. But, I'm enjoying seeing more of him now."

"Well good. So, how can I help you?"

"I heard about your debate team. It's really been doing well."

"Oh, thank you. We may go to State this year."

"I know. That's so exciting. I'm particularly

interested in one of your students, Blinh Lai. I've heard he is quite amazing."

"Oh, yes. He's brilliant for sure. Such a quick learner and so focused."

"I'd like to meet him. You know the Democratic Party is always looking for new talent."

"Yes. Well, there is a debate at home this Friday. How would you like to be one of the judges?"

"Oh. That would be wonderful. Do you think I'm qualified?"

"Sure, of course, you are. I'll put you down. Come about an hour early so I can give you a little orientation."

"I will. Thank you."

Evelyn hung up excited about her meeting with Blinh Lai. She was sure she was finally on the right track and would soon be in a position to find out what was going on at the Timber Creek Ranch.

†††††

Romas and most of the Tarizonians still thought that Sheriff Wade Wilkins hadn't fully recovered after his mysterious accident. It was common knowledge that he could walk but only very slowly and his mind wasn't right. The story that was circulating was that Evelyn had realized that her father could not continue as Sheriff so she had convinced him to take an early retirement. It was assumed that his retirement ended the investigation of his bizarre accident. They had no idea that Sheriff Wilkins hadn't resigned, was mentally and physically fine, and was heading a secret task force with the Sheriff's office and the FBI looking into the unsolved murder in Mineral Wells and the strange weapon used to temporarily incapacitate the witnesses to it.

Romas hoped the investigation was over but didn't entirely believe that Evelyn or the new Sheriff would give up that easily. After consulting with the other leaders of the

GOT, it was decided that someone needed to befriend Evelyn Wilkins, to keep a close eye on her and, if the investigation were ongoing, dissuade her from pushing it further. Blinh Lai volunteered for the job as he had met Evelyn once and thought she was attractive. His father and mother supported the move because they wanted Blinh to be sheriff someday, and they thought Evelyn might pave the way for that to happen.

✝✝✝✝✝

Bellah spotted Tom Schell waiting for her when she left gym class. Her pulse quickened as she wondered how she looked after an hour of playing volleyball and a shower without time to fix her hair. He smiled as he approached her.

"Hey," Tom said. "I was hoping to catch you."

"Oh, hi Tom," she replied with a pleasant smile.

"What's going on?"

"Just the usual. Hey, I checked the newspaper and we are in luck."

She frowned. "How's that?"

"Goldfinger is up!"

"Goldfinger?"

"Yeah. James Bond, 007, you know."

"Oh. That's a movie?"

"Yes. James Bond is a British spy. It's supposed to be totally awesome. You want to go?"

She nodded, thinking a spy movie might be instructive. "Well, sure, sounds interesting, but I'll have to check with my parents to make sure it's okay. They will want to meet you."

"Okay. No problem. How about 5:00 p.m. on Saturday, if that works. I can pick you up and meet your parents then. After that, we'll have time for dinner before the movie."

"Sounds good. I'll check and let you know."

Bellah already knew it would be fine with her parents, but she didn't want to seem too eager. Her mother had warned her that men would take you for granted if you didn't make every date a little bit of a challenge.

"Great!" Tom said. "I'll give you my number so you call me when you find out."

She shook her head. "No. That's alright. I'll tell you in class tomorrow."

Tom shrugged. "Okay. See you tomorrow then."

When she got home she called her mother. "Mom. Are you going to be here this weekend?"

"We can be if you need us. There are always things that need to be done at the ranch."

"Good. Tom is taking me out on a date and I figured you and Dad would want to meet him."

"Yes. Absolutely. When is this happening?"

"He's picking me up at 5:00 p.m. on Saturday. We are going to see a spy movie if you can believe that."

Sarna laughed. "Good. So you can pick up some pointers."

"Yeah, maybe."

"Okay, I'll check with your father, but I'm sure it won't be a problem. We'll come up Saturday morning so we'll be there in plenty of time."

"Good. I'll see you then," Bellah said and hung up.

†††††

Evelyn arrived early for the debate tournament and got the short course from Mrs. Meadows on how to judge a debate. Twenty minutes before the debate was to start, Blinh Lai showed up and Mrs. Meadows introduced them.

"I'm so glad to meet you," Blinh said. "Aren't you the Sheriff's daughter?"

"Yes."

"Sorry about his accident," Blinh said. "I read about it in the paper."

254

"Oh, thank you."

"How's he doing?"

"Not well," Evelyn lied. "He's never really recovered from the concussion."

"That's terrible."

"So, I hear you are quite the debater?"

Blinh blushed. "Who told you that?"

"Your debate coach. She told me you're one of the best she's seen in years."

"Oh, really?"

"That's one of the reasons I came tonight. I wanted to see if you had any interest in politics."

"Politics?" Blinh repeated thoughtfully. "Well, maybe."

"The Democratic Party is always looking for potential candidates. You should consider a career in politics."

Blinh nodded. "Yeah. It sounds exciting."

"Let's get together after the debate. I'd like to get to know you better."

"Sure," Blinh replied. "I'd love that."

"Good. I'll catch you after the debate."

Blinh agreed and they went out to Dairy Queen when the debate was over, each with their own agenda. Over the next few weeks they spent more and more time together and became inseparable.

††††††

On Friday, Bellah caught Tom after gym class and told him she got permission to go out with him. He was thrilled and promised Bellah a memorable evening. On Saturday, Tom arrived at the ranch at 5:00 p.m. as promised. He came in a red Ford Mustang convertible. Many of the children playing out front rushed over to see the fancy sports car. Bellah looked on approvingly as he got out amongst all the excited children. He shook his head and walked over to her.

"You have quite a family?" Tom said.

"Oh, they belong to the ranch hands. I just have my brother Blinh. My parents are in the house. Come on up."

Tom nodded and followed Bellah up to the big ranch house. Markis and Sarna were waiting on the front porch.

"Mom. Dad. This is Tom Schell."

"Good afternoon," Tom said. "It's so nice to meet you."

"Yes. Likewise," Sarna said. "Bellah has told us all about you."

Tom looked at Bellah. "She has, huh?"

Bellah nodded. "Of course. You were my hero helping me out on my first day at school."

"Oh, that was nothing. It was my pleasure."

"So, where do you live, Tom?" Markis asked.

"Actually, just a few miles down the road. We have a ranch too."

"Really? Is it an active ranch or just a place to live?"

"No. It's active. We raise cattle and horses."

"Bellah tells us your father is a state senator?" Sarna said.

Tom smiled proudly. "Yes. He's our representative in Austin. It's an exciting job. Unfortunately, we don't see much of him because of it."

"Well, public service is always a sacrifice."

"Ah. We should get going," Bellah said. "We want to get some dinner before we go to the movie."

"Sure," Sarna said. "It was nice meeting you, Tom. You two have a nice evening."

"We will," Tom promised. "It was a pleasure meeting both of you."

Tom and Bellah waved goodbye and walked quickly back to the Mustang. Tom opened Bellah's door causing her to smile broadly. The children moved away as Tom did a quick u-turn and drove back down the driveway in a cloud of dust. Twenty minutes later they were being seated at Shakey's Pizza in Mineral Wells.

"So, what kind of pizza do you like?" Tom asked.

"Oh, I like pepperoni or sausage. We didn't have pizza in Hungary."

"Really. That's terrible."

"Yes. If I ever go back to the homeland I'm going to open a chain of pizza restaurants. I'll make a killing."

Tom laughed. "I bet you would."

"So, tell me what you father does as a state senator? I'm really curious."

Tom shrugged. "Well, every year the state legislature meets to pass new laws or change old ones. He has to study all of them and then vote for or against them. Of course, he has to consult with the people in our district to get their opinions on each piece of legislation."

"I bet it must be a very lucrative job."

"No. Not really. State legislators don't get paid much."

"But what about the bribes and gifts?"

Tom laughed. "Bribes? No. That doesn't happen—well it happens, but my dad doesn't take bribes."

"He doesn't? Then how do you live if the government doesn't pay that much?" Bellah asked.

"Ah. Well. My dad has an insurance business that does quite well. Being a state senator isn't a full-time job."

The waitress finally came and took their order. While they ate they talked a while about Tom and his family. Then Bellah told Tom about her life in Hungary. She followed her memorized script but added a few real personal stories without mentioning that they took place millions of miles away in another solar system. After the movie, Tom asked if Bellah wanted to come by and see his ranch since it was on the way to her place. It was late, but

Bellah didn't have a curfew so she agreed.

The road into Tom's ranch was paved and followed a white post and rail fence up to the main house. A bright front porch light illuminated the big circular driveway. Tom pulled up, killed the engine and then rushed around to open Bellah's door. She smiled appreciatively and stepped out of the car.

"Wow! This is quite a place. It puts our ranch to shame."

"What are you talking about? Your ranch is great. You've got so much going on. Our place is dead when Mom and Dad are gone."

Bellah raised her eyebrows. "Are you alone here?"

Tom shook his head. "No. There are a ranch foreman and a cook. The housekeeper is just here during the day."

"So, where do they sleep?"

"In the bunkhouse behind the barn."

Bellah laughed. "So, you brought me home on our first date and we are all alone in the big beautiful house?"

Tom shrugged. "Well, I guess."

Bellah shook her head. "So, you think I'm going to be your Bond girl, huh?"

"No. Not at all," Tom said. "I'm sorry. Do you want me to take you home?"

"No, silly. I'm just kidding. I'm dying to see the inside."

Tom sighed. "Good. Come on in, then."

Tom opened the front door and they stepped inside. Bellah marveled at the lavish interior. It reminded her of her home back on Tarizon. Suddenly, she felt a little homesick.

"Come on. I'll show you around."

Bellah nodded and followed Tom into the next room. It was filled with several gun cabinets and there was a bear's head mounted on the wall.

"As you can see my Dad is a big hunter. He collects guns too. Vintage guns from the old west as well as the latest military assault rifles."

"Oh. Wow! I love to shoot," Bellah said she admired the collection.

"Really," Tom said. "You hunt?"

"Sure, but game is in short supply back in my country, so I did mostly target shooting. I was the best shot in my unit."

"What unit?" Tom asked.

"Ah. Our local militia. Everyone over age twelve is part of the militia and must go through rigorous military training."

"Seriously? I didn't realize that about Hungary."

"Yes. We live between Germany and Russia, so we are always in fear of invasion."

"Boy. I bet you are glad to be in America."

Bellah nodded. "So, we should go hunting sometime, huh?"

Tom nodded. "Sure. That would be great."

Bellah smiled. "Good. So, let me see your bedroom. I want to see how messy you are."

Tom laughed. "Well, you are out of luck. The maid cleans my room every morning and I've been out all day today, so I haven't been here to mess it up."

"So, we better go mess it up then," Bellah replied. "Your maid needs to earn her pay."

"Absolutely," Tom agreed taking Bellah's hand and leading her to his bedroom.

At midnight, when Bellah finally made it home, Sarna was waiting anxiously.

"So, how was your date?"

Bellah smiled. "Perfect. Tom's very nice and you should see their ranch. It's quite lavish."

"So, how did you two get along?"

"Don't worry. He's already in love with me. He'll do anything I ask."

"Nice work, honey. I'm proud of you."

Bellah yawned. "Thank you. I'm so tired. Tom wore me out. I think I'm going to go to bed."

"Sure. Good night."

As Bellah went to bed she wondered if this was the life she wanted. Seducing Tom was easy enough, but she didn't get much satisfaction from it. In time she feared she'd be bored to tears with him. She wanted to do something more exciting and, hopefully, more important than seducing a politician's son. She prayed she'd find a way to do it.

27
Bitter News

Once inside his compartment, Sandee went to the kitchen to get them something to eat. It had been a busy day and they hadn't eaten since breakfast. Salina had wanted to hire a housekeeper for them, but Sandee had thought that to be a frivolous expense since they were so rarely home. After he'd found a piece of meat for Snowflake, he was rummaging around the cooler when there was a knock on the door. Annoyed, he stopped what he was doing and went to answer it. When he opened it, his driver was standing there nervously.

"Can't you leave me alone for five loons?" he scolded.

"Sorry, First Minister but there has been an explosion."

"An explosion? Where?"

"Back at your offices. It happened shortly after you left."

Sandee's face turned ashen and he began to tremble. "Was anyone hurt? Tell me nobody was hurt."

"I don't know for sure, but they are reporting that Salina was killed?"

"What? No! Not Salina! It can't be!"

"It's just speculation, I'm sure. But a woman was killed in the blast, and she is the only woman not accounted for."

"Take me there! Take me there, now!" Sandee screamed.

On the way to the office building, they heard sirens

and could see heavy smoke over the city. Sandee thought of Whisper's concern that something had been wrong. He wondered if Whisper had been killed too.

"Why did I just ignore Whisper? I should have stayed with him and helped him figure out what was wrong."

"If you had stayed back to assist him, you may well have been killed too. It was Whisper's job to protect you, so he did the right thing and you were right to leave," Snowflake responded.

When they got two blocks from their destination, they were stopped by public enforcers, who refused to let them pass. Frustrated, Sandee bolted from the Grinden and started running down the street with Snowflake on his heels. When he got near his office building, a member of his security detail recognized him and escorted him to a temporary command center that had been set up. When he saw the Ambassador there sitting on a bench with Whisper at his side, he rushed over to them.

"Is it true? Please tell me it's not true."

The Ambassador looked over at him with grief-stricken eyes, and Sandee instantly knew his beloved Salina was truly dead. Tears welled in his eyes and he angrily wiped them away with the sleeve of his shirt.

"I can't believe she is dead," the Ambassador said. "Many of the staff had left the room, but Salina stayed behind with a few others to finish up. She didn't suffer. The blast was so strong it killed them all instantly."

Sandee slammed his clenched fist against the wooden bench, startling the Ambassador. He was angrier than he'd ever been in his life. He stood up and began pacing. Finally, he stopped and, looking up toward the heavens, silently screamed, "Pelgrem! How could you let this happen? I loved Salina. I needed her. How do you expect me to do this hopeless task without her?"

He waited a moment but there was only silence.

"Answer me!" he screamed out loud this time.

Everyone in the room turned and stared at him. Sandee ignored them, continuing to look upwards toward the heavens.

"Answer me now or strike me dead. I don't care which," he silently pleaded. But Pelgrem didn't answer him nor did he strike him dead. There was nothing but silence in the room and he felt alone, helpless and betrayed.

28
Saying Goodbye

Salina's funeral was held at the National Cathedral in downtown Ya Lat. The thousands of mourners who lined Central Boulevard joined the solemn procession as it passed until it stretched several kylods through the city. For security reasons, the Chancellor, Ambassador, Sandee, and other government officials were brought to the Cathedral in armored vehicles before the funeral parade arrived. Security forces surrounded the Cathedral, adjacent buildings were closed and jet copters flew overhead looking for potential threats.

Pelgrem funeral services were usually short affairs but Salina had been a popular public figure and many wanted to speak about her life. Sandee sat nervously waiting for his turn to speak. Since the bombing, he hadn't been able to sleep and had little appetite. Finally, his time came and he slowly made his way to the lectern. He looked anxious and disheveled.

"Many cycles ago when I was just a boy wandering in the woods with a pack of rhutz, I met Salina Gill. When I told her my crazy story she didn't laugh or doubt a word I said. Instead, she embraced me and offered to help me in any way she could to make my peace mission a success.

"It is a monumental understatement to say I wouldn't have made it this far without her. Only Whisper has helped me as much in this quest for peace.

"It's difficult for me to fathom going on without her. I'm not sure it is even possible. The emptiness and despair

I feel right now are overwhelming and debilitating. I have no will to go on. Perhaps we should just give up and admit defeat. Tarizon is lost. It's just a matter of time before we all will die and our planet will join those billions of other uninhabitable planets that roam the galaxies.

"Salina, I am sorry I failed you. My friends and followers, I'm sorry I wasn't the leader you needed to bring about peace. Pelgrem, I'm sorry I wasn't the man that could save Tarizon.

"Goodbye, my love. Perhaps I will join you soon. Fear not, wherever you have gone, I will find you and we will be together for eternity."

An eerie silence fell over the crowd as Sandee stepped down from the pulpit and returned to his seat. Moments later the crowd erupted in hushed debate over what they had just seen and heard. Was the peace movement really dead or was this just a threat to scare the masses into action? There was no consensus.

Sandee, the Ambassador and Salina's sister Arvis Gill stayed to witness the atomization of Salina's remains following the ceremony. With so many people dying each cycle on Tarizon, this quick and effective procedure for the disposal of human remains had become mandatory in Lyon.

The witnesses were led to a small room in the basement of the Cathedral. Two technicians carried her body into a clear cylinder chamber in the center of the room and put it on a white table. When they had cleared the cylinder, the operator pushed a button, there was a flash of light, then a dry cloud of debris began swirling around the cylinder. When the debris settled, the body was gone.

A tear ran down Sandee's cheek and Arvis fainted. The Ambassador caught her and pulled her into his arms. Sandee helped him get her to a chair. Then, without a word, he turned and left with Snowflake and his security detail scampering to keep up.

29
Depression

Depression quickly consumed Sandee, and for nearly twenty days he stayed in his compartment, eating very little and refusing to communicate with anyone. Even Whisper could not get through to him telepathically as Sandee had thrown up an impenetrable wall in his mind. Each day Sandee would sit in a chair next to the window and stare down at the crowded street below, but see nothing. His thoughts were consumed exclusively with memories of Salina.

On the street below his compartment, hundreds milled around waiting for some word from Sandee about the future of his peace mission. Many had followed him all over Tarizon and could not believe he had given up. So, instead of going home they prayed to Pelgrem for Sandee to recover from his grief and get on with his mission to save Tarizon.

Arvis visited Sandee every day. She had promised her sister that if anything ever happened to her that she would look after Sandee. In the past, Sandee would get so caught up in his work that he would forget to eat or sleep. Arvis made sure Sandee didn't starve. She brought him food or cooked for him every day and wouldn't leave him at night until he was asleep.

After a while, Sandee began to open up to Arvis and they would talk about Salina or what was going on in the General Assembly in his absence. It was on the twentieth day after Salina's death that their discussion turned to Sandee's future.

"You can't just quit now," Arvis argued. "Salina would want you to go on. She loved you but she loved God too, and she'd want you to keep your promise to Him."

"Why can't Pelgrem just make people want peace? He's a god, isn't he? Can't He do anything?"

"No, I don't think so. He made each of the life-forms on Tarizon free and independent. All He can do is show us the way we should live our lives, and hope that we pay attention. He came to you because the human race wasn't listening to Him. He needed a leader the people could see, hear and touch, someone they could interact with. You are his messenger and if you quit now all hope for peace on Tarizon will be gone."

"Why did He pick me?" Sandee complained again. "What did I do to deserve this curse?"

Arvis shook her head. "You could have died with your family. Would you have preferred that fate?"

Sandee sighed. "No."

"He called on the rhutz to save your life, so you could save millions more. That makes you the most important person on the planet. If I were you, I'd be grateful."

"I am grateful," Sandee replied, "but why did He have to take away Salina? I miss her so much."

Arvis put her arms around him and squeezed him tightly. "I know. I miss her too. Unfortunately, many more will lose their lives before this is all over."

Whether Arvis's words were prophetic, or just a coincidence nobody knows, but on the following day, shocking news from Synclare dominated the news. Just after breakfast, Sandee's wrist array alerted him to the breaking story. He told Arvis to turn on the VC. She did, and the image of Veile Shante appeared in her studio. As she was speaking, viewers could see the image of three mushroom clouds billowing ominously over Roshaunda. Veile gasped in horror at the sight, and then grimly began reading the story.

"There was a devastating nuclear strike by Soni against the holy city of Roshaunda in Synclare just loons ago. Hundreds of thousands are presumed dead as the strike took the nation by complete surprise. Not only was there no warning of the attack, but our sources tell us that a Soni advance team infiltrated Synclare's Central Command Center, and sabotaged their missile defense system. With no warning and no defenses operational, most of the city's districts were obliterated, hundreds of thousands killed, and many more wounded.

"Just after the strike, Soni troops began pouring across the border between the two countries, however, reports from the front line indicate they were met with stiff resistance and, for the moment, their advance has been stopped.

"One of the bombs vaporized Synclare's Capitol Building, but there is no word as to the fate of the Synclare government. Informed sources have reported to us that the Chancellor, at least, was not at the Capitol when the attack occurred. Any government officials at or near the capitol were surely killed. Fortunately, the attack took place when the General Assembly was not in session, so many lawmakers were back in the home districts when the attack took place.

"Stay tuned for updates as they come in."

Arvis turned off the VC and looked at Sandee. He had buried his face in his hands. There was a knock on the door. Arvis opened it and saw it was Ambassador Talvihn. She stepped back, and let him in.

"Have you seen the news?" the Ambassador asked.

"Yes, we were just watching it," Arvis replied.

"I came to discuss what should be done."

"It's a little late," Sandee said. He looked pale and broken.

The Ambassador stared at Sandee for a moment. He could see now that Sandee had been devastated by what had happened.

"All those people are dead because I let my grief debilitate me. Again, I have failed Pelgrem!" Sandee said bitterly.

"It's not your fault," the Ambassador reasoned. "Even if you'd gone to Soni before the attack, there is no guarantee you could have done anything to stop it."

"You don't know that. Instead of feeling sorry for myself, I should have been there trying to talk some sense into them. That would have been the right thing to do."

"You're only human, you had to grieve. Quit beating yourself up, and move on."

"Indeed, that is what I must do," Sandee said, taking a deep breath. "Should I go to Soni now?"

"It would be very dangerous. I'm sure any day now Synclare will be retaliating."

Sandee took a deep breath. "True, but I have to try something."

"Perhaps you should go to Synclare and convince them not to retaliate. Someone has to take the first step in bringing about peace."

Sandee nodded. "It won't be easy to convince them, but I think you are right. We have to end this madness now."

That afternoon, for the first time since Salina's death, Sandee went out on his balcony and looked out over the sea of faces of those who hadn't given up on him. It was Fall and getting cold, but he managed a smile and a wave before he went back inside. The crowd responded with cheers and chants of "Peace Now!" As he stepped back into his compartment he felt much better. His depression was gone and he began to feel excited about his upcoming trip to Synclare. There was still hope of bringing peace to Tarizon. He just had to be patient.

Since Roshaunda had been destroyed by the recent nuclear strike, the Capitol had been moved north to Kinomba. Soni controlled the entire southern half of Synclare now and Sandee would have to get to Kinomba from the North Sea through Pohl. This was a long trip by ship which was the safest method of transport, but Sandee didn't think he'd get there in time to stop the retaliation if he took such a slow mode of transportation.

With half the world at war, flying was a very dangerous way to travel. Most nations would shoot down any unknown aircraft crossing through their airspace. Even if permission were sought and acquired, there was no guarantee that hostile forces in the area might attack, thinking they were enemy planes. So, the only solution was to fly well out to sea and not over any nation's airspace. This meant Sandee had to fly over 2,000 kylods across the North Sea to the city of Rappadat in Pohl, and then travel by jet copter to Kinomba. Going out over the North Sea was way out of the way and stretched the aircraft's range to the limit. And there was no guarantee once they got to Pohl that they'd be allowed to land or be provided fuel for their return trip to Ya Lat.

Nevertheless, the Ambassador volunteered his private air transporter for the peace mission, and they were off three days later. Arvis volunteered to come along as Sandee's personal assistant, while Whisper and several other rhutz agreed to act as his bodyguards. The Ambassador, his staff and a small security detail filled out the rest of the entourage. Three fighters were provided by Lyon's air force to act as escorts for the diplomatic mission and to report back to the Chancellor should anything go wrong.

They had attempted to communicate with the Synclare government about their mission but hadn't gotten a response. This was understandable since the government had been forced to move in such a hurry and was undoubtedly in disarray. So they contacted the government of their northern neighbor, Pohl. Pohl and Synclare had been allies in the past, so it was hoped they would be able to assist in making contact.

As they approached Rappadat they held their breath. Pohl hadn't promised anything when they got the Chancellor's communique other than to pass on the message. Sandee hoped and prayed they'd let them land and continue on by jet copter to Kinomba. When the pilot radioed the airport, there was a long delay before they responded with landing instructions.

"Thank God!" the Ambassador said. "I was afraid we'd have to land on the beach."

Sandee sighed. "Yes. That would have ended our peace mission pretty quickly."

"What are you going to do now?" Arvis asked.

"I'm hoping they've sent an emissary to deal with us," the Ambassador replied. "We'll know soon enough."

After they'd taxied up to the terminal, a security transporter pulled up, and four men got out into the cold night air. Three of them wore grey and black security uniforms, heavy jackets and were armed with lasers. The other donned purple diplomatic attire. When the pilot opened the door and lowered the stairs, the security guards ran up and rushed inside the plane as if to seize control of it. Sandee raised his hands in a gesture of surrender. They ignored him and rushed by to search the cabin. When the men were satisfied there were no threats within the plane, they disembarked. The diplomat then walked up the stairs and into the aircraft. The Ambassador greeted him.

"Hello. I'm Ambassador Talvihn from Lyon."

The man bowed slightly and replied, "I'm Vice Minister Trill Lankershank."

"I trust you were expecting us?" the Ambassador said.

The diplomat nodded. "Yes, but we never agreed that you could come. We are not involved in the war between Soni and Synclare. I'm afraid we cannot help you."

"Although we would like your support, that's not why we are here. This is simply the quickest way for us to get to the new government in Kinomba. We were hoping to acquire the use of a few jet copters for the remainder of our journey."

Trill frowned. "What exactly do you hope to accomplish by contacting the Synclare government? Their capital city has already been destroyed. It's a little late to be on a peace mission."

"We understand that," Sandee replied.

"Oh, I'm sorry," the Ambassador said, stepping aside and gesturing to Sandee. "This is Sandee Brahn. I'm sure you've heard of him."

"Yes," he said bowing slightly to Sandee. "I am familiar with your peace mission and I support it."

"Thank you," Sandee replied.

"But, I'm not optimistic about your chances of success."

"I can understand that," Sandee said. "But we have to try for the sake of Tarizon. Don't you agree?"

"I suppose so, but I'm not sure I can get you jet copters. The diplomatic corps does not have automatic access to them. We can only get them from the military, and they are rather stingy about granting such use in these uncertain times."

"Speed is important," the Ambassador stressed. "If we have to go by surface transporter it could take several more days and I'm sure Synclare will be retaliating soon."

"Yes. That's likely."

"We can't let that happen," Sandee said. "We have to stop this insanity now or there will never be peace on Tarizon."

Trill sighed. "Let me see what I can do. I have a few friends in the army who owe me favors. This might be a good time to collect them."

"Thank you!" Sandee replied appreciatively.

They were escorted off the plane and taken by transporter to an empty army barracks where Trill said they could relax while he checked on the jet copters. Whisper and the other rhutz remained outside to survey their surroundings and try to make contact with the local rhutz population.

Shortly after Trill had left, three women showed up at the barracks door and inquired if Sandee Brahn were there. Sandee immediately got up and greeted them. They each were carrying two bags of food and drink which they took to a table inside. The eldest of the women said her name was Landa Lanorf.

"How did you know I was here?" Sandee asked.

"We heard rumors of your mission to Synclare days ago, and have been watching the skies praying for your safe arrival."

"Well, thank you for coming, and for bringing us food."

"It is the least we can do after all that you have sacrificed on our behalf."

Tears welled in Sandee's eyes. "Yes, I miss Salina terribly. We can't let her death be in vain."

"Tell us what we can do, and we will gladly do it," Landa promised.

"Spread the word that we are here and that we need everyone to speak up for peace. If enough voices are raised the politicians and military officers responsible for this war will have to listen. We have the power to stop them, we just need to unite and show them our strength."

Within a kyloon, more than a dozen rhutz had shown up and hundreds of additional followers had arrived. The three security officers Trill had left stood by the door to the barracks and eyed the crowd and rhutz warily. They looked up when they heard the sound of jet copters in the distance.

The Ambassador and Sandee had heard the sound too and came outside. Soon three copters were landing on a parking lot two hundred strides to the north. Trill stepped out of the first copter and the crowd parted to let him walk through and join them.

"Pelgrem must really be with you," Trill said. "Look at this crowd."

"Yes," Sandee replied with a warm smile. "He is."

"Well, there were three copters available when I got to the base. That's very unusual."

"Excellent," the Ambassador said. "Did your friend give you any trouble when you called in your favor?"

"No. Apparently, the unit commander is very nervous over the situation in Synclare and is hopeful your peace effort will be successful. So far Pohl has not suffered a nuclear strike, and everyone wants to avoid such a disaster at all cost."

"That's a relief," Sandee said. "I feared the government would be controlled by war profiteers and would be hostile to our efforts."

"No," Trill assured him. "Our military seeks only to protect the government and the people."

"So, do they know where we can find Synclare's government?" the Ambassador asked.

"Yes. They've sent us escorts who know the precise locations to make sure we get there safely."

"We?"

"Yes, they're insisting I go along to introduce you to whoever is in charge now. We're not certain who that is, but I know most of their senior leadership."

"Excellent," the Ambassador said. "Glad to have you on the mission."

"They've also alerted the Synclare air command that we will be coming, so they will let us through."

"That's good to hear," the Ambassador said, appearing somewhat relieved. "Now all we have to worry about are Soni fighters."

"That is a real danger, I'm afraid," Trill said, "but our pilots will be flying low and it will be difficult for a fighter to spot us."

"We should go then," Sandee said. "We only have a few more kyloons of daylight. I don't want to get there after dark and miss talking with them today. They may be planning a retaliatory strike in the morning."

"Sure. Get your people aboard. We're ready," Trill assured them.

Sandee and the Ambassador went inside the barracks, and soon everyone was streaming out toward the three jet copters. Within a few loons, they were onboard and heading south, gliding just above the trees, toward Synclare. As Sandee looked out over the thick forest below, he felt his stomach twist. How would he convince Synclare not to retaliate? Those left in the government would be under tremendous pressure to make Soni pay for what they had done. Would they even consider his pleas for restraint, or was he wasting his time? A sudden wave of hopelessness washed over him.

"Remember, Pelgrem is with you!" Whisper thought. *"He will show you the way."*

Sandee looked over at Whisper but her thoughts did little to comfort him.

30
Politics & Business

A lot had happened since the Tarizon Evacuees' 1962 landing at Possum Kingdom Lake. After they purchased the Timber Creek Ranch, they were finally able to house everyone comfortably and keep a low profile while they all adjusted to their new home on Earth. With the help of the previous owner, Jaime Briggs, they learned the cattle business and even a little farming. By the time Jaime's consulting contract ended, the ranch was doing quite well. Not surprisingly, once they were on their own and free to implement their advanced technology, production increased dramatically. Amongst the settlers were some very talented scientists, engineers, chemists, and biologists who watched and learned from Briggs but had to act dumb so he wouldn't get suspicious. Once he was gone, they made dramatic changes to the operation of the ranch with the result that production doubled within two years.

In 1964 Eroh and Ritz were starters on the Mineral Wells High School Football team but at mid-season the GOT made them fake injuries and quit the team because their notoriety was bringing too much scrutiny on the Tarizonian community. Rammel and Blinh didn't have that problem as the debate and moot court teams didn't get much press. They both remained on their teams and did quite well until their graduation in 1965.

The two oil wells on the property turned out to be a lucrative bonus. Once the GOT Board learned how oil leases worked, they bought out their own oil lease from the production company that had drilled their wells for a small bag of diamonds. The oil executive on the receiving end of the diamond exchange thought he'd made out like a bandit until he found out a year later that the sellers had increased production from 10 to 150 barrels a day.

After meeting Blinh at the debate tournament Evelyn and he began to date and within a year they had gotten engaged. Blinh knew he had to keep Evelyn very busy so she'd forget about her father's mysterious accident. While Wade was Sheriff, Evelyn and he had been heavily involved in the Democratic Party. But after the accident, Evelyn seemed to have lost interest in politics. Once they were engaged, however, Blinh insisted they attend all the local party meetings and rallies. Since she knew everyone on the local political scene, she introduced Blinh to the party bosses and many of the local politicians.

Blinh was gregarious, liked parties and social events, so he was an instant hit with many of the Democratic Party leaders. In fact, it wasn't long before people were suggesting he should run for office. Evelyn at first resisted that idea claiming she hadn't fully gotten over her father's accident, but in time she warmed to the idea and suggested he should run for Sheriff. The interim Sheriff, Walter Hudson, had been a disappointment to the Party and they were looking for someone to run against him in the primaries.

Normally the GOT Board would not encourage one of their group to get involved in politics, but the prospect of having one of their own as County Sheriff excited them. As Sheriff, Blinh could provide much-needed security for the Tarizonians while they were assimilating, and he would be in a position to warn them if trouble was brewing. So, with Evelyn's support and the encouragement of the GOT Board, Blinh put his hat in the ring.

The incumbent Walter Hudson immediately jumped on Blinh's youth and inexperience in law enforcement as a reason not to vote for the newcomer. Anticipating this line of attack, Evelyn asked the Mineral Wells' police chief to hire Blinh and put him through their police training program. He did, and Blinh passed with flying colors. With this experience and training behind him, Evelyn on his arm at every event, and so many local Democratic leaders behind him, when election day rolled around few voters seemed concerned about Blinh's youth or lack of experience.

Evelyn organized a watch party on the day of the primary election and invited everyone she knew to come to join them while they waited for the election results. The party was held at the local VFW hall, and when Blinh and Evelyn arrived, the place was packed, and the music was loud.

Seeing them walk through the door, Bellah and her date, Tom Schell, came over. Upon graduation, Tom had joined his father's casualty insurance business to help run things when Sam was in Austin performing his duties as a state senator.

"So, the hour of reckoning has come," Bellah teased.

"I guess so," Blinh replied. "I hope I don't get my ass kicked."

"No way," Evelyn assured him. "You're going to win by a landslide."

"She's right," Sam agreed. "You're a shoo-in, so let's go get some beers and get this party rolling."

After they'd gotten their drinks, they found a table and huddled around it. "So, how are things out at the ranch?" Tom asked.

"Busy," Blinh replied. "Another well came in this week."

"Another one. Wow! That's the sixth or seventh this year isn't it?"

"Eleventh," Bellah corrected.

Tom shook his head. "You are one lucky son of a bitch. We've had three dry holes on our property and we're not three miles from your place. My dad sunk over a hundred and fifty-grand into those wells."

Blinh shrugged, "Well, we have the best geologist in the business. He told us exactly where to drill and how deep we'd have to go."

"You drilled the well yourself?"

"Ah, yeah we have some guys on the ranch who used to work on a rig."

"Huh. You're going to have to give me your geologist's number. Maybe he can figure out where the oil is hiding on our property."

"Sure, but he's pretty busy. Good luck booking him. I remember we had to wait quite a long while before he came out."

"Hmm. My dad is going to be pissed when I tell him about this. He'll want to come over and talk to your crew tomorrow."

"Oh," Bellah interrupted. "Not tomorrow. There's a going-away barbeque for some of our friends."

"Oh, where are they going?"

"They have to report for duty. They were drafted into the Army and are leaving for boot camp."

"Really? Well, later in the week, then."

"Sure. We'll talk to the rig foreman and see when it would be a good time for you to come."

A man went up to the microphone and tapped on it three times. "May I have your attention, please. I'm Joe Bean, the county chairman, in case you don't know me. During the night I will be announcing election results as the precincts report, and I just got my first one handed to me." He held up a piece of paper and began reading. "In the 15th precinct in the race for sheriff, the vote is 88 for Sheriff Hudson and 77 for Blinh Lai."

There were boos and groans of disappointment.

"Shoot," Evelyn said. "Oh, well. The 15th precinct

isn't very important."

Tom stood up and smiled. "Anybody need another beer?" he asked.

"I could use one," Evelyn said and stood up. "I'll come with you. I need to use the ladies' room."

Tom looked at Bellah expectantly.

"I'm good," Bellah added.

"You can get me another one," Blinh replied.

Tom and Evelyn left and headed toward the bar.

"You shouldn't brag about our production," Bellah admonished. "We don't need people snooping around the ranch."

"You should talk! Why did you mention the going-away party?"

"I needed an excuse to keep Tom's Dad from coming over. In a few days, hopefully, he'll forget about our new wells."

"Well, I don't know the point of trying to hide our oil wells. Anybody with a pair of eyes can see the rigs popping up. We can't really hide what we are doing. Plus, the noise the rigs make while we are drilling can be heard five miles in every direction."

"I know," Bellah replied. "Just don't draw any more attention to it."

"Okay. So, what's the final count of new recruits entering the Army?" Blinh asked.

"Sixteen."

Blinh laughed. "The Board is going to be livid when they find out sixteen of our citizens are going into the U.S. Army."

"Yeah. Can you imagine what they'd do to us if they knew we were behind them being drafted?"

"Or, what they'd do if they knew Dad ordered us to do it."

Bellah stood up. "There's Ritz," she said as she waved

to him. "Over here." Ritz saw her waving and came over.

"Where have you been?" Bellah asked. "You're an hour late."

"Yeah. I went to my first Klan meeting. I didn't realize it would last so long."

"You joined the Ku Klux Klan?" Bellah asked incredulously.

"I did. You know they have the same problem here on Earth with darkies and Jews as we have with Seafolken and the mutants back on Tarizon."

"You're not supposed to join any political organizations, Ritz," Bellah reminded him. "The Board will be angry if they find out, and your father will have a stroke."

"Too bad. If Blinh can join the Democratic Party and run for Sheriff, I ought to be able to burn a few crosses with my Earth-friends."

Blinh laughed. "He's right, Bellah. It's only fair."

Bellah shrugged. "Well, I'm not going to say anything to anybody, obviously. I'm just worried the Board might find out and restrict you to the ranch, or, worse yet, your father finds out and kills you."

Ritz laughed. "Don't worry. I wear a white robe and a hood at our gatherings, so nobody will know I'm even there."

Bellah shook her head and looked away. She saw Tom and Evelyn returning and smiled.

Tom walked up and put two bottles of beer down in front of Blinh and Ritz.

"Thanks," Blinh said.

"I saw you finally made it," Tom said to Ritz, "so, I brought you one, too."

"Great. Thanks. I did work up quite a thirst. It gets hot wearing those thick robes and a hood."

"Robes?" Tom asked.

"Nothing," Bellah said, frowning at Ritz. "He's

joking."

Joe Bennett stood in front of the microphone and tapped it a few times. "Okay, I have two more precincts in, Precincts 11 and 3. With those two added the vote tally stands now at Sheriff Hudson with 232 votes and Blinh Lai with 201."

There were sighs of disappointment. Evelyn grimaced. "Those must be areas out in the country where you're not well known, Honey," Evelyn explained. "Wait until the Mineral Wells' precincts come in."

"I hope you're right," Blinh replied. "I'm starting to get nervous."

"It wouldn't be the end of the world if you lost," Tom suggested. "You've got a good job with the Mineral Wells Police Department."

Evelyn glared at Tom, and Bellah jabbed him in the shoulder.

"Okay, I'm just saying," Tom said meekly.

"Who would vote for that bastard Hudson?" Ritz asked. "I heard he makes more under-the-table money from pimps and madams than the county pays him in salary."

"Where did you hear that?" Blinh asked skeptically.

"From my dad," Ritz replied. "One of the madams is a patient."

Blinh laughed. "Your father has a madam for a patient?"

"Of course, he does. There's an arrangement. I'll explain it to you later."

Blinh frowned.

Evelyn sighed. "Yeah. They offered my dad money all the time to leave them alone, but he wouldn't take a dime. He tolerated prostitution more than I would have, but he said as long as nobody got hurt, they didn't use drugs, and they kept a low profile he wouldn't make them a high priority."

"I don't know if I agree with that policy," Blinh said. "I thought I had to swear to uphold the law."

"You do, but there are limited resources, so you have to set priorities."

Blinh nodded thoughtfully.

There was some static from the microphone. They looked up and Joe Bennett was getting ready to announce some more results. "Ladies and Gentlemen, we have quite a few new precincts reporting. Let's see, there's Precincts 7, 9, 13, 18, 21, and 26. To save time I will just give the totals right now: Hudson 3,731 and Lai 4,216."

There were screams of delight and applause from the crowd. Evelyn and Bellah stood up and clapped. Tom offered his hand to Blinh to congratulate him. Blinh accepted it and they shook hands vigorously.

"See," Evelyn said. "I told you that you'd win."

"It's not over yet. There are still a few precincts out," Blinh noted.

"Don't be such a pessimist," Evelyn complained. "You're only going to widen your lead, Honey."

Blinh raised his eyebrows. "If you say so."

Evelyn turned out to be right, and at 10:32 p.m. Hudson conceded the race. It was a monumental day in American politics, yet there were no TV broadcasts or newspaper headlines reporting the event. Nobody even suspected that on May 7, 1965, an extraterrestrial being had been elected to political office in the United States!

31
Flight to Synclare

Their flight to Synclare was uneventful until they caught sight of the Kinomba River in the distance. Suddenly, two Soni fighters appeared on their radar. The pilot's voice crackled over the com-system, "Fasten your seatbelts and brace yourself, enemy fighters coming at us, taking evasive action."

Sandee tightened his grip on the arms of his seat. The jet copter veered violently to the right then dipped down into a canyon. Sandee saw two missiles fly by and heard thunderous explosions as the first missile hit a tree and then another struck a huge boulder. Arvis grabbed his hand and held it tightly.

He looked over at her. "It's okay," Sandee assured her. "Pelgrem will protect us."

She flashed a smile, but it didn't last. He put his arm around her and drew her close. The copter lurched left and then shot upward barely clearing a wooded hilltop. There were more explosions beneath them. Sandee looked out the portal and saw the Kinomba River. The copter dipped down and flew just twenty feet above the water.

It was quiet for a few loons, and then the pilot's voice came over the com-system once again. "I think we lost them," he advised.

The Ambassador breathed a sigh of relief and looked over at Sandee and Arvis with a grin. "Thank God! I don't think I have ever prayed so hard in my life."

Sandee smiled. "Good. Consider it practice for later

on when we start negotiating."

The copter veered right and headed back over the treetops. The sun was setting and it was starting to get dark. After another kyloon, they saw Kinomba ahead. It was an old city built mainly of wooden, single story homes and businesses. Streets and highways were interwoven through the city in random meandering patterns. Sandee thought it looked beautiful from above, but rather inefficient for getting around the city quickly.

When they finally reached the reported location of the new government on the south side of the city, they landed their copters in an empty field and got out to regroup. Many local citizens were watching them curiously from a distance, but no one approached them.

"I guess we need to figure out who is in charge," the Ambassador said.

"I'll find out," Trinh said, and then dashed off to the closest group of people watching them. After talking to one of them, he returned and pointed west. "The new government complex is about a kylod this way. Unfortunately, I'm told it's closed for the day."

The Ambassador frowned. "Then I suppose we better start looking for a place to stay for the night."

Just then an ATV came up from behind them and skidded to a halt. They all turned around and stared at a public enforcer as he got out and approached them, "Who are you?" he demanded. His name tag revealed he was PE Rhint Slepp.

Trill stepped up. "Vice Minister Trill Lankershank from Pohl's Foreign Office. We are here to meet with Chancellor Tranille."

"Who is we?" Slepp asked irritably.

"Oh, sorry. This is Ambassador Talvihn, and First Minister Sandee Brahn from Lyon."

The PE frowned. "Why are you here? Don't you know

what's happened?"

"Yes, the nuclear strikes. That's why we came."

"I seriously doubt the Chancellor has time to see you."

"It's urgent," Sandee said. "Can you take us to him?"

The PE shook his head. "No. We can't get past security at this late hour. Besides, the Chancellor doesn't live in the government compound at night."

"Where does he go?"

"That's kept secret. There are many assassins lurking about."

Trill sighed. "Is there somewhere to get lodging for the night?"

"No. With the government in town every available room is taken."

"That's okay," Sandee said. "This won't be the first night I have slept under the sky. Is there any rain in the forecast?"

"No, but there is radiation fog heading this way. If you get caught out in the open when it comes, it will make you very sick. You should get back in your jet copters, and go back to Pohl. There's nothing you can do here."

As they were arguing a woman stepped up to Sandee and asked, "Are you Sandee Brahn?"

Sandee smiled. "Yes, I am."

The woman knelt and said, "It's an honor to be in your presence."

The PE looked at the woman angrily and said, "Get up! Leave us. He's going back to Pohl."

The woman stiffened. "But this is Sandee Brahn. You can't send God's messenger away."

"There's no place for him or his entourage."

"They can stay with me," the woman said.

The PE looked at Sandee and his entourage and laughed. "Right. You have room for what . . . twenty guests?"

"I can take two or three, and I'll find others who will

take in the rest."

"Thank you," Sandee said. "That is very generous of you. What is your name?"

"Coraleeta Winzell, but please call me Cora."

"I don't know what we would have done had you not shown up."

"Oh, it's nothing. I'm the lucky one to have crossed your path. Let me make a few calls to arrange everything."

Cora punched a code into her communicator and after a tik began talking. After a few loons, she looked up. "Come. We must get all of you under shelter quickly. The radiation cloud will be here soon."

"Okay, Cora," Sandee said. "Lead the way."

By this time a crowd had gathered around them, and as Cora led them away the crowd followed. They were in a residential neighborhood, and as they walked people came out of their houses as if a parade were passing by. Many joined the procession as it made its way through Kinomba. When Cora got to her home, she invited Sandee, the Ambassador, and Trill inside. The others were escorted to other homes in the neighborhood where Cora promised they would be safe for the night. Whisper and the other rhutz stood guard outside. After they'd each been shown to their rooms and freshened up, they assembled in the dining room where Cora's daughters had prepared them a meal.

"This is so generous of you," Sandee said as he looked at the impressive array of meats, vegetables, and desserts.

Gesturing to two young ladies Cora replied, "You can thank my daughters, Mara and Sutra. I called them first, and told them we were having company."

The two girls smiled as Sandee looked over at them. "Thank you. This looks very appetizing."

"Their mates were called back into military service last cycle when Soni started making threats against us. I never thought we'd be in danger here or I wouldn't have invited them to come here. We were shocked when the government decided to move to Kinomba and put us all at risk."

"Well, if we are successful, there won't be any further escalation of the fighting."

"That's good to hear," Cora said. "Why don't you tell us all about that while we eat?"

Sandee agreed and everyone took a seat. After Sandee thanked Pelgrem for delivering them safely to Kinomba and into Cora's home, they all began eating diligently. A while later, Sandee began explaining his plans.

"I know your government is planning retaliation for Soni's nuclear strike, but that will just lead to another counterstrike and thousands more will die in the process. We have to bring an end to this now."

"Yes, I agree," Cora said. "But that will be a hard sell to our generals."

"Indeed it will, but have you heard about our success in Lyon? Finally, after many cycles of hard work our government firmly supports peace."

"Yes, that's wonderful."

"And the North Sea Alliance is close to joining the Peace Movement as well. That would mean nearly a third of Tarizon's nation-states are with us. So, we are at a crossroads here and now. That's why it is so important to put an end to this Soni-Synclare war immediately."

"I can see that," Cora said. "Is there anything we can do to help?"

"Yes, the people of Synclare need to rise up and show their leaders that they want this war to stop. That's what finally happened in Lyon, and the government could no longer ignore us."

"You have many followers here. I am sure they will be glad to help. You just need to tell them what to do."

"If it wasn't too dangerous, I would have them follow

us tomorrow when we go to meet the Chancellor. If he sees thousands of his citizens standing with us, he will be forced to listen."

"Don't worry," Cora said. "While you are sleeping tonight, I will get the word out. I'm certain tomorrow the streets will be filled with your followers."

"No. You can't ask them to do that," Trill said. "It is too dangerous with the radiation levels so high. They should stay indoors where they have some protection."

"Although our homes do provide some protection, we can't stay in them all the time, and we don't," Cora replied. "We have to go to work and go about our daily routines to survive. There are drugs and protective clothing to help us endure the high radiation levels."

Sandee smiled. "She's right. We all must be brave and selfless. We are doing Pelgrem's will so He will protect us."

Cora nodded and stood up. "If you will excuse me, it's getting late. I better start getting the word out about tomorrow. Mara and Sutra will make sure you have everything you need tonight to be comfortable."

"Thank you," Sandee said. "You have been very kind and generous. Your good deeds will be rewarded."

Cora shrugged. "A peaceful world will be ample reward for me."

Cora left, and while Mara and Sutra began cleaning up, Sandee, the Ambassador, and Trill moved to the living room to drink Sankee and discuss how best to approach Chancellor Tranille in the morning, should they be lucky enough to see him. Once they had agreed on a strategy, Sandee went to bed but he couldn't sleep. There was simply too much at stake, and he was worried that Synclare might launch their retaliatory strike before they even got an audience with the Chancellor.

32
Retaliation

Spring 6 BU

Sandee was awakened by the sound of barking outside his window. When he peered out he saw two rhutz fighting over the hind leg of a range deer. He looked at his wrist array and saw it was nearly time to get up. It would be light soon and he wanted to get an early start on their journey to the government complex.

When he made it to the dining room he saw that the Ambassador and Trill were already eating. "Good morning," he said as he sat down at the dining room table next to them. "I can't believe I slept this late."

"We wanted you to be rested," Cora said as she brought him a plate of pollo eggs and pribett strips. "It's going to be a long day."

"So, what about you, did you get any sleep?" Sandee asked.

"No," Cora replied. "I'll sleep once you've convinced the Chancellor to stop this senseless war."

Sandee sighed heavily. "Yes. We will all sleep better once that happens."

"I told everyone to gather along the streets leading to the government complex. We will pick them up on our way. I'm hopeful the turnout will be satisfactory."

"I'm sure it will," Sandee said smiling. "Pelgrem will make sure of that."

"I hope so," Cora said warily. "I see the rhutz are in force."

"Oh, really?" Sandee said.

"Yes, there are hundreds of them outside. Didn't you hear them barking?"

Sandee laughed, "Yes, I did but I didn't know there were so many. Whisper is a pretty good recruiter and when your life-form can communicate with their minds it makes the task a bit easier."

When they had eaten, they all gathered outside. It was a cold winter day and the sun was nowhere to be seen. Sandee pulled on his heavy coat and began the long trek to the government center. Whisper and the other rhutz led the way followed by Sandee, his entourage and a growing crowd of Synclare's citizens following in the rear. By the time they got back to where they'd left their helicopters the night before the crowd stretched behind them for nearly two kylods.

As they approached they saw Enforcer Slepp standing in front of his patrol vehicle with several other enforcers with grim looks on their faces. "Good morning," Slepp said as they approached.

Sandee nodded, "Good morning, Enforcer Slepp. I hope you have good news for us."

PE Slepp shook his head. "Not yet. I advised the Chancellor's chief of staff of your arrival and desire to meet with the Chancellor, but I have not gotten a response as yet. I'm afraid they don't understand why you are here since Soni started the war and are the aggressor."

"Well, we will explain all of that when we meet," the Ambassador replied.

"That's what I told him, but he said to keep you here until I got word that they were ready to receive you."

"We have to speak to the Chancellor before any retaliation takes place," Sandee insisted.

Enforcer Slepp looked nervously over the large crowd following Sandee. "I guess we can proceed to the government compound," Enforcer Slepp replied, "but I can't guarantee you will get past the front gate."

"That's okay," Sandee said. "We'll worry about that when we get there. Let's go."

Enforcer Slepp and the other enforcers got into their patrol vehicles and drove ahead of the procession as it slowly made its way to the government complex. All along the way, people continued to join the group until its numbers swelled into the tens of thousands. Along the way, a herd of zodillo joined them, walking in single file parallel to the main procession.

When they finally reached the front gate a kyloon later, it was heavily guarded and they were told to halt. Sandee obeyed and halted the procession, then sent Trill to see if they were going to be let in. He came back with a member of Chancellor Errol Tranille's staff. Trill introduced him as Sall Banus, Deputy Chief of Staff.

"I'm afraid you have wasted your time," Banus said. "The Chancellor does not have time to meet with you. We are about to launch a counterattack on Soni. It's too late for talk. Nothing you say could change his mind."

"I must see him. He cannot launch a counterattack. We have to put an end to hostilities at once."

"You should have told that to Chancellor Marcez before he started this war. It's too late now."

Sandee knew that Chancellor Illeez Marcez of Soni was a good friend of Cornelius Bruda and a staunch enemy of the peace movement. That was another reason he had elected to go to Synclare first rather than to Soni once hostilities had broken out.

"I know," Sandee said. "It is partially my fault for grieving too long for my mate who was brutally murdered by the same people who were behind the attack on Synclare. I'm deeply sorry I let you down."

"Well," Banus said, "I can't fault you for being human and Synclare is a peace-loving state, so I appreciate what you have done to bring peace to Tarizon. But it's too late, the General Assembly has already authorized us to retaliate and the order has been given."

"Let us in, please," Sandee pleaded. "When Chancellor Tranille sees how badly his citizens want peace, perhaps he will postpone the retaliation and sit down and listen to me."

"No! I have my orders. Now turn around and get your followers out of here. You have endangered their lives by bringing them here. Once the retaliation has begun, this complex will be Soni's number one target."

Sandee took a deep breath. He looked over at Whisper and then at the Zodillo to his left. "Clear a way for us, my friend," he thought.

The Zodillo started forward toward the blockade in front of them. Then Whisper and the other rhutz began running through the blockade like water through sand. The enforcers and soldiers raised their weapons to fire on the crowd but the rhutz quickly disarmed them with their invisible hands. Without weapons, they rushed to their patrol vehicles to make a hasty retreat. Some managed to get away but others were crushed under the Zodillos' massive feet.

The procession moved deliberately through the front gate and quickly surrounded the temporary government building. The yellow, two-story, pre-fabricated structure which had been assembled in just a few days, glistened in the morning sun. As the procession came to a halt, the crowd began to chant. "Peace now! Peace now! Peace now."

After a few loons, Sandee was lifted on top of one of the zodillo's back where he was given an amplifier to address the crowd.

"Citizens of Synclare. Thank you for coming out today in the name of peace," Sandee began.

"Peace now! Peace now! Peace now!" the crowd screamed in unison.

"Chancellor Tranille. Your people are calling you. They want peace. Retaliation will bring nothing but more endless bloodshed. It's time to stop this senseless killing. Come out here or invite me in so we can discuss a road to peace. We've never been so close as we are today to bringing a lasting peace to Tarizon. Come out. Postpone your retaliation for a few kyloons. You can kill your enemies later if we can't convince you to cease hostilities."

Sandee waited a moment for a response, but there was none. The crowd started chanting again, "Peace now! Peace now! Peace now!"

Sandee raised the amplifier to his lips and continued, "We are not here in rebellion. You and your government are not in danger. We want nothing from you but your ear. Please talk to us so we can show you a way to peace. Come! Come out and talk."

The crowd quieted in anticipation of a response, but nothing happened for several loons. Finally, a door opened and an aide motioned for Sandee to come in. He quickly slid off the zodillo and walked over to the open door. Trill, the Ambassador, and Whisper went inside. The door closed and the crowd began their chant once again, "Peace now! Peace now! Peace now!"

Sandee and his party were led through a narrow hallway to a large conference room and told to be seated. They all took a seat and waited. After a while, they began to get restless as neither the Chancellor or anyone from his staff made an appearance.

"What is this?" Sandee asked. "Is he going to talk to us or not?"

"It shouldn't be much longer," Trill replied. "You

forced his hand, so some discourtesy would be expected."

Sandee shook his head. "We don't have time for games or petty antics."

The door suddenly flew open and a short man with puffy red cheeks appeared. He was dressed in a purple Chancellor's robe with a gold fringe. They all stood up. After scanning the delegation he walked to the head of the table and took a seat. "You may be seated," he said irritably.

They all sat back down and when the room was quiet the Chancellor spat, "Now. What is the meaning of this?"

"My apologies for the manner in which we forced this meeting," Sandee said. "But it is urgent that you do not retaliate against Soni and we thought that was what you were about to do."

"It was and this delay could cost lives. Are you prepared to take responsibility for that?"

Sandee ignored the question and replied, "We are very close to bringing peace to Tarizon but continued hostilities between Synclare and Soni could jeopardize that effort."

"We have to retaliate," Chancellor Tanille replied. "Soni must be punished for its unconscionable acts of aggression."

"Yes, that has been the way of Tarizon for centuries, but look where it has brought us. Our planet is on the brink of becoming uninhabitable. Millions of citizens have already died and millions more will succumb to this insanity."

Chancellor Tanille took a deep breath and frowned. "That may be true, but we have no other alternative. If I don't retaliate, Soni will unleash their armies on us and all will be lost."

"Not necessarily," Sandee said. "If you take this first step by refusing to retaliate for the good of Tarizon and ask Soni's Chancellor to join you in peace talks, you will be seen as a very courageous leader and your people will support you."

"I'm not so sure about that. They are more likely to think me a coward."

"Look out your window. The peace movement in Synclare is very strong and growing stronger each day. Your people are tired of war and the havoc it has brought on the world. They will support you in this effort."

"Chancellor Marcez will never agree to a cease-fire, let alone an end to hostilities. Nothing less than total surrender will satisfy him and his generals."

"I know. He is a very belligerent man, but the peace movement in Soni is just as strong as it is here. Soon he will have no choice but to listen to his people."

"Soon perhaps, but not today, I fear."

"I think you're wrong. Now is the moment," Sandee assured him.

"If we postponed our retaliation, what would be the next step? I just can't see Chancellor Marcez coming to the table to talk about peace."

Sandee smiled. "The Ambassador and I would immediately go to Soni and invite Chancellor Marcez to join in peace talks. The leaders of our peace movement in Soni will rally the people and they will march on Shisk, just as we have done here today. They will have no choice but to agree to, at least, talk."

"Even if he agrees to talk," Chancellor Tanille replied, "he'll have the upper hand since Soni now controls the Tazi Strip. What incentive can you offer him to make him agree to withdraw his battleships and let our ships pass freely?"

"It would be Soni's chance to help save the planet."

"I agree, but he's obviously not convinced the situation is so dire or he wouldn't have attacked us. He thinks the environment will recover once this final war is over. So, I'm sure he won't agree to a cease-fire."

Sandee swallowed hard. He knew the Chancellor was

right, there was little chance that Chancellor Marcez would agree to peace talks, and even less likely that a final resolution of the Tazi Strip dispute could be reached. But he had to try to get the parties together whether the odds of success were good or not. It was that or give up.

He started to admit that the odds of success were not good when he felt Whispers' thoughts in his head. *"Don't be discouraged. I am feeling good about these peace talks. Remember Pelgrem will be there to guide us. This must be part of His plan or we wouldn't be here today."*

Sandee took a deep breath. *"Okay, my friend. I hope you are right."*

"Alright," Chancellor Tanille said. "I'll give you two days to get Marcez to agree to peace talks. If he doesn't agree by then the war will go on."

Sandee nodded. "Thank you, you're making the right decision. This will go down as a historic day in the history of Tarizon."

"Well, we'll see," he said warily as he got up to leave.

As they shook hands and said goodbye, the weight of the task before Sandee hit him like a brick. He was glad they had cleared this first hurdle but terrified of the daunting task ahead. The situation seemed impossible, yet he had no choice but to push on. The fate of Tarizon depended on it.

33
Task Force

The day after the primary election, the Special Timber Creek Task Force met again at the FBI's Fort Worth Field Office. Wade Wilkins, Evelyn Wilkins, Curt Gibbons, Sheriff Hudson, Special Agent Glenn Johnson, Special Agent Hal Bennett, and several others.

Sheriff Hudson was angry, "So, what happened? I thought Blinh Lai was supposed to lose."

Evelyn shrugged. "Well, it turns out my fiancé has charisma. I'm sorry. I didn't figure he had a chance. Don't worry, he'll be behind bars long before general election time. I'm sure the Democratic Party will put you back on the ballot once he has been exposed."

"They better. I kept my mouth shut just like you asked."

"So, what exactly have we learned these past few weeks?" Agent Bennett asked.

Evelyn pulled out a notebook and began summarizing her findings. "The Timber Creek Ranch consists of approximately 800 acres of pasture, 5 acres of structures including the homestead, two single-family residences, a barracks for ranch hands housing approximately 50 persons, two large equipment sheds, two stock ponds, and an assortment of horses, cows, pigs, chickens, and other livestock."

"What about their oil operations?" Sheriff Hudson asked.

Evelyn flipped a page in her notebook. "Ah. . . . they have eleven wells in operation and one being drilled, as I understand it."

"So, who are these people, and where did they come from?"

"Blinh is very vague on this subject, but he claims they are all from Hungary. I have heard him speak Hungarian and it seems natural for him. Of course, I don't understand Hungarian so he could be speaking Swahili and I wouldn't know the difference."

"But there is no record of any of them entering the United States," Agent Bennett interjected.

"What?" Sheriff Hudson asked. "How is that possible?"

"They may have crossed the border from Mexico and moved to Palo Pinto county undetected. It's not that hard to do."

"When they first got here, I observed them snooping around my office at the courthouse looking at birth and death records. I think they may have forged their birth certificates and Social Security cards. With those documents, it wouldn't be hard for them to get a Texas driver's license or passport."

"They traded diamonds for cash at a local pawn shop in Palo Pinto, and other pawn shops in surrounding counties reported they did business with Rammel Garciah and others too," Wade added.

"You think they are diamond smugglers?" Sheriff Hudson asked.

"Maybe," Wade replied. "One of our pawnbrokers who did business with them indicated he had a big sack of them the first time he came in. They must have been worth hundreds of thousands of dollars."

"We have checked with our offices in DC and there aren't any reports of any large diamond heists in the United

States in the two years preceding their arrival here," Agent Johnson said.

"Another thing of interest," Curt interjected. "I have been out at the ranch on a stakeout for the last several weeks, and I want to tell you they have a lot of traffic going in and out of that place. I think there are hundreds of people living there, and they all have old cars that have been fixed up and supercharged."

"What does that mean?" Agent Johnson asked.

"It means the cars look like real clunkers but run like the latest Cadillacs fresh out of Detroit. The ranch hands all drive very fast, too. I've thought about stopping a few of them for speeding, but I would have blown my cover."

"That's not a bad idea," Sheriff Hudson said. "Let's pull one over and impound it so we can take a look at what's under the hood."

"Good idea," Agent Johnson said. "Why don't you do that?"

Curt nodded. "Consider it done."

"All these people you have observed coming and going from the ranch, where do they go?" Agent Bennett asked.

"Some are going to school, others to their jobs and some are just out shopping, eating at restaurants and normal stuff like that," Curt replied.

"Have you talked to any of their employers?"

"Yes," Curt replied. "They seem to be good, dependable workers. I haven't heard any complaints from the ones I have interviewed."

"So, has Blinh given you any hints as to what he plans to do if he were elected Sheriff?"

"Not really," Evelyn replied, "but his friends out at the ranch are very excited about it, I know that."

"What about doctors and dentists? They must get medical treatment, right?" Agent Bennett asked.

"Yes, but they have their own doctors and dentists

and they never go to anyone else."

"All right. Let's keep digging," Walt said. "Evelyn, see if you can get an invite to the ranch. Maybe they will give you the grand tour now that you've helped their boy win the primary."

"I already plan to do that," Evelyn replied. "I'll let you know when I get it set up."

The meeting broke up with the understanding that everybody would keep digging for a few weeks and then meet again. Special Agents Bennett and Johnson indicated they'd get with INS to see if there was any record of the Timber Creek residents with authorities in Hungary.

34
Jealous Neighbors

The following day, Romas was surprised when he was informed he had a visitor waiting for him in the main house. He'd been out at a new tank they'd just completed and filled to provide water for their growing herds of cattle and for irrigation during the hot Central Texas summers. When he walked in the room, he recognized the tall, lean, dark-haired man. He didn't know him but had seen him around.

"Hi. I'm Romas Garciah, can I help you?"

"I hope so. I'm Sam Schell, Tom's father. He's friends with your son Rammel as well as Bellah and Blinh Lai."

"Oh, yes. I thought you looked familiar. So, what brings you out our way?"

"Tom's been telling me about all the oil wells you've been drilling. Apparently, you've been successful at finding oil."

"Yes. We've been fortunate."

"That's amazing. They've drilled several wells on my property and none of them have produced anything but oily salt water. My geologist tells me there's nothing down there, but I'm only three miles down the road from you. That doesn't make sense."

Romas shrugged. "Well, I'm not a geologist, but I have been told that a lot of times it's just a matter of luck whether you find a productive zone or not. There were three producing wells on our property when we bought it, so we knew the oil was down there. It was just a matter of drilling down to the right depth."

"Luck, huh? Well, I could use some of that. In the

meantime, could I get your geologist's name? I'd like to hire him to take a look at my properties."

"Ah, well. He works out of Austin. I'll contact him and tell him to call you."

"What's his name?"

"I'm afraid I can't disclose that. He actually works for a major oil company and he was doing a little moonlighting when he came here. I'll tell him to call, but I can't promise he will."

"Well, he'd better call. I have friends at the Railroad Commission. I understand you drilled these wells yourself. I'm sure you are aware of all the rules and regulations involved here. Have you gotten all your permits and filed all the required reports?"

Romas sighed. "Okay. Give me a week or two to make contact. Maybe he can come to take a look at your place. I'll try to convince him. There is no reason to get upset."

"I'm not upset. I just want my fair share of the pool of oil that's running underneath our properties."

Romas nodded. "Right. I understand. I'll be in touch soon."

Sam left and Romas went straight to the telephone to call Rammel, but Rammel denied telling anyone about the oil production on the ranch but suggested he call Bellah. He dialed her number.

"Hello."

"Bellah, this is Romas Garciah."

"Oh, hi, Mr. Garciah. What's going on?"

He told her about State Senator Schell's visit.

"Oh, I'm so sorry. Blinh mentioned to Tom that a new well came in at our victory party the other night. I guess Tom told his father."

"You kids have been warned about this. We can't afford to be under close scrutiny. Now Sam is threatening to bring in the Texas Railroad Commission. This could put us all in danger."

"I know. I don't know what to say. I had no idea Blinh would bring it up."

"Well, I guess I need to have a talk with our new Sheriff nominee. He's going to have a lot of responsibility once he is elected and that will bring opportunity to our community, but also some risk."

"I'll tell him you called."

"Thanks."

Romas hung up the phone, wondering if backing Blinh Lai for Sheriff had been a mistake. It was too late to change that decision, so he called Jox Machlyn and suggested he call a special meeting of the GOT Board. He agreed and said they'd all meet on board Earth Shuttle 7 in two hours.

When Romas made it to the Captain's Conference Room five of the nine members of the GOT Board were present. He was the sixth member and the other three were in Austin.

"Alright. Let's open the connection with Austin," Jox said.

Captain Linde hit a few buttons on his controller and the big VC monitor lit up. The other three GOT Board members smiled when they saw the connection had been established.

"Hello, everyone," Jox said. "Sorry to call this meeting on such short notice, but something urgent has come up."

"It better be good?" Markis asked. "I was in the middle of a golf game when I got the summons."

"Golf? Well, that's important," Jox said sarcastically. "Anyway, at Blinh Lai's election night party the other day, he apparently bragged to his friend Tom Schell that another well had come in at the ranch. Of course, Tom's father is a state senator and owns a ranch just down the road from Timber Creek. Unfortunately, the production company that has the lease on his property has drilled three dry holes."

"So, everyone knows that drilling an oil well is risky," Sarna noted. "It's not our fault they can't find oil."

"No. Of course not," Jox continued, "but we are using technology that is twenty years ahead of anything they have here on Earth. We can't have people snooping around our rigs."

"What does he want?" Rama asked.

"He wants to talk to our geologist," Romas replied. "He thinks maybe our geologist could help him find oil on his property."

"That can't happen," Jox said.

"No," Markis agreed. "So, what does our geologist suggest?"

Everyone looked at Paya Alt. When jobs were being assigned on the Ranch, he had given the responsibility for oil production on the Ranch since he owned an oil company back on Tarizon.

"Why don't we drill a well for Senator Schell?" Paya suggested. "If we control the drilling, nobody will be able to see our technology. Plus, there's a lot of oil in Texas, so why not build a big oil company and make lots of money."

"Well, we're not here to make money," Romas said. "But I like your idea. Do you think you could drill a producing well on his ranch?"

"I'll have to do some testing, but the pool of oil we are exploiting is big; I'm sure part of his ranch must be over it. We'll just have to figure out where that is."

"Good," Romas said. "I move we drill a well for Senator Schell, for now, to get him off our back. We'll see how that goes, and later on, we can decide whether we want to build an oil company."

Several people raised their hands to support the motion.

"Alright," Jox said. "The motion has been made and

properly supported. All those in favor record your vote."

Nine lights all lit up green on the Captain's console.

"It's unanimous then," Jox ruled.

"I'd like to bring up another matter as long as we are all together," Romas said.

"Okay. What is it?"

"Fifteen of our young men have just this week received a draft notice. We've done everything possible to avoid this happening, yet somehow it has. The prospect of our children being taken away to serve in the U.S. Army is bad enough, but there is a more urgent problem, not just for them, for all of us. In ten days, these young men must report for a physical exam. If they show up and are examined there is a strong possibility the slight differences between our anatomy and that of Earth humans will be noted. If it were just one person it might be overlooked, but if fifteen show up with the same anomalies, it is likely to spark an investigation."

"So, how did it happen that these boys were drafted?" Captain Linde asked.

"We don't know. They didn't register yet somehow got on the draft board's list."

"So, are you saying this was a deliberate act?" Jox asked.

"Well, even if these boys had registered for the draft, the odds that 15 men from our community would be drafted in the same month would be astronomical."

"Who do you think did this?" Captain Linde asked.

Romas shrugged. "I have no idea."

"So, the immediate question is how do we make sure these boys pass their physical exams?" Jox said.

"Let me take care of that," Markis said. "We managed to get two of our doctors licensed to practice medicine in Texas. It wasn't easy, but we worked it out. I'll figure out a way to substitute one of our doctors for the Army doctors giving the physical exams."

"You sure you will be able to do that from Austin?" Romas asked.

"Positive. Don't worry about it. I'll take care of it."

"All right, then. Is there any more business?" Jox asked, looking around the room and then up to the VC monitor. "Hearing none, the meeting will be adjourned."

After the meeting, Romas met with Paya and Jox to discuss how to handle Senator Schell.

"We're going to have to get an attorney to make sure everything we do is legal," Romas warned. "Senator Shell may get the Texas Railroad Commission involved."

"Talk to Evelyn Wilkins," Jox suggested. "She should be able to recommend a good attorney."

"As long as you keep him away from our operations, I don't care about the legalities," Paya said as he stood up.

Romas left the shuttle and while he was walking through the caves he worried about how Markis Lai was going to handle the Army physical exam problem. Markis seemed confident he could take care of it, but Romas wasn't so sure. He could think of many things that could go wrong, and if they did, he just hoped their thriving little community wouldn't be exposed.

35
Getting Legal

The next day Romas contacted Senator Schell and gave him the good news. He told him their geologist had agreed to come out to his ranch and do some testing. They scheduled the visit for the following week to give them time to consult with an attorney. Romas was worried about hiring the attorney. He knew an experienced oil and gas attorney would have questions about their history and current well operations. He'd be curious as to how they'd managed to drill so many wells by themselves. Romas would have to come up with a creative story. He could do that, but he just hoped the attorney would buy it.

Reluctantly he picked up the phone and called Blinh Lai. He was glad Blinh and Evelyn had gotten engaged. They seemed happy together and it seemed to him that she'd gotten over her obsession with her father's accident.

"Blinh. This is Romas Garciah. Congratulations on your primary victory."

"Oh, thanks. I appreciate your support. I didn't think you or the Board would let me run."

"Well. It was a gamble, but it's a great opportunity for you and for our community. Do you expect any problem when the general election rolls around? I understand you will have a Republican opponent."

"Yes, Roger Glasgow, but the Republican Party hasn't won a county office in the last ten years, so I'm not worried."

"Good."

"But you didn't call me to talk politics, did you?"

"No. I didn't."

"So, what can I do for you?"

"Right. Well, it seems our oil and gas business is getting some outside scrutiny, so the Board thought it was time to get our legal affairs in order. We thought Evelyn might be able to recommend a good oil and gas attorney, someone who will be discreet and not too nosy."

"I'd heard about that. That's good news."

"Yes. It is. It will be good for the community."

"Okay. Let me ask her, and I'll get back to you."

"Thanks," Romas said. "Did I say we're in a hurry?"

Blinh laughed. "No, but I figured that was the case."

"Good. Thanks again."

Romas hung up the phone and started thinking about what he should be doing while he waited for Evelyn's recommendation. The oil company would need a name. He thought about that for a moment and decided to look at the current listing of oil and gas exploration companies in the phone book. He figured it should be a common American name so it wouldn't be conspicuous in a list. Many of the names were mere initials. He liked that idea. After playing with different names and their initials, he decided the official name of the company would be APC, Inc. To the Tarizonian community, it would be known as Amerizon Production Company.

The next morning Blinh called him back.

"I talked to Evelyn and she says the man you need is Willard Winston in Palo Pinto. He represents a lot of the small independent oil companies in this area and understands the need for discretion. Apparently, many of these companies are owned by officers and directors of some of the major oil companies, and they can't afford to have their participation known."

"Why is that?"

"She said it was a violation of their duty of loyalty to

compete with the company that employed them. Also, she said some investors might be in a shaky marriage and wouldn't want their spouses to find out they had oil and gas interests. There is a myriad of reasons for secrecy in this business."

"Okay. Great. I think I can articulate a good reason for the need for secrecy in our case, something that will make sense to him. Thanks for getting back to me so quickly."

"Not a problem."

Romas disconnected and then dialed Winston's office. He made an appointment for the following day. The moment he hung up, the phone rang. He picked it up.

"Mr. Romas."

"Yes."

"This is Blinh. I'm at the Central Medical Clinic in downtown Mineral Wells. You know, that's where our guys were having their Army physicals done today."

"Oh, right."

"I think I'm going to need your help. My father gave me instructions on what to do, but there have been complications. The clinic is on fire. Can you get over here?"

"What? On fire? Did you call the fire department?"

"Yes, they are on their way."

"Is anyone inside?"

"Yes, the doctor."

"Has anyone tried to rescue him?"

"Another officer and I tried to get in, but the flames were too intense."

"Okay. Just act dumb. You know nothing about this. I'm on my way. Thanks for calling."

Romas called Celius and Rammel and told them to come immediately and bring a memory gun and a flight suit. A few loons later they all climbed into their enhanced Ford pickup and tore off toward Mineral Wells. As they raced into town at 90 mph, Romas briefed them on Blinh's call.

"Was the fire planned?" Celius asked.

"I don't know, but nobody was supposed to get hurt."

"What can we do now?" Rammel asked. "If he's already dead we're screwed."

"Not necessarily, maybe his death won't be linked back to us."

When they arrived at the medical center, two Mineral Wells fire trucks were on the scene fighting the fire. Blinh and another Mineral Wells police officer were keeping spectators away from the blaze. They parked their truck across the street and rushed over to Blinh.

"So, what happened?" Romas asked.

"My Dad told me to make sure I was the only cop in the vicinity of the medical clinic at 9:00 a.m. I was supposed to stand out front and tell anyone who tried to enter that the clinic was closed until noon. At about 11:00 a.m. some of our boys started leaving and they were all gone by 11:30 a.m. At 11:45 a messenger from the base came and picked up the completed physical exam paperwork. It happened right after the messenger left."

"What happened?"

"A car came racing down the street full of teenagers, it screeched to a halt in front of the medical center, and two guys wearing President Johnson masks jumped out holding Molotov Cocktails. They screamed some obscenities and then threw them through the window of the clinic. The burning bottles exploded, and a raging fire ensued. I rushed to the door to see if I could get in and help the doctors and medical staff escape, but it was locked."

"Locked? Oh, my God! You sure every one of our guys was out of there?"

"Yes, they all had left."

"Who was inside?"

"A doctor, a nurse, and a receptionist, I believe."

Romas shook his head. Static came from Blinh's radio and then a voice said, "All units. An explosion and fire have been reported at the U.S. Army Recruiting Office. Available officers, please respond."

"These could be Vietnam protesters," Blinh suggested.

Romas frowned. "Right. They just happened to show up when our guys were having their physicals."

Blinh shrugged. "It's possible."

"So, your Dad didn't tell you his plan?"

"No. He just told me to stand out front and keep people out until noon."

"Well, it looks like his plan worked, but I wish he had come up with one that didn't involve killing innocent people."

"Maybe we should go," Celius suggested. "People may wonder why we are here so far away from the ranch."

"You're right, but first we need to go inside."

"The building's on fire!" Celius exclaimed. "You can't go inside."

"Sure, I can. That's why I brought a flight suit."

Celius sighed heavily. "You're crazy."

"What about the firemen?" Rammel asked.

"Our memory guns should give us five or ten minutes inside. I'll go in while you two stand watch."

Romas turned to Blinh. "Play dumb. You know nothing about this."

"Yes, sir. I'll call you later with an update," Blinh said and walked away.

"Ready," Romas said.

Rammel nodded and they all got back in the truck and drove around to the back of the building. A lone fireman was dragging a hose into the alley as they drove up. He put his hand up and yelled for them to turn around and leave. Rammel got out and fired his memory gun at the fireman. The fireman dropped to the ground like a punctured balloon. While Rammel and Celius dragged the fireman out of sight,

Romas put on the flight suit and entered the building through the back door.

Inside the fire was raging and the smoke made it difficult for Romas to see, but he scarcely felt the heat since the flight suit had been designed to protect against the heat of reentry from space. The hallway from the back door led to a work area surrounded by an office and three treatments rooms. Romas found the doctor on the floor of his office. He checked for a pulse but felt nothing.

Romas had planned to avoid the reception area for fear of being seen by the firemen fighting the blaze, but he decided to stick his head in for a second and scan the room for any evidence that might need to be destroyed. As he stuck his head around the corner he saw movement. A woman was on the ground crawling toward him. He immediately rushed over to her, picked her up, and rushed her outside.

"Rammel. Come here. Help me," Romas whispered.

Rammel came over and helped lay her down next to the fireman."

"Is she alive?" Celius asked.

"Yes, but she needs immediate medical attention."

"What should we do?" Celius asked.

"Just leave her here," Rammel replied. "When the fireman wakes up he'll think he rescued her."

"Good thinking, son," Romas said. "I'm going back inside and finish what I was doing. I'll be right back."

"Hurry," Celius said. "The fireman will be waking soon."

A few minutes later Romas exited the structure and got in the truck. Celius breathed a sigh of relief.

"Are you okay?" Celius asked.

"Yes. I'm fine. I didn't see anything in there that would compromise us."

"Good," Rammel said. "But why did innocent people

have to be killed?"

"They didn't," Romas replied angrily. "It's Markis and Sarna's doing. They have a callous disregard for human life. Unfortunately, there are many who share their views."

"That's terrible," Rammel said shaking his head. "Do you think Blinh and Bellah feel the same way?"

Romas shrugged. "It's quite likely. Children often share their parents' values."

"People like that are dangerous and wouldn't think twice about stabbing you in the back if it advanced their agenda," Celius added.

"Okay. So, what is their agenda anyway?" Rammel asked.

"I'm not exactly sure," Ramos replied, "but I don't think they ever intend to leave Earth. If I'm right, then their agenda will be to gain as much power, influence, and money as possible, and at any cost."

"That sounds about right," Celius agreed.

When they got home, they turned on the TV just as the 6:00 p.m. news was coming on.

"Our top stories today are the two deaths as a result of the attacks on the U.S. Army Recruiting Office in Mineral Wells and a nearby medical clinic where draftees were getting their physicals in preparation for military service.

"Shortly before lunch, five young males wearing President Johnson masks drove by the Central Medical Clinic in a stolen Ford Mustang convertible. The vehicle stopped in front of the clinic, two men jumped out of the car holding Molotov Cocktails and threw them through the window of the clinic. When the fire was finally put out hours later, two bodies were found inside. The identities of the victims have not yet been released.

"The car then traveled about a mile to the recruiting

office and repeated the attack. No one was killed at the recruiting office, but three staff members suffered minor burns and injuries.

"No groups have claimed responsibility for the attack, but local officials believe this was an anti-war protest by left-wing radicals opposed to the Vietnam War and compulsory military service. Local officials further advise that they have requested assistance from the FBI in investigating these acts of terror."

Romas turned off the TV angrily. "Well Markis' plan sure worked out well, didn't it? What an idiot! As the Americans say, we've jumped out of the frying pan into the fire."

"What are we going to do?" Celius asked worriedly. "The FBI won't be as easy to deal with as the Sheriff and the local police."

Romas shook his head. "I don't know. I hope there is a way out of this, but there may not be. We'll just have to wait and see what happens."

That night Romas tossed and turned trying to sleep. When he did finally fall asleep, he had a nightmare about an FBI Swat Team raiding the ranch and arresting every one of them. He woke up with a start and saw on his clock radio it was only 4:30 a.m. Then he started worrying about the Texas Railroad Commission and imagined the Texas Rangers paying them a visit and shutting down all their oil wells. Finally, it began to get light outside, so he got up and went outside and jogged around the perimeter of the ranch as he often did in the morning.

Willard Winston's office was across the street from the Palo Pinto County Courthouse. It was a storefront office sandwiched in between a title company and an accountant's office. The receptionist smiled at Romas, Celius, and Paya as they entered the office.

"Good morning," she said. "Can I get you a cup of coffee or a soda?"

"No, thanks," Romas said. "We're fine."

"Okay. Have a seat and I'll tell Mr. Winston that you are here."

"Thank you," Romas said.

Two minutes later, they were escorted into a small conference room and told that Mr. Winston would be right with them. There was a large painting of a drilling rig in operation and anxious oilmen and investors crowding around in anticipation of striking oil. The painting reminded Romas of the first well they had drilled and how exciting it was when it came in. His reminiscing was interrupted by the door opening. A short, robust man with a red face and thinning hair walked in smiling.

"Good morning. I'm Willard Winston. You must be the Garciahs."

Romas stood up and introduced himself and the others.

"So, Evelyn tells me you've had some success drilling oil wells."

"Yes," Romas replied. "Paya is our geologist and production engineer. He's gotten pretty good at finding oil. We have eleven wells in production now."

"Wow. That's extraordinary. What kind of production are you getting out of them?"

"Well, you know, that's one of the reasons we are here. We want to keep our affairs private. We've already got a neighbor who is jealous of our success and wants us to tell him all of our secrets."

"Right. So, you've developed some new drilling techniques?"

"Yes," Paya said. "I've been doing this for years now and, you know, I'm always experimenting. About a year ago I had a breakthrough, something revolutionary, and we want to keep it to ourselves."

"You could patent it." Winston suggested.

"Yes," Romas said, "but doesn't that mean we have to disclose the new technology to the government patent office?"

"Yes. That's right, but then you will own the technology and can sell or license it to others. If anyone uses it without your permission, you can sue them for damages."

Romas shook his head. "No, we'd rather just keep it a secret, so no one can copy us. Can you help us do that?"

"Sure. If you want to keep it as a trade secret, that's fine."

"We want to set up an oil company, so we can acquire leases and drill on lands we don't own. We want to call it APC, Inc. if that name is available."

"I will check with the Secretary of State and see if it is. You may need some other entities as well, a limited partnership and one or more subsidiary corporations. And, of course, you'll need offshore bank accounts to shelter your money, unless you want to pay exorbitant taxes. I assume you haven't done any legal work in conjunction with your existing wells?"

"No. We haven't. That's why we are here. We need to get legal. Someone has threatened to report us to the Texas Railroad Commission. For what, I don't know, but we want to avoid trouble."

"Okay. Well, you've come to the right place. We'll take good care of you, but I've got to warn you, it's going to be expensive. We bill at $150 per hour plus expenses and we'll need to get a retainer of $25,000."

"That's fine. Just keep us out of trouble," Romas said feeling much relieved. By the end of the meeting, Willard Winston had impressed him with his knowledge, experience, and confidence, and he hadn't balked at their insistence on secrecy. He had assured them if they were willing to pay his fees and make a few political contributions to the right people, there wouldn't be any problems with the Texas Railroad Commission. Although the fees were high, they'd be inconsequential considering the revenue APC would be generating. So, with little fanfare, the first corporation, wholly owned by aliens from another planet, had been formed in Texas and would soon be a major player in the American oil and gas industry.

36
Peace Talks

Cornelius Bruda looked out over the large expanse of smoking rubble that days earlier had been the site of Soni's Capitol Building. The retaliatory strike was unexpected as Sandee Brahn and his delegation had been in talks with Chancellor Illeez Marcez of Soni and Mayor Vill Linell of Shisk trying to set up parameters for peace talks between the two nation-states. Unfortunately, the discussions had dragged on too long and Chancellor Tranille's patience wore out.

Rather than an aerial strike which Leode Barkha, the man in charge of Shisk's defenses, had expected and could have easily repelled, the attack came from the Coral Sea to their flank as thousands of Seafolken soldiers emerged from the docks and swarmed Shisk's west gate. With the bulk of Shisk's army to the north and east between Shisk and Synclare, the attack was a complete surprise. The soldiers easily overtook the few guards on duty at the west gate and in just a few loons the soldiers had made it to the Capitol Building itself and had it surrounded.

Capitol Security and the small contingent of Soni forces on duty attempted to repel the invasion but they were no match for the well-trained Seafolken soldiers with their uncanny strength, near bullet-proof skin, and telekinetic abilities. Once inside the government compound, the Seafolken soldiers easily took out local air defenses and then called in low trajectory missile strikes from their ships patrolling offshore. In just a few loons the Capitol Building stood in ruins.

Ordinarily Bruda would have enjoyed this escalation of hostilities as he indirectly supplied munitions to both sides, however, today he was in town to promote peace. In fact, he was on his way to the Citihead's office where Chancellor Illeez Marcez, Sandee Brahn, Vice Minister Trill Lankershank of Pohl, and Sall Banus, Deputy Chief of Staff of Synclare and others were meeting to try to negotiate a cease-fire.

Their Grinden made its way slowly through the mass of citizens who had followed Sandee Brahn's procession to the Municipal Auditorium. After almost a kyloon of tedious driving, they pulled up in front of the huge complex and came to a stop. Two PE's stationed in front of the building opened the doors for Bruda and his contingent while six more helped restrain the crowd.

"Peace now!" they chanted in unison. "Peace now!"

Bruda winced from the blast of summer heat that engulfed him as he stepped up onto the curb. He looked around at the crowd anxiously. Following him out of the vehicle were General Bakker, Tributon's First Minister Solis Landy, and several aides. The two PE's escorted them inside the auditorium and directed them to take the elevators to the 6th-floor conference center. They stepped inside, pushed the appropriate button and soon walked into a noisy waiting room where numerous politicians, military officers, journalists, and interested citizens were waiting anxiously for the talks to begin. An usher greeted them as they came out of the elevator and instructed them to follow him. They did and he took them directly to the main conference room through tall double doors made of bronze.

Chancellor Marcez looked up as the big doors creaked and Bruda stepped into the room. Smiling broadly, he immediately went over to him and shook his hand.

"Cornelius, it's so good to see you. Thank you for coming."

"It is an honor, Illeez. I'm glad to be here. I'm sorry about your Capitol Building. We just saw what's left of it. It was such a magnificent structure."

"Yes, indeed. It's been the centerpiece of Soni for over two hundred cycles. I can't believe it's gone forever."

Bruda shook his head. "Well, don't worry. Soon we will be building an even bigger and more magnificent Capitol Building, but not for Soni. We are going to be building it for Tarizon."

Chancellor Marcez frowned. "What are you talking about?"

"What I'm telling you, Illeez is that it is time for peace. We have no choice. The people are weary of war and will put up with it no longer. We barely made it here today there were so many of Sandee Brahn's followers in the streets."

"I know, but—"

"The good news, my friend, is that by embracing the peace movement now we can participate in the creation of a new world government and make sure our interests are protected."

"A world government?"

"Yes. How else can we bring about peace? We need a central world authority with a strong military to enforce the peace. It's the only way."

"But I'm not sure I want to give up our autonomy to a world government. What if the wrong people get control of it?"

"That's why it's important that we are the driving force behind it. That way we can make sure that, in the end, we will be in control. And, of course, why not make Shisk the Capital of Tarizon."

"I like the sound of that," Chancellor Marcez admitted.

"Can you imagine how much money there is to be made on building and equipping a new global army? I think we shall call it Tarizon's Global Army or "TGA" for short. What do you think?"

A smile came over Chancellor Marcez's face and he nodded. "Okay. I see the possibilities, but what if Sandee Brahn and his followers end up controlling this new government?"

"It's a risk, I'll admit, but remember Sandee is a man of God. He will act fairly and honestly, whereas we will not be subject to any such constraints."

They both laughed heartily and then turned when the big double door swung open again and Sandee Brahn and his entourage entered the auditorium.

"Let's discuss this later," Chancellor Marcez suggested, putting his hand on Bruda's shoulder and giving it a gentle squeeze.

"Of course," Bruda said looking over at Sandee and wondering how this man had eluded all the assassins he had hired to end his life.

"This way," the escort said to Bruda and escorted them to their designated seats at the table.

"Holy one! It's an honor to meet you at last," Chancellor Marcez said as he extended his hand.

Sandee grasped it and held it for a polite moment. "The honor is mine. Thank you for agreeing to meet."

"You have many followers in Shisk, I see. It's been a long time since our streets have been so full."

"The people are anxious for peace. They want you to realize that."

"I get it. I do, but what about our Capitol Building? Am I to ignore such a crime against our nation?"

"There is going to have to be a lot of forgiveness if we are ever going to have a lasting peace."

"Well, perhaps so. Why don't you take your seats and maybe we can start with agreeing on terms for a cease-fire for now."

Sandee nodded and they all took their assigned seats at the table. When every seat had been taken the big doors were closed and Trill stood.

"Greetings to everyone. Thank you for coming today. I am Vice Minister Trill Lankershank of Pohl. The Chancellors of Soni and Synclare have asked me to preside over these peace talks. As you know, we are all here today at the urging of the First Minister of Lyon, His Holiness, Sandee Brahn, for the purpose of discussing the possibility of a cease-fire between Synclare and Soni.

"Unfortunately, as many of you have seen, Soni's Capitol Building lies in ruins due to an unfortunate attack just days ago by Seafolken allies of Synclare.

"Obviously, this is no way to start off peace talks, but, to be honest, I fear we wouldn't be talking here today had the attack not occurred.

"Synclare held off its retaliation for over sixty days at the request of Sandee Brahn hoping Soni would agree to these talks, but they did not have the decency to even respond."

"Alright!" Sandee interrupted. "We are not here to lament history. We are here to ensure that Tarizon has a future and the first step is to stop this senseless war."

"Agreed," Chancellor Marcez acknowledged. "Let's get to the issues."

"Yes, of course," Trill replied. "The main issue is the Tazi Strip which has belonged to Soni for over a thousand cycles, yet Synclare recently seized control of it and claimed ownership."

Sall Banus shook his head. "That's a lie! The Tazi Strip has been part of Synclare since the borders of the nation-states were formed over a century ago. It was specifically given to Synclare so it would have access to the Coral Sea since Synclare is otherwise landlocked."

"Okay. Again. We are not here to discuss history,"

Sandee interjected. "Let me ask a question. It is my understanding that the critical issue boils down to who has access to the Tazi River. Is that correct? The Tazi Strip consists of a strip of land four kylods in width with the river passing through it."

"Correct," Banus said. "It was carved out specifically to give Synclare access to the Coral Sea."

"Okay," Sandee said. "So, why can't both nations use the river? It's a very wide river. I have traveled on it myself."

There was a moment of silence. "That might be agreeable as long as Synclare acknowledges that the Tazi Strip is the sovereign territory of Soni and agrees to allow\ inspections and pay appropriate tariffs and fees," Chancellor Marcez said.

"No," Banus said, "Synclare might be willing to let Soni use the river but it will remain under the control of Synclare. We will not be subject to tolls, arbitrary inspections, and harassment."

"Why can't it be considered joint territory?" Sandee suggested. "Then an independent authority can be charged with overseeing it with expenses and revenue to be shared equally."

"That sounds like an excellent idea," Bruda said. "Over the past several centuries hundreds of wars have been fought over local issues like the Tazi Strip. And these wars are fought because the leaders of these nation-states are unwilling to sit down and work out reasonable solutions to them. The result has been millions of death and a planet that is in crisis."

"Forgive me," Ambassador Talvihn said. "But it is no secret that Bruda Industries has supplied most of the weapons for these wars, at least the most recent ones."

Bruda smiled. "That is true. That is our business and we have done well, but there comes a time when profits must take a back seat to the welfare of the planet. I agree with

His Holiness, that it is time for peace. If Tarizon becomes uninhabitable then there will be profits for no one."

Sandee smiled. "I'm glad you finally understand that. Does that mean you are joining our peace effort?"

Bruda grinned. "I guess it does, but let me finish my thought. Like creating an independent authority to govern the Tazi Strip, Tarizon needs a central government to settle local disputes and to end warfare forever."

The room fell silent.

"You're suggesting we establish a world government?" Chancellor Marcez asked.

"Yes, precisely."

"Well, that's an interesting idea, but I don't see that ever happening."

"Perhaps not, but I think it is an idea that should be considered if you are serious about putting an end to war on Tarizon. What do you think, Your Holiness?" Bruda asked.

Sandee thought a moment. "I don't know, but I look forward to discussing it as a possible mechanism for bringing peace to Tarizon. Thank you for suggesting it."

Bruda nodded. "Yes. Bringing peace to Tarizon will be a complex and delicate process. I look forward to working with you to make it a reality."

"As do I," Sandee replied suspiciously.

By the end of the day, the parties had agreed on the terms of a cease-fire which included the establishment of an independent authority to manage the Tazi Strip and coordinate shipping on the Tazi River. More importantly the nations of Soni, Synclare, Lyon, Pohl, and Tributon agreed to sponsor a peace summit of all the nation-states of Tarizon the following spring in Lyon for the purpose of considering the abolition of nuclear warfare, undertaking joint efforts to restore Tarizon's ecology, and the creation of a worldwide authority to arbitrate serious disputes between nation-states that might lead to war.

Sandee was astonished but elated by this sudden turn of events. Now, for the first time, he was confident his peace mission would be a success. It was now just a matter of time before all the nation-states would come onboard. But he hadn't given much thought to how peace would be maintained once the fighting had stopped. After all, he reasoned, that was up to the politicians to figure out. But when he got back to Lyon, Chancellor Linzcot asked him that very question.

"I don't know. I guess that's what we are going to have to figure out before the spring peace summit," Sandee replied.

"I don't like Cornelius Bruda's world government idea. That's a lot of power to place in the hands of a few elected officials."

"As long as they are elected and their terms aren't too long, why would it be different than what we have now?"

"There'd have to be a new mandate and to be effective a majority of the citizens of Tarizon would have to adopt it," Chancellor Linzcot noted. "That would be a monumental task. I don't know if it is really feasible."

"That is a task I would gladly assume," Sandee said. "We already have an organization equipped to do it. Once you get agreement on the content of a supreme mandate, my followers and I will travel to every corner of the world to make sure it is ratified."

"Assuming you do get it ratified, how will this new worldwide military be controlled? I fear with all that power the generals could take control and no one could stop them."

"True enough. That is something you politicians have to figure out. I know it won't be easy, but there must be a way for it to be done."

"I hope so," Chancellor Linzcot replied. "But I can't help thinking Bruda is counting on us not being able to do it."

37
New Developments

Wade Wilkins called the Timber Creek Task Force meeting to order. They were all crowded into a small office at the Palo Pinto County Sheriff's office. Evelyn Wilkins started the meeting.

"I thought we should meet because there have been some new developments. I'm sure you are all aware of the recent attacks against a medical clinic and recruiting station in downtown Mineral Wells."

There was a murmur of acknowledgment and many heads nodded.

"Well, we believe our suspects at Timber Creek may be responsible."

"How is that?" Evelyn asked.

"It turns out all of the persons getting physicals at the time of the attack were from Timber Creek," Wade said.

"Really? So, why would they attack the clinic and the recruitment center?" Evelyn asked.

Wade shrugged. "It beats me, but it can't be a coincidence."

"No, it can't," Agent Bennett agreed. "But there is substantial evidence it was carried out by an anti-war group."

"Maybe the anti-war protesters only planned to hit the recruitment center and the Timber Creek protesters coordinated their attack to make it look like they were part of the peace movement," Sheriff Hudson suggested.

"Yeah, but why attack the medical clinic?" Evelyn asked. "All of the recruits passed their physicals."

"Right," Agent Johnson said thoughtfully.

"The other development was dropped into my lap," Evelyn noted. "Blinh got a call a few days ago from Romas Garciah wanting the name of a good oil and gas lawyer. They thought maybe I knew somebody. They told Blinh they had developed some new revolutionary method of extracting oil from old wells. In fact, they increased production ten-fold on the three wells that were on the property when they bought it. Since then they've drilled eight more wells all with equal production and the landowners around them were starting to take notice. That's why they needed a lawyer."

"So, you are telling us they drilled eleven oil wells without getting permits from the Texas Railroad Commission?" Sheriff Hudson said.

Evelyn nodded. "Yes. So, I referred him to Willard Winston. Of course, everything they tell him will be attorney-client protected, but as soon as they start registering those wells with the TRC we should learn a lot."

"They must be rolling in cash," Agent Bennett said. "I wonder if this is some kind of money laundering operation? Maybe those wells aren't producing a damn thing, but they want everybody to think they are."

"That would be pretty clever," Agent Johnson agreed.

"No," Evelyn said. "They are going to start drilling wells for other people. Blinh got that much out of them."

"Well, they didn't come from Hungary," Agent Johnson advised. "The authorities there can't find a trace of any of them."

"I pulled over one of the ranch hands who was driving a little erratic and impounded his car," Curt Gibbons said. "Our mechanic said he's never seen such a clean engine. It looked like it was fresh off the assembly line."

"So, it's not hard to clean an engine," Sheriff Hudson

said.

"The car was eleven years old and when you turned it on it purred like a kitten."

"Huh. These people are quite extraordinary whoever they are," Agent Johnson acknowledged thoughtfully.

"Well, maybe so, but they've broken a lot of securities laws, so why don't we raid the place?" Wade suggested.

"They haven't filed any income tax returns either; not one of them," Agent Bennett advised. "We could prosecute them for that, and we'd have a good excuse to go in and search the whole damn place for records of undisclosed income."

"All right," Agent Johnson said. "I'll get with the United States Attorney in Fort Worth. Sheriff, you talk to your local prosecutors and see what our options are."

Sheriff Hudson nodded. "No problem. I should be able to get with them next week."

The meeting broke up and Evelyn went back to her office at the county courthouse. She felt exhilarated. Finally, she was going to make the bastards who tried to kill her father pay for what they'd done. She couldn't wait to look them in the eye as they were hauled off to jail.

38
The Return

As promised, two months later ATC had its first well in production on Senator's Schell's ranch and two more were in the planning stages. Needless to say, there had been no complaints from the Texas Railroad Commission and Paya had applications from over a hundred Texas landowners anxious for their properties to be evaluated for possible leasing. The prospects for the Tarizonian community had never been better until something quite unexpected happened. Captain Linde advised the Board that he'd gotten a communication advising that Earth Shuttle 3 was approaching Earth and was about a week out.

"Why is it coming?" Romas asked.

"The message was brief and did not state a purpose for the visit," Captain Linde replied. "It may be another load of settlers. That would be my guess."

"We hadn't planned a second ship," Romas reminded them.

"No, but if things are deteriorating on Tarizon as fast as we expected, it's not surprising that others have organized evacuation shuttles."

"That's quite possible," Jox agreed. "If we get another two thousand settlers, what will we do with them?"

"Actually, it might be a blessing," Paya said. "With ATC growing so rapidly, we'll be needing a lot of new labor."

"True," Romas agreed. "Let's just hope the new settlers have been properly orientated for life on Earth. If not, they'll need weeks of training before we can let them out amongst the local population."

With so many housed on the ranch, it had always been a busy place, but with preparations being made for a new load of settlers, busy had turned to hectic. Fortunately, the new arrivals could remain on the ship for a while so new housing could wait a bit. Food, on the other hand, would be needed immediately. The shuttle would likely be nearly out of rations when it arrived and feeding two thousand hungry travelers would be no small task.

Because only one shuttle could land at Cactus Island at a time, Earth Shuttle 7 had left Cactus Island and gone to its back up landing site at Lake Tawakoni. On the day of the Earth Shuttle 3's arrival, hundreds of settlers were gathered in the caves under Possum Kingdom Lake to greet the visitors and find out why they had come. Speculation had been rampant on the subject with most believing that life on Tarizon had finally become intolerable and evacuation was now the only viable option. They expected Earth Shuttle 3 was but the first of many more Earth shuttles to come. Others thought the arriving shuttle had been sent simply to check up on how the mission was going and return to report back to the GOT members who were still on Tarizon. But no one expected the message Captain Sparken had for them the moment he stepped off the shuttle.

"I have great news," Captain Sparken advised. "Peace has come to Tarizon! Sandee Brahn has done it!"

The crowd stirred in shock and confusion. "Done what?" someone asked.

"There hasn't been a bomb dropped or a shot fired on Tarizon for nearly a cycle. There's going to be a World Council constituted to consolidate all the nation-states into one world government."

"How could that be?" Romas asked incredulously. "When we left there were at least seven or eight wars in progress."

"I know. It's amazing."

"Who is Sandee Brahn?" Celius asked.

"That's right," Captain Sparken said. "You left before he started his peace movement. Sandee Brahn is a messenger from the God Pelgrem. Pelgrem came to Sandee in a dream after his family was slaughtered by deserters from the Lecton Army. He was but twelve years old at the time. Pelgrem assigned him the task of bringing peace to Tarizon, and a rhutz named Whisper was commanded to be his companion and protector. They traveled together for several cycles to every corner of Tarizon warning everyone that if peace didn't come to Tarizon soon, the planet would become uninhabitable.

"Although he drew large crowds and provoked much debate, nothing really changed. So, Sandee decided to run for office and that's when the movement finally got traction. Eventually, he was appointed First Minister of Lyon. It was only after that happened that he began making progress at getting world leaders to join his peace mission. The states of the North Sea Alliance were the first to join as everyone expected, but it was after the states of the Dark Sea Alliance joined that peace really became possible."

"That's wonderful," Celius said smiling excitedly.

"Yes, it is. So, it's important for all of you to return to Tarizon to put your substantial power and influence to work to make sure this peace effort is not derailed. There will never be another chance to save Tarizon."

"Yes, of course," Jox said, "but I'm afraid not everyone will be anxious to return to Tarizon. We have all worked very hard to adapt to the American way of life and to be accepted into the community. Most of our people are happy here and our future here is bright. Even if peace is possible on Tarizon, it's not a sure thing."

"I understand," Captain Sparken said, "but I'm sure many will want to return. I know the GOT still has a big stake in Tarizon's future."

"Yes, we do," Romas agreed. "Give us some time to consider all of this. In the meantime, we can show you and your crew around so you can see what we have accomplished here. Then you will understand why some of us may not want to return."

"We'd like that," Captain Sparken said. "Let me secure the ship tonight, and then first thing in the morning we'll come out to your ranch. I'm anxious to see it."

That night there were endless discussions about the possibility of saving Tarizon and whether to stay or return. Jox and Romas wanted to return to Tarizon and bring as many Tarizonians back with them as possible, but they agreed no one would be forced to return if they didn't want to.

Paya announced he wanted to stay and continue to run the oil company, and most of the men running the rigs agreed. They felt the revenue from the ATC would be important for those who remained on Earth.

Rama Sloken said he would stay and continue to run the ranch, however, his son Ritz wanted no part of ranching. He wanted to return to Tarizon and join the peace movement.

Eroh told his father and mother that he wanted to stay on Earth and help Rama run the ranch. Romas and Celius were upset by their son's decision and tried to talk him out of it, but he refused to change his position. Rama promised he would look after Eroh, so Romas promised to keep an eye on Ritz when they got to Tarizon.

Bellah was still going out with Tom and everyone thought they would eventually marry, but she wasn't so sure she wanted that anymore. Tom was handsome and rich but lacked ambition. He wasn't like his father at all. He'd been given everything he needed or wanted in life and never learned how to fend for himself. If they were married, she feared he'd want her to cook, clean and raise his children while he tended to the family business or hung out with his friends at the country club. That prospect gave her nightmares.

Her parents urged her to stay and marry Tom even if she didn't love him. They wanted to exploit the Schell family's wealth and political connections, but Bellah said she'd have to think on it a bit before she made a decision. Markis and Sarnia Lai, of course, planned to stay on Earth to carry out their secret mission. They used the success of their real estate investments as the official reason.

Since the Tarizonian settlers had come to Earth, their numbers had grown from a little over 2000 to nearly 6000. At the end of the day, only about 1700 of those wanted to return home. Romas was disappointed but not surprised by this development. Many indicated if the World Council was successful and a lasting peace did come to Tarizon, they might reconsider.

The next day Romas and Jox escorted Captain Sparken and his First Officer Remmi Talke around the ranch. In the afternoon they took them to Palo Pinto where they visited Blinh Lai. The soon to be Sheriff told them he intended to stay on Earth and run for re-election. He felt it important for those who stayed behind to have a friendly Sheriff to have their backs.

When they returned to the ranch that night, it was agreed that the shuttle would make its return trip to Earth in seven days. This would give all those going home time to settle their affairs, say goodbye to family and friends and pack their belongings. Unfortunately, that all changed when Romas got a call from Blinh.

"Everyone must leave immediately. I just found out that a joint task force with the Sheriff's department and FBI has been investigating our activities for months. Apparently, they have gathered enough evidence against us to get a search warrant and start making some arrests."

"How did we not know about this?" Romas asked.

"I don't know. Evelyn is in on it. Her father hasn't retired. In fact, he's leading the task force."

"Skutz!" Romas exclaimed bitterly. "Damn your father. This is his fault. I'm tempted to call Evelyn and tell her where to find him."

"Yeah. Well, you can't do that. It would be treason."

"I know. But it would serve him right."

"I'm going to have to disappear too. Evelyn's been playing me."

"I'm sorry, Blinh. Destroy anything you have that would be sensitive and then get over here to the ranch to help us evacuate. I'll call over to Cactus Island and make sure the shuttles will be ready to take off as soon as we can get everyone aboard."

"I'll come over and help, but then I'm going to Austin."

"That's your decision, just get over here as fast as you can and make sure Evelyn doesn't know you are on to her."

Romas hung up and went to tell the others the bad news. He couldn't believe they'd have to abandon the ranch and shut down ATC. Then he had an idea.

39
The Escape

The next morning, Blinh, Markis, and Sarna readied a caravan of vehicles from the ranch heading for Austin. Bellah wasn't planning to go with them. She still didn't know whether to stay on Earth or go back to Tarizon.

"Why don't you want to stay?" Sarna asked. "You and Tom are getting along so well. He's perfect for you."

"You mean he's perfect for you and your mission."

"It's your mission too. Soon, Tarizon will be uninhabitable and millions will have to be evacuated to Earth. We must pave the way for that eventuality."

"What about Sandee Brahn and the peace movement?" Bellah asked. "Captain Sparken seems convinced that this new world government is really going to happen. If he's right, then Tarizon will be saved and no one will be coming to Earth."

"I'm not as optimistic as Captain Sparken. Even if a Supreme Mandate is adopted and a world government established it will take decades to rebuild the planet's infrastructure, clean up the environment, and restore agriculture and industry to adequate levels to sustain the population. In the meantime, anyone who wants to lead a decent life will want to come to Earth."

"Actually, if you want to go back to Tarizon, that's fine," Markis interjected.

Sarna glared at him.

"The danger of a one world government," Markis explained, "is that the wrong people might get into power. If that happens life on Tarizon will change drastically, and not for the better. Sandee Brahn and his followers will want to treat the mutants and Seafolken as equals and guarantee civil liberties for everyone. If that happens, we will end up having to feed and house millions of them at our own expense. Most of them are unemployable and in poor health. The cost to sustain them will be staggering."

"So, how do we make sure the right people take over this new government?" Bellah asked.

"There are many people back on Tarizon working on that. If you went back, you could join them. It would be important and exciting work. You wouldn't be bored."

"Then that's what I will do—go back to Tarizon and do something important."

"Bellah, no!" Sarna protested. She glared icily at Markis. "As Tom's wife, you will have much power and influence here on Earth."

"I don't want to be an American housewife. That would be almost as bad as being a slave on Tarizon."

"No. You know nothing of slavery," Sarna replied. "Many wives control their households and their husbands obey them. Of course, they won't admit it, but that is the truth."

"Maybe so, but Tom isn't the type to take orders. He's spoiled and always gets his way. We'd be at each other's throats. It wouldn't work. I'm going back to Tarizon."

Sarna let out a cry of despair. She knew she'd lost the fight and wouldn't see her daughter again for a very long time. Tears began to flow down her cheeks. Bellah sighed. "Oh, Mother. I'm a woman now. You have to let me go."

They embraced.

"I know," Sarna said. "It's hard. Wait until you are a mother."

"When you get back to Tarizon," Markis instructed, "you and Ritz should contact Cornelius Bruda and fill him in on what we are doing here on Earth. Tell him you want to help in the fight for control of this new world government that is being established to rule Tarizon. He'll find important jobs for both of you."

"I thought Ritz wanted to join the Peace Party?" Bellah replied.

Markis laughed. "That's what he wants everyone to think, but don't believe it. He's with us, I promise you. I've known him since he was a toddler. If he joins the Peace Party he'll do it so he can spy on them or subvert their efforts in some manner."

"Well, what could one person possibly do to make a difference?" Sarna spat. "You're both being foolish."

Markis didn't respond but smiled knowingly.

40
Raid on Timber Creek

Two days later at first light, the Timber Creek Taskforce including officers from the Sheriff's Department, Texas Rangers, and the FBI descended upon Timber Creek Ranch. They searched the main houses, the outbuildings, the barns, and the bunkhouses, and the huge equipment buildings, but found nothing. The entire ranch was deserted.

"Where did everyone go?" Agent Bennett asked irritably. "Wasn't someone watching this place?"

"Yes, there were two deputies out here the past two days," Evelyn replied. "They said everything was quiet."

"Where are these deputies now?" Agent Bennett asked.

"Ah. I don't know. They didn't report this morning. I assumed they were on their way to the rally point to come out here."

"Damn it!" Wade exclaimed. "They outsmarted us again."

As they were talking they all spotted a pickup truck coming up the dirt road slowly. When the truck reached the group of angry law enforcement officers, it stopped. Senator Schell stepped out.

"What's going on out here?" the Senator demanded.

"What are you doing here?" Wade asked.

"This is my place now. I just bought it yesterday."

"You've got to be kidding me," Evelyn spat. "How did that happen?"

"Ah. Romas Garciah contacted me and said they needed to raise some capital for their new oil and gas company and had decided to sell the ranch. They said they had a buyer, but he needed ten days to close. They asked if I was interested, and if so, how long would it take me to close. I said 24 hours. They liked that, so we agreed on a price and we closed yesterday afternoon at Willard Winston's law office."

"Did you pay by check?" Agent Bennett asked.

Senator Schell shook his head, "No, they gave me wiring instructions and I wired the money yesterday."

"How much?"

"A little over 2 million."

"Do you still have the wiring instructions?" Evelyn asked desperately.

"Yes, but it went to an intermediary bank in the Cayman Islands. I'm sure the money is untraceable. You know Willard. If he set them up an offshore trust, you'll never find that money."

✝✝✝✝✝

At the same time, the members of the Timber Creek Task Force were lamenting their failed operation, Earth Shuttle 3 was taking off from Cactus Island with all of the Timber Creek evacuees. They were headed for Lake Tawakoni in East Texas. There they would start over and try not to make the same mistakes they'd made at Possum Kingdom Lake.

Earth Shuttle 7 had departed the previous night with Romas Garciah, the GOT leadership and all those returning home to Tarizon to join the peace efforts there. There was great optimism amongst those on board, and as each was placed into deep space hibernation they prayed to Pelgrem that they'd awake back on Tarizon to witness the beginning of a new age of peace, cooperation and restoration.

41
First Draft

Sandee Brahn brushed the snow off of his shoulders and stomped his feet as he entered the Nepat Assembly Hall with Whisper on his heels. It had been snowing hard for kyloons and the rush of hot air that enveloped his body felt so good he paused a moment to enjoy it. Suddenly, Whisper shook his fur vigorously drenching Sandee's back side.

Sandee whirled around and scowled at him. *"Hey, boy! Look what you did."*

Whisper looked up and thought. *"Sorry, it was just instinct. I wasn't thinking."*

Sandee shook his head and then smiled. *"It's okay. It will dry. Come on. We're late."*

The leaders of the peace movement had been working for nearly thirty days on a draft of a Supreme Mandate to be introduced at the World Conference. In attendance were delegates who Sandee believed favored the creation of a true democratic world government that would be responsive to the will of the people and protect the individual rights of each citizen. Although he welcomed Cornelius Bruda's unexpected support for the cause, he didn't trust him and hadn't invited him to Nepat. In fact, the time and location of the conference had been a well-guarded secret.

Sandee and Whisper rushed across the foyer and entered the Citihead's Conference Room. The meeting hadn't started yet, so delegates were milling around and talking. Arvis stood up when she saw Sandee and Whisper enter. They walked over to her.

"Anything happening yet?" Sandee asked.

"Yes, Romas Garciah and his son, Rammel are here."

"What? They're back from Earth?" Sandee asked.

"Yes," she said pointing to the other end of a large wooden conference table where the two men were surrounded by excited delegates.

Sandee had never met Romas Garciah since he'd left for Earth before the peace movement began, but he'd heard lots of good things about him. He walked over to the cluster of excited delegates. Seeing Sandee join them, Ambassador Talvihn said, "Romas. I'd like to introduce you to Sandee Brahn."

Romas turned and smiled at Sandee. "Yes. This is the man I came to meet. Ever since I landed all I have heard about is the Savior of Tarizon."

Sandee laughed. "Well, I wish that was the case and we could all go on vacation. Unfortunately, there is much work yet to be done."

"Of course," Romas agreed, "but without your heroic effort, my boy and I wouldn't have been able to come home."

"Well, you should thank Pelgrem. He set this all in motion."

"I have. Believe me."

"Good. So, how did things go on Earth?" Sandee asked.

Romas laughed. "Well, we assimilated into the general population of Texas, more or less, and I don't think we did any permanent damage to the planet."

Everyone laughed.

"You'll have to tell me all about it sometime," Sandee said.

"It would be my honor," Romas replied.

Ambassador Mill Talvihn of Lyon, who had been elected chairman of the committee, stood and called the meeting to order. Everyone took their seats. When the room quieted, the meeting began.

"I want to welcome Romas Garciah, his son Rammel, Jox Machlyn, Ritz Sloken and Captain Linde who have just returned from Earth."

Everyone stood up and clapped.

"Thank you for joining us in this very difficult task of writing a Supreme Mandate for the establishment of a centralized world government. Obviously, this is important work and your input in the process will be greatly appreciated."

There were murmurs of agreement amongst the members.

"Just to bring you up to date, let me summarize where we are at this time. So far, our version of the Supreme Mandate will provide for a centralized executive branch which is to be called Central Authority. It will be administered by the Supreme Chancellor who will be elected by the people every seven cycles. The legislative branch of government will be comprised of 500 assemblymen apportioned between the states by population. There will be a judiciary to interpret the Supreme Mandate and laws that are enacted by the General Assembly. It shall be called the Supreme Council of Interpreters and each state will have an inferior judicial body to be known as the State Council of Interpreters.

"This is not an uncommon form of government on Tarizon, so it shouldn't cause any concern amongst the voters."

"What about the military?" Captain Linde asked.

"Yes, the military will be under the control of the Supreme Chancellor and his designated general staff. We are going to call it Tarizon's Global Army or the TGA.

"Included in the Supreme Mandate will be the usual provisions guaranteeing each citizen certain rights: to speak freely, travel at will, associate as they wish, bear arms, reside wherever they can find accommodations and, if they are charged with a crime, to trial by their peers.

"The topic that is under discussion today is the definition of citizen. Each of the nation-states have different definitions. Some recognize Seafolken as citizens and others do not. Some exclude mutants and slaves. None of them include the rhutz or zodillo as citizens even though many believe each to be a sentient life-form."

"They all should be citizens," Sandee argued. "Their life on Tarizon is no less important than the life of each human. They should have an equal say on who rules over them."

"No offense to Whisper, but no rhutz or zodillo has ever voted in any election on Tarizon, so there is no justification for that to change now," Ritz Sloken noted.

Several members verbalized their agreement.

"I agree with His Holiness on this point," Romas said, "however, I promise you, if the rhutz and zodillos are considered citizens and allowed to vote, the Supreme Mandate will never be ratified. We should not push our luck. Bruda and his gang will never go for it. Having Seafolken, slaves and mutants within the definition of a citizen will be difficult enough getting past them."

"You may be right," Sandee confessed, "but shouldn't we at least try?"

"Why don't you leave them out, too?" Ritz suggested. "There's no use making the ratification process any harder than necessary."

"No," Romas said, glaring at Ritz. "Seafolken, mutants and slaves are all human beings. They must be included in the definition."

Many of the delegates vocalized their agreement.

Ritz shook his head and walked away. Rammel watched him worriedly. Ritz had been excited about the prospects of peace. Then he remembered that Ritz had been friends with Blinh and Bellah. *Had they been a bad influence?*

Romas turned back to Sandee and continued, "I just worry that issues like this will get us bogged down and the delegates won't be able to agree on a final draft of the Supreme Mandate that can be presented to the people. Then we will be back to square one."

Sandee nodded. "You may be right. I will defer to your political expertise."

Romas nodded. "Thank you. After the Supreme Mandate has been adopted, the General Assembly can propose amendments, so giving the vote to the rhutz, zodillos and other life-forms may be something to consider in the future."

For the rest of the day and late into the night the members discussed the remaining issues before them and just before daybreak the next morning agreed on a final draft of the new Supreme Mandate to be presented at the World Conference. There was great celebration when the last vote was cast and when the cheers and applause had subsided, Sandee Brahn stood to speak.

"Members and friends I want to thank all of you for your hard work and dedication in making today's momentous accomplishment a reality. Just two cycles ago I was on the verge of accepting defeat and giving up on our quest for peace as being hopeless. But for almost one full cycle now there has not been a single bomb dropped, missile launched or even a shot fired between enemy combatants on Tarizon."

There were applause and cries from the members.

"I want to thank my Chief of Staff, Arvis Gill, for helping me get through my grief when her sister, Salina Gill, the mother of our peace movement, was assassinated. If she hadn't been there to push and prod me out of my depression, many thousands would have died this last year and Tarizon may have been pushed over the brink."

There was cheering and applause for Arvis. Tears were running down her cheeks. The people around her were smiling and hugging her.

"And, of course, I can't forget Whisper who has been with me from the beginning—a constant companion, advisor, and protector. Without Whisper none of us would be here today."

Whisper glanced around the room unsure how to react as everyone was watching him and clapping. Finally, he bowed his head slightly in acknowledgment.

"Finally, I want to thank Pelgrem, the God of Pharidon who came with our people ages ago on their journey to Tarizon. I'm not sure how He picked me out of billions of inhabitants of Tarizon to lead this movement, but I am honored that He did and I hope He is pleased with what we have accomplished."

There were more cheers, clapping and words of encouragement from the crowd.

"So, go home and sell your constituents on our new draft of the Supreme Mandate. Our final task is to get it approved and then ratified by the people. It will not be an easy task, but it can and will be done. I am certain of it!"

Everyone came to their feet cheering and clapping. Many were hugging and weeping incessantly. Sandee smiled broadly, feeling as happy as he had ever felt in his life. Ritz Sloken got up and moved toward him quickly. Sandee opened his hands to embrace him but instead of an embrace, Ritz pulled out a laser he had concealed his coat, pointed it at Sandee and said, "Pelgrem can't protect you from this!"

Ritz pulled the trigger and Sandee was jolted backward, his body jerking and twisting uncontrollably.

There were gasps from the crowd and cries of horror and despair. Whisper immediately went for Ritz's arm but he'd anticipated the attack and quickly pivoted. He pulled the trigger again, this time the laser blast riddled Whisper's body. Whisper barked and wailed as his coat of fur burst into flames. Suddenly, Rammel Garciah came up from behind and got Ritz in a choke-hold while others pulled the laser out of his hand. Ritz was quickly wrestled to the ground and pinned there by Rammel and Trill Lankershank.

An emergency casualty team had been on standby and was there in just a few tiks, but there was nothing they could do. Both Sandee Brahn and Whisper were already dead and there weren't going to be any miraculous recoveries this time. It was all over for the Savior of Tarizon and his protector. In the end, Pelgrem hadn't been able to protect them. The question now was whether the peace movement was now dead as well?

When the public enforcers arrived they took Ritz Sloken into custody. On the way to their transporter someone asked him, "Why? Why did you do this?"

Ritz looked back at the man evenly and replied. "Just following orders."

"Orders?" he asked. "Whose orders? Who do you work for?"

Ritz laughed eerily. "All men who are pure in body and soul."

Romas's stomach twisted and he winced in pain and anger. He already knew Markis Lai was behind the attack. He had gotten to Ritz through Blinh and Bellah, and that it shouldn't have ever happened. He knew he'd been stupid not to warn Sandee and his security detail about Ritz Sloken and his questionable intentions. But he'd thought Ritz was all talk and posed no immediate danger. It never occurred to him that the son of someone as kind and honorable Rama Sloken would ever commit cold-blooded murder.

Romas fell to his knees, overwhelmed with guilt, and cried out in despair, "No! Please Pelgrem. Don't let this be on me!" But no one heard him in the chaos that ensued.

Romas knew his error in judgment had cost Sandee his life and seriously jeopardized Tarizon's chances for peace. Now the daunting task of getting the Supreme Mandate ratified and bringing about a lasting peace was squarely on his shoulders. He'd have to make it happen or he'd be responsible for the dire consequences of its failure.

42
The Purist Party

A little more than 500 kylods away at the Bruda Ranch on the Pollo River in the White Mountains of Northern Tributon, Cornelius Bruda, his son Progasis, Petri Volk, General Bakker, Bellah Lai and other members of Bruda's military-industrial alliance were also meeting to organize a political party in opposition of the Peace Party. They too had started work on a draft of the new Supreme Mandate that they hoped would be presented to the people of Tarizon for ratification.

It was a public meeting and there were members of the media in attendance observing the proceedings. Just shortly after the members had elected officers and agreed to call themselves the Purist Party, a messenger rushed in and whispered something to Bruda who, having just been elected Party Chairman, was seated at the head of a large conference table. He stood up.

"Ladies and gentlemen, I have just been informed that there is breaking news relevant to the formation of our new government. Please turn your attention to the VC monitor behind me."

Bruda turned around and looked at the huge VC monitor expectantly. The screen flickered, there was static and then it came to life. The scene was the front of the Nepat Assembly Hall. A large crowd was milling around anxiously. Police and firemen were going in and out of the building. Billows of smoke would escape every time the door was opened. Veile Shante, dressed in a light blue blouse with navy pants, was holding a microphone waiting to give her report. The screen changed to the face of the network news director.

"Hello. I'm Tone Wajh. Sorry to break in on our regular programming, but we've got developing news in Nepat, Rigimol. Let's go to Veile Shante in Nepat for a report." The screen flipped back to the front of the Nepat Assembly Hall.

"Thank you, Tone. I'm here in front of the Nepat Assembly Hall in Rigimol where members of Sandee Brahn's Peace Party had just completed a draft of a new Supreme Mandate for presentation to the upcoming World Conference. Apparently, His Holiness Sandee Brahn was thanking the members and supporters for their hard work when one of the members of the group rushed up to him as if to embrace him, but instead pulled a laser gun and shot him. We are told Whisper the rhutz was also shot when he tried to intervene in the assassination attempt. This is not confirmed, but there is talk that Sandee Brahn may not have survived."

The room was dead silent as everyone looked on in disbelief.

"I am told that Sandee Brahn has been taken to the Waltk Casualty Center in Nepat for emergency treatment but the Center has yet to issue a statement as to Sandee's condition. We do have confirmation that Whisper the rhutz is dead.

The crowd stirred.

"The charred remains of his body are apparently still inside the Center.

"As you can see, there is much sadness and grief here amongst the delegates. Particularly, as the members and guests were celebrating a milestone, the first draft of the Supreme Mandate to be the cornerstone of a proposed world

government that was hoped would finally bring a lasting peace to Tarizon.

"The assassin is yet to be identified, but we understand it was someone well known to party members, someone they trusted and did not fear.

"It is unclear what the loss of the leader of the peace movement will mean for the upcoming World Conference. As you know, Sandee Brahn started the peace movement when he was just a boy of twelve. He claims that the God Pelgrem came to him in a dream and assigned him the task of bringing peace to Tarizon. While there are those who are skeptical of that claim, few dispute that he is the architect of the cease-fire between Soni and Synclare and the cessation of hostilities all over Tarizon in anticipation of the World Conference set to convene soon in Shisk."

Shante grimaced and put one hand to her ear. *"Oh! I just got word. The casualty center has just reported that Sandee Brahn has died of his wounds!"*

Shante started to choke up. *"Excuse me. This is a horrible moment for me and, I'm sure for all of you. Oh, my God! . . . Yes, I am sad to report that Sandee Brahn, who has survived four previous assassination attempts, did not survive this fifth one today."*

Tears began to flow down Shante's cheeks. *"I'm sorry. That's all for now. This is Veile Shante in Nepat. Tone, back to you."*

The screen went blank and the gathering erupted in excited chatter. After a few tiks, Bruda raised his hand to quiet the gathering. When the room was quiet, he said, "Well, that was certainly stunning news from Nepat. Sandee Brahn was a great man and his assassination is certainly an outrage, particularly from someone within his own inner circle. Such treachery is unimaginable."

There were nods and murmurs of agreement.

"Obviously, we are all too shocked and saddened to continue our work today," Bruda continued. "We should all go and contemplate the events of this tragic day. We will convene again tomorrow morning. Thank you."

Bedlam broke out amongst the members. Many hustled off to get more information on the assassination. Others stood around speculating as to what would happen to the peace initiative now that Sandee Brahn was dead. Bruda gathered his papers together and put them in his satchel. General Bakker came up to him and whispered. "I compliment you on keeping a straight face."

Bruda smiled and replied, "It wasn't easy, I promise you."

Petri Volk walked over and said, "I thought you gave up on assassinating Sandee Brahn when we embraced the peace movement?"

Bruda shook his head. "No. I never said that. Do you think I want Sandee Brahn around when the people elect their first Supreme Chancellor?"

"Good point," Petri said in a low voice. "So, how did you pull it off?"

"Did you not hear the reporter? It was someone in Sandee's inner circle. Clearly, I had nothing to do with it."

Petri nodded. "Right. Of course not."

They grinned at each other and then quickly walked out of the conference room, and walked across a courtyard to Bruda's office.

Once inside and away from the media, they each grabbed a Tekari and gathered around Bruda's desk.

"So, what does this mean, Dad?" Progasis asked.

Bruda smiled at his son. "It means we don't have to worry about Sandee Brahn becoming the first Supreme Chancellor of Tarizon. That's what would have happened had he run."

"Really?"

"Yes. He would have initially refused to run, claiming he had brought about peace and his job was done, but then his political allies would convince him that he was the only candidate they could put up who was guaranteed to win."

"Oh," Progasis said.

"So, he'd finally, reluctantly, give in and run. Then the other problem is with his popularity, he'd probably get whatever language he wanted in the Supreme Mandate and there would be very little we could do about it. If he wanted to be King he could insist on broad, far-reaching powers that would ensure he'd control the new government indefinitely."

Progasis nodded. "Oh. So, you had no choice but to get rid of him."

"Exactly. Now we have leveled the playing field and have taken Pelgrem out of the equation. Religion has no place in politics. There is no proof that Pelgrem even exists or, if he does, that he came with our ancestors to Tarizon."

"Who was the assassin?" Petri asked. "Anybody I know?"

"No, he just recently returned from Earth, so he can't be traced back to us. His name is Ritz Sloken."

"So, he was recruited on Earth?"

"Yes."

"How did you manage that?"

"You know me, I have spies everywhere," Bruda said.

"Right, but this was a suicide mission, right? How do you recruit people to do something that is likely to kill them?"

"I don't know that it was a suicide mission," Bruda replied. "Let's find out. Turn on the VC and see if there is an update."

Progasis got up and turned on the VC. It immediately lit up. On the screen was Veile Shante again taking the viewers, tik by tik, though the events of the morning.

Finally, she got to the arrest and identification of the assassin.

"The assassin has now been identified as Ritz Sloken," she advised, *"the son of one of the members of the GOT who, just a few days ago, returned from Earth. Members and supporters of the Peace Party that we have talked to today are baffled by Sloken's acts. Reportedly, he was a strong supporter of Sandee Brahn and his peace movement.*

"Of course, that's what he claimed. We don't really know much about him."

Shante grimaced as she listened to something in her earpiece. "Ah. . . . I'm just getting a report that Ritz Sloken has escaped. Apparently, he was taken into custody by two local public enforcers to be transported to Nepat's detention center, but the officers were imposters.

"The actual officers who were assigned the duty of transporting Sloken have been found dead, apparently killed by laser blasts to their abdomen just as Sandee Brahn was killed.

"That's all for now. Back to you, Tone."

The screen changed back to the news anchor. Bruda gave Progasis a nod and he turned off the VC.

"So, it wasn't a suicide mission," Petri said.

"No, suicide missions are for fanatics. We are businessmen and smart enough to know that anything we want to do can be accomplished by careful planning and discipline."

"So, what's our next move?" General Bakker asked.

"We need to finish our draft of the Supreme Mandate and then start planning for the World Council. While everyone else is mourning the loss of Sandee Brahn, we will be making sure we have a majority of the delegates on our side. That won't be easy, but it will be a lot easier now with His Holiness out of the picture."

"We are about done, aren't we?" Petri asked. "What issues are left?"

"Several, but the most important is the definition of citizen. In other words, who will be allowed to vote," Bruda said. "We want to exclude Seafolken, slaves, mutants and all non-human life-forms. The slaves and mutants will be a drag on the economy. Most of them are unemployed and generally unhealthy. They'll expect the new government to let them into the domed cities and take care of them. The cost to do that would be staggering. We don't want that. It's going to take all our resources to ensure all normal, healthy humans survive, considering the dire state of the environment."

"So, what will happen to those who are not given citizenship?" Progasis asked.

"They will have to fend for themselves like many of them do now. It won't be our problem. As it is, we will have to build many more domed cities where the air, water, and food supply can be filtered and protected from the toxins in our atmosphere. It will be a monumental task, but absolutely necessary if we want our families to have comfortable, healthy and productive lives in the future."

"When you say fend for themselves, do you mean the new central authority won't govern them?" Petri asked.

"Right. Our new military, the TGA, will maintain order outside the domed cities. But the mutants and others living on the outside will have to figure out how to govern themselves and survive on their own."

There was a moment of silence as everyone contemplated what would be tantamount to a death sentence for millions of mutants, Seafolken, and other life-forms.

Seeing their discomfort, Bruda added, "It's not much different than what's happening now, but we will have to kick out all the mutants and Seafolken living in the domed cities now. We don't really have any other choice. There simply aren't enough resources to save them. We are simply protecting and preserving the lives of all healthy and pure human beings on Tarizon. It's the best way to ensure the survival of the human race."

"What about the right to bear arms?" General Bakker asked. "I've been wondering if we want the civilian population to have weapons. On the one hand, we will profit by millions of citizens purchasing them, but how can the TGA keep the peace if every dissident has an arsenal of weapons?"

"If it were just about profits, I'd say let every citizen be armed, but we can't forget why we decided to support the peace movement. We want to ultimately control the new central government. Once we are in control, we want to stay in control. If our enemies are well-armed, they may try to revolt."

"But what if the Peace Movement's candidate wins? Won't we want our supporters to be armed in case we need to revolt?" Progasis asked.

Bruda laughed. "Don't worry, son. It doesn't matter what the Supreme Mandate says about the right to bear arms. We will always have what arms we need. After all, we'll still be manufacturing and warehousing them."

Progasis nodded. "Right."

Bruda looked at his son thoughtfully. The questions he'd asked were troubling, and he wasn't sure his answers had been necessarily correct. A lot hinged on who was elected the first Chancellor since he would be setting up the new Central Authority and be in charge of the creation of the TGA. Realistically, even with Sandee Brahn dead, the Peace Party candidate would be difficult to beat. So, they had to prepare for the worst—Tarizon's first Supreme Chancellor coming from the Peace Party. That would mean they would want a Supreme Mandate that guaranteed them as much freedom and privacy as possible so the new government couldn't hinder them in the realization of their business and political goals and objectives.

"In closing," Bruda said. "Remember this. As Purists, we will always be successful because we are strong, resourceful and willing to do whatever it takes to win! Whatever it takes, or in Tari, Eek n badden!!"

"Eek n badden!" they all proclaimed.

43
Filling the Void

While the public enforcers were working the crime scene, the bodies were taken to the Public Crime Lab for processing. When that had been completed the next day, they were taken to Nepat's airport to be flown back to Ya Lat where a funeral was in the planning stages. Ambassador Talvihn, Romas Garciah, Arvis Gill and their staffs accompanied the bodies back to Lyon. Thousands of people lined the streets of Nepat along the route to the airport where they knew the procession of Grindens carrying the bodies would have to travel. It would be their only chance to say goodbye to their fallen heroes.

All over Tarizon, there was sorrow and outrage over the assassinations. In Ya Lat, hundreds of thousands of citizens were already converging on the airport in anticipation of the arrival of Sandee's and Whisper's bodies. In Tarizon's largest cities, Shisk, Vaceen and Shini, the city squares and downtown areas were filled with tens of thousands of citizens mourning Sandee's death and demanding that the assassin be caught and brought to justice.

Marches, protests and vigils were being held in almost every city on every continent from Queenland to Pohl and from Quori to Darkland. People everywhere were grief-stricken and shaken to the bone by these senseless killings, and had to find a release for these emotions or go mad. Fear gripped the hearts of everyone out in the streets. Fear that, without Sandee and Whisper, the lasting peace that was so close to fruition after 100 cycles of war, would be stolen from them in the final hours.

Once in the air, the Ambassador, Arvis, and Romas discussed the future of the Peace Party. They knew Sandee would want them to press on without him and do whatever was necessary to finish the job he had started.

"You knew Ritz Sloken, didn't you?" Arvis asked Romas.

"Yes," Romas said. "He's Rama's son. He's always been a decent boy, however, I did hear some rumors about him that were disturbing."

"Did you ever speak of our leader when you were on Earth?"

"Only recently, after we got word of the cease-fire between Soni and Synclare and the agreement to constitute a World Council to draft a Supreme Mandate for ratification."

"Was his father upset over the creation of a world government?" Arvis asked.

Romas thought a moment. "Not to my knowledge. He never spoke for or against it,"

"Did anyone speak against it?"

"Yes, Markis Lai and his mate, Sarna were very outspoken about it. They thought Sandee was a fraud and only out for his own power and glory. There were others who felt the same way, too. Their children, Blinh and Bellah, of course."

"Could any of them have influenced him?" Arvis asked.

"Possibly. The Lai children and Ritz spent a lot of time together, so they were pretty close."

"I didn't think Sandee could be killed," Arvis said. "I really thought Pelgrem would protect him."

"Perhaps this was Pelgrem's plan," the Ambassador suggested.

"What do you mean?" Arvis asked. "Who will lead us with Sandee gone?"

"Sometimes when a great man sacrifices himself for a cause, his influence grows tenfold."

"You mean, he becomes a martyr."

"Yes. Maybe a martyr is what was needed to finish the job."

"Maybe, but we still need a living leader. Someone from the Peace Party should be our first Supreme Chancellor. We can't let Bruda and his generals get control of the government. They would never let go of power once they got it."

"You're right about that," Romas agreed.

"What about you?" the Ambassador suggested.

"Me? What about me?" Romas said.

"Maybe you should be our new leader," the Ambassador said.

"Yes. That's a good idea," Arvis agreed.

Romas shook his head. "No. I'm an interpreter, not a politician. We need someone with charisma and proven leadership skills; someone the people will love and respect, but also someone who respects the law."

"Chancellor Linzcot," Arvis suggested. "He was the first Chancellor to come out in favor of the peace movement and he is loved and respected by the people of Lyon."

"I don't know him," Romas said. "But perhaps he is the one we are looking for. When we get to Lyon, I shall be anxious to meet him."

"He's certain to be there when we arrive," Ambassador Talvihn said. "I'm sure you will like him."

"I'm sure I will."

As the plane made its approach to Ya Lat's airport, they were all amazed to see the thousands of citizens below who had converged on the airport to pay their last respects to their fallen hero, His Holiness Sandee Brahn. After the plane landed and had taxied to the terminal, the Ambassador held a brief media conference from the top step of the disembarkation stairway.

Someone handed him an amplifier and he held it up to his lips and began, "Thank you for coming out here today to show your love and respect for Sandee Brahn. This is a difficult time for all of us. We are all still in shock. It's hard to understand how a heinous act like this could happen, and it's tempting to blame it on those who have been perceived as the enemies of peace. But you know Sandee wouldn't want you to lash out at anyone until you had proof they were responsible. Be assured, the person or persons responsible for the assassination of His Holiness and Whisper the rhutz, will be brought to justice.

"In the meantime, Sandee wouldn't want us to be distracted from our primary objective. He'd want us to carry on and complete his mission of peace by going through with constituting a World Council, adopting a supreme mandate and getting it approved by the citizens of Tarizon. This must be our primary focus.

"In the next few days, a new leader will be selected to carry our torch of peace. I'm not sure who that person will be, but whoever it is, he will need your complete and unrelenting support. Can I count on you?"

"Yes," a few in the crowd yelled!

"I'm sorry," the Ambassador said. "I couldn't hear you. I said, can I count on all of you to support our new leader and be relentless in your pursuit of peace on Tarizon?"

Everyone in the crowd responded, "Yes!"

"Good. Because the task at hand will be much more difficult without Sandee's guidance. So, your hard work and support will be critical to our success. Please pray to Pelgrem for His help in ensuring the peace we enjoy today will soon become permanent," the Ambassador concluded.

As the Ambassador descended the stairway, the

crowd started chanting, "Peace now! Peace now! Peace now!"

Soon a new motorcade of Grindens was driving out of the airport toward central Ya Lat. After dropping off Sandee's and Whisper's bodies at the disposal center, the Ambassador and the others went to the Chancellor's office where Chancellor Linzcot was anxiously waiting.

Chancellor Linzcot embraced Arvis and then shook each of the other's hands. "We are so stunned by this tragedy," he said shaking his head. "It's unfathomable."

"Yes, it is," Romas agreed.

"I'm so baffled how one of our own could have done this. Did he give us no hint of his intentions?"

"Perhaps he did and I missed it," Romas admitted. "I'm afraid I look for the good in people and sometimes overlook their shortcomings. He said he wanted peace for Tarizon, but now we know that was a lie."

"Well. That's what Pelgrem taught us, but I'm afraid that won't work in the current political environment," Chancellor Linzcot said, "Have a seat. We have much to talk about. Can I get you some Sankee or something stronger?"

"Sankee is fine," the Ambassador said. The others agreed.

"So, who do you think was behind the assassination?" Chancellor Linzcot asked.

"We talked about that on the way here from Nepat," Romas said. "I think Markis Lai's boy, Blinh, must have turned his friend. They were good friends on Earth."

"But why kill Sandee now? Everyone seems to agree there has to be peace."

"Right. I think they were afraid Sandee couldn't be beaten if he ran for Supreme Chancellor. They figured they at least have a shot at defeating a lesser-known figure."

Chancellor Linzcot nodded. "They are probably right, and whoever we pick to run is going to be looking over his shoulder a lot."

"Yes. Security is going to be a nightmare. There is so much at stake in this first election."

"I'm worried about the delegates to the Organizing Committee of the World Council. I have polled them and right now eighteen of the thirty-one support the Peace Party and our agenda, but what if Bruda and his thugs get to some of them? Each state will give their delegate a security detail, I'm sure, but I fear they will be no match for an MIA assault team."

"I'll get with Rack Brodie and see if he has any suggestions," Arvis said.

"We should enlist the help of the rhutz. They could provide a pack of rhutz to help protect any delegate no matter in what state they reside," Romas added.

"So, who are you looking at to run for Chancellor?" Chancellor Linzcot asked.

"Actually," Romas said, "we were thinking of you."

"Me? Oh, no. I was going to suggest you, Romas. You have a reputation of being a very honest and wise man."

"No, I'm not a politician. I have never run for office. We couldn't take a chance on a novice. Plus, I have been harshly criticized for abandoning Tarizon at a time of need. I frankly didn't believe Tarizon could be saved. I'm glad I was wrong and was able to come back to support the peace movement, but my vulnerability precludes my candidacy. You, however, are the perfect candidate."

"He is right," Ambassador Talvihn agreed. "You were the first political leader to join the Peace Party and were instrumental in getting other world leaders to join. You are the perfect person to run."

"Well, I can't say I haven't thought about it," Chancellor Linzcot admitted. "Setting up this world government is going to be a very delicate business."

"Yes, you're absolutely right," Romas agreed. "That's why we need you."

"Even if the citizens of Tarizon approve the Supreme Mandate, that doesn't mean the elected officials and state militias will automatically turn over their access codes and their weapons. There could be resistance and we won't have an army put together yet to deal with it."

Romas sighed. "Yes. There will have to be much planning done to ensure the transition takes place quickly and peacefully, but realizing how difficult a challenge will be is the first step in overcoming it."

"True enough. I'll have to talk to my family, of course, but I suspect they won't be opposed to the idea. I will need a lot of help in pulling this off."

"Oh, yes," the Ambassador said. "You'll have all the help you need."

"Absolutely," Romas said.

The Chancellor looked at Arvis. "Well, Arvis, you know the Peace Party better than anyone. Are you ready to get me up to speed?"

"Yes, sir. We can start first thing in the morning."

"Good. There's no time to lose."

44
The Last Tribute

The population of Ya Lat swelled from its usual 1.2 million to over five million with the onslaught of mourners from every corner of the planet wanting to pay their last respects to the Savior of Tarizon. Unfortunately, with Sandee's death, it was unclear as to whether Tarizon would be saved after all. There was talk of postponing the convening of the World Council in light of the assassinations.

Organizers were in a panic now that their leader was gone. It was a complicated process getting 31 governments to agree on a date, location, and governing rules for the convention to constitute a World Council. Sandee Brahn had enjoyed so much respect and admiration of the people that state leaders had usually accepted his judgment on convention issues with little opposition, but after his death, the new leadership got much less cooperation. Bickering and infighting over every issue quickly became the norm and many wondered if the whole process would come to a halt.

Cornelius Bruda and his entourage arrived in Ya Lat the day before Sandee's funeral. He knew with the leaders of every nation-state on Tarizon being in Ya Lat at the same time, there would never be a better opportunity to forge relationships and alliances to ensure the final draft of the Supreme Mandate adopted by the World Council, would be to their liking. He had also heard that the Peace Party would be announcing their candidate for Supreme Chancellor and, if that happened, it would be important that an opposition candidate is announced soon thereafter. They couldn't let the

Peace Party get the jump on them. There was simply too much at stake.

That night Bruda hosted a dinner and strategy session at a local tavern. Bruda, his son Progasis, Petri Volk, General Bakker, Cameela Bruns, Bellah Lai, Chancellor Marcez, Mayor Vill Linell, General Barkha, and others were in attendance. After dinner, they got down to the important issues that confronted them.

"Thank you all for coming tonight," Bruda began. "I trust your dinner was enjoyable."

There were nods and smiles of appreciation.

"Ordinarily I would have provided after-dinner entertainment, but there are too many important issues that need to be discussed and decisions that must be made in the next few days to allow it. My apologies."

"No. Let's get down to business," Petri agreed. "We can party after the World Council meets and we have a Supreme Mandate to our liking."

"Yes, that's right," General Bakker agreed.

"Okay, the first order of business is to determine who should be our candidate for Supreme Chancellor," Bruda said. "Rumor has it that the Peace Party will be announcing their candidate tomorrow. We don't have to announce ours tomorrow but we shouldn't wait too long."

"We should announce our candidate as well," Petri Volk said, "while all the world leaders are in Shisk."

Many members nodded their agreement.

"Anyone disagree?" Bruda asked.

"Shouldn't our party have a convention to elect its candidate?" Cameela asked. "That way you get a lot of free publicity and you can keep your candidate in the public eye for several days."

Bruda looked at her thoughtfully. "Yes, of course. I wonder why the Peace Party isn't doing that?"

"Because Pelgrem is calling the shots," Bellah Lai replied sarcastically. "You don't need a convention when you have God behind you."

There was a roar of laughter.

"I suppose," Bruda said. "We will also need to set up an organization in each state to recruit candidates for local office and make sure the new Supreme Mandate is ratified. Since you brought it up, Cameela," Bruda said, "I appoint you to organize it."

There was more laughter.

Cameela blushed.

"No. I'm serious," Bruda said. "I don't know anyone better suited for the role as Cameela. She's as shrewd a woman as I know and a great organizer."

"Thank you," Cameela said meekly. "But I have no political experience."

"Don't worry. You're not running for office. That's going to be Chancellor Marcez's job. He'll announce he is seeking the Purist Party's nomination for Supreme Chancellor and you can announce when and where the party convention will be."

Cameela nodded warily. "Okay. I suppose."

"I'll help you," Bellah said. "It will be exciting."

Cameela smiled.

"Thank you, both of you," Bruda said. "Now since our last meeting was cut short, we didn't get to discuss the location of our new capital city. Rumor has it that the Peace Party wants it to be in Lyon or Rigimol, but I believe it should be here in Soni where we have the greatest political support. So, I believe Shisk should be our new world capital."

There were nods of approval, so Bruda continued, "General Bakker, you and I need to contact as many military leaders as we can find in these next few days. We need to know who to support for leadership positions in the new central command."

"Yes. I have a list already prepared, and my staff is setting up meetings as we speak."

"Good. That may be our most important task."

The General nodded.

"Chancellor Marcez. I assume you will be talking to the other chancellors about the delegates they are sending to the Organizing Committee meeting to constitute the World Council," Bruda asked.

"Yes, that's my top priority right now. Unfortunately, if the Organizing Committee for the World Council met today the Peace Party would defeat us."

"We can't let the Peace Party control the Committee," Bruda exclaimed. "They want to give mutants, slaves, and Seafolken the right to vote."

There were cries of anguish from everyone.

"What do you suggest?" Chancellor Marcez asked.

Bruda thought a moment. "Leave that to me," Bruda said. "How many delegates do we need to turn or eliminate?"

"Four or five would be ideal, but if any of them die or cannot serve their Chancellor will just appoint a replacement."

"If they can find someone stupid enough to accept the appointment," General Bakker noted.

Everyone laughed.

"Alright," Bruda said. "Let me worry about the delegates. Now, you all have your assignments so get to work. And remember we cannot be stopped and we cannot fail because we'll do whatever it takes for victory."

Everyone stood, raised a clenched fist, and yelled, "Eek n badden!"

"Eek n badden!" Bruda screamed raising his clenched fist.

"Eek n badden!" everyone echoed.

After the party meeting broke up, Bruda and General Bakker moved to a private room where General Barkha was providing entertainment for a group of generals and their staffs representing Quori, Darkland, Merria, and Rour. Scantily clad women were everywhere dancing, serving drinks and attending to every wish and desire of their guests.

"Alright, soldiers," General Bakker said. "Party time is over. Let's get down to business."

The music stopped and the women quickly disbursed. The soldiers reluctantly took seats where they could listen to Bakker.

"Thank you all for coming tonight. I trust you enjoyed the entertainment."

There were nods of assent and many smiles.

The General cleared his throat. "I know you are all here to pay your respects to Sandee Brahn. His assassination is a great tragedy for Tarizon, and it is right to honor him. But he is gone and we can't bring him back, so after the funeral, new leaders will have to be chosen to guide Tarizon into its future.

"Our sources tell us the Peace Party candidate for Supreme Chancellor will be announced tomorrow. Whoever he turns out to be, he will be banking on the support of all of Sandee's followers to sweep him into power. If this happens, it will be a disaster for Tarizon.

"It's no secret the Peace Party's objective is to minimize the army's power and authority. You can bet if the Peace Party candidate is elected our new TGA will be nothing but a peacekeeping force. You will be spending the bulk of your time on disaster relief, traffic duty and keeping mutants from killing each other. There won't be any need for new weapons, ships, or aircraft, and those we have will not be maintained.

"In addition, I'm sure you know that the Peace Party wants to free the slaves, let mutants and Seafolken vote, and guarantee them the same rights and freedoms that we enjoy."

Many groaned, shook their heads and mumbled their displeasure.

"I urge you to join the new Purist Party. We will build a strong TGA and arm it with the latest weapons, ships, and aircraft available."

General Bakker turned to Bruda. "You all know Cornelius Bruda and Bruda Industries. He is the new Chairman of the Purist Party so you can rest assured our party will fight for a strong TGA to keep all our citizens safe. And, when I say citizens, I mean humans as God made them, pure and perfect, not mutants or Seafolken or inferior life-forms like the rhutz or zodillo."

Many nodded, cheered and clapped.

"So, if you are with us, help us and we will make sure you get the best assignments when the new TGA is formed. Thanks again, for coming. If you want to hang around a while, I'll send the girls back out."

There were cheers and clapping, then the music started back up and girls began streaming out of a back room into anxious arms. Bruda smiled, turned and left the room with General Bakker on his heels.

<h1 style="text-align:center">45
The Funeral</h1>

On the day of Sandee Brahn's funeral, the streets of downtown Ya Lat were clogged with citizens hoping for a glimpse of Sandee's final journey on Tarizon. The streets had been closed since daybreak, but even without traffic, there was barely room to move anywhere downtown. Fortunately, Mayor Linell had provided Romas and his entourage a hover taxi that brought them in over the crowds to the Pelgremist Cathedral where a memorial service was to be held.

The church, which took up almost a full city block, was nearly full when they were escorted to their reserved seats in the third row. Sandee and Whisper were laid out in two elegant coffins at the front of the church, framed by arrangements of silk flowers handcrafted to look like Sky Blossoms which once grew abundantly on Tarizon.

The Ambassador nodded at Mayor Linell and Cornelius Bruda who were seated in the second row. Anger welled in the Ambassador as he peered down at Bruda who he was sure was responsible for Sandee's assassination. He looked over at Arvis and shook his head. She took a deep breath and let it out slowly.

"I can't believe Bruda has the nerve to be here," the Ambassador whispered.

"And in the second row with friends and family," Romas added. "What a travesty."

"I'd like to kill the skutz," Arvis whispered angrily. "He deserves a slow and painful death."

A moment later a priest, adorned in a purple robe and

a thick gold necklace, took the pulpit. He stood there silently until the crowd quieted. Looking out over the crowd, he finally smiled and raised his hands to the heavens and said, "Oh, mighty Pelgrem, bless these friends and citizens of Tarizon who have come out today to honor your messenger and servant, Sandee Brahn."

The priest lowered his hands and continued, "Thank you for coming today. This outpouring of love for Sandee Brahn, that we have seen these past few days, is a tribute to the power of our God Almighty Pelgrem. Seventeen cycles ago Pelgrem came down from Heaven and appeared before a young boy still reeling from the loss of his mother, father, and siblings, and said unto him; go out onto the world and seek peace in my name in order to save our people from self-destruction. And with only a rhutz to guide and protect him, Sandee Brahn obeyed his God and took on this seemingly impossible task without argument or complaint.

"I know you must be thinking, how could Pelgrem allow his servant and messenger to be murdered? Well, I can't answer that. Only Pelgrem could do that, but He will not. Instead, He asks each and every one of us to have faith. Faith in Pelgrem's plan to bring peace to Tarizon. Apparently, Sandee's death was a necessary sacrifice. This is, of course, sad but it's an honor, too; to be able to give one life so that millions can live. There is no doubt that Sandee Brahn's name will be honored and cherished until the end of time."

The priest continued his sermon for nearly a kyloon and then released the pulpit to friends and followers who wanted to reflect on their encounters and experiences with Sandee. After the last speaker left the pulpit there was music, songs, and prayers for Sandee and Tarizon.

At the conclusion of the ceremony, a long line of mourners began streaming by Sandee's and Whisper's coffins. The line stretched outside the church for several kylods and didn't seem to shrink in length as new citizens joined the line all afternoon and into the evening. At midnight, the church was closed and the last mourners were allowed to view the bodies. Many disappointed citizens were turned away.

The following afternoon the Peace Party held a news conference to assure the citizens of Tarizon that the peace process would continue, despite Sandee Brahn's assassination. Cornelius Bruda and his entourage watched the coverage of the news conference on the VC in the hotel bar.

"This is Veile Shante coming to you live from the Capitol Building in Ya Lat, Lyon. As you know yesterday Sandee Brahn and Whisper were honored at a memorial celebration at the Pelgremist Cathedral. Due to Sandee's death, the Peace Party has called this news conference which will begin momentarily.

"Speaking today for the Peace Party and answering questions will be Lyon's Chancellor Linzcot who was the first Chancellor on Tarizon to embrace the Peace Party and its mission to end war on Tarizon. With him are Lyon's Ambassador Talvihn, Arvis Gill, Romas Garciah and the rhutz known as Snowflake."

Chancellor Linzcot went to the podium and looked out over the dozens of reporters, cameramen, and spectators who had assembled for the media conference.

"Good afternoon," he said smiling warmly. "Thank you for coming out today. I called this news conference because I know there is a lot of fear and confusion amongst our citizens about the future of the peace process now that Sandee Brahn is no longer here to lead us going forward.

"Let me affirm to you that the Organizing Meeting for the World Council will be held in Shisk on the tenth day of

the third phase, cycle 20237 as previously agreed by all the nation-states last cycle in Shisk. This means we have less than two cycles for the completion of a world census, apportionment of delegates amongst the states, and the election of delegations to the World Council. There will be no delays or postponements. This is our one chance to adopt a Supreme Mandate for ratification by the states. In order for the Supreme Mandate to become effective and a world government formed, it must be approved by a majority of citizens in each state. This will be no simple task. It will take a monumental effort by all of us to achieve, but with the help of our God, Pelgrem, it can be accomplished.

"Now, the ratification of the Supreme Mandate is just the first step. Once it has been ratified the people of Tarizon will have to elect a Supreme Chancellor who will set up the new government or Central Authority as it is to be called. The election of this first Supreme Chancellor will be the most important vote any citizen of Tarizon will ever cast.

"I know we all assumed and expected that Sandee Brahn would be our first Supreme Chancellor, but that can't happen now, so we must choose another. That is why I am announcing today that I will be the Peace Party's candidate for Supreme Chancellor.

"As you know, once a Supreme Mandate is ratified, the members of the World Council will become the first World Assembly and it will immediately get to work enacting all the laws that will be needed to run the new government.

"As you know, I was the first Chancellor of any nation-state on Tarizon to support Sandee Brahn and join his Peace Party. I agreed with Sandee that if we allowed the many wars in progress on Tarizon to continue, Tarizon would be on its way to self-destruction. Something had to be done, so I made a commitment to the Peace Party and did all I could to encourage and support it, including appointing

Sandee as First Minister of Lyon.

"For many cycles, I have worked closely with Sandee in his efforts to bring peace to Tarizon, so I knew him and those around him as well as anybody. That knowledge and familiarity with him will uniquely qualify me to continue his work and preserve his legacy without interruption.

"Thank you," Chancellor Linzcot concluded. "Now, I will take a few questions."

Many reporters raised their hands. Chancellor Linzcot pointed to a reporter he knew as Riki Tilbet. "Riki."

"Mr. Chancellor. Do you intend to find Sandee's assassin and bring him to justice?"

"Well, that will have to be done by the authorities in Nepat and Tributon since Sandee was assassinated there, but I will provide any cooperation requested."

The reporters raised their hands again and the Chancellor pointed to Veile Shante. "Yes, Veile."

"Mr. Chancellor, Do you expect anyone to oppose you in the race for Supreme Chancellor?"

The Chancellor nodded. "Oh, yes. I'm certain there will be many other candidates. The Supreme Chancellor will have enormous power and there will be many coveting the job, some because they believe their election would be for the good of Tarizon, but many, I'm afraid, for their own personal gain and satisfaction.

"Personally, I only care about the welfare of Tarizon and its citizens. I believe in personal freedom, democracy, equality of all sentient life-forms and the end to slavery. I have been a public servant for many cycles so it will be easy for voters to look at my record and know that I am an honorable man who deserves their trust."

The news conference continued for some time as the reporters had an endless supply of questions. Finally, Chancellor Linzcot grew weary and said, "Thank you. That will be all for now."

"Veile Shante came back on and summarized the Chancellor's statement. Then she noted, "So, the race for Supreme Chancellor of Tarizon begins. This has been Veile Shante coming to you live from the Capitol Building in Ya Lat, Lyon."

Bruda respected Chancellor Linzcot as an adversary. Although he had tried on numerous occasions to buy his support for various arms contracts with Lyon, Linzcot had always refused. Such integrity was rare on Tarizon and Bruda didn't know what to make of it. He was used to getting what he wanted simply by passing out money and power but he knew that wouldn't work in this case.

Bruda turned to Petri Volk and said, "Well, that's no big surprise. He's definitely their best candidate, but he's no Sandee Brahn."

"No," Petri agreed. "And he's not well known outside of Azollo."

"We must thoroughly investigate his past. There must be secrets he's kept hidden over the cycles. Now is the time to expose them."

"What if he doesn't have anything compromising in his past?" Petri asked. "I don't remember hearing about anything."

"Then we'll have to be creative and conjure up something," Bruda replied with a grin. "He's a proud man, and his pride will make him vulnerable."

Petri laughed. "Right. We'll have to get someone to infiltrate his inner circle in order to pull this off, and I know just the person to do it, too."

"Who did you have in mind?" Bruda asked with a grin.

"Bellah," Petri replied.

"Your granddaughter, really?"

"Yes. She's just back from Earth and nobody knows what she looks like. She'd love an assignment like that."

"But the people returning from Earth know what she looks like."

"True, but none of them were from Lyon. She'll be a stranger in Ya Lat, and we'll give her a new identity just in case."

"What about her mate? Won't he object?"

"She hasn't mated. She was engaged on Earth but that was ended when she returned to Tarizon."

"And you're okay with it? You're not worried she might be exposed to danger?"

"No. She's always been a clever girl. As I understand it, she had seduced the son of a very powerful man on Earth and was about to exploit that relationship when news of the unification effort reached her. Apparently, she is quite good at seduction and manipulation."

"Great. Set up a meeting then. This might take some time to plan, and it will need to be carefully orchestrated, so we better get started soon."

"Yes, of course," Petri replied. "I'll get right on it."

Petri picked up his Tekari and took a drink.

"Father," Progasis Bruda said. "I'd like to do something exciting as well. I've served a tour of duty in the TNA as you asked, but I don't want to be career military or a businessman either. I want to be a delegate on the World Council."

Bruda looked over at his son and frowned. "You think you'd like politics?"

"Yes. It's exciting and I want to be part of the new world government."

"Well, you'll definitely be at center stage where many important decisions about Tarizon's future will be made."

"Do you think it is possible?" Progasis asked.

"Well, there will be 500 delegates to the World

Council allocated by relative population amongst the 31 nation-states. So, I figure Tributon will get at least 30 or 40 delegates. If you want to be a delegate, I will support you, but it won't be an easy job. You'll have to devote every waking hour for the next two cycles getting elected. After that, the real work begins."

Progasis swallowed hard. "Right. I know it will be a challenge, but that's okay. I can do it. I'm ready."

Bruda shrugged. "Well, good. If that's what you want."

"It's settled then. I can run?"

"Why not," Bruda replied with a grin.

Petri raised his bottle of Tekari. "Here's to Progasis Bruda, the first Purist candidate to be a delegate to the World Council!"

Bruda and the others raised their bottles and joined in the toast. Friendly banter and applause broke out and Bruda felt proud of his son. He liked the idea of having someone on the World Council he could really trust; someone who was bound to him by blood rather than money. But did his son know what he was getting himself into? Bruda didn't think so, but he supposed it was time for him to grow up, and what better way than in the line of fire.

46
The Mole

Bellah Lai, known to the campaign staff as Bellah Surro, approached Chancellor Linzcot who was seated at his desk in his Lyon office reading a thick report. She handed him a cup of Sankee. He smiled broadly as he took the drink. He'd instantly liked this beautiful and charming woman who had recently joined his staff. Arvis had hired Bellah as one of many campaign aides to assist in the handling of Linzcot's calendar and logistics for his campaign to be Tarizon's first Supreme Chancellor.

"Thank you, Bellah," he said. "Let me know when everyone has arrived for the staff meeting."

"Yes, sir," Bellah replied. "I believe everyone is here but General Mulhford. He called and said he'd be here in about ten loons."

"Good," he mumbled. "I need to get through this report before the meeting starts."

Bellah nodded, turned and left the room. Fifteen loons later she returned and advised him that they were ready for him. He stood up and followed her down the hall to the conference room. She opened the door for him but didn't follow him in the room as the meeting was confidential and only top staffers had been invited.

"Can I bring you more Sankee, sir?" she asked before closing the door.

"Yes, please. I could use another cup."

Bellah went back to the Chancellor's office and retrieved his cup. Adroitly, she switched his cup for an identical one she'd earlier hidden in one of his desk drawers. The cup had an embedded microchip that would silently broadcast the meeting to a recording device in a hover taxi parked down the street. After delivering the cup of Sankee to the Chancellor, she left the room and breathed a sigh of relief. This was the first dangerous thing she'd done, and she was glad the task was over. She wondered what would be next.

In attendance at the meeting were a representative from each of the states as well as Ambassador Talvihn, Arvis Gill, and Snowflake.

Linzcot cleared his throat. "Alright. Let's get started. This will be the first of many meetings to plan and prepare for the upcoming World Council organizing convention. Obviously, nothing like this has ever been done on Tarizon, and the job will be quite daunting.

"Phase One will be constituting a World Council. To do this we will have to come up with a way to identify who will be entitled to vote. Once we know who the voters are, we must then develop an effective way for them to cast their ballots.

"Next we must decide the qualifications for delegates, determine how many will be elected, and apportion them equitably between the nation-states.

"Finally, we will have to set dates for the beginning and end of campaigning. Once the delegates are elected, then the elected delegates of the World Council will take over and Phase Two will begin.

"In Phase Two, leadership will have to be determined and then the delegates will have to draft and approve the content of the Supreme Mandate. Once the proposed Supreme Mandate is approved it must be submitted to the citizens of Tarizon for their ratification.

"Phase Three will be the election of a Supreme Chancellor and Vice-Chancellor and the formation of Central

Authority.

"Thankfully, today we are only dealing with Phase One."

There were sighs of relief and laughter among the delegates.

"To get things started," Linzcot continued, "Ambassador Talvihn has some ideas that he would like to share with the delegates."

Linzcot looked over at the Ambassador and smiled. Talvihn stood up and said, "Thank you, Chancellor Linzcot. Delegates and friends. Don't be discouraged by the enormity of this task. The difficult part has already been done. The people of Tarizon have spoken and they want, no, they demand peace."

There were shouts of agreement.

"So, let's give it to them by getting the World Council constituted quickly and effectively. In this vein, I have a number of ideas I would like you to consider.

"First, every human being of every race and gender including mutants and Seafolken must be allowed to vote. That means slavery must be immediately abolished. This is our chance to create a real democratic government so it must be all inclusive to be legitimate and sustainable."

There were cries of anguish and excited whispers.

"I know this will be a bitter pill for some to swallow, particularly if they engage in the slave trade, but we can't impose a world government on a class of human beings who haven't consented to it. On the other hand, we cannot give the right to vote to non-human life forms as it would be too complicated and there is simply no precedent for it. I know many of you want all life forms to have the right to vote and enjoy the protections of the Supreme Mandate, but if we insist on that the Supreme Mandate will never be ratified. We must be realistic. What I propose is a common-sense compromise, and I would urge you to adopt it."

"Now, once we have defined our voters, we must come up with a voting mechanism for the election of the delegates, the Supreme Chancellor and other officers. Realistically, to do this we must conduct a census for the entire world. We cannot rely on the existing nation-states to certify their electorates because there is no uniformity in the way each state determines who can vote, and no way to verify the integrity of their voting systems.

"I know this will be an enormous task, but we simply have no other choice. Because time is limited, I suggest we conduct the world census, and at the same time put in place the mechanism for casting ballots."

There were frowns and looks of confusion on many of the delegates' faces.

Talvihn smiled. "Okay, bear with me. I know it sounds impossible to do all three things at once, but it's really not. Let me explain. Citizen Registration Centers or CRCs will be set up at convenient locations throughout each state. Registrars at these CRCs will process all those who come in, and at the same time provide them with a wrist array for voting in future elections. These wrist arrays will be surgically implanted in each person's body and will deactivate if removed. They will ensure that each citizen only votes one time during a prescribed voting period, and ensure there is no voter fraud."

Many of the delegates stiffened and squirmed in their chairs.

"I know this sounds radical, but it's the only way to be sure we get a quick and accurate vote. These wrist arrays will also be necessary for our new Central Authority to keep track of our citizens. Not only will these wrist arrays be used for voting, but they will also monitor health, provide communication, and be a critical element in the world's new banking system."

Many hands shot up. "Now I know you all have

questions and there is much to discuss. Later in the week, we will bring in experts to further explain the census and the use of wrist arrays. All your questions will be answered then."

Linzcot nodded. "Thank you, Mill. I have one question. What if a citizen objects to having a wrist array surgically implanted? Will he lose his right to vote?"

Talvihn nodded. "I'm afraid so. This system will only work if every citizen participates. But, even if some people refuse and give up the right to vote, if the Supreme Mandate is ratified, I'm sure the new Central Authority will require everyone to have a wrist array or some kind of implant so it can keep track of its citizens."

"What about the cost?" a delegate asked.

"Fortunately, these wrist arrays, if manufactured in large quantities, are relatively cheap. They will certainly be much cheaper than organizing a traditional election."

The meeting went on for several kyloons and when it was about over Linzcot introduced their new head of security, Rack Brodie. "Mr. Brodie and his staff will have a very difficult job," Linzcot said. "You can bet the Purists will use every dirty trick they can imagine to compromise us and give them an advantage when the elections roll around."

"That's correct," Brodie said. "You should all be very paranoid from now on. Assume everyone you don't know is your enemy. Always stay close to your security detail. Don't stray away from them. Such carelessness could be fatal.

"Now, obviously, everything discussed here is confidential. Don't ever talk about what goes on at these meetings with anyone except fellow delegates. Your compartments and transport vehicles should be swept for listening devices often. But, just to be safe it would be better not to talk about confidential matters at home or when you are traveling.

"Now, I will want to meet with each of your own

security details to coordinate our activities. If you have any questions, don't hesitate to let me know. Thank you."

When the meeting finally concluded for the day, Bellah cleaned up the conference room and disposed of the Chancellor's cup. Before she left for the day, she went to the Chancellor's office and stepped inside. Brodie was just leaving. Linzcot looked at her and smiled.

"Bellah. What can I do for you?"

"Oh, actually, I was going to ask you that question. Is there anything I can do for you before I leave?"

The Chancellor didn't respond but gave Bellah a hard look. Finally, he said, "Ah. No, but thank you for your help today with all the delegates. You are very good at making people feel at ease."

"Thank you. I learned that from my mother. She was a great hostess."

"Do you like to travel?" Linzcot asked thoughtfully.

"Sure. Who doesn't?"

"Good. I might take you with us on the campaign trail. We will be hosting many important people and you would be a big help, I'm sure."

"Oh! I would like that."

"Alright. I'll tell Arvis to add you to my travel staff."

"Thank you!" Bellah replied excitedly. She knew he liked her and didn't think it would be too hard to get into his bed, but she had to be careful because Brodie was always around and wouldn't tolerate any intimacy between them. She'd have to wait for the right moment.

Linzcot nodded and Bellah turned and left. She couldn't help but feel ecstatic over her new assignment. On her way home to her compartment, she stopped at a café for dinner. She was joined by her friend Shellee, who in actuality was her Purist handler.

"So, did the transmission go okay?" Bellah asked.

"Yes. It was perfect. No problem switching mugs?"

"No. Everyone is so busy they don't pay much attention to me."

"What about Brodie? He seems pretty intense."

"Yes. I don't think he trusts me, or anyone for that matter."

"Well, that's his job and he just blew it."

They laughed.

"Yes, he did," Bellah agreed. "And I also managed to get an invite to join Linzcot on the campaign trail."

"Seriously? Shellee asked.

"Yes. I'm going to be helping him wine and dine VIPs. He likes how I make people feel at ease."

Shellee laughed. "If they only knew what you were up to."

"Yes, indeed."

"But, that does present a problem."

"What problem?"

"Here in Lyon nobody knows you, but once you get out on the road you may run across someone you knew back on Earth. If that happens, they will wonder why you're working for the Peace Party."

Bellah shrugged. "True, but most of the returnees from Earth came from Tributon and Rigimol. I don't think there will be any danger until we go to those states. When that happens, I will just have to lay low and avoid any of the people I know. They won't recognize my name and I have changed my appearance, so it may not even be a problem if they did see me."

"I don't know. You are a gorgeous woman and men never forget women like that."

Bellah sighed. She knew Shellee was right, but she'd just have to take the risk. She liked doing something important, something that would make a difference and she wanted most of all to make her parents understand why she had to return to Tarizon.

47
Integrity of the Vote

As expected Chancellor Marcez was nominated at the Purist Convention to be its candidate for Supreme Chancellor should a Supreme Mandate be ratified. But the constitution of the World Council was the immediate concern. Bruda had promised Chancellor Marcez that he would somehow get four or five delegates to switch their vote or not show up to vote.

Bruda delegated the task to General Bakker and Petri Volk. They intern recruited military allies in each state and formed a task force to locate and assess the most vulnerable delegates. The committee worked diligently for several weeks and when they were ready to make their recommendations they met with Bruda.

"So, how are we going to make sure we control the Committee?" Bruda asked.

General Bakker cleared his throat. "It's not going to be easy. Each delegate has a security detachment, an entourage of deputies and there will be a lot of media coverage."

"Okay," Bruda replied irritably. "What's our plan?"

"Well, many of the delegates committed to the Peace Party will be staying at the same place, the Baccaluna Hotel. We have bribed one of the security officers there and enlisted his assistance in gaining entry during the night before the Committee meets."

"How many peace delegates do you plan to kill?" Bruda asked.

"We won't have a lot of time, but with a little luck we should be able to take out four or five."

"Good. That should give us the leverage we need to control the Committee."

"Don't you think they will simply postpone the meeting?" Petri asked.

"They might try, but that would require a vote of the Committee. So, if we are successful we can insist on the meeting going forward. If not, then we'll have no choice but to let the process continue."

"There is something else you should know about," Petri advised. "We have learned that the Peace Party will be advocating a world census. It was Ambassador Talvihn's opinion that a worldwide census would be necessary to determine who can vote and to guarantee the integrity of the election. He apparently doesn't have confidence that each state could conduct a fair election."

"He's probably right," General Bakker replied. "Many of them could not."

"Right. He also is advocating a state of the art voting system, a wrist array that is permanently embedded in the arm, and acts as a communication and health monitoring device which will give each voter the ability to cast his vote electronically. It would be permanent and perhaps useful to Central Authority if a Supreme Mandate is adopted."

"Wouldn't a system like that be vulnerable to hacking or jamming?" General Bakker asked.

"Ambassador Talvihn says no," Petri advised. "Apparently, it's a state of the art system that cannot be impaired in any way. There will be approximately 30 orbiting satellites to capture the votes. Each wrist array will upload its vote to three randomly selected satellites within range. The three uploads will be compared for accuracy by the compiling computers, so if there is a discrepancy it will be immediately detected. Because there will be millions of wrist arrays uploading votes, it would be nearly impossible for a hacker to impact the election process.

"There will be three compiling servers, too, so again a hacker would have to compromise all three of them to impact the vote. Of course, each server will be heavily guarded and their locations will be kept secret. They should all agree on the vote but if they do not, the discrepancy can be addressed and resolved quickly.

"To further ensure that the system will work as promised, the manufacturer will keep a testing facility open until thirty days prior to the election, so any state can send technicians in for training or to test the system. Hopefully, if there are any flaws or inadequacies in the system, they will be detected early on and resolved prior to the election. Finally, there will be an integrity committee made up of representatives of all the states to monitor the compiling of the vote," Petri concluded.

"You should check on this manufacturer," Bruda said, "and make sure they are independent and unbiased. If they are, then it sounds like a reasonable plan."

"I will do that," Petri promised.

"I like the idea of having each citizen tagged and monitored. That could be very useful once we gain control of Central Authority," Bruda noted. "We should thank the Ambassador for coming up with such a great idea."

They all laughed.

48
First Vote

The Baccaluna Hotel had a long tradition of hosting the most wealthy and influential visitors to Shisk. Discretion and security were always guaranteed, and their record was untarnished. At 0300 kyloons the chief security guard on duty disabled the hotel security systems for forty-five tiks. At that precise moment the back door to the kitchen opened and twelve men, dressed head to toe in black and armed with laser pistols for close quarter combat, entered the hotel. They quickly moved to the lobby and then to the stairwells.

Their prey was on two separate floors, so they split up when they reached the third floor. Six waited at the door to the third floor while the others climbed to the fifth floor. At the same precise moment, they entered each floor heading for their prearranged targets. Their plan was to quickly breach each suite door, and murder anyone they found inside. Instead, much to their shock and distress, their lasers inexplicably jerked from their hands and they were immediately attacked by angry rhutz who started systematically ripping them apart until each rhutz heard a voice in their head that said, "Stop!" They obeyed.

The elevator bell on the third floor rang, the door opened and Rack Brodie stepped out leading a squad of hotel security. They quickly surrounded the intruders, secured them, and led them away. The assassins on the fifth floor suffered a similar fate.

Romas Garciah breathed a sigh of relief when he heard what had happened. He hoped there weren't other attacks planned but they were ready for them if they came. During breakfast the next morning, Brodie called to tell Romas what they'd learned after the interrogation of the assassins.

"They don't know who hired them," Brodie said. "We gave them truth serum so I think they are telling the truth. Apparently, someone paid them quite handsomely in untraceable gold and jewels to kill everyone on those two floors."

"Okay. Turn them over to the local authorities, and get back here. Bruda isn't one to give up easily."

"So, nobody was hurt?" Artis asked.

"None of our people. The rhutz detected the intruders the moment they entered the hotel. We were expecting some kind of an assault, so we were ready for them."

"Thank Sandee," Artis said.

"Yes. I hope he is up there with Pelgrem watching over us."

"I'm sure he is," Artis assured him.

At 1100 kyloons the convention was called to order. The secretary then reported that all of the appointed delegates were in attendance and the Convention to Constitute a World Council was ready to conduct business.

To the shock and surprise of Romas Garciah and other Peace Party members in attendance, the Purists endorsed Ambassador Talvihn's proposal to implant a wrist array in every citizen who was determined to be eligible to vote during the world census.

Unfortunately, there was no consensus on who should be considered a citizen of Tarizon and allowed to vote. After kyloons and kyloons of debate Ambassador Talvihn's proposal to allow all human beings no matter their age, gender, health, race, religion, status, or lifestyle, came to a vote. This definition was expressly intended to include Seafolken, mutants, and slaves.

"Delegates shall now cast their votes on Resolution 1," Bruda advised. "You will have five loons to vote."

Each of the thirty-one delegate's names was on a tally board at the front of the meeting hall. Lights began to blink on beside each name. A tally updated after each vote. The vote immediately flashed as 11 in favor and 13 opposed. There was a flash and the vote changed from 14 in favor and 14 opposed. There was a long silence. A clock counted down the tiks to when the final vote would be counted. At 31 tiks the vote changed to 15 in favor and 15 opposed.

The crowd stirred in anticipation of the final vote. Delegates strained to see the one who hadn't voted. All eyes focused on one man. The delegate from Morissee in Lower Azollo. The man swallowed hard. The clock ticked down to 3. The man cast his ballot and the tally board flashed once again to 16 in favor and 15 opposed.

There were screams of joy and ecstasy mixed with moans of disappointment and despair. Romas, Arvis, Chancellor Linzcot, and Ambassador Talvihn raised their hands high in celebration and slapped each other on the back. Many other delegates were celebrating too. The Chairman banged the gavel.

"Alright! I'll have order," the Chairman spat. "The resolution is adopted."

The meeting went on for several kyloons as there were many other issues that had to be decided. When the meeting ended it had been determined that the census would begin in sixty days and would go on for two cycles. Ninety days after the census was complete there would be an election of delegates to the World Council. The sole purpose of the World Council would be to draft a Supreme Mandate. Once the Supreme Mandate was drafted, there would be a worldwide vote by wrist array. Each citizen could vote on the prescribed date at any time during Tarizon's 27-hour day. If the Supreme Mandate was ratified by a majority vote, Tarizon would have a single world government to be called Central Authority.

When the meeting ended, Romas, Rammel, Ambassador Talvihn, Arvis, and Chancellor Linzcot adjourned to brainstorm in a private suite at a local tavern.

"That was close," Romas observed. "For a moment there I thought someone had gotten to our delegate from Morissee. Why did he wait to the last loon to vote? Yesterday he confirmed he was voting for the resolution."

"Maybe it made him feel important to cast the deciding vote," Arvis suggested.

"Or he's going to think we owe him something now," Ambassador Talvihn said.

"It doesn't matter," Chancellor Linzcot said. "That was a crucial vote and will make it much easier for us to get the Supreme Mandate that we want adopted and put before the people for ratification."

"Yes. You're right about that," Romas agreed. "But we can't afford to celebrate too long. We have a census to conduct and a lot of campaigning to do for delegates to the World Council."

"Yes, and I'm worried about our candidates running for delegate positions to the World Council," Arvis said. "How will we protect them?"

"It won't be easy, but it has to be one of our top priorities," Romas said.

"How did they find out where we were staying? It wasn't public knowledge."

"It might have been a good guess. We often stay at the Baccaluna."

"Was anyone surprised by the Purists' endorsement of Ambassador's Talvihn's proposal?" Arvis asked.

The Chancellor's eyes narrowed. "You're right. I was

expecting a fight. What are you thinking?"

"That they had advance knowledge of the plan and had thoroughly vetted it."

"It is a good plan," Ambassador Talvihn reminded them. "I doubt they could have come up with anything better."

"That's true," the Chancellor said. "But it's a complicated process and we only made the proposal ten days ago."

"They obviously have known about it much earlier," Arvis said.

"So, what are you saying?" Romas asked. "Do you think we have a mole in our organization?"

Arvis shrugged. "Maybe, or the plan was leaked by one of our contractors."

Romas stared at Arvis. "You better have everyone in the Chancellor's campaign staff checked out. I'll do the same thing with our staff at the Peace Party. If we have a mole, we better find out who it is fast."

The Chancellor nodded. "Yes. Please do. I don't want any unpleasant surprises down the road."

49
Delegates

When Bruda was growing up he hated that he never saw his father and was given so much responsibility to care for his mother and siblings. He often complained that he had no childhood at all. So, unlike his father, Cornelius Bruda spent a lot of time with Progasis and they developed a close relationship. This made for a happier family life but it left Progasis with little drive, confidence or ambition.

So, his father had been surprised when Progasis announced he wanted to be a delegate to the World Conference. This pleased Bruda but also presented him with the difficult task of preparing his son for such an ambitious undertaking. He couldn't afford to back him for such an important position and then have him fail.

Tributon had been allotted 31 seats on the World Assembly and there were already 121 candidates running for those seats. There would be just one vote so the top 31 would get Tributon's seats. Tributon, however, was not a Purist stronghold. It was part of the North Sea Alliance and one of the first states to join the peace movement. Consequently, Sandee Brahn's Peace Party would be strong here and their candidates difficult to beat.

On the day Progasis filed his papers officially entering the race, Bruda hosted a strategy session followed by a rally to celebrate his son's entry into the political arena. Before the meeting began, everyone gathered in Bruda's media room to watch the news report on the commencement of the campaign for delegates to the World Council.

"This is Alli Daun coming to you from Vaceen, Tributon. We are in front of the World Election Bureau's offices where candidates had been filing their papers to run for one of the 31 seats allocated to Tributon for the World Council which is to convene in just 90 days.

"The world census was completed just 30 days ago and has been certified by the General Assembly's of each of Tarizon's 31 states. Today, campaigning began for the 500 seats up for grabs. In Tributon there are expected to be 81 candidates for the 31 seats. Both the Purist Party and the Peace Party have released their slates leaving 19 independent candidates. The 31 delegates with the most votes will represent Tributon at the World Council.

"Leading the Purist's slate is Progasis Bruda, the son of Cornelius Bruda of Bruda Industries. At the top of the slate for the Peace Party is Rammel Garciah, the son of Supreme Councilor Romas Garciah, who recently returned with his son from Earth.

"It's difficult to predict how the vote will finally turn out because of a large number of independent candidates. Many are well known and influential members of the community but, so far, have not expressed their opinions on the issues that will be addressed by the World Council as it struggles to draft a Supreme Mandate.

"Around the rest of the globe, the scene is similar with large numbers of candidates seeking a seat on the World Council. Although the campaign is just beginning, experts are predicting the Peace Party will win the states of the North Sea Alliance which would give them 165 seats. The Purists are expected to win states who belong to the Dark Sea Alliance which would give them 139 votes. All of this assumes each party gets all the votes allocated to that state,

which may not happen due to the independent candidates running. This means there are 196 contested races that are impossible to predict at this time.

In ten days the Vaceen Citiheads will be sponsoring a debate between a representative of the Peace Party, the Purist Party, and the Independents. We will be bringing you live coverage of the debate so be sure and tune in.

"This is Alli Daun reporting."

"So, who is going to represent the Peace Party in the debate?" Petri asked.

"Progasis," Bruda said. "That's who the press will be expecting, so we don't want to disappoint them."

Progasis looked a bit shaken but didn't say anything.

Petri looked at Progasis and asked, "Can you handle it? The Purists will put up someone strong, I'm sure."

Progasis nodded tentatively.

"Rammel Garciah is my guess," Bruda said. "That's why Progasis must step up. I'm not a politician nor is Romas. Our sons are going to have to lead the fight before the World Council."

"But Progasis, you're just 21 aren't you?" Cameela asked. "And Rammel is about the same age, isn't he?"

"Yes," Progasis replied.

"So, they are both older than Sandee would have been had he lived to address the World Council," Bruda noted. "I'm sure he would have done fine."

"Yes, but he was before the public every night and gave thousands of speeches. Shouldn't you let him get a little experience under his belt before you toss him in the ring?" Cameela asked.

"Nonsense," Bruda said. "If you want to teach a child how to swim, you throw him into the river. I'm sure Progasis will do fine."

Progasis swallowed hard, then stiffened. "Don't worry

about me. I'm not afraid of Rammel Garciah."

"That's the spirit," Bruda said.

"I know a good speech coach," General Bakker said. "I'll have him put together a team to get you ready."

"Thanks," Progasis said.

"Has anyone done an analysis of 196 uncertain seats?" Cameela asked.

"Yes," General Bakker replied. "We are working on that right now. It looks like they have split evenly three ways."

"What are we going to do to get them to swing in our direction?"

Bruda frowned thoughtfully. "I think all these independents are hoping to get elected so they can sell their vote to the highest bidder. If I'm right we will be able to buy those votes."

"What's to stop the Peace Party from buying them?" Cameela asked.

"Their moral code. Don't worry. We'll be the only serious bidder, so we should be able to pick up any independent seats without much trouble. It will cost us, but it will be worth the investment."

"You're assuming the independent voters are dishonest and would be susceptible to a bribe. I'm sure most of them are honest."

"Every man has his price, as they say," Bruda replied. "But if bribery doesn't work there are other ways to turn people into puppets."

Cameela raised her eyebrows and replied, "This could all backfire on us, though, if we are caught."

"Don't worry. That won't be a problem. The Peace Party and the Purists aren't the only actors on the stage. The Nationalist Party will soon be joining us, and I hear they are a nasty bunch."

"The Nationalist Party?" General Bakker asked. "I

haven't heard of them."

"That's because you haven't organized them yet. So, you better get busy," Bruda snapped.

The General's eyes widened. "Oh, yes. You're right. I've got work to do."

50
Rammel Garciah

Rammel Garciah stood tall at the podium, his moot court experience on Earth having given him confidence and poise. But even so, he felt nervous and afraid. This was a real battle against a ruthless and amoral opponent, and the stakes had never been higher. Peace would be the inevitable victor no matter who prevailed, but the future of democracy, personal freedom, and social justice were on the line.

"Alright," Romas said. "Now, under the rules of the debate, you each will have fifteen loons to make an opening statement. Then the moderator will introduce an issue that will be considered at the World Council. Each of you will then have ten loons to address that issue. Finally, there will be a challenge round where each of you will have five loons to attack the opponent's position and a final rebuttal round of two loons."

"Right," Rammel said. "I got it."

"So, do you know all the issues cold?"

He nodded. "Yes, Father. Don't worry. I've got this."

"Well, your opening statement was perfect. I couldn't have done better myself."

"Thank you," Rammel said as he stepped down from the podium.

"Okay, the others are waiting for us in the conference room. We should go."

The two walked briskly out of the general hall and down a corridor to Conference Room 2. Mingling around inside the conference room were Celius Garciah, Solis Landy,

Snowflake, Tobin Sandista, Jox Machlyn, Captain Linde, and Major Zitor. They comprised the Peace Party leadership in Tributon and were responsible for delivering 31 Peace Party delegates to the World Council.

Tobin Sandista had been recruited to communicate with the rhutz, and in particular, Snowflake who had been assigned to be Rammel's protector. He was a brilliant scholar and had been a clerk for Romas when he was Supreme Councilor of Tributon. Romas had tried to recruit him to run for a delegate position but he declined on the grounds he didn't have the temperament for it. He enjoyed his privacy and wasn't particularly comfortable with people. However, he did love animals, so he jumped at the chance to use his powers of telepathy to communicate with the rhutz.

Romas took a seat at the head of the conference table and said, "Thank you all for coming. Our first order of business will be to view and approve a campaign ad we just received from Chancellor Linzcot's office. They are suggesting we use it to kick off the campaign for delegates to the World Council. Celius, would you play the ad?"

Celius pushed a button on her wrist array and the screen lit up. An image of a smiling Arvis Gill appeared.

"Citizens of Tarizon," she began. "This is Arvis Gill speaking to you from the Peace Party headquarters in Ya Lat, Lyon. As you may remember I am Salina Gill's sister, and when she was assassinated I took over as Sandee Brahn's personal secretary.

"Today campaigning begins for candidates seeking to become delegates to the World Council. This is a very important day for Tarizon. In just a few phases a World Council will finally be constituted, and it will begin work on drafting a Supreme Mandate upon which a new era of world peace will be built.

"I congratulate all of those seeking a delegate seat and

wish them well. But I have a few words of caution for the citizens of Tarizon about these candidates for a seat on the World Council. The Peace Party will have a slate of candidates for each of the 31 states. These candidates have been thoroughly vetted and you can rest assured they will vote in a manner consistent with the beliefs of his Holiness, Sandee Brahn. They will vote to make sure the Supreme Mandate provides for freedom, democracy and social justice for all.

"The Purist Party will also have a slate of candidates for each state, and you can rest assured they will not vote in a manner consistent with the beliefs of Sandee Brahn. It is well known that they oppose the abolition of slavery, equal rights to Seafolken and mutants, and seek to limit the personal freedoms the citizens of Tarizon have enjoyed for centuries.

"So, the choice will be easy between the candidates of the Peace Party and the Purists, but there are also a lot of independent candidates running as well. Be wary of these candidates and don't believe everything they tell you. Many are only seeking office for their own personal gain. Some want to be in a position of power so if the vote is close on an issue they can sell their vote to the highest bidder. There are also many independent candidates who are really Nationalists and do not want a unified world government. That is fine if they disclose that to the voters, but many will not. So, be wary of these independent candidates even if they are well-respected members of the community. They may have a private agenda.

"If you truly want a lasting peace for Tarizon, I urge you to vote for the delegates endorsed by the Peace Party. Only if the Peace Party candidates control the World Council can we be assured of a great Supreme Mandate that will create a strong government that can maintain world peace

*but also ensure freedom, democracy and guarantee the civil
rights of all citizens of Tarizon.*

"Thank you, and may Pelgrem be with you."

The VC went blank and there was a buzz of
excitement in the room. Romas smiled broadly. "Well, that
was well done. I think we should run it on all the media
outlets for the next few days."

"Do you think the ad will be enough? It sounds like
this is going to be a very serious problem," Jox noted.

"No. It won't solve the problem," Romas
acknowledged. "We just need to make voters aware of it, so
they will support our slate of candidates."

"What about this Nationalist Party?" Solis asked.
"Does it really pose a threat?"

Romas nodded. "Yes. There are always those who
oppose change. It's man's worst fear, fear of the unknown.
But, they have a point. If the Purists get control of the World
Council and draft a Supreme Mandate we can't live with, we
may end up teaming up with the Nationalists to make sure
the Supreme Mandate isn't ratified."

As the meeting dragged on Rammel realized how
critical it was for the Peace Party delegates to get elected.
He felt an enormous burden on his shoulders and worried
that he might not be up to the task. Then he remembered,
Pelgrem had been guiding Sandee Brahn, so surely He would
be looking out for all the delegates seeking to bring a lasting
peace to Tarizon. This gave him solace, and, in the coming
weeks, helped him sleep at night.

51
The Debate

Most men and women on Tarizon were mated before the age of twenty. When Rammel returned from Earth he met a girl named Petrina who worked as a press aide for the Peace Party. They were both over twenty and unmated, so they began dating. They hit it off quite well, so it wasn't long before they fell in love and were mated.

Petrina was a good cook and had made Rammel a nice breakfast. He usually ate a hearty breakfast each day, but today he wasn't hungry. It was the day of his debate with Progasis Bruda. To make matters worse the election was only ten days away, so his performance today could be critical to electing the 31 Peace Party delegates to the World Council.

Rammel grabbed a cup of Sankee and took it into the media room. He wanted to check the news on the VC to see what they were saying about his debate scheduled to start at 1300 kyloons.

Petrina followed him in with his breakfast. She set it down on a side table next to him.

"You need to eat. It's going to be a long day and you're going to need your strength."

"Okay," Rammel replied as he switched on the VC. It immediately came to life with the scene of an unruly crowd in Mapi, Quori protesting the upcoming election. They had surrounded the Peace Party headquarters and were taunting the candidates and workers coming in and out of the building.

The screen switched to a male reporter, in white pants, shirt, and sandals, standing a few strides away from the demonstration and holding a microphone.

"This is Ruhle Zinni for the Global News Channel. The scene you are watching is in Mapi, Quori where a lone gunman claiming to be a Nationalist opposed to the formation of a world government, has entered Peace Party headquarters with a laser pistol and began shooting at everyone he encountered. Witnesses indicate he shot seven party members including two candidates for delegate seats on the World Council.

"Local Public Enforcers responded to the attack and killed the gunman whose identity has not been disclosed. Two of the seven victims were killed and the others are being treated at the Central Casualty Center in Mapi where they are expected to recover.

"One of the two killed was a Peace Party candidate and the other a security guard. Witnesses claim the man broke through the PE security line and followed a group of party members entering the building. Just as soon as he was admitted into the lobby he began shooting.

The screen switched to the scene of a burning building.

"Today's violence has not been restricted to Quori. What you are looking at now is a light manufacturing business in Zarne, Darkland owned by Pollis Rawli, a Peace Party candidate. Candidate Rawli claims to have been approached by two men who offered him a large sum of money if he would withdraw his candidacy. When he refused, they said he'd regret his decision. Today, someone set his factory on fire and left a note threatening to kill him and his family if he remained in the race."

The screen returned back to the reporter. *"These are just two instances of many attempts to subvert the upcoming election of delegates to the World Council. Spokesmen of the Nationalist Party, as well as the Purist Party, have denied any involvement in these incidents.*

"This afternoon in Vaceen, Tributon the long-awaited debate between Rammel Garciah and Progasis Bruda is set to take place. The two candidates will debate some of the most controversial issues that will have to be addressed by the World Council when it is finally convened later this cycle. This is Ruhle Zinni reporting for the Global News Channel."

Rammel turned off the VC and looked at Petrina. "I can't believe the skutz killed one of our delegates," Rammel said angrily.

"I'm so worried about you," Petrina said. "What if there are demonstrators at the convention center? Will you still have the debate?"

"Yes. We can't let a few dissidents distract us from our objective. We only have a few more days to convince the voters to elect the Peace Party candidates."

"But if you show up and get killed that will be one less Peace Party delegate."

"I'm not going to get killed," Rammel assured her. "The auditorium will have tight security and I have Autumn to protect me."

Petrina nodded but didn't look convinced.

"It is getting late. We need to go."

"Finish your breakfast," Petrina urged.

Rammel reluctantly sat down and took a few bites. Then he stood up and said, "All right. Let's go."

The big Grinden was waiting outside when they exited the lobby of their compartment building. The doorman opened the door and they got in. Autumn was sitting in the front passenger seat. Soon, they were speeding down Central

Avenue toward the auditorium. As they got nearer to the facility the crowds grew thick and the jeers and taunts got louder and louder.

"Keep Quori Free," many were chanting. Others held signs that read, "No Mandate!" Rocks and bottles were thrown at them as they went by. One of them hit the window startling Petrina. "Oh, Sandee help me!" she screamed.

Rammel took her hand and said, "Don't let these sligots upset you. They are paid Purist agitators, I'm sure."

When they finally got to their destination there was a line of public enforcers in riot gear protecting the entrance. The Grinden pulled into the driveway and stopped, and they were hustled into the building by security officers. Romas and Celius greeted them as they were escorted into the waiting room.

"Are you two all right?" Celius asked with concern in her voice.

"Yes," Rammel said. "The PE's have everything under control."

"Have you seen the news?" Romas asked. "This is going on all over Tarizon."

"Yes. We were watching the Global News this morning at breakfast. The Nationalists claim to be responsible for killings in Mapi, but I'm not so sure."

"No. I'm sure it's the Purists," Romas agreed.

"I can't believe they killed one of our delegates," Petrina moaned. "Why would they do that?"

"They can't beat us by legitimate means," Romas replied. "So, they are using every underhanded trick they know to get delegates. Every one of our delegates who is killed, accepts their bribes, or resigns from the race is one more delegate they will control once the World Council meets."

"Can't we do anything about it?" Celius asked.

Romas shook his head. "There's no way to prove it.

They cover their tracks very well. We just have to make sure we have impregnable security for every delegate."

A man stepped in the room and advised them the debate would commence in five loons. Celius and Petrina hugged Rammel, wished him well as he gathered his notes together, and watched him follow the man to the stage. When he was gone, they immediately left the dressing room and found their seats in the audience.

A few loons later the curtains opened to three podiums with the moderator in the middle and Rammel and Progasis on both sides.

"Good afternoon. I'm Rill Lindes and I will be the moderator in this debate between Rammel Garciah of the Peace Party and Progasis Bruda of the Purist Party. As you know in just nine days the election of delegates to the World Council will take place. Today's debate will be on five crucial issues that will be addressed by the World Council as it works to draft a Supreme Mandate.

"The purpose of today's debate is to explore and contrast the positions of the Peace Party and the Purists so the voters will have a better idea of how to vote on Election Day.

"At this time I would like to introduce Rammel Garciah appearing on behalf of the Peace Party. Mr. Garciah please give your opening statement."

All eyes focused on Rammel as he began. "Mr. Lindes, ladies and gentlemen, and citizens of Tarizon. It has been fifteen cycles since the God Pelgrem appeared to Sandee Brahn and Whisper the rhutz and tasked them with bringing peace to Tarizon. It's been a long and arduous road, and there have been many casualties along the way, especially the loss of our leader Sandee Brahn, but we are getting close and we cannot let up now.

"We need to elect the Peace Party slate of delegates to the World Council. Only by electing a majority of Peace

Party delegates can you be assured that Sandee Brahn's mission of bringing a lasting peace to Tarizon will be realized.

"But peace is not the only concern we have. It is imperative that the Supreme Mandate be written to provide a strong democratic government elected by the people. It should also guarantee personal freedom for all human beings, the right to privacy, to speak freely, to gather, to move at will, to practice a religion, to a fair trial, and to conduct any lawful business,

"Now, the Purists will tell you they want peace, and many of these same guarantees that I just mentioned, but not for everyone. They want nothing to do with the mutants, the Seafolken and any other disadvantaged class of human beings that might be an inconvenience to the government.

"But we'll be talking more about that later, I'm sure. For now, I just want to remind you this election is about creating a strong democratic government that will serve the people, bringing about lasting peace so that Tarizon's ecosystem can heal and all life forms on Tarizon can flourish. Thank you."

There was a rousing round of applause from the audience. When the room quieted, the moderator continued. "Speaking for the Purist Party is Progasis Bruda. Mr. Bruda, you may now make your opening statement."

Everyone's attention went to Progasis who looked a little nervous. He cleared his throat. "Mr. Lindes, ladies and gentlemen, and citizens of Tarizon. We are all, of course, indebted to Sandee Brahn for recognizing that after a hundred cycles of war, Tarizon's very existence was in peril. We are grateful that he started the peace movement and that it grew under his stewardship. But, as you will recall, it was only when the Purist Party got behind the movement that it finally got traction. In fact, if you are honest, you will acknowledge that we wouldn't be here today, on the eve of the commencement of the first World Council, had it not been for the tireless efforts of the Purist Party.

"So, we all agree Tarizon needs peace, and that peace can only be sustained if there is a strong worldwide, central government to peacefully resolve disputes between nations. Disputes that in the past have caused endless wars costing millions of lives and gravely injuring our planet.

"Where we disagree with the Peace Party is on how to maintain the peace, restore the world's infrastructure, cleanse the planet of radiation, toxins, and pollution, and provide for the citizens of Tarizon in the process.

"I know that the Peace Party likes to talk about ensuring freedom, justice, and democracy but we have to be realistic. Tarizon is in crisis. What we have to think about is survival. It is naive to think that just because we have stopped fighting that all our problems will suddenly be solved. We need a Supreme Mandate that will provide a framework for a government that will have the strength and flexibility to do what is necessary to build a viable future for the human race. Thank you."

There were cheers and a generous round of applause for Progasis. He nodded at the crowd and smiled broadly, satisfied and relieved that he had done well.

The moderator waited for the applause to end, then he said, "Alright. Now I will suggest various issues that will come up at the World Council as it drafts the Supreme Mandate. Then I would like each of you to give us your thoughts on the issue. The first issue is whether the usual three branches of government, the executive, legislative, and judicial should be equal in authority or if one or more should be subservient to the others. Mr. Bruda. You can go first."

Progasis took a deep breath and then replied. "The executive branch should be preeminent with the legislative and judiciary given a supporting role. Tarizon is a dying planet and only bold, quick and decisive action will bring it back to life. When you have three equal branches of government, getting anything done is slow and tedious. We don't have the time for the luxury of endless debate and consideration of each issue. In the Purist view, the World Assembly would enact or change the laws, and the judiciary would resolve civil disputes and try persons accused of crimes, but the Chancellor as leader of the executive branch would be left to rule Tarizon through the new Central Authority without having to answer to the World Assembly or the Council of Interpreters."

"Thank you," the moderator said. "Mr. Garciah."

Rammel nodded. "One of the great dangers of a world government is if too much power is given to the executive branch or, in this case, the Chancellor, he might be tempted to abuse his position, usually by citing some kind of emergency or urgent need for action. This is how kings and dictators are born. It's our position at the Peace Party that there should be three equal branches of government, each a check and balance on the other. It is imperative that the people retain control over their government. To further assure that power, we will propose short terms of office so that our leaders will have to go back to the people frequently to get their continued consent to govern."

"Thank you, Mr. Garciah. Now, the next question deals with personal freedom. Should the Supreme Mandate guarantee that a man and woman can mate freely or should that be left to the World Assembly to determine? Mr. Garciah, you may respond first."

"The Supreme Mandate should guarantee the personal freedoms of every human being whether it be picking a mate, where to live, their occupation, their religion, to speak freely, and to travel at will.

"The people will not ratify the Supreme Mandate if it doesn't provide these protections. The right to freely mate has been a tradition on Tarizon throughout its history and was how it was done on Pharidon before that. No man or woman should have to mate someone they do not love. That is the law given to us by Pelgrem Himself."

"Thank you, Mr. Garciah. Mr. Bruda. Your response."

Progasis thought a moment and then replied. "Actually, if you study our modern history you will find that in the last five cycles sixty-seven percent of the matings on Tarizon have been abandoned. Studies by scholars indicate this is due to the fact that human beings are not very good at selecting their mates, so the matings are often doomed from the start. And we all know the tragic results of a failed mating—violence against the weaker mate, neglect of children, distraction on the job, depression, anxiety, poor health, and the list goes on and on.

"The Purist Party proposes that all citizens in the future would be mated by state of the art computer programs. A comprehensive analysis of every citizen would be made, and by comparing and analyzing this data, men and women would be mated with the most compatible person possible. The result would be much happier and productive citizens, and an improved and more nourishing environment for their children."

There was silence from the audience, and then someone asked in a loud voice, "Can that computer find me a new mate?"

Everyone laughed and there was another round of applause. The debate went on for nearly two kyloons. When it was over, the local Peace Party officials and supporters gathered at a local tavern to unwind from the ordeal and watch the media's reaction to it.

"You did well, son," Romas said enthusiastically.

"Thank you, but Progasis didn't do so bad himself."

Romas nodded. "True. You both articulated your positions well. But, the people are not stupid. They will not want to give the new government too much power and end up as slaves."

"I hope you're right."

The news was coming up on the big VC mounted on the wall of the tavern. Everyone quieted to listen to the report.

"This is Ruhle Zinni for the Global News Channel. In Vaceen noisy Nationalist protesters surrounded the Central Auditorium where two candidates debated important issues that will have to be determined at the World Council once its delegates are elected.

"Local Public Enforcers and event security personnel wearing riot gear held off the unruly crowd so that the important debate could go forward. Midway through the debate, protesters broke through security and began streaming into a side entrance of the venue. Much to their shock and dismay, they were met with a pack of local rhutz providing security for the Peace Party at the event.

"The ensuing confrontation resulted in the death of two of the protesters and serious injury to eleven others. Public enforcers arrested and jailed thirteen uninjured protesters for trespass and failure to abide by orders of public enforcers.

"The debate between Purists representative Progasis Bruda and Peace Party representative Rammel Garciah was a spirited affair with both debaters highlighting their positions on the many difficult issues that the delegates to the World Council will have to address.

"During the debate, Bruda attacked Garciah and the Peace Party as being naive to think the new government would be able to guarantee equal rights to all human beings including mutants and Seafolken when the planet was in such peril. He said the new central government would have to make hard decisions if Tarizon was to survive, and that

some citizen's rights might have to be sacrificed for the greater good.

"Garciah countered that the new central government had to represent all human beings equally as that was implicit in the worldwide vote for a World Council. He stressed that the new Supreme Mandate must provide for checks and balances between the three branches of government to make sure the citizens of Tarizon always control the government.

"This has been Ruhle Zinni for the Global News Channel. Thank you and good evening."

Rammel campaigned tirelessly twenty kyloons per day up until Election Day. He knew this was the most important election in the history of Tarizon and defeat was not an option. As the election drew near, Nationalist protests around the globe increased and they became more violent. Reports of attempts on the lives of delegates became more frequent, attempts to bribe them happened almost every day, and there were even reports of delegate's spouses and children being kidnapped to force delegates to withdraw from the race. Rammel knew these were all Purists tricks to thwart the will of the people. Unfortunately, there was nothing the Peace Party could do about it other than to redouble their efforts to keep their candidates safe.

52
Election Day

On Election Day there wasn't much for the candidates to do. Every citizen's wrist array would sound an annoying alarm every kyloon starting at 800 kyloons until the citizen voted. The alarms would continue until 2000 kyloons at which time the computers would calculate the vote.

The vote tabulation was to be broadcast on the Global News Channel throughout the day with a final tabulation at 2200 kyloons. The leaders of Tributon's branch of the Purist Party, Cornelius, Progasis, Petri Volk, General Bakker, and Cameela Bruns gathered at the Bruda Ranch to watch the results come in and to discuss strategy for the World Council.

They had just enjoyed a lavish breakfast and had taken their Sankees into the media room to begin their discussion. The media room had a large glass window with a view of the snow-capped White Mountains. It used to be a spectacular sight but not anymore since all the trees had died for lack of sun and the sky had turned grey.

"So, how is it looking?" Cameela asked.

Bruda shrugged. "Not so good, I'm afraid. As hard as we tried to discredit the Peace Party, it is still very popular."

"The race should be close, though, shouldn't it?" Progasis asked.

"Yes. I'm sure you will be elected as a delegate since you did well in the debate. I'm just worried you may be one of the few Purists from Tributon who get elected. We'll do much better in Soni and the Dark Sea Alliance states."

425

"So, if we don't get a majority of delegates, how are we going to get a Supreme Mandate we can live with?" General Bakker asked.

"Well, once the delegates get elected they still have to make it to Shisk so they can participate in the World Council. It's going to be a long, hard journey for most of the delegates and a lot can happen along the way," Bruda noted.

"Sure, but if a delegate doesn't show up, he'll be replaced, right?" Cameela asked.

"Right, but the replacement will have to be elected and that will take 30 days. In the meantime, the Council continues its work without interruption."

"There will also be independent candidates who won't always agree with the Peace Party's position," Petri said. "If there are enough independents elected, the Peace Party won't have a majority and they will be forced to make concessions."

Celius turned on the large VC monitor and the Global News Channel's Election Central studio came into view.

"This is Ruhle Zinni for the Global News Channel. Peace Party candidate Rammel Garciah is the leading candidate for a seat on the World Council with 252,501 votes as of 900 kyloons. The next twenty-five leading candidates are also from the Peace Party. Progasis Bruda and two other Purists are in the running with Independent candidate Lilar Ingot."

"We picked up four Peace Party seats so far," Bruda noted. "Four of their candidates couldn't handle the pressure and dropped out."

"If that holds throughout the day Progasis will be elected," General Bakker said. "I hope some others will make it."

"If not from Tributon, there will be others from the

states in the Dark Sea Alliance," Petri Volk added.

"Worldwide the Peace Party delegates are leading in 231 races and the Purist in 193. The strong showing of independents in 76 races may deprive the Peace Party of a majority in the World Council."

"As you can see the new voting by wrist array has turned out to be quite effective, so far. Let's just hope it continues to function as well as the day goes on. Many experts worried that the system that relies heavily on satellites and regional computer processing centers might be vulnerable to cyber attack."

Progasis looked at his father. "You're not going to try a cyber attack are you?"

Bruda shook his head. "We thought about knocking out some Peace Party strongholds, but that could invalidate the entire election, and we don't want that. This worldwide central government is going to be a good thing for us either way. If we don't end up controlling the government right away, it will still be dependent on us supplying its new military."

"And we will have many friends in the new TGA," General Bakker noted.

"Yes," Bruda agreed. "As I said, the Peace Party may think it's in control but it's only an illusion."

✝✝✝✝✝

The Peace Party leaders gathered at Rammel Garciah's home overlooking Wedding Cake Falls on the Lienh River near Paceka, Tributon. The river ran over three 50' tiers of rock that looked like a wedding cake with water cascading down each layer. From a distance, the rushing water looked like white frosting covering each layer.

Across the falls, on a huge rock pedestal above the river sat a castle built by King Kial who once ruled Tributon before the hundred cycles of war. When the king was deposed, the castle was turned into a Pelgrem monastery.

After an afternoon feast on a deck with a great view of the river and the falls, Rammel and the others moved indoors to a media room to watch the election returns.

"This is Ruhle Zinni for the Global News Channel. Peace Party candidate Rammel Garciah continues to lead the pack for a seat on the World Council with 1,752,521 votes as of 1500 kyloons. The next twenty-three leading candidates are also from the Peace Party. Progasis Bruda and three other Purists are in the running with Independent candidate Lilar Ingot and one other."

"Congratulations, son," Celius said. "I think you've made it."

Rammel shrugged. "I hope so, but there still are a lot of votes that haven't yet been cast. How many voters are there?"

Romas thought a moment. "I think the Tributon Census showed about 10 million eligible voters, so we are at about fifty percent."

"I wonder how many will actually vote?" Celius said.

"Most of them, if they haven't cut off their arms to stop the wrist arrays from constantly beeping," Petrina said.

They all laughed.

"Worldwide the Peace Party delegates are leading in 227 races and the Purist in 196. This shows a slight gain by both the Purists and the Independents and may deprive the Peace Party of a majority in the World Council."

"I wonder who hasn't voted. I would think most people would have voted early. What's the point of waiting?" Petrina said.

"If they are undecided they might wait until the last loon hoping to get some last loon clarity," Celius replied.

"So, if this turns out to be the final percentages, where does that leave us in the World Council?" Rammel asked. "It would have been so much easier with a majority."

"I have people researching the independent candidates," Romas replied. "As soon as we know which of them have been elected, we can figure out who might want to join us in a coalition. We're going to need 20-25 independent delegates to get our version of the Supreme Mandate adopted."

"I have just been advised by election officials that there have been reports of attacks on several of the satellites receiving data from wrist arrays on the ground in Lower Serie and Darkland," Ruhle Zinni reported. *"Apparently two satellites have been destroyed by rockets fired from high altitude fighters. It is unclear how this will affect the voting that is just a few kyloons from being concluded."*

"Oh, no!" Celius said. "I was afraid something like this would happen."

"It's the Nationalists, I bet," Rammel said. "If the World Council doesn't meet, they win."

"Don't panic yet," Romas said. "This type of attack was anticipated. We discussed it at planning meetings I attended. They must have a plan to deal with it."

"I hope so," Petrina moaned. "We are so close to victory. They can't take it from us now."

"An anonymous spokesman for the Nationalist Party has just claimed responsibility for the satellite attacks and promised they would take whatever action as is necessary to stop the World Council from meeting. They claim the voting is rigged and the entire election process is a sham."

For over a kyloon there was no word as to how the loss of two satellites would affect the election. Citizens all over the globe wondered if the entire peace effort would be thwarted by saboteurs. Then at 1800 kyloons, they got some good news.

"An election spokesman has just informed us that backup satellites have been deployed to receive transmissions from Lower Serie and Darkland and that election officials expect the vote to be completed, but there would be no more interim reporting. A final report of the vote is planned for 2350. Stay tuned for further updates."

"Thank God!" Petrina said.

"I wonder what else the Nationalists have planned?" Rammel asked worriedly.

"I don't know what else they could do," Romas said. "The processing centers are well guarded and they wouldn't know which citizens haven't voted, and if they did it wouldn't be practical to attack each individual. So, I don't see what else they could do."

For the next few kyloons until 2350 kyloons they all waited impatiently for the final vote tabulation, so they could all move to the next stage of Tarizon's slow path to a lasting peace. Finally, at 2380 the final vote came in.

"The final worldwide vote is in. The Peace Party delegates have won 229 seats, the Purist 197, and the Independents 74. Since 251 seats would constitute a majority, the Peace Party will not have a majority in the World Council and will have to get support from the Purists or Independents to get its version of the Supreme Mandate adopted."

"Alright! It's not a perfect result, but we still came out on top," Romas said. "Congratulations to everyone. Now the real work begins."

There were congratulations all around and then someone turned on the music and drinks were passed around. The party lasted several kyloons but many left early wanting to get a head start on their next daunting task—drafting Tarizon's new Supreme Mandate.

53
World Council

As Romas studied the list of independent delegates to the World Council, he came across a name he recognized. Trill Lankershank had been the Vice Minister of Pohl. He'd never met him but Romas knew he had helped Sandee with setting up the Soni-Synclare Peace Accord. He told his secretary to set up a meeting.

The next day they met at one of the Peace Party conference rooms at the Baccaluna Hotel.

"Vice Minister, it's so nice to finally meet you," Romas said as he shook Trill's hand.

"Yes. I'm honored to meet you. I was so saddened by His Holiness' assassination. I know you were there when it happened."

Romas nodded. "Yes, I'm still haunted by the moment," Romas admitted. "And, it was all my fault. I should have known Ritz was trouble." Romas took a deep breath, and then forced a smile."So, I'm curious why you decided to run as an independent. I'm sure the Peace Party would have welcomed you as a delegate."

Trill nodded and smiled. "They offered a delegate seat to me, but I don't want to be committed to one party line. I think there are a lot of issues that need to be fully debated. I'm not sure either party has all the answers."

Romas nodded slowly. "Yes, you have a point. It's only a fool who thinks he has the solution to every problem."

"I respected the Purist Party for adopting

Ambassador Talvihn's census and voting plan even though it was a Peace Party proposal. It showed they are not necessarily the scoundrels all of you say they are."

"Well, that shocked me too, but I think they backed it because it was a brilliant plan."

"Exactly my point. They saw the wisdom of the plan, and even though it must have pained them dearly, they got behind it. That is the attitude I hope everyone has at this convention."

"Yes. You're right. Everyone must have an open mind," Romas agreed. "That leads me to the second reason for this meeting."

Trill raised his eyebrows. "Okay. I'm listening."

"Since you have some admiration for both the Peace Party and the Purists, I can't think of a better person to be Chairman of the World Council."

Trill laughed. "Well, I don't know about that."

"We don't have a majority, so it would be difficult to elect one of our own for the post. We might be able to pull it off, but it could take days or even weeks which would be a waste of precious time. But, if you run and we back you, I'm sure the other independents will support you. That way we can get on with drafting the Supreme Mandate without further delay."

"That does make sense, but I don't know if I'm the right man."

"I think you are, and I think you know it too."

Trill laughed. "Okay, the thought may have crossed my mind," he admitted.

They both laughed heartily and then Romas took Trill and introduced him to the Peace Party delegates from Tributon who were assembled at one of the hotel bars. While the delegates and Trill were getting to know each other, Romas went to see Cornelius Bruda.

He had prearranged the meeting, so Bruda was

waiting for him at a bar in the Purist hotel, the Areon Plaza about a kylod away. Romas brought his security detail as a precaution. Bruda stood when he saw Romas approaching. The two shook hands like old friends.

"So, you made it back from Earth," Bruda teased.

"Yes, I hadn't anticipated you would embrace the Peace Movement. Had you told me, I wouldn't have left."

"Well, Sandee Brahn proved to be a formidable adversary, and the people were tired of war. So, I didn't have much choice. It's the will of the people that's important, right?"

Romas stifled a laugh. "Yes, I hope you mean that."

"Why wouldn't I? We both just want what's best for Tarizon. And, of course, a lot depends on your definition of people."

They both laughed knowingly.

"So, what brings you into the enemy camp?" Bruda asked. "This is not a social call, I'm sure."

"No. I wanted to suggest something to you."

"Alright. You have my undivided attention."

"As you know, our first hurdle to getting the World Council moving toward its primary objective is to elect a chairman."

"Yes. That will have to be done, but if you're here to tell me you're running and you want my vote, I'm afraid I must disappoint you."

"No. No, I'm not running. Although, I could and I might win eventually, but that's not a good way to start off this historical gathering."

"True. So, what do you propose?"

"I'm here to tell you that we are going to back Trill Lankershank of Pohl for the job. He's an independent and, if even half of the other Independents vote for him, we could elect him."

"He worked with Sandee, didn't he?"

"Yes, he helped Sandee get the Soni-Synclare peace talks set up, but he's never been a member of the Peace Party. He has an open mind on most of the issues that will be raised in drafting a Supreme Mandate."

"So, if he can win so easily, why are you here? You don't need us."

"Because I think his election should be unanimous. That will get the World Council off on a good footing, and tell the world that the delegates have only one agenda, to draft the best Supreme Mandate possible to ensure peace, happiness and prosperity for all the citizens of Tarizon."

"That's an interesting idea," Bruda admitted.

"And neither I nor the Peace Party will try to take credit for the unanimous vote. We will agree that it was a mutual decision and issue a joint press release to that effect."

Bruda nodded. "I'll have to meet with Lankershank and confirm what you have said. I'll do that and then talk it over with Progasis and the other delegates. I'll get back to you tomorrow."

"Thank you," Romas said and stood up. "I look forward to working with you on other issues as they come up."

"Likewise," Bruda said warily.

The next day Romas got word that the Purist Party had agreed to support Trill Lankershank for the Chairmanship of the World Council. When the World Council convened three days later, Trill Lankershank was unanimously elected as Chairman. After the vote, he took the podium and addressed the delegates.

"First, I want to thank you for your support and promise you that I will work tirelessly to bring about a consensus on this most important task of drafting a strong and enduring Supreme Mandate for Tarizon.

"To get this job done it will be imperative that we all

keep an open mind, listen to each other and try to understand the other's arguments and perspectives on the issues. That way compromises can be struck and issues can be resolved. It's not going to be easy to draft a document that will both ensure a strong and stable government and one that will be responsive to the will of the people. But it can be done, so let's do it!"

There were cheers from the delegates.

"One other thing; I know during the campaign there have been demonstrations, accusations of bribery and intimidation and even violence toward fellow delegates. Overnight, Nationalist extremists have vowed to disrupt this convention and prevent it from adopting a Supreme Mandate. Let me be clear, in this forum everyone will act with decorum, mutual respect, and dignity.

"Security will be tight, and we will not tolerate any disruption, displays of animosity or intimidation against other delegates. Finally, there will be no weapons of any kind allowed in the council hall, the surrounding grounds and meeting rooms. During these deliberations, the use of telepathic communication or telekinetic powers by delegates, their staff, or visitors is strictly prohibited. We will have rhutz and Seafolken assigned to security to detect any such activity. Violations of any of these rules will result with immediate expulsion from these proceedings.

"Thank you, now I believe the first item of business is to draft a Supreme Mandate. The chair recognizes the delegate from Tributon, Rammel Garciah who would like to speak to that issue."

Rammel got up from his chair and moved to the podium. "Fellow delegates, I place before this great body a draft of a Supreme Mandate supported by the Peace Party and endorsed by Sandee Brahn himself before his tragic assassination. You all were provided with a copy of this document when you first arrived in Shisk, and it has been a matter of public record for some time. So, I move that it be adopted."

There were cheers as delegates began standing. "I support the motion," a delegate said. "I support Rammel Garciah's motion!" another delegate yelled. Others echoed their support for the motion."

Trill went to the podium. "The motion has been made and properly supported. We will now have the debate. Mr. Garciah. You have a statement in support of the motion?"

"Yes. Thank you," Rammel said. "Mr. Chairman and fellow delegates. Sandee Brahn and members of the Peace Party drafted this Supreme Mandate presented to you today to create a new world order on Tarizon. It is designed to provide a strong world government that will be able to preserve the peace so that our planet can heal, our infrastructure can be restored, business and commerce can flourish, and our people can once again enjoy their lives without fear of military attack, famine, disease, or government oppression.

"Under this proposed Supreme Mandate there would be three equal branches of government, the executive, judicial and legislative. The executive branch would be led by a Chancellor who would be elected by the people for a term of six cycles. It would be his duty to oversee and administer the government bureaucracy which will be called Central Authority.

"The judicial branch would consist of a Supreme Council of Interpreters appointed by the Chancellor. Each Supreme Councillor would have a term of twelve years to preserve the continuity of law. Beneath the Supreme Council of Interpreters would be inferior courts as needed in each state and regional appellate courts to resolve conflicting decisions of the lower courts.

"The legislative branch will consist of a World Assembly. This body will serve as the first World Assembly once a Supreme Mandate is adopted by the people. Each assembly member will serve for a term of four cycles.

"It will be the World Assembly's job to enact the laws needed to govern the people, regulate business and commerce, provide for peace and security, and raise funds for government operations.

"Finally, the proposed Supreme Mandate has provisions to guarantee a wide range of basic civil rights to each citizen. Citizens are broadly defined in the document as any human being no matter his economic condition, sex, age, race, religious preference, or general health. This is consistent with the agreement of the organizers of this World Council and must be a fundamental principle of the Supreme Mandate.

"Of course, this is just a summary of the provisions of this opening draft of the Supreme Mandate. I believe it will provide a solid foundation for the establishment of a new government designed to bring about a lasting peace on Tarizon. I urge you to support it!" Rammel concluded.

There was a noisy round of applause and yells of support mixed with a few heckles from those opposed to the motion. Rammel stepped down from the podium and Trill replaced him.

"Alright. Thank you, Rammel. The next person who has asked to speak on this issue is Progasis Bruda. Mr. Bruda."

Progasis strolled to the podium and smiled to the delegates. "Thank you, Mr. Chairman. At the same time that the Peace Party was drafting the Supreme Mandate that is now before the Council, the Purists were doing the same thing. As you can imagine our two documents are quite different."

There was laughter.

"So, obviously we do not support the Peace Party's draft that is now on the table, at least without some modifications. Accordingly, I propose some amendments to their draft. I believe you have all been provided a copy of those proposed amendments. To summarize, we propose to amend the current draft on the table by (1) increasing the term of the Chancellor to ten years, (2) eliminating the need for an election of a Supreme Vice Chancellor by making the Vice Chancellor the candidate who comes in second in Supreme Chancellor's race, (3) eliminating the definition of "citizen" and leaving that term to be defined by the World Assembly, (4) striking any reference to the guarantee of civil liberties and leaving that to the World Assembly as well, and (5) to make the Supreme Vice Chancellor the Chairman of the World Assembly.

"If these changes are made the Purist Party believes that the Supreme Mandate as amended would be fair, just and serve the people of Tarizon well. So, I, therefore, move to so amend the Peace Party's draft of the Supreme Mandate as stated."

A delegate stood up and said, "I support the motion." A second delegate rose and said, "I also support the motion." Others got up and echoed their support.

Trill approached the podium and took the mic. "Alright, there is an amendment before the Council that has been properly supported. Is there any debate?"

"Yes," Chancellor Illeez Marcez announced. "I would like to address the delegates in support of this Amendment."

"Very well," Trill said. "You have the floor Chancellor."

Chancellor Marcez of Soni approached the podium and took the microphone. "Mr. Chairman, fellow delegates. As you know when this World Council finishes its draft of the Supreme Mandate, I intend to run for Supreme Chancellor."

There was an enormous round of applause and cheers from many of the delegates.

"So, I am particularly interested in the provisions that are adopted relative to the powers and duties of the Supreme Chancellor."

There was laughter.

"As we all know Tarizon faces many staggering, seemingly impossible challenges ahead, yet the survival of our planet depends on us solving them effectively. To form a new world government and solve all of Tarizon's critical challenges won't happen overnight or even in six cycles. Therefore, I support extending the term of the Supreme Chancellor to ten cycles. That probably isn't long enough, but I understand the need to give the people the right to make a change if the elected Supreme Chancellor does not perform as needed.

"Now, as to the election of the Supreme Vice Chancellor, there is a good reason to support the Purist position on this. If the Supreme Chancellor and Vice Chancellor run as a team the Vice Chancellor will be elected as a matter of course whether he is the best person to lead the government or not. It would make much better sense for the candidate who comes in second in the chancellor's race to automatically become Vice Chancellor. That way the Supreme Chancellor will always be someone chosen by the people. So, I support the second amendment to the draft of the Supreme Mandate before this body.

"As to the 3rd Amendment, there has been much debate during the campaign on the definition of a citizen. I think it was correctly decided that all humans be allowed to vote for delegates to this convention. Now, no one can say that the final draft of the supreme mandate when it is finally adopted by this body is not legitimate.

"But, now we have a different issue. Is it possible to save every human being on Tarizon given our limited resources and the time it will take to rebuild our infrastructure, increase food and industrial production and cleanse our rivers, oceans, and atmosphere? Reportedly there are over a billion mutants on Tarizon. Many have extraordinary powers and abilities, but most have severe defects, are sick and require tremendous medical resources to even keep them alive. I know this is a very emotional issue, but the time may come that we have to make a choice between letting some die so that many more can live. In that case, I think the General Assembly should make that decision on a case by case basis and not dictate it now as a moral certainty."

There were applause and shouts of agreement from several delegates.

"The argument on the 4th Amendment is similar to the 3rd. To deal with our enormous problems, our new government must be strong, swift and flexible. We can't afford to get bogged down or sidetracked because of guarantees of personal civil liberties. What is best for all citizens should be our primary concern. So, I support this amendment.

"Finally, the person who comes in second in the race for Supreme Chancellor will obviously be a very talented and capable person. It makes perfect sense that his talents not be wasted while he stands ready to serve if something happens to the Supreme Chancellor. If the vice-chancellor automatically becomes the chairman of the World Assembly those qualifications and talents won't go to waste. So, I support that amendment as well. Thank you," Chancellor Marcez concluded."

There was a standing ovation as Chancellor Marcez left the podium and Trill returned. "Thank you, Chancellor," Trill said. "Now I have been advised that Chancellor Rikin Linzcot of Lyon would like to speak on this issue."

Chancellor Linzcot walked slowly to the podium as delegates stood, clapping and cheering. He nodded his appreciation. When he started talking the auditorium fell silent. "Mr. Chairman, fellow delegates, It is an honor to be here today at such a historical moment in the history of Tarizon. As you know, I had the pleasure of working with Sandee Brahn when he was an Assemblyman in the Lyon General Assembly. I was skeptical of his peace movement at first, but as I got to know him I realized he was truly a man who had been touched by the God Pelgrem. So, I vowed to do whatever I could to help him bring peace to Tarizon.

"Since he no longer can lead the peace movement, I believe it is my duty to step in and make sure the job is finished. That is why I am running for Supreme Chancellor. Now I was with Sandee Brahn when this version of the Supreme Mandate was drafted. It reflects the type of government that Sandee Brahn believed would best bring about a lasting peace to Tarizon.

"But peace without the guarantee of freedom, democracy, and justice is worthless. So, I oppose the proposed amendments to the draft of the Supreme Mandate before the Council. The term of the Chancellor should be short so every elected Supreme Chancellor will have to face the voters often. This will not be a hindrance to good men but only those who don't listen to the will of the people.

"I oppose the idea of making the loser of the election the Vice-Chancellor. If the duly elected Supreme Chancellor dies while in office, why should a successor who has an entirely different political philosophy step in? Should not the policies supported by a majority of the citizens be continued until the end of the term? Of course, that's just common sense.

"As to the definition of citizen, that issue has already been decided and should not be revisited by the World Assembly. Every human being on Tarizon should be treated the same, and that should be guaranteed by the Supreme Mandate.

"Nor should we take out the provisions guaranteeing

the right to privacy, freedom to speak freely, the right to travel and live anywhere, the right to a fair trial, to assemble, and to vote. These are fundamental human rights that no government has the right to abridge. Therefore, we should leave this provision the way it was originally proposed. Thank you."

The crowd gave Chancellor Linzcot another standing ovation and there were many others cheering and dancing excitedly in the aisles. When the crowd grew silent, Trill returned to the podium and invited another delegate to speak. This went on for kyloons until it was time to adjourn for the day. After the council had adjourned, Romas and Rammel took Chancellor Linzcot out to dinner. After they finished their meal, they retired to the hotel bar to discuss the day's events.

"So, how long is Trill going to allow the delegates to debate these amendments?" Rammel asked.

"Until everyone who wants to speak has been given the opportunity," Romas said. "We listened to thirteen speakers today and Trill said there were seventeen more who have signed up for a slot."

"So, another day and a half," Rammel moaned.

"You better hope all the amendments lose, because if there are any amendments that stick it might not be approved. Then we would be back to square one," Chancellor Linzcot noted.

The World Council listened to delegates debate the merits of the Purist Party amendment for another day and a half until it finally came to a vote. Trill took the podium.

"Alright, it's time to vote on the amendments proposed by delegate Progasis Bruda. Unfortunately, the vote will have to be delayed as there seem to be 27 missing delegates. Please be patient as security is searching for them now."

Progasis turned to his father and asked, "What's up?"

"Things were going a little too smoothly so some of the delegates we had converted to our side were getting a little rebellious. We had to remind what they had at stake."

Progasis frowned. "Was that really necessary? We seem to be doing quite well."

"Exactly," Bruda spat, "and I want to keep our momentum going."

Ten loons later, Trill was back up on the podium. "Alright. Thanks for your patience. The missing delegates have been found. They were trapped in an elevator and there were some ventilation issues, but they seem to be okay now."

There was excited chatter from the delegates.

"Alright. I'll have order, please. Now, you will have five loons to vote. Use your wrist arrays."

"Point of order," Progasis Bruda yelled from the floor of the convention hall.

Trill pointed to Progasis and said, "Alright, state your point of order."

"Rather than vote on all of the amendments together, I want them to be split up and voted on separately," Progasis advised.

"Well, that's not how they were proposed, but I suppose it doesn't make any difference since you could propose them again separately later. ... Alright, we'll vote on each one separately.

"Please vote now for or against the first amendment to extend the term of the Supreme Chancellor from six to ten cycles."

The tally board behind the podium lit up immediately. After one loon the vote was 141 in favor and 181 opposed. There was an excited conversation amongst the delegates. After two loons the vote was 231 in favor and 261 opposed. The vote didn't change after three loons but at four loons it changed to 237 in favor and 263 opposed.

"Alright, the first amendment fails."

There were cheers by some and cries of disappointment and frustration by other delegates. Trill waited for silence and then said, "Alright now we will vote on the second proposed amendment to provide that the candidate for Supreme Chancellor who comes in second by the popular vote will become Vice Chancellor."

The tally board lit up again. After one loon the vote was 101 in favor and 121 opposed. There was a muffled conversation amongst the delegates as many struggled with how to vote. After two loons the vote was 191 in favor and 211 opposed. After three loons, the vote was 241 in favor and 229 opposed. The room grew quiet in anticipation of the final vote. At four loons it was 248 in favor and 247 opposed. The last loon dragged on and the members grew restless as they waited for the final tally. Finally, the tally board blinked and the final vote was 251 in favor and 249 opposed.

Trill took the podium. "Alright. The second amendment carries."

The room erupted in conversation. Trill waited a moment and then said, "Alright. I'll have order, please. Let's vote on the third amendment to eliminate the definition of "citizen" and leave that up to the World Assembly."

The tally board lit up once again and this time the decision became apparent after just two loons when the vote tally blinked at 111 in favor and 287 opposed. The final tally was 201 in favor and 299 opposed. The fourth amendment to strike any reference to the guarantee of civil liberties went down in the first loon 139 in favor and 299 opposed. The final tally was 161 in favor and 339 opposed.

Romas was relieved these two amendments had been defeated for had either passed it would have likely doomed passage of the Peace Party's draft of the Supreme Mandate. With just one Purist Party amendment passing it was going to be difficult enough. He prayed this last amendment would be defeated as well.

Trill took the podium for the vote on the final amendment to make the Supreme Vice Chancellor the Chairman of the World Assembly. "You will have five loons to vote. Please cast your votes now."

The tally board lit up once again and this time after two loons the tally was close at 111 in favor and 112 opposed. After three loons the tally board blinked and the vote was 244 in favor and 244 opposed. The auditorium became still in anticipation of the final tally. Finally, the tally board blinked one last time and the final result was 251 in favor and 249 opposed.

Bedlam broke out as the impact of the vote took hold. The Purists were up on their feet clapping, cheering, laughing and parading around gleefully. Rammel sat rigidly and stoned-faced wondering if he could vote in good conscience for a Supreme Mandate that gave so much power to the opposition.

Trill went to the podium and announced, "Amendments two and five are adopted and amendments one, three, and four are denied. Due to the late hour, we will adjourn until tomorrow at which time we will proceed with consideration of the Peace Party's draft of the Supreme Mandate as amended."

As Rammel was leaving Romas advised them there would be a strategy session in his suite 1900 loons. He nodded and then went to find Petrina so they could get some dinner before the meeting. When they got back to their suite they decided to order room service so they could watch the news coverage on the VC.

"This is Ruhle Zinni for the Global News Channel. Chances for the adoption of a Supreme Mandate to create a new world government for Tarizon may have dimmed today.

"After yesterday's apparent attempt to suffocate 27 delegates from Quori by sabotaging their elevator and

shutting down its ventilation system, the World Council continued its debate on the Peace Party's proposed version of a supreme mandate. Fortunately, none of the delegates were seriously injured. Yesterday, during debate on the proposed draft of Progasis Bruda, the Purist Party spokesman and delegate proposed five amendments. They were debated and today two of the five were adopted.

"The first of the two amendments make the candidate for supreme chancellor who comes second in the popular vote the Supreme Vice Chancellor. The Peace Party opposed this amendment because they claim it will undermine the will of the people who supported the policies of the winner of the election. They contend that if the elected chancellor should die in office, the Vice Chancellor should step in and carry on those same policies ratified by the people.

"Some delegates even claim that this provision will put a target on the back of any elected Supreme Chancellor as one bullet would be all it would take to overturn an election.

"The second amendment makes the Vice Chancellor automatically the Chairman of the World Assembly. Again, many Peace Party delegates contend this provision will thwart the will of the people by giving the losing candidate power to undermine the relationship between the Supreme Chancellor and the World Assembly.

"The question for the Peace Party tonight is whether they can support the version of the Supreme Mandate that is now before the Council. If they can't, it will likely be rejected and the World Council will have to start all over. If that happens, some say the process of adopting a Supreme Mandate may take months or cycles, if it can be accomplished at all.

"Delegates today are on edge after yesterday's attack on the Quori delegates. Many wonder what the Nationalist protesters have in store for them today.

"This is Ruhle Zinni reporting from Shisk, the proposed capital of Tarizon should a Supreme Mandate ever be adopted."

"I'm really worried," Petrina said. "After all that Sandee has sacrificed to bring peace to Tarizon, it may all go up in flames today. We can't vote for a draft that includes those provisions."

"I know," Rammel agreed. "It would make the Supreme Chancellor's job very difficult and quite dangerous. On the other hand, if we lost the election we would still have some power. It works both ways."

"No, it doesn't because we would respect the will of the people and accept their decision, but the Purists would not. You know if they lost they would be plotting every loon for ways to kill the Chancellor or subvert his power."

There was a knock on the door. Rammel thought it would be room service so he opened it without checking to see who was there. He was shocked to see Progasis Bruda.

"Progasis, what are you doing here?" Rammel asked.

"Let me in. I don't want to be seen."

Rammel opened the door a little wider and Progasis stepped in. Petrina's eyes widened.

"Sorry to intrude, but we need to talk."

"Okay," Rammel said motioning toward a sofa and chair. Progasis took the chair and Rammel and Petrina sat on the sofa.

"I know you can't support the draft of the Supreme Mandate that will come to a vote tomorrow."

"That's probably true," Rammel agreed. "But we haven't decided yet."

"My father won't like it, but I think I can talk him into a compromise if it would do any good. That's why I'm here. I don't want to propose it if it wouldn't be enough to gain the Peace Party's support."

"What are you proposing?"

"A simple amendment to our amendment which made the Supreme Vice Chancellor the Chairman of the World Assembly. The amendment would provide that the Chairmanship of the World Assembly would be on a ceremonial position only and that the delegates to the World Council would have the exclusive power to pick their own leadership and establish their own rules."

"So, the Supreme Vice Chancellor would not have a vote and wouldn't have any control over the body?"

"That's correct. So, what do you think? Can you live with that? As I said, my father might go for it, and I'll recommend it to him if it will be enough."

"We're meeting with the delegation later tonight. I'll discuss it with them and let you know."

They shook hands and Progasis left. As he was leaving, their dinner arrived. They ate slowly and thoughtfully thinking about the proposal. When they were finished Rammel said, "Well, let's find out what the others think."

Petrina nodded and they got up to get ready for the meeting. When they got off the elevator where the Peace Party had its suite they were mobbed by reporters.

"Mr. Garciah, is the Peace Party going to support the latest draft of a Supreme Mandate?"

"We don't know yet. That's why we're meeting."

"Mr. Garciah, are you worried about another attack tomorrow by the Nationalist protesters?"

"No. Our security should be able to protect us. We won't be intimidated by anyone."

When they got to the door of the suite they entered making sure no reporters followed them inside. Rack Brodie immediately greeted them and apologized for the presence of the reporters.

"They're not supposed to be on our floor. I have a call

into hotel security to have them removed."

Rammel nodded. "Where's my father? I have important news."

"He's on the balcony with Chancellor Linzcot."

"Thanks," Rammel said. He looked at Petrina. "Let's get a drink and then we'll go tell my father and the Chancellor the news."

Petrina nodded and they went to the bar. Once they had a drink in hand, they headed for the balcony. The Chancellor smiled when he saw them enter.

"Rammel. Petrina. It's good to see you," the Chancellor said jovially.

"Well, you may not like the news we bring," Rammel said.

"What news?" Romas asked.

Rammel told them of Progasis' recent visit.

"So, why didn't Cornelius come to me?" Romas asked.

"It wasn't his idea and he may not like it, but Progasis really wants the Supreme Mandate to pass and is sticking his neck out."

"Maybe, maybe not. This may be what they intended all along; for us to think they were compromising."

"But they will be compromising," the Chancellor noted, "since the amendment passed."

Romas took a slow deep breath. "I suppose you're right, but I still feel like we are stepping on a landmine."

"Don't worry about me. If I get elected Brodie assures me he can keep me safe," the Chancellor said.

"Do we know who was behind the attack on the Quori delegation?" Romas asked.

"I heard Quori voted unanimously for both amendments," Petrina advised. "So, my bet's on the Purists."

The Chancellor raised his eyebrows. "Really? I know at least half of that delegation are members of the Peace Party."

"That's why I'm not crazy about this compromise," Romas said. "Bruda will do anything to get what he wants."

"But it may be the best deal we can get," Rammel warned. "If a Supreme Mandate is not approved tomorrow, it may never happen."

"Well, let's put it to a vote of the full delegation. This isn't something we should be ramming down anyone's throat," Romas replied.

For over a kyloon the Peace Party considered Progasis' proposal. In the end, they agreed to support it. So, Rammel contacted Progasis and told him of their decision. He promised them he'd convince his father to go along with it. Rammel was sure that had already been done.

54
The Final Vote

It seemed like an ordinary day in Shisk. Citizens were going about their business as usual, but everyone knew life was about to change dramatically all over Tarizon if a new Supreme Mandate was finally approved by the World Council.

Rammel could feel the tension in the air as he entered the Council Hall. Security was tight with extra rhutz and Seafolken soldiers brought in to sweep for bombs, weapons or other devices that the Nationalists could use to disrupt the proceedings again.

Once the hall was declared safe the delegates were seated and Trill once again took the podium and called the World Council to order. "Fellow delegates, citizens of Tarizon, before we vote on the Peace Party's amended draft of a Supreme Mandate for Tarizon, I have been advised that independent delegate Lilar Ingot would like to propose an amendment to the draft that is currently before the Council. Mr. Ingot, you have the floor."

The tall, lanky delegate walked confidently to the podium and spoke into the microphone. "Mr. Chairman, fellow delegates and citizens of Tarizon. I move that Amendment #5 to the original draft of a supreme mandate currently on the table be amended to add in the word "titular" before the words "Chairman," such that the amendment will read "The Supreme Vice Chancellor shall be the titular Chairman of the World Assembly."

A delegate rose, "I support the amendment!"

A second delegate announced his support as did

numerous others. Trill went to the podium. "An amendment has been made and properly supported. Is there any debate?" Trill gazed out over the delegates. "Hearing none, please cast your votes now. You have five loons."

The tally board came to life and after the first loon the vote was 257 in favor and 121 opposed.

Trill leaned into the microphone and said, "The amendment has carried." A moment later he advised, "The final vote was 321 in favor and 177 against with 2 abstentions."

The hall erupted in conversation. Trill said, "Alright. Silence, please. Now we will vote on the draft of the Supreme Mandate that is currently on the table. You will have five loons to vote. Cast your votes now!"

The hall became very still, as all eyes focused on the tally board. After one loon the vote was 101 to 129. There were shouts of delight and others of anguish. At two loons the vote shifted to 159 to 149 and the Peace Party delegates clapped and yelled their approval. After three loons, the tally board showed 201 approved and 189 opposed.

Many delegates began to pace back and forth the stress finally getting to them. Romas looked up at the tally board with obvious concern. Progasis sat nervously in his chair seeming to ignore the numbers flashing on the board. He suddenly got up and walked swiftly out of the auditorium. Rammel looked at Petrina and shook his head. The tally board blinked for the fourth time to disclose a razor-thin margin of 247 approved and 237 opposed.

Everyone was on their feet now as the moment of truth was at hand. The Peace Party candidates began chanting 'Peace now! Peace now!' As the tally board blinked for the last time there was a loud piercing noise that echoed through the hall. The rhutz immediately began running toward the sound.

Delegates began grabbing at their ears as they felt

intense pain. The lights in the hall began to flicker and then failed. The tally board went blank. Then there was an explosion that rocked the hall and sent debris hurdling in all directions. A brick struck Romas' shoulder and he fell to his knees in pain and shock. Rammel suffered a direct hit to his head, went limp, fell to the ground and didn't move.

Dust filled the air and was so thick it was difficult to see or breathe. Those who were not knocked out by the blast stampeded to the nearest exits. There were screams of terror, cries of anguish and pain, and whimpers from fallen rhutz.

Progasis, Cornelius and Chancellor Marcez were not in the main hall when the explosion occurred. Neither was Chancellor Linzcot who was watching from his room at the insistence of Rack Brodie.

Chancellor Linzcot stared at the VC in disbelief. Brodie got on his communicator, contacted hotel security and demanded backup to his suite be sent up immediately. The image on the VC changed to the outside of the council hall where Ruhle Zinni, covered in dust and debris, was holding a microphone.

"This is Ruhle Zinni with the Global News Channel in Shisk. We are outside of the World Council chambers where a final vote was being cast to approve or disapprove of a draft of a Supreme Mandate to be submitted to the citizens of Tarizon. Just as the final vote was being cast there was a shrill noise and then a violent blast that sent projectiles and debris everywhere. Many delegates were struck and wounded, I saw some who appeared dead. Luckily for me, I was far enough away from the blast not to be seriously hurt."

The screen shifted to the chaotic scene at the main entrance to the council hall where emergency personnel were arriving and victims were being helped out of the building and into casualty transporters.

"The blast occurred before a final tally had been posted, so we don't know if the Supreme Mandate passed or not. The vote appeared to be close. Earlier, a last loon compromise between the Peace Party and the Purists seemed to suggest approval was imminent."

Ruhle touched his earpiece as if he was listening to someone.

"I have just been advised that the Chairman of the World Council, Trill Lankershank was pronounced dead on arrival at the Southwest Casualty Center. That's the first confirmed death from this vicious attack on the World Council.

"There was also an attack yesterday against the Quori delegates, but officials investigating the attack still do not have any suspects."

Brodie went to the door when his backup security detail arrived. He let two in and told the others to stay in the hall. Then he got on his phone and called Rammel Garciah's security chief.

"Pranhk Rizte here," he said.

"Pranhk, how is Rammel?"

"He's going to be okay. Just has a bruised shoulder. Petrina is okay as well. Just a broken ankle from some brute who ran her down."

"What about Romas?"

"He has a concussion. He's awake now. I think he'll survive. Did you hear about Trill?"

"Yes, that's so horrible. How did he die?"

"A pipe struck him in the side of the head. He died instantly."

"Oh, my God!"

"What about Chancellor Linzcot?" Pranhk asked.

"He was here at the hotel, so he's alright. Any word on how the vote came out?"

"No. I haven't heard a thing."
Brodie hung up the phone and turned back to the VC.

"We have updated casualty figures on this horrific attack on the World Council. Seventeen have died and thirty-seven are now being treated at local casualty centers.

"We are going live now to the Public Enforcer's office in southwest Shisk where Mohda Grean, Deputy Chairman of the World Council, is holding a news conference."

The screen shifted to an array of microphones in front of the Southwest Headquarters of the Public Enforcer's office. A middle-aged woman was at the microphone.

"Ladies and gentlemen. As you know there has been another attack on the World Council this morning. Seventeen citizens are dead on account of this latest horrific act including the Chairman of the World Council, Trill Lankershank.

"These attacks by the Nationalist protesters have been designed to disrupt the movement to centralize Tarizon's government in order to put an end to global wars and finally bring peace to Tarizon. On that score, I'm happy to announce that the vote was not compromised by this cowardly act. As you may remember voting is now conducted by wrist array, so when each delegate voted his vote was immediately transmitted to a local satellite network. We have now taken that data and calculated the vote.

"The final vote to accept or reject the latest version of the Supreme Mandate is 254 in favor and 246 opposed. The next step is for the new Supreme Mandate to be ratified by the people. That vote is set to take place in thirty days.

"Violence has plagued Sandee Brahn's peace movement from the outset. There were several earlier attempts on his life, his chief of staff, and constant companion Salina Gill was killed by a bomb hidden in his

conference room, and then he, of course, he and Whisper the Rhutz were assassinated.

This is Ruhle Zinni with the Global News Channel in Shisk."

Romas and Rammel went home to Tributon to recuperate after the World Council was over, but were back in Shisk 30 days later for the worldwide vote to ratify the new Supreme Mandate and the launch of Chancellor Linzcot's campaign for Supreme Chancellor.

Bellah Lai, with whom Chancellor Linzcot had become quite fond, felt sick that day and stayed home. She knew Romas and Rammel would recognize her, so she had no choice but to avoid them.

Recent public opinion polling commissioned by various press outlets indicated the Supreme Mandate would be adopted by the people, and their polling turned out to be accurate. In the end, over 70% of the voters approved the new Supreme Mandate and it became the law of the land. Now, the final and most important question was about to be decided. Who would be the first Supreme Chancellor of Tarizon?

While Chancellor Linzcot and his supporters were celebrating the commencement of his campaign, Bellah was home tweaking her plans to compromise and discredit him. And she couldn't wait to get started and make her father proud.

55
The Final Campaign

By far the most important political race in the history of Tarizon was underway the moment the Supreme Mandate was adopted by the people. There were three main candidates who the media was taking seriously in the race; Chancellor Linzcot from Lyon, Chancellor Marcez from Soni and the independent candidate Lilar Ingot from Vada.

At the outset, the race was Chancellor Linzcot's to lose with media polling showing that if the election were held today he'd get 55% of the vote, Marcez 35%, and Ingot 10%. While everyone knew Marcez and Linzcot's views on the issues, Ingot had kept his positions close to the vest while the World Council drafted the Supreme Mandate.

Due to the poor state of Tarizon's infrastructure, its dangerous atmosphere, the lack of any commercial air travel, limited ground transportation due to fuel shortages, and general civil unrest outside the domed cities, none of the candidates were planning to do much traveling. The campaign would be primarily conducted by VC. But, there was one planned event that all the candidates would be attending, the official designation and celebration of Shisk as the capital of Tarizon. This week-long event would culminate with the election of the Supreme Chancellor.

This was perfect for Bellah Lai because no one in Lyon knew her. As Chancellor's Linzcot's personal secretary she was always at his side but rarely seen in public. During media appearances, she kept her distance so she wouldn't be seen in any of the camera feeds. Bellah's mother and father were well-known Purists and friends of Cornelius Bruda, so she knew if anyone who had traveled to Earth with the GOT saw her they would immediately recognize her and know something was wrong.

Up until now, her job had been to spy on the Peace Party and Chancellor Linzcot. But with the campaign now underway, her job had been expanded to finding dirt on him that might taint his reputation, personally compromising him, or, if need be, killing him.

At first, she didn't think her job would be that difficult until she met Rack Brodie. He was suspicious of her from day one and watched her like a hawk. Then after the campaign for delegates to the World Council was over, Linzcot managed to get Autumn the rhutz transferred to his security detail. Autumn was suspicious of her too, and she felt him on more than one occasion trying to probe her mind. Luckily, she had the gift and knew how to protect her thoughts.

Once the Supreme Mandate had been ratified the World Council became the World Assembly and started operations immediately. Its job was to draft and enact all the laws that would be needed to operate the new world government. Trill Lankershank's death meant Mohda Grean, another independent delegate, became the first Chairman of the World Assembly.

Chairman Grean immediately appointed Rammel Garciah to be the Chairman of the Judicial Affairs Committee which would be drafting the laws needed to fund and operate Tarizon's new judicial branch of the government. Then he appointed Progasis Bruda to be Chairman of the Military Affairs Committee whose job it would be to fund and draft the laws regulating Tarizon's Global Army or TGA.

The independent Candidate for Supreme Chancellor Lilar Ingot was born and raised in the city of Plumma, Vada. His family had been wealthy before Vada and Lower Serie went to war twenty years earlier, but his family had lost everything in the last nuclear strike that ended the conflict with Vada's defeat.

Ingot was blessed with good looks and charisma which made him a popular man. He was the town's citihead for many years before he ran for Vada's General Assembly and won easily. During his tenure in the General Assembly, he was assigned to the Military Procurement Committee and met Cornelius Bruda who did much business with Vada's military.

Bruda appreciated the influence Ingot would have getting military procurements for Vada approved, so he immediately put him on his secret payroll. When the new world government was proposed, Bruda suggested he should run as an independent candidate for the World Assembly. Ingot loved the idea, particularly when Bruda tripled his monthly paycheck.

Before Ingot left Shisk for the long flight home to Plumma, he had a secret meeting with Bruda and General Bakker aboard their transport plane getting ready to take them back to Tributon.

Ingot stepped inside the plane and was shown to a small private room. He went inside and found Bruda and General Bakker sitting in lounge chairs each with a bottle of Tekari.

"Lilar. Thank you for coming. Would you like a Tekari?" Bruda asked.

Ingot nodded. "Sure, why not?"

Bruda pointed to a small refrigerator and Ingot opened it and pulled out a Tekari.

"Have a seat. So, what did you think of the World Council?"

Ingot took a seat across from them.

"It was pretty exciting."

"It ended with a bang, didn't it?" General Bakker said

with a grin.

They all laughed.

"So, did everything work out the way you planned?" Ingot asked.

"Yes," Bruda replied. "Everything is falling into place nicely. Linzcot will be exposed as the fraud that he is and be forced to resign, or he'll be dead."

Ingot laughed. "How will you manage that?"

"We have someone in his inner circle ready to take him out of the race one way or another."

"So, if he is out of the race, won't the Peace Party back somebody else?"

"Yes," Bruda said. "That's why we will expose him first and force him to resign, but if that doesn't work then the alternative will be to terminate his candidacy."

Ingot swallowed hard. "Okay. So, where do I fit in? I doubt I could beat the new Peace Party candidate even if it's a last loon pick."

"You won't have to," Bruda said with a smile. "You'll be the Peace Party's new candidate."

Ingot frowned. "Excuse me?"

"From now on I want you to echo whatever Chancellor Linzcot says on the campaign trail, except you will propose different ways to achieve the same result. That will explain why you didn't join the Peace Party. You're independent and like doing things your own way."

"I see. So, if Linzcot is out of the picture you want the Peace Party to come to me to be their replacement candidate."

"Exactly. Do you think you can do that?"

Ingot shrugged. "Sure. Why not? It seems pretty straightforward."

Bruda leaned over and slapped Ingot on the knee. "That's what I want to hear. Depending on how the election goes, you'll either be Supreme Chancellor or Supreme Vice

Chancellor. Do you think you can handle that?"

"I'm sure if I need help, you'll provide it, right?"

Bruda laughed.

"I'm going to enjoy working with you, Lilar. Now get out of here and start campaigning."

"Yes, sir," Ingot said getting up. He smiled and then walked to the cabin door, lowered his head and disappeared.

"So, what do you think, General?" Bruda asked.

"He'll be fine if he doesn't let getting elected go to his head and think he can cross us," General Bakker replied.

"Don't worry about that. He's not that ambitious. He's a man who likes luxury and the illusion of being powerful. He doesn't really want to do the hard work."

"I hope you're right."

"If not, he's not bulletproof, right?"

They both laughed heartily.

†††††

Chancellor Linzcot sat in his chair behind his desk. There were only two weeks left until the election and he was studying his appearance schedule. His wrist array began to beep. He squinted and then stood up. Bellah came rushing into the room.

"Sir. Mr. Brodie wants you to come to the media room immediately. There's something you need to see."

"What is it," Linzcot said irritably.

"I don't know, sir. He didn't say."

Linzcot left his office with Bellah following close behind. When they got to the media room Brodie had a news report on pause. He looked concerned.

"What's going on?" Linzcot asked.

"I don't know. I just got an alert that we needed to watch this report."

Linzcot sighed and took a seat in front of the VC. "Okay. Let's take a look."

Bellah sat down next to the Chancellor and Brodie

tapped his wrist array. The VC came on with the news reporter sitting behind his desk.

"This is Liree Tonn reporting for the Global News Channel with this campaign alert. A messenger delivered a package to our Shisk offices today containing old shipping receipts dating back to the cycle 20212 from Pompelus Trading Company formerly owned by Rikin Linzcot, the Peace Party Candidate for Supreme Chancellor.

"The significance of these records is that they document the transport of five hundred Seafolken slaves down the Mulga River to the Dark Sea twenty-one cycles ago. According to local business records, this would have been at a time Chancellor Linzcot owned and operated the company.

"Chancellor Linzcot has campaigned for the abolition of slavery and it's one of the foundations of the Peace Party's platform. This revelation that Chancellor Linzcot at one time was a slave trader will certainly shock his followers and undermine their enthusiasm for his candidacy.

"Of course, these records will have to be carefully inspected and analyzed for their authenticity, and everyone will be anxious to hear the Chancellor's reaction to the discovery, but if it turns out Linzcot was a slave trader this election may be over for him.

"This is Liree Tonn of the Global News Channel reporting from Ya Lat, Lyon."

"Where did they get this garbage?" Linzcot spat. "I've never owned a slave in my life."

"Have you ever heard of the Pompelus Trading Company?" Brodie asked.

"Sure. I owned that company but we raised pribett and pollos in the Black Hills of Darkland. We transported them down the Mulga River to Zarne where they were sold at auction."

"So, someone found these old records and then altered them to make it look like you transported slaves rather than pribett."

"Perhaps. We'll have to get access to those records to be sure that's what happened," Linzcot said frantically. "Call that reporter and set up a meeting. Half of my following are Seafolken, slaves or mutants. If they think I was a slave trader, they'll never vote for me."

"I'll get right on it," Brodie replied.

"Is there anything I can do?" Bellah asked feigning concern.

Linzcot looked at her and sighed. "Get Arvis and Ambassador Talvihn in here. I'm going to need their advice."

"Right away, sir," Bellah said and ran off to get them.

A few loons later she returned with them, and Linzcot replayed the news report again.

"This will be devastating to your campaign if we don't take quick action," Ambassador Talvihn said.

"I know. But what can I do other than deny it?"

"Did you have business associates or friends back then who were familiar with your operation?"

"I don't know. That was twenty-five cycles ago. I'll have to think about it."

"We should schedule a media conference for later today so you can at least deny these accusations," Arvis said. "Every loon that goes by without you denying that you ever were a slave trader increases the chance that people will begin to believe the report."

"Right. You better get that set up," Linzcot said worriedly.

Arvis and the Ambassador left the room and Autumn strolled in wondering what all the commotion was about. Bellah came up from behind and put her arm on Linzcot's shoulder. "This is so unfair, Chancellor. I'm so sorry you're having to go through this. You're such a good man."

Linzcot looked at Bellah awkwardly and smiled. "Thank you. This is so ridiculous. I have never owned a slave."

"I know," Bellah replied patting him on the shoulder.

Autumn growled and Bellah stepped back. The Chancellor looked curiously at Autumn and asked, "What's wrong girl?"

Autumn sat and looked up at him. Then Brodie entered the room. "What's wrong with Autumn?"

"I don't know," Linzcot said. "She just started growling."

Brodie looked suspiciously at Bellah then turned away. "I talked to Romas Garciah. He knows some Seafolken from Darkland. He's going to see if he can find any who knew the slave trade in that region 27 cycles ago. If so, they would know whether you were a slave trader or not."

"I assure you I wasn't."

"I believe you, but it will sound better if it came from a knowledgeable Seafolken."

"Right," Linzcot agreed.

Later that day Chancellor Linzcot held a media conference at a local VC studio. Arvis and Ambassador Talvihn were at his side. Brodie, Autumn, and their security detail surrounded the building and kept a close eye on everyone in attendance.

"Citizens of Tarizon," the Chancellor began. "Today there was a news report that suggested I once was a slave trader. This is absolutely untrue, so I called this media conference to make that clear.

"I have never owned a slave, let alone traded them like merchandise. I have always opposed the slave trade and I personally led the fight to abolish it in Lyon cycles ago.

"The records that were sent to the Global News Channel offices were altered or fabricated by someone who wants to undermine my campaign for Supreme Chancellor. It is true I owned Pompelus Trading Company back then but it dealt strictly in pribbets and pollos and nothing more.

"We will be launching an independent investigation into where these documents came from, how they were altered, and who is behind this sinister attempt to undermine our election process. We will get to the bottom of this I promise you.

"Thank you," the Chancellor concluded.

†††††

Romas entered his son's temporary offices in Soni's General Assembly Hall. It was being loaned to the World Assembly until its new facility could be designed and constructed. His secretary greeted him warmly and showed him into Rammel's office.

"Father, come in. How are you?"

"Not so good, actually," Romas said.

"What's wrong?"

"I just talked to Rack Brodie and he says someone has delivered some papers to the media that indicate that Chancellor Linzcot was a slave trader."

"What! That's impossible."

"Yes. It's obviously a fabrication by someone, probably Cornelius Bruda, if you want my guess."

"That sligot! I can't believe he thinks he can get away with it."

"He's very cunning. We'll never be able to prove he did it. The question is what else does he have up his sleeve?"

"Do you have any ideas? I would have never thought of accusing Chancellor Linzcot of being a slaver. That's a joke."

"Yes, but some people will believe it and don't think the fake shipping reports will be the last of the evidence they dig up to support their accusations."

"So, what do we do?" Rammel asked.

"I have some Seafolken contacts in the Dark Sea Alliance looking into it. They should be able to help us out. What's worrying me is the amendment that we were forced to accept making the runner-up in the election the Supreme Vice Chancellor."

"Yes, I don't like that provision at all. I wish we could do something about it. You don't think Bruda would try to have Chancellor Linzcot assassinated, do you?

"I wouldn't put it past him," Romas replied. "The question is how and when he would try."

"If he tried it before the election we could endorse another candidate."

"True, but Progasis might be able to beat someone we get to replace Linzcot at the last loon."

"So, how would they get to Linzcot?" Rammel asked. "We've got tight security."

"Unless they have someone in the inside," Romas said thoughtfully. "That would be the only way they could pull it off."

"Everyone on the campaign staff has been thoroughly investigated and we have Autumn there and a pack of rhutz for backup."

"True, but I still can't get over Ritz Sloken being there right under our noses," Romas said. "I don't want to make that same mistake again."

"Right. Whatever happened to him? I know he escaped. Have the Public Enforcers been able to find him?"

"No. I'm sure he's in hiding."

"What about Bellah? Has anyone seen her around?" Rammel asked.

"Bellah," Romas repeated thoughtfully. "Yes, where is Bellah? That's a good question. We better get someone to locate her so we can keep an eye on her."

"Yes. She's a sly one. The first day at Mineral Wells High School she hooked up with the richest and most powerful student at the school. I was surprised when she dumped him and came back to Tarizon."

"Maybe she thought she had something more important to do here," Romas said. "If so, we better find out what it is."

56
Slander

Chancellor Marcez stepped before the microphones. Two days after the story on Chancellor Linzcot broke he'd scheduled this media conference. He'd waited to see how Linzcot responded before making the next move. Linzcot's response had been about what he expected so he thought it was time to drive another nail into his coffin.

"Citizens of Tarizon. I called this media conference today to comment on the recent revelations about the Peace Party candidate for Supreme Chancellor, Rikin Linzcot. Many of us suspected all along that he had been less than candid with the public in this election. He has been very outspoken about how he and the Peace Party are so morally superior to the rest of us. They are the champions of civil rights and the protectors of the people. Then we find out Linzcot as a young man made his fortune trading slaves."

Marcez shook his head slowly.

"What a disgrace this is for a man who claims to have such integrity. Of course, he denies he was a slave trader. He called a media conference immediately and claimed the records were altered or forged. He promised to get to the bottom of this shameful attack on his integrity. Well, I'm sorry to be the bearer of bad news, but shortly after the story broke we were contacted by one of Chancellor Linzcot's ex-employees, a mutant named Sigand Zuree. Mr. Zuree is here today and would like to tell you what he knows about Pompelus Trading Company."

A tall, stout mutant dressed in rags and relying heavily on a staff to walk, made his way to the microphones.

His face was marked with ugly scars and burns from living outside the domed city. His long grey hair was tangled and matted. He cleared his throat, looked down at a script someone had prepared and began to read.

"My name is Sigand Zuree. I'm from Zarne on the east coast of Darkland. I came to know Rikin Linzcot when he was running a company called Pompelus Trading Company out of Pompelus, Lyon. He hired me in the spring of 20211 as a slave handler. I worked for him for more than two cycles and my job was to buy slaves brought in by cargo ship to Zarne and then bring them up the Mulga River to ranchers in the Black Hills who had ordered them. It was a very lucrative business and I was well paid."

Zuree looked up from his paper and gave everyone a toothy grin and concluded by saying, "I will say that Mr. Linzcot was a fine employer and told me to treat those Seafolken slaves with dignity and respect."

There was laughter from the news reporters in attendance.

"I'm sorry, but I won't be answering any questions. I just wanted to confirm that all you've heard recently about Chancellor Linzcot is true. Thank you."

Zuree turned and slowly hobbled away from the microphones. Security personnel swarmed around him, took both arms and quickly escorted him away from the press. Marcez came back to the microphones and began fielding questions from reporters who were eager to find out how he thought this might affect the election.

†††††

Bellah watched the Chancellor as he listened to the media report in shock and dismay. She stifled a smile.

The Chancellor turned off the VC angrily and stood up. "I have never seen that man in my life!" he screamed. "He never worked for me. This is an outrage."

"I know," Ambassador Talvihn said shaking his head.

"It's all a set up designed to crack your hardcore supporters and discourage them from voting."

"We've got to do something and do it fast. The election isn't too far off."

"Shall I schedule another media conference?" Arvis asked.

"No," Ambassador Talvihn replied. "Let's schedule an interview with a friendly VC reporter in a few days. By then Romas Garciah's Seafolken friends from Zarne should be here. We can bring them to the interview."

"Are you sure they are coming?" Linzcot asked.

"Yes, they left this morning. They should be here tomorrow afternoon."

"Do you know what they are going to say?"

"No, but Romas wouldn't be sending them if it wasn't positive."

"Should I meet them at the airport or transport station?" Bellah asked.

"No," Rack Brodie replied. "I've already arranged for them to be picked up. I'll take them to a safe house and from there right to the VC studio."

Bellah smiled. "It's almost lunch. Is anybody hungry?"

"No. I lost my appetite," Linzcot said.

"Why don't I take you home?" Arvis said. "You need to rest for your appearance tonight. We can get something to eat on the way home."

"That sounds good," Linzcot replied. "I am a bit tired."

Bellah was frustrated that she couldn't find out when the Seafolken were coming or where they were staying. She had hoped to give that information to Shellee. But as the election got closer and closer it seemed to be harder and harder to get any useful intelligence. She wondered if they were on to her. She voiced that concern to Shellee when they met at a sankee shop near her compartment.

"What do you have for me today?" Shellee asked.

"Nothing much. I know Romas Garciah has arranged for some Seafolken from Darkland to come in and meet with the press in a couple of days, but Brodie is picking them up and taking them to the safe house. From there he'll take them to the studio."

"Where's this safe house?"

"I don't know. Brodie wouldn't say nor would he tell when and where the interview will take place. I don't think they trust me."

"Well, they may have figured out who you are. It's a little surprising you haven't already been discovered. I'm sure they have people rechecking all the campaign staff."

"So, what should I do?" Bellah asked.

"We knew we were going to have to pull you out anyway before the campaign moves to Shisk. It would be too dangerous for you to go there as the Chancellor's personal secretary. If you haven't already been discovered, you surely would be recognized there by someone. So, the committee has decided to reassign you, and I think you will like the assignment."

"What is it?"

"You're going to meet up with your old friend, Ritz Sloken."

"Ritz? Is it safe for him to come out of hiding?"

"You'll both be disguised and will remain in the shadows most of the time."

"What's our assignment?"

"You'll be informed when the time is right. For now, I'm to take you to Shisk and find a place for you and Ritz to stay during the celebration."

"Right now?"

"Yes. Go to the compartment and pack a bag. Don't leave anything behind that is important to you. You won't be coming back."

Bellah raised her eyebrows and then stood up. "Okay.

Where should we meet?"

"In front of your compartment in fifty loons. A public transporter will pick you up and take you to the airport. I'll meet you there."

Bellah nodded and left. She wondered what this new assignment was going to be, and how Ritz Sloken fit in. She hoped it was something important as she was frustrated she hadn't been able to do more to derail Chancellor Linzcot's campaign.

††††††

Rack Brodie and two of his security detail waited at the transport station as if they were there to pick up the Seafolken who were coming to meet with the press. They knew they were being watched because the local rhutz had been at the station all night looking for Purist agents. They'd detected several and informed Autumn.

At the same time, at a private airstrip thirty kylods away, Ambassador Talvihn, his security chief and Autumn were meeting the two Seafolken who Romas had arranged to fly in. He was taking them straight to the studio as soon as they arrived so there would be no opportunity to prevent them from being interviewed.

The friendly reporter they'd lined up was Veile Shante who had covered Sandee Brahn before he ran for the Lyon General Assembly. When she was told there were security concerns, she took one of the studio's mobile units and set up a temporary studio in a vacant compartment. When the Ambassador and his guests arrived, she was ready for them.

They exchanged introductions. "I'm so glad you called me. I couldn't believe the slanderous attack on Chancellor Linzcot. It was so outrageous."

"Yes, a total fabrication. Unfortunately, some people will believe anything. Hopefully, today we can set the record straight."

Rhod Selps, a Seafolken from Dark Uzza stood seven feet two with pale blue eyes and short brown hair. He looked like any other human except for his pale green complexion, gills, and feet and hands that expanded when placed in water.

"Mr. Selps," Veile said. "Let's start with you."

Rhod nodded and walked over to the chair facing the cameras. He sat down awkwardly.

"Alright. Thirty tiks," the Director said.

Veile took the seat next to Rhod, tossed her hair into place and then smiled.

"Ready in 3...2...1," the Director said.

"Good afternoon. This is Veile Shante coming to you from Ye Lat, Lyon where I am going to interview two citizens who claim to have information about an allegation that has recently surfaced about Chancellor Linzcot. An anonymous person left a package containing records that appeared to show that Chancellor Linzcot at one time owned a company called Pompelus Trading Company that engaged in the slave trade in Darkland, Azollo some twenty-five cycles ago.

"Shortly after that revelation, Marcez, a candidate for Supreme Chancellor held a media conference and produced a man, a mutant named Sigand Zuree, who claimed that he once worked for Pompelus Trading Company as a slave handler.

"Chancellor Linzcot has denied that he or his company has ever traded in slaves, and today he has sent me two witnesses who he thinks can shed some light on the actual facts. The first witness is Rhod Selps, a Seafolken from Dark Uzza.

"Mr. Selps. First, why don't you explain how you came to have relevant knowledge to these allegations against Chancellor Linzcot."

"Certainly. Twenty-five cycles ago I was a spotter for the Dark Sea Alliance. The Dark Sea Alliance is an organization of free Seafolken who fight slavery. Slave trading had been outlawed in Darkland for many cycles but the slave lords paid bribes to the public enforcers so they could keep trading. It was my job to locate Seafolken who were still enslaved and help them obtain their freedom."

"I see. So, how does Chancellor Linzcot fit into all this?"

"The Deep Sea Alliance has no funding, and everything we do depends on contributions from governments, businesses, and individuals. Chancellor Linzcot was a big contributor to the Dark Sea Alliance back then, and I knew him well. The idea that he was a slave trader is ridiculous. He's always been a champion of freedom and I will be voting for him for Supreme Chancellor"

"Thank you, Mr. Selps. Alright. We'll take a break and be back in a loon with our next guest."

Brulh Ragon was about the same in size and appearance as Selps but he had black curly hair and a sharp chin. He switched places with Selps and a technician attached a microphone to his collar.

The Director counted down again and part two of the interview began. "This is Veile Shante back with my next guest Brulh Ragon from Pompelus, Lyon. Mr. Ragon, how do you know Chancellor Linzcot?"

"I used to work for him when he owned Pompelus Trading Company. In fact, I was one of the original employees."

"So, did Pompelus or Linzcot ever engage in slave trading?"

"No. Absolutely not. We dealt in livestock and food stocks. There were many Seafolken working there but they were all paid a fair wage and treated well."

"Do you know this mutant Sigand Zuree fellow?" Veile asked.

"No. He didn't work there while I was there, and I

was there the entire time Chancellor Linzcot owned the company. I left after he sold out to go into politics."

"Well, thank you for coming in and shedding some light on the situation. I guess the voters will have to decide who to believe.

"This is Veile Shante in Ya Lat, Lyon."

After the interview, they took Ragon and Selps back to the airport because Ambassador Talvihn didn't want them to be hounded by reporters or targeted by the Purist Party thugs that had been lurking about. Several hours later Brodie and his security team came back to Peace Party headquarter relieved their deception had worked.

As a result of the interview, large crowds of mutants and Seafolken gathered in front of Purist Party headquarters in Ya Lat, Shisk and other major cities across Tarizon in protests of this blatant attempt to defame their hero, Rikin Linzcot. As campaign workers came in and out of these buildings the protesters chanted, "No more lies! No more lies!"

57

Supreme Chancellor

Bellah Lai and Shellee landed two days later at a private airstrip in the Weeping Mountains owned by one of General Bakker's friends in the Soni air force. The Capital City Dedication was just getting underway 120 kylods to the west in Shisk. Bellah was anxious to see Ritz Sloken as so much had happened since they had left Earth. He was waiting for her in a big mountain cabin overlooking the plains of Soni. She ran up to him and they embraced.

"Wow! It seems like forever since we were back on Earth," Bellah said as she gave him a once over.

"I know. You look good," Ritz noted.

She shrugged. "Well, I had a cozy assignment spying on Chancellor Linzcot. Being a pretty little assistant was my job."

Ritz laughed. "So, how come you got reassigned?"

"Well, I couldn't get close enough to the Chancellor because Arvis Gill or Rack Brodie was always there. Neither one of them liked me. Then they assigned Autumn to the detail, and he followed the Chancellor like his shadow was a potential assassin."

"Oh, well. He'll get what's coming to him," Ritz said.

"What about you? Taking out Sandee Brahn? I couldn't believe it when I heard it. How did that happen?"

Ritz smiled proudly. "Actually, that was your father's idea."

"Really? He didn't mention it to me."

"No. Only he and Cornelius Bruda knew about it.

Bruda sent a messenger aboard Earth Shuttle 3. He went to your father and told him Bruda needed someone to infiltrate the Peace Party and get close to Sandee Brahn. So, your father talked to me about it and I agreed to do it."

"So, that's why you suddenly became a fan of the peace movement. I wondered about that."

He nodded proudly. "Yes. I couldn't believe Romas and the others accepted me in their group so readily."

"He obviously hadn't heard about your Klu Klux Klan activities back in Texas."

"No. I only shared that with you and your brother. I assumed you wouldn't mention it to Rammel or Eroh."

She shook her head. "No. I knew better. So, what have you been doing since the assassination? Have you been hiding here?"

"No. Bruda thought I might like a little recreation, so he sent me to flight school."

"Flight school?" Bellah repeated.

"Yes. He sent me to a base on Pogo Island where I learned to fly fighters."

"Wow. That sounds like fun."

"It was, particularly on our days off."

"Really? What was so fun on your days off?"

"A bunch of the guys would take the T29s up almost into space where the hibernation pods were in orbit."

"Un huh."

"Then we'd search for them. There are thousands of them up there."

"So I heard."

"If we found one, we'd use it for target practice."

Bellah's eyes widened. "You what?"

"It's hard to find them, but if you do they are easy to blow up."

"But they have families in them?"

"So? They gave up on Tarizon so who's going to miss

them, right? Most of them are mutant lovers anyway."

Bellah swallowed hard. "I suppose."

"Anyway, I'm so glad to finally get a new assignment. It's nice up here but I am starting to get really bored."

"Is the hunting around here any good?"

"No, not really. The forests have been slowly dying and the water is still toxic. The only animals I see are a few rhutz now and again. I wanted to do a little rhutz hunting, but Shellee wouldn't let me stray too far. I don't know how they manage to stay alive without clean water."

"Let's go inside," Shellee suggested. "We have a lot of planning to do."

They all went inside the spacious cabin. A fire was burning in the fireplace.

"So, what's our assignment?" Bellah asked.

Shellee sighed. "Well, it seems our efforts to undermine Chancellor Linzcot's support amongst the Seafolken and mutants has failed. They responded much quicker than we anticipated they could. So, Linzcot has recovered all the ground he initially lost. That means we must go to our final option."

"Which is to remove him from the race?" Bellah asked.

"Right," Shellee replied.

"How are we going to manage that?" Ritz asked.

Shellee explained their assignment to them. They were to leave in two days for Shisk. In the meantime, they rested, got familiar with the weapons they'd be using for the assignment and worked on their disguises. Every security detail in Shisk would have seen both their faces in their briefing materials, so the disguises had to completely obscure their facial features.

The next day Ritz and Bellah left their mountain safe house as a Seafolken and his mate from Lower Serie. Their credentials said they were from Uihya where they worked as fishing guides on the Serie River. If their best friends had seen them they wouldn't have recognized them.

They arrived at the northeast gate to Shisks' dome at 1200 kyloons the next day. They displayed their credentials and were let in without incident. The streets were clogged with people arriving for the great celebration. Shellee had arranged a hotel room for them downtown near the Assembly Hall. After waiting over a kyloon they were able to get on the subtram to take them downtown. Luckily, Shellee had arranged for their luggage to be delivered to their rooms before their arrival. She'd arranged bribes to key hotel personnel to avoid screening. In the luggage amongst their clothes and toiletries were an assortment of rifles, lasers and light explosives which they would need to carry out their assignment.

Ritz and Bellah decided they might as well do a little partying since that would be expected of them as tourists. So, they went to a few of the parades, some exhibits, toured the historic sites of Shisk, and drank a lot at the local taverns. It was an enjoyable week for both of them, and they were sorry when it was over. Now, they had to focus on taking Rikin Linzcot out of the race for Supreme Chancellor.

✝✝✝✝✝

Rack Brodie was not happy about this last week of the election campaign. He cursed the person who dreamed up having a dedication ceremony for the city during the last week of the campaign. Shisk normally had a population of 2.1 million but on the last day before the election there were 3.7 million under the city's dome and another 1.1 million camped outside hoping somehow to get in for the festivities.

Both candidates were scheduled to speak before the World Assembly the night before election day. Progasis Bruda was scheduled first at 1700 kyloons and Rikin Linzcot at 1900 kyloons. The World Assembly Hall was brand new since the old structure had been destroyed by Seafolken troops at the end of the Soni-Synclare War. It was built in anticipation of its being the home of the World Assembly so it had a stunning design and state of the art security.

Rack deployed a pack of rhutz around the perimeter of the building who would be searching for anyone carrying weapons, bombs, or poisonous gases of any sort. Several dozen Seafolken were also circulating amongst the crowd scanning minds for hostile intent. The World Assembly's regular security force was at the gates, on the walls, and on duty throughout the hall.

Everything looked fine, but Rack was still uneasy. He had a bad feeling about this event the moment it was announced and had worried about it every day. At 1830 kyloons Chancellor Marcez ended his speech and left the World Assembly Hall. Once his transporters had left the building, Rack called for Chancellor Linzcot's driver and told him to bring in Linzcot. Soon, the Chancellor was in the building and on his way to the stage.

✝✝✝✝✝

Ritz, looking like any other Seafolken security guard, had been given an access pass to patrol inside the Assembly Hall. He made his way to the roof maintenance access door on the upper deck. He used an access card Shellee had given him, stepped inside and climbed up five flights of stairs to the roof. From his pocket, he took out plans of this part of the roof and studied them. The map showed an access point for one of the banks of lights that illuminated the stage. He found it, swung it open and crawled inside.

Just inside the door was a fully loaded R5 sniper rifle manufactured by Areon Armaments with an M13 silencer. Ritz picked it up and began crawling toward the end of the bank of lights. When he got there he peered out and saw that he had a clear shot to the speaker's podium. He noticed several people standing around but Linzcot had not yet arrived. While he was waiting he checked his rifle, made

483

sure it was loaded, and examined the silencer. When he was satisfied everything was in order, he began positioning himself for the shot.

†††††

Bellah, also in her Seafolken disguise, joined the line of Seafolken security officers patrolling the perimeter of the Assembly Hall. She walked quickly to where the transport vehicles brought in guests to the underground parking garage. She stood as if she was watching for intruders or unauthorized personnel.

At about the same time Chancellor Linzcot was moving toward the stage to give his address, Chancellor Marcez was getting in his Grinden to leave the World Assembly Building. Once Progasis and his aides were all inside their Grinden, the driver accelerated up the driveway to where Bellah was stationed.

When Bellah saw the Grinden coming up the driveway she readied herself to complete her assignment. Just as the Grinden was about to pass, she aimed her TL 5 laser rifle at the windshield and fired. The laser beam punched a hole in the bulletproof glass the size of a man's head. The Grinden swerved, ran off the driveway and into the wall. Bellah pulled out a pocket bomb with a yellow stripe and tossed it toward the hole but it missed, bounced off the windshield and then exploded in front of the Grinden.

Two Seafolken guards grabbed Bellah's arms and wrestled her to the ground. Soon, she was cuffed and turned over to two public enforcers who showed up on the scene. After the fires from the pocket bomb were extinguished, the driver opened the Grinden's door and got out. He ran to the passenger door, opened it and inside he found Chancellor Marcez a little shaky but not seriously injured. Without any further delay, the security team raced Marcez to another Grinden and he was rushed back to the safety of his hotel.

†††††

Inside the Assembly Hall, there was a commotion from behind the stage. Ritz looked through his sights and moved the rifle toward the noise. He saw a crowd of people moving out toward the podium. In the midst of them was Linzcot, but Ritz didn't have a clear shot because there were too many people around.

Finally, Linzcot emerged from the crowd and began waving. Everyone suddenly was on their feet clapping and shouting their approval of the front-running candidate for Supreme Chancellor of Tarizon. Ritz aimed the rifle at Linzcot's heart and started to pull the trigger when he heard a vicious growl and felt a stinging pain in his leg. The distraction caused him to miss Linzcot and hit a spectator in the first row. Ritz rolled over to defend himself but another rhutz joined in the attack and sunk his teeth into his neck before he had a chance to pull his pistol. In a few tiks, Ritz Sloken was dead.

✝✝✝✝✝

Cornelius Bruda and Petri Volk rushed into the media room at Bruda's White Mountain ranch in Northern Tributon. They were anxious to see if Ritz and Bellah had been successful in taking Linzcot out of the race. When the VC lit up the camera was focused on a chaotic scene in front of the World Assembly Building.

"This is Veile Shante of the Global News Channel with the latest news from around the world. In Shisk just loons ago there were assassination attempts against Supreme Chancellor candidates Rikin Linzcot and Chancellor Bromas Marcez. The attacks came just before Linzcot was scheduled to speak before the World Assembly and as Marcez was leaving the complex after his address.

"The assassins were disguised as Seafolken security guards and apparently had been moving freely in and around the assembly hall. One of them positioned himself in

a bank of lights over the podium with a sniper rifle and took aim at Linzcot. Fortunately, a rhutz on patrol discovered the intruder and attacked him about the same time he took his shot causing him to miss Linzcot. Another rhutz joined in the attack and killed the unidentified assassin.

"At about the same time Marcez's Grinden was attacked by the other would-be assassin with a laser rifle. The rifle punched a hole in the windshield but the Grinden swerved and avoided the pocket bomb that had been tossed at the hole in the windshield. The bomb exploded outside the heavily armored vehicle and did not injure Marcez."

"The second attacker turned out to be a woman but her identity has yet to be released. The first attacker's body has been transported to the Public Enforcer's Central Evidence Lab for an autopsy.

"Although no organization has claimed responsibility for this attack, experts believe this was yet another attack by Nationalists who oppose the imposition of a world government on Tarizon. Fortunately, both candidates survived and the election is but a day away, so maybe this will be the end of senseless violence on Tarizon.

"This is Veile Shante with the Lyon News Agency coming today from Shisk, the new world capital."

"Skutz!" Bruda spat. "I hate those damn beasts from hell. One day I hope we exterminate every last rhutz on the planet."

"Well, it almost worked," General Bakker said shaking his head. "It was really a brilliant plan to make it look like both candidates had been attacked."

"Don't worry," Petri Volk said. "Even if we lose the election Marcez will be Vice-Chancellor and just a heartbeat away from being Supreme Chancellor. We'll have plenty more opportunities to rid the planet of Rikin Linzcot."

"Weren't you worried Marcez would be injured when the assassin fired the laser through the windshield?" Cameela asked.

"No," Bruda replied. "The laser couldn't penetrate the limdidium shield between the driver and the passengers. The only danger was that pocket bomb getting through the windshield, but Bellah was warned not to let that happen."

"What's going to happen to her?" Cameela asked.

"Oh, don't worry about her," General Bakker said. "We always have a contingency plan. By now she's escaped and on her way to a safe house."

Cameela smiled. "You are amazing, General."

"Why thank you, Cameela. That's nice of you to say."

"Not so amazing actually since Chancellor Linzcot is still alive," Bruda spat.

The room went silent.

The next day Bruda and the Purist Party senior staff watched the election returns with keen interest. They were not optimistic that Chancellor Marcez could win but were hoping that the race would be at least close. After the first kyloon 11% of the population had voted and Linzcot led with 44% of the vote, Marcez had 32% and Ingot came in with 11% with all others splitting the remainder votes fairly evenly.

At midday, 62% of the citizens had voted and Linzcot had increased his lead to 47% with Marcez having 33%, and Ingot with 12%. Bruda and the others were hoping that Linzcot would not get a majority of the votes so they could claim he wasn't the choice of a majority of citizens on Tarizon, but by early evening he had stretched his lead to 52% over Marcez who was still at 33%.

Needless to say, the mood at the Bruda ranch was somber, but not defeated. They hadn't been able to defeat the Peace Party even without Sandee Brahn, but they remained confident that in time the Supreme Chancellor would be a

Purist.

†††††

As the voting closed in the last time zones on Tarizon, the senior staff of the Peace Party watched from the ballroom of the Baccaluna Hotel in Shisk with great anticipation. Rikin Linzcot was about to become the first Supreme Chancellor of Tarizon and a new era on Tarizon began. Whether it would be one of peace or continued warfare was uncertain, but everyone at the Peace Party's victory celebration was more than optimistic.

The World Assembly as one of its first acts discontinued use of the Pharidon Calendar and replaced it with the Unification Calendar. Henceforth, days on Tarizon would be counted starting with the year the Supreme Mandate was ratified. So, when the final tabulation came in giving Rikin Linzcot the victory with 54% of the vote, it was year 0 A.U. on Tarizon.

After the final vote came in Supreme Chancellor Rikin Linzcot took the stage to make his first speech as Supreme Chancellor.

"Ladies and gentlemen, distinguished guests and citizens of Tarizon, I want to thank you for granting me this great honor of leading Tarizon into a new era of peace, healing, and hope. To all the rhutz, Seafolken and security personnel who helped save my life yesterday and who have protected me during this campaign, I will forever be indebted.

"Thanks to our fallen leader, Sandee Brahn, we are here today to set in motion the building of a new government committed to peace, freedom and equal rights for all citizens. The people have ratified a strong and fair Supreme Mandate that will provide a great foundation upon which to build an effective and stable government.

"It's not going to be an easy task, as there is so much work to be done to build this government from the ground up. The good news is we are not going to be burdened with outdated policies, procedures, and precedents of the past that have no relevance today. I want to build a lean, efficient and fair Central Authority so we can start rebuilding our infrastructure, cleaning our rivers and streams, helping farmers and ranchers increase their production, and get our industrial production booming again.

"To do all of this I will need the cooperation of all citizens of Tarizon, as well as the leaders of all the 31 states of Tarizon. It won't be easy for some to relinquish their power and authority as they must do under the Supreme Mandate, but that is the first task that must be accomplished.

"We have already begun the process of creating a worldwide military force. It will be known as the TGA or Tarizon's Global Army. Once its commanders have been selected, it will take over all armed forces throughout Tarizon.

"So, a lot will be happening starting today and it is bound to get confusing and frustrating at times. Please be patient and cooperate fully with all the fine men and women who will be assisting me in getting our new government off to a fast start.

"Again, thank you for your support, hard work and sacrifice in making this day possible. All of you through your hard work and diligent support of the Peace Party has made this day possible. I thank you, your children thank you and Pelgrem thanks you.

"For He came to a small boy in a dream and thrust upon him the task of bringing peace to a dying planet, so it could be saved. And the boy, Sandee Brahn, protected by a rhutz named Whisper set out to fulfill this task.

"Sandee Brahn and Whisper have done their job and now it is up to us to maintain peace on Tarizon until the beauty, bounty, and magnificence of our planet is restored.

Thank you!" Supreme Chancellor Linzcot concluded.

The crowd went wild and the party began and lasted throughout the night. People all over Tarizon celebrated this great victory for weeks to come as they felt confident for the first time that their lives were about to get so much better.

Epilogue

Bellah Lai sat solemnly in the back seat of the public enforcer's patrol unit with mixed feelings. She'd performed her assignment perfectly and done Tarizon a great service, but now must face the consequences of her actions. If the Purists won the election she was sure Cornelius Bruda would figure out a way to get her released from prison, but she knew that depended on how Ritz had done, and she had no idea if he had been successful.

The Public Enforcer's face was hidden by a helmet, so she didn't know what he or she looked like. The Seafolken had roughed her up a bit during the arrest, but she'd managed to get in a few blows herself. Her hand was bleeding from the exchange, and not all the blood was hers.

The PE started the engine and drove off. Bellah wondered where they would be taking her. She imagined hours of intense questioning and, if she didn't cooperate, they'd give her the truth serum that would make her spill her guts. She hated the idea of that; giving up all her secrets and not being able to do anything about it.

The patrol unit made a hard turn onto the main boulevard that intersected the city from east to west and accelerated quickly. She was surprised at this because she had anticipated only a short drive to the PE station. As the loons ticked by she became concerned. Where are they taking me? She wondered if they were taking her to a military base for more intense questioning. That thought scared her. In the city under the dome there would be rules and procedures to protect her, but out on a military base they might give her the truth serum, get what information they wanted from her, and then kill her.

She noticed they were getting close to the east exit from the dome. The PE unit didn't slow down and soon they were outside the city in the tube. Soni was one of the few states where the tubes were still functional. Once out of the tube the unit slowed and turned into a fueling station. The woman parked behind the station, got out, and opened Bellah's door. Bellah just stared at the officer wondering what was going on. The officer removed her helmet and Bellah began to laugh.

"Shellee? What the hell?"

"You didn't think we'd leave you to rot in prison, did you?"

Bellah shrugged. "Well, I was wondering."

"There's a jet copter just outside the tube that's going to take us to the safe house."

"Thank you. So, where's Ritz? Did he get extracted."

Shellee swallowed hard. "No. I'm afraid he didn't make it out."

"Oh no, what happened?"

Shellee told her. They both were quiet on the ride back to the safe house. Bellah felt angry that Ritz had died and Chancellor Linzcot hadn't even been hurt. Her anger turned to depression and despair. She thought back to the time she had spent there with Ritz while they were training for the mission. She had never felt so connected to another human being. They were a team working together to fulfill a critical mission.

The intensity of their relationship had spilled over into the bedroom on more than one occasion. It was the best sex she'd ever had, and she doubted she'd experience anything like it again. She wondered what her next assignment would be, or since her cover had been blown, would she have to go back to Earth.

"So, what's going to happen now?" Bellah asked.

"We wait for instructions," Shellee advised. "We are not sure if your cover was blown. If it wasn't, then you can do whatever you want. If it was, then you may want to go back to Earth. Either way, you're going to have to change your lifestyle quite a bit."

"Change my lifestyle? Why?"

"Things change when you have a baby," Shellee said.

"What? Who's having a baby?"

"You. I've been monitoring your wrist array and it's reporting that you are pregnant."

Bellah looked down at her wrist array and began tapping on it. "How does this thing even work? I haven't paid much attention to it since it was implanted."

Shellee laughed. "I'll show you when we get back to the safe house."

"I'm pregnant!" Bellah repeated shaking her head in dismay.

"Yes," Shellee said. "And it's a recent event, so I figure the father must be Linzcot or Ritz."

"Ritz. I could never get a moment alone with the Chancellor."

"So, you'll be raising him alone."

"It's a boy?" Bellah asked.

"Oh, right. Yes. It's a boy."

"Wow! I can't believe it."

"So what will you call him?" Shellee asked.

Bellah thought a moment and then replied, "Videl." I have always liked that name."

"Since you were not mated, he'll have to take your surname."

"Right," Bellah agreed.

"Videl Lai," Shellee said, "the son of Sandee Brahn's assassin. I bet he'll make his mark on history?"

Bellah smiled confidently. "Oh, you can count on that."

About the Author

William Manchee is a consumer lawyer by trade and practices in Texas with his son Jim. Originally from Southern California, he lives now in Plano, Texas. His undergraduate degree is from UCLA and he graduated from law school at Southern Methodist University.

Manchee discovered his passion for writing in 1997 when he represented a romance writer in an estate matter and became familiar with her exciting life. Curious as to whether he could write, he gave it a try and was quickly hooked. He finds it not only fun but also therapeutic. Since he found practicing law to be a more stable career than writing novels, he practices law by day and writes at night. His works have received considerable critical acclaim and have been reviewed in *Publisher's Weekly*, *Library Journal*, and *Foreword Magazine*.

<u>The Tarizon Saga</u>

Supreme Mandate (2019)
Shroud of Doom (2013)
Desert Swarm (2014)
Cactus Island (2006)
Act Normal (2007)
The Liberator (2008)
Civil War (2009)
Conquest Earth (2010)